TREASURE AND TROUBLE THEREWITH:
A TALE OF CALIFORNIA
1917

TREASURE AND TROUBLE THEREWITH

A Tale of California

By Geraldine Bonner

EDITED WITH AN INTRODUCTION BY DAN COYNE

WHITLOCK PUBLISHING
ALFRED, NEW YORK

Treasure and Trouble Therewith: A Tale of California
By Geraldine Bonner, First published by D. Appleton and Company,
New York and London, 1917.

First Whitlock Publishing Edition 2019

Whitlock Publishing
www.whitlockpublishing.com

Editorial Matter ©Daniel Coyne
Cover Art: Library of Congress
Detroit Publishing Co. *City Hall.* 1905
Meyron, Charles. *San Francisco.* 1856.

ISBN: 978-1-943115-32-7

This book was set in Adobe Caslon Pro on #50 acid-free paper that
meets meets ANSI standards for archival quality.

TREASURE *and* TROUBLE THEREWITH

Aknowledgements:

I'd like to thank Dr. Grove for helping me put this book together and encouraging me to try my hand at publishing.

INTRODUCTION

Two folksy train robbers make off with twelve thousand dollars cash and fall into a mosaic of interconnected characters, each of them finding their aspirations and successes more vacant than originally thought. Set in San Francisco leading up to the 1905 earthquake, *Treasure and Trouble Therewith* provides a broad portrait of early twentieth-century Californians, and a new lens through which to view California.

INTRODUCING CALIFORNIA

California holds a curious and sometimes contradictory place in the American consciousness. At the farthest end of the territory, it represents total sovereignty and opportunity. After being acquired as a state, gold miners first flocked westward seeking metal fortune, but as the gold mines dried up, Americans began heading west in search of different commodities: they looked to California for wealth, fame and oppurtunity.

In many ways, the self-creation myth of America is strongest in California. In the 19th century, the recurring depictions of its beautiful and undeveloped nature were more connected to the pastoral image America had of itself than the populated and developing northeast where society was beginning to stratify and become set in its ways. Even today, California as an image is often seen as the wide open frontier full of possibilities rather than constraints—unless you think about traffic and housing costs. That sunny ideal is deceptive. As Bonner shows, the prosperity and freedom of the western territories bred greed and violence which was so much in contrast with the beautiful land. To begin with, that trope of the untamed and undeveloped West waiting to be tapped into is a historical reimagining. The reality of the huge population of native Americans who lived on the pacific coast, the first Spanish colonies at Santa Cruz, and California's time as a part of Mexico are easily forgotten in Panovision with a John Ford movie. By 1900, San Francisco numbered almost 350,000 people and Geraldine Bonner, unlike many of the Californians who wrote before her, steered from wide open plains and focused on the booming cities and the vices simmering within them.

At the start of the twentieth century, California was producing distinctive literature, the most notable being Frank Norris' *McTeague*, a meditation on greed and violence in San Francisco. Along with Norris, Bret Harte and Geraldine Bonner were using California to inform stories of grifters, gamblers and gold miners. They wrote in contrast to the idealized western territory—instead of Huck Finn's desire to "light out on the territory," the idea that there is a virgin land somewhere, these Californians explored the seedier parts of the golden state. These writers, each born far from the West, adopted California as their home, but in their work they explored the falsehoods and shortcomings of perhaps the most iconic American image: the wide open West.

BRIEF BIOGRAPHY

Geraldine Bonner was born on Staten Island in 1870, where she lived until she was ten. Her father, whose literary influence Bonner pays tribute to in *Treasure and Trouble Therewith*, had been an editor and writer for several New York publications—first *The New York Herald* and later *Harper's Weekly*. At some point, he became an operator on Wall Street, at which—according to his obituary—he "made a fortune."[1] Unfortunately this success was short lived, and her father's career in finance collapsed spectacularly. After his firm sunk, and owing $400,000 of loans in addition to the stocks and securities of nearly every firm on Wall Street, he fled to Canada without his family.[2] A few months later the family reunited in America, heading west to seek new fortunes and escape an unlivable situation in the Northeast. They first emerged in Kansas City, very much like the hopeful Missouri pilgrims of Bonner's subsequent work, *The Emigrant Trail* (1930), and later stayed for two years in a mining camp in Colorado (gold miners are a recurring theme for Bonner). The family settled in San Francisco where her father returned to news-

1 San Francisco Call, Volume 85, Number 157, 6 May 1899
2 New York Times, 7 May 1899

paper work and under his guidance, Geraldine began writing herself. While Bonner does not appear heavily in this West Coast creation myth, her family's story is very much tied into the aspirations of California and informs her unique take on them. Here, her family found a place for the ruined to start again.

By seventeen, Geraldine had begun contributing to *The Argonaut*, which her father edited. She began publishing short stories in *Collier's Weekly*, *Harper's Magazine* and *Lipinscotts*[3]. In 1900, at the age of thirty, she published her first novel, *Hard Pan*, under the pseudonym "Hard Pan." Here she began exploring the fascinations of California, and, as would become characteristic in her work, its shortcomings.

HER WRITING

As a writer, Bonner faced criticism on several fronts. By some, she was characterized as overly romantic, and by others she was a writer guilty of creating characters too ugly and too unpleasant. A review of her novel *The Pioneer* captures her place in early 20th century literature.[4] First stating that "the red, red west" has been a topic and setting overworked and drained of artistic value, the review acknowledges Bonner's contributions as a writer not just of romances, but of "character [studies], both regional and personal."[5] In some ways not taken seriously the way her male contemporaries were—she was also more flexible as a writer and made forays into genre novels, writing romances and detective fiction in addition to her more literary works. In a style combining elements of realism with the outlandishness of California, she was certainly unique but not always perfect: as the title suggests, her style can be overwrought and antiquated.

LITERARY CONTEXT

Bonner was working within specific ideas of innocence and fortune laid out by writers before her. To say all American literature comes from Mark Twain is a simplification, but for simplicity,

3 Literary News, Volumes 24-25
4 The Craftsman, Volume 8
5 The Craftsman, Volume 8, 1905

Huck Finn introduces many of the thematic issues which Bonner and so many others unpack—specifically the innocence of America pertaining to individual characters in addition to the land those characters inhabit. As an ideal, America and its untamed territories were pure and divorced from the stifling society of Europe. When Huck memorably wishes to "light out for the territory"—as does Holden Caulfield—he is setting up a place connected to a pastoral tradition and separate from the constraints of the civilized world that has made him an outcast. This idea is so American, that a free world exists where anyone and everyone can pursue fortune. The territory Huck alludes to is a place of sovereignty where a poor and uneducated orphan is no longer stigmatized and held back by his societal maladies; it is a place where he can escape and be free. In the national consciousness, California embodies that idea, even if its continuous development has changed the pastoral aspect.

The ideal of the western frontier as a place of true American values is not just false in real life, but myopic in literature. Bonner rebels against the frontier image, weilding more understanding of American life than simple and young innocence. In *Treasure and Trouble Therewith*, California fortune seekers are lampooned when she displays accumulating wealth as vapid. Although she only critiques a small portion of that frontier image (boundless wealth), Bonner's disagreement made room for other writers to explore the limits of the West. The right to "light out" is reserved for men. In California, only the white are able to find legitimacy and fortune in the great expanse of the "red, red west." This realization that an iconic American image is flawed has created great literature. Carson McCullers explores this same desire to go westward in her book, *The Member of the Wedding* with a pubescent girl who rather than live out her own fantasies of "lighting out," is relegated to a kitchen where she can become a woman, get married, and obey the Law. So, with Bonner having her down-on-luck train robbers take twelve thousand dollars in cash in order to find their own fortune and remake themselves, she's following a narrative laid out before her while opening new territory for later writers to explore.

As the title suggests, wealth proves to be unsatisfying. Perhaps Bonner's family history of fortune and collapse fed into her story, but it's also related to greed, an often understated or celebrated part of American culture. The title, *Treasure and Trouble Therewith*,

is actually taken from a psalm in the Bible which says, "better is little with fear of the lord than great treasure and trouble therewith."
This can explain the moralizing tone of the novel, and Bonner's in-
spiration for attacking material wealth. When looked at biblically,
the California promised land is not virgin, but a rapidly populating
cesspool where the freedom of those western pilgrims has lead to
sin. Surprise surprise, stealing a whole train car worth of Wells Fargo cash does not bring fulfillment—lighting out on the frontier has
proved just as dissatisfying as life in the East, only with more sunshine and better views of the ocean.

CONTEMPORARY TIMES

This notion of California as a place of hope as well as darkness
has proved rich in pop culture. Recall the famous Dorothea Lange
picture "Towards Los Angeles" where two depression-era men are
walking past a huge billboard that says, "Next time take the train.
Relax." As a place of self-creation and fulfilment, especially in show
business, California still holds that dream, but with the space Bonner made, many have given their own take on the shortcomings of
the Golden State.

Moving from the gold rush and early industrialists, California
became the center of a counterculture revolution in the sixties, which
valued personal freedom and liberation, searching for the same thing
as the first western settlers, only in a different context. Today, California is ground zero for celebrity culture and America's fetishiza-
tion of fame. While note necessarily a product of freedom, celebrity
does have its roots in the original fortune seekers.

More recent California literature has responded directly to the
tradition laid out by Bonner, Harte, and Norris, and it has done so
in a new California with hippies rather than gold miners, trust fund
teenagers rather than industrialists. Joan Didion's collection of essays,
Slouching Towards Bethlehem, gives a picture of instability and change,
cutting through the smoke of the idealized hippie lifestyle. Bret
Easton Ellis' first novel, *Less Than Zero*, looks at the vacant life of the
rich and famous of Los Angeles. Just like the train robbers of *Treasure
and Trouble Therewith*, their success is dissatisfying and empty.

IN FILM

More to Bonner, the California darkness she explored has been regurgitated and built upon in movies, most notably film noir. The most essential of those films have dealt with the chiaroscuro of sunny Los Angeles. In *Sunset Boulevard*, where Joe Gillis, the struggling screenwriter from Ohio, is taken in by silent-movie queen Norma Desmond in his attempt to escape debt and find some legitimacy in Hollywood, Gillis is playing into an old story. Gillis, like so many others, has been seduced by the dream of California but has found its reality more artificial and less satisfying than he expected. Similarly, Desmond, a monster made by the fame and glory of Hollywood, has been ruined by her success and is unable to give up the fame and legitimacy she once had. Rather than the simple path of fame, wealth, and satisfaction that has been advertised to them, here are two freaks made from this dream they have California. While Bonner never covered show business, her plots involving hope and fortune which ultimately turn sour was pioneered the tradition of disproving this very American dream. From the first Puritan settlers in New England, who saw going west from England as a chance at freedom to practice their religion, to the waves of poor hopefuls wishing to make some mark, the dream has always been myopic, something one could argue is more national propaganda than anything else. But, as America has grown, it has been unable to grow out of the notion that there is something better out west.

So if the futile dream Bonner explored was built upon in *Sunset Boulevard*, then human corruption—another piece of *Treasure and Trouble Therewith*— is expanded in *Chinatown*. Rather than the emptiness of Hollywood stardom, *Chinatown* focuses on pulling back the facade of Los Angeles to expose its ugliness, along with the shortcomings of prosperity. Nowhere is the corruption of wealth more clear than in Noah Cross, John Huston's character. He is a wealthy industrialist whose money and influence have led to a perverted sort of California legitimacy. He sums this up with his famous line that "politicians, ugly buildings and whores all get respectable if they last long enough." Like those train robbers who rip off a Wells Fargo car, Cross has achieved success through unscrupulous means, and like them he is corrupted by his fortune. But in a turn from Bonner, who takes an almost a binary, biblical view of good and evil, Cross is presented as something far more interesting than an unsatisfied dreamer. He is someone who seemingly takes joy in the corruption, or has been so consumed by it that it's the only thing left pushing him forward. Within the broken system, he wins. This moves away from our clichéd view of American innocence set out in *Huck Finn*, which Bonner carries on with a moral hand guiding her characters through their crises, where their most existential want is redemption or salvation. In *Chinatown*, greed and lust have taken control of someone who has achieved the dream, and rather than portray him as a tormented soul, a hopeful like a character out of Fitzgerald, he is only more powerful by it. There is no redemtion like Bonner offers. Perhaps California has only gotten that much darker since 1917.

TYING THINGS UP

In the tradition of critiquing and examining the westward drive of Americans, *Treasure and Trouble Therewith* is a key piece. The ideas laid out here have been built upon and imagined in new contexts and mediums. Geraldine Bonner took aim at the American institutions of wealth and freedom and sought the truth in them. In her critique, Bonner made space for later writers and artists to continue exploring American society, and she gave her readers a more critical eye for examining themselves.

Note on the Text

I have been faithful to the original text as much as possible, keeping the phrases, vocabulary and punctuation originally layed out to best preserve the author's work and intention.

TREASURE AND TROUBLE THEREWITH

THEREWITH

A Tale of California

GERALDINE BONNER

CHAPTER I

HANDS UP

THE TIME WAS LATE AUGUST some eleven years ago. The place that part of central California where, on one side, the plain unrolls in golden levels, and on the other swells upward toward the rounded undulations of the foothills.

It was very hot; the sky a fathomless blue vault, the land dreaming in the afternoon glare, its brightness blurred here and there by shimmering heat veils. Checkered by green and yellow patches, dotted with the black domes of oaks, it brooded sleepily, showing few signs of life. At long intervals ranch houses rose above embowering foliage, a green core in the midst of fields where the brown earth was striped with lines of fruit trees or hidden under carpets of alfalfa. To the west the foothills rose in indolent curves, tan-colored, as if clothed with a leathern hide. Their hollows were filled with the darkness of trees huddled about hidden streams, ribbons of verdure that wound from the mountains to the plain. Farther still, vision faint, remote and immaculate, the white peaks of the Sierra hung, a painting on the drop curtain of the sky.

Across the landscape a parent stem of road wound, branches breaking from it and meandering thread-small to ranch and village. It was white-dusted here, but later would turn red and crawl upward under the resinous dimness of pine woods to where the mining camps clung on the lower wall of the Sierra. Already it had left behind the region of farms in neighborly proximity and the little towns that were threaded along it like beads upon a string. Watching its eastward course, one would have noticed that after it crested the first rise it ran free of habitation for miles.

Along its empty length a dust cloud moved, a tarnishing spot on the afternoon's hard brightness. This spot was the one point of

1

energy in the universal torpor. From it came the rhythmic beat of flying hoofs and the jingle of harness. It was the Rocky Bar stage, up from Shilo through Plymouth, across the Mother Lode and then in a steep, straining grade on to Antelope and Rocky Bar, camps nestling in the mountain gorges. It was making time now against the slow climb later, the four horses racing, the reins loose on their backs.

There was only one passenger; the others had been dropped at towns along the route. He sat on the front seat beside Jim Bailey the driver, his feet on a pine box and a rifle across his knees. He and Jim Bailey knew each other well, for he had often come that way, always with his box and his rifle. He was Wells Fargo's messenger and his name was Danny Leonard. In the box at his feet were twelve thousand dollars in coin to be delivered that night to the Greenhide Mine at Antelope.

With nothing of interest in sight, talk between them was desultory. Jim Bailey thought they'd take on some men at Plymouth when they stopped there to victual up. The messenger, squinting at the swimming yellow distance, yawned and said it might be a good thing, nobody knew when Knapp and Garland would get busy again. They'd failed in the holdup of the Rockville stage last spring and it was about time to hear from them—the road after you passed Plymouth was pretty lonesome. Jim Bailey snorted contemptuously and spat over the wheel—he guessed Knapp and Garland weren't liable to bother him.

After this the conversation dropped. The stifling heat, the whirling dust clouds broken by whiffs of air, dry as from a kiln and impregnated with the pungent scent of the tarweed, made the men drowsy. Jim Bailey nodded, the reins drawing slack between his fingers. Leonard slipped the rifle from his knees to the floor and relaxed against the back of the seat. Through half-shut lids he watched the whitened crests of the Sierra brushed on the turquoise sky.

The horses clattered down a gulley and galloped across a wooden bridge that spanned a dead watercourse. The ascent was steep and they took it at a rush, backs humped, necks stretched, hoofs clattering among loosened stones.

A sudden breeze carried their dust ahead, and for a moment the prospect was obscured, the trees that filled the gulley, bunched at the summit into a thicket, just discernible in foggy outline. The horses had gained the level, Jim Bailey, who knew the road in his sleep, had cheered them with a familiar chirrup, when the leaders stopped, recoiling in a clatter of slackened harness on the wheelers. The stage came to a halt so violent that Jim Bailey lurched forward against the splashboard, the reins jerked out of his hands. He did not know what had happened, could see nothing but the horses' backs, jammed together, lines and traces slapping about their flanks.

Afterward, describing it at Mormons Landing, he laid it all to the dust. In that first moment of surprise he hadn't made out the men, and anyway who'd have expected it—on the open road in the full of the afternoon? You couldn't put any blame on him, sprawled on his knees, the whole thing coming so quick. When he picked himself up he looked into the muzzle of a revolver and saw behind it a head, only the eyes showing between the hat brim and a gunny sack tied round the lower part of the face.

After that it all went so swift you couldn't hardly tell. He didn't even then know there were two of them—heard the feller at the wheel say, "Hands up," and thought that was all there was to it—when the one at the horses' heads fired. Leonard had given an oath and reached for his gun, and right with that the report came, and Leonard heaved up with a sort of grunt, and then settled and was still. The other feller came along down through the dust, and Jim Bailey, paralyzed, with his hands up, knew Knapp and Garland had got him at last.

The one at the wheel kept him covered while the other pulled out the box. He could see him plain, all but his face, a big powerful chap, shoulders on him like a prize fighter's, and freckled hands covered with red hair. He got the box out with a jerk and dropped it, and then, snatching up a stick, struck the near wheeler a blow on the flank and jumped back into the bushes.

The horses started, mad, like they were locoed; it was a wonder the stage wasn't upset, racing this way and that, up the bank and down on the other side. Jim Bailey crawled out on the axle, picked up the dragging reins and got back just in time to keep Leonard from bouncing out. He heaved him up and held him round the body, and when he got the horses going straight, took a look at him. That first time he thought he was dead, white as chalk and with his eyes turned up. But after a spell of going he decided there was life in him yet, and holding him with one arm, stretched the other over the splashboard, shaking the reins on the wheelers' backs, and the way those horses buckled to their work was worth gettin' held up to see.

Half an hour later the Rocky Bar stage came like a cyclone into Mormons Landing, Jim Bailey hopping like a grasshopper on the front seat, and on his arm Danny Leonard, shot through the lung. They drew up in front of the Damfino Saloon, and Mormons Landing, dead among its deserted ditches, knew again a crowded hour of glorious life. Everybody came running and lined up along the sidewalk, later to line up along the Damfino Bar. The widow woman who ran the eating house put Danny Leonard in her own bed and sent one of her sons, aged six, to San Marco for a doctor, and the other, aged eight, to Jackson for the sheriff.

Before night fell the news had flashed through the countryside. On ranch piazza and in cabin doorway, in the camps along the Mother Lode and the villages of the plain, men were telling one another how Knapp and Garland had held up the Rocky Bar stage and got away with twelve thousand dollars in gold.

CHAPTER II

THE TULES

THE PLACE OF THE HOLDUP was on the first upward roll of the hills. Farther back, along more distant slopes, the chaparral spread like a dark cloth but here there was little verdure. The rainless California summer had scorched the country; mounded summit swelled beyond mounded summit all dried to a uniform ochre. But if you had stood on the rise where the stage stopped and faced toward the west, you would have seen, stretching to the horizon, a green expanse that told of water.

This was the tules, a vast spread of marsh covered with bulrushes, flat as a floor, and extending from a distant arm of the bay back into the land. It was like a wedge of green thrust through the yellow, splitting it apart, at one end meeting the sky in a level line, at the other narrowing to a point which penetrated the bases of the hills. From these streams wound down ravine and rift till their currents slipped into the brackish waters of the marsh. Such a stream, dried now to a few stagnant pools, had worn a way along the gulley where the holdup had occurred.

Down this gulley, the box between them, the bandits ran. Alders and bay grew thick, sun spots glancing through their leaves, boughs slapping and slashing back from the passage of the rushing bodies, stones rolling under the flying feet. The heat was suffocating, the narrow cleft holding it, the matted foliage keeping out all air. The men's faces were empurpled, the gunny sacks about their necks were soaked with sweat. They spoke little—a grunt, a muttered oath as a stone turned. Doubled under the branches, crashing through a covert with closed eyes and warding arm, they fled, now and then pausing for a quick change of hands on the box or the sweep of a sleeve across a dripping brow. Nearly a half hour from the time

5

they had started they emerged into brighter light, the trees growing sparse, the earth moist, a soft coolness rising—the creek's conjunction with the tules.

The sun was sloping westward, the sky infinitely blue and clear, golden light slanting across the plain's distant edges. Before them, silent, not a breath stirring the close-packed growth, stretched the marshes. They were miles in extent; miles upon miles of these level bulrush spears threaded with languid streams, streams that curved and looped, turned back upon themselves, narrowed into gleaming veins, widened to miniature lakes on whose bosom the clouds, the birds and the stars were mirrored. They were like a crystal inlay covering the face of the tules with an intricate, shining pattern. No place was ever more deserted, alien, uninhabitable, making no compromise with the friendly, fruitful land.

Against the muddy edge a rotten punt holding a pole swung deliberate from a stake. The men put the box in, then followed, and the elder, standing in the stern, took the pole and, pushing against the bank, drove the boat into deep water. It floated out, two ripples folding back oily sleek from its bow. After the Indian fashion, the man propelled it with the pole, prodding against the bottom. He did it skillfully, the unwieldly hulk making a slow, even progress. He also did it with a singular absence of sound, the pole never grating on the gunnel, feeling quietly along the soft mud of the shores, rising from the water, held suspended, then slipping in again as noiseless as the dip of the dragon flies.

No words passed between them. Sliding silent over the silent stream, they were like a picture done in a few strong colors, violent green of the rushes, violent blue of the sky. Their reflection moved with them, two boats joining at the water line, in each boat two figures, every fold of their garments, every shade and high light, minutely and dazzlingly reproduced.

Highwayman is a word of picturesque suggestion, but there was nothing picturesque about them. They looked like laborers weather-worn from wind and sun; the kind of men that crowd the streets of new camps and stand round the cattle pens at country fairs. Knapp, sitting in the bow, was younger than the other— under thirty probably. He was a big-boned, powerful animal, his thick, reddish hair growing low on his forehead, his face, with its wide nose and prominent jaw, like the study of a face left in the rough. In his stolid look there was something childlike, his eyes following the flight of a bird in the air, then dropping to see its reflection in the water.

Garland was older, fully fifty, burly, thickset, strong as an ox. His hat lay in the bottom of the boat and his head, covered with curly, grizzled hair, was broad and well-shaped. A corresponding grizzle of beard clothed his chin and fringed a straight line of lip. The rest of his face showed the skin sun-dried and lined less from age than a life in the open. Wrinkles radiated from the corners of his eyes, and one, like a fold in the flesh, crossed his forehead in a deep-cut crease. His clothes were of the roughest, a dirty collarless shirt with a rag of red bandanna round the neck, a coat shapeless and dusty, and overalls grease and mud-smeared with the rubbing of his hands. His boots were the iron-hard clouts of the rancher, his hat a broken black felt, sweat-stained and torn. Passing him on the road, you would have set him down as a farm hand out of a job.

The boat had passed beyond the shelter of the hills to where the tules widened. Pausing, he glanced about. Far to the right he could see a small white square—the lodge of a sportsman's club which in the duck shooting season would disgorge men and dogs into the marsh. It was closed now, but on the plain beyond there were ranches. He dropped to his knees, shipped the pole, and drew from the bottom of the boat a piece of wood roughly shaped into a paddle. Here in the heart of the tules, where a head moving over the bulrush floor might be discerned, sound would not carry far. He dipped in the paddle, the long spray of drops hitting the water with a dry, running patter.

The man in front moved and looked ahead.

"We'd ought to be near there."

"A few yards over to the right," came the answer, and with it the boat took a sharp turn to the left, nosing along the bank, then stole down a waterway, a crystal channel between ramparts of green. This looped at a right angle, shone with a sudden glaze of sun, slipped into shadow and, rounding a point, an island with a bare, oozy edge came into view.

A deep stroke of the paddle sent the boat forward, its bow burrowing into the mud, and Knapp jumped out and beached it. The place was a small islet, one side clear, a wall of rushes, thick as grass, clothing the other. Over the water line the earth was hard, its surface cracked and flaked by the sun. On this open space lay two battered kerosene oil cans, their tops torn away, and a pile of stones. The hiding place was not a new one and the properties were already prepared.

With a knife and chisel they broke open the box. The money was in small canvas sacks, clean as if never used before and marked with a stenciled "W. F. & Co." They took it out and looked at it; hefted its weight in their hands. It represented the first success after several failures, one brought to trial, others frustrated in the making or abandoned after warnings from the ranchers and obscure towns-folk who stood in with them. Knapp had been discouraged. Now he took a handful and spread it on his palm, golden eagles, heavy, shining, solid. Swaying his wrist, he let the sun play on them, strike glints from their edges, burnish their surface.

"Twelve thousand," he murmured. "We ain't but once before got that much."

The elder, pulling the gunny sack from his neck, dropped it into one of the oil cans, pressing it against the sides like a lining.

"I can get the ranch now; six thousand'll cover everything."

"Are you honestly calculatin' to do that?" Knapp had reached for the other can. With arm outstretched, he looked at Garland, gravely curious.

"I am. I told you so before. I had a look at it again last week. They'll sell for four thousand, and it'll take five hundred to put it into shape. I'll bank the rest."

"And you'll quit?"

"Certain. I've had enough of the road."

The younger man pondered, watching the hands of his partner fitting the money bags into the can. "Mebbe you got the right idea," he muttered.

"It's the right idea for me. I'm not what I once was, I'm old. It's time for me to lay off and rest. I can't keep this up forever and now I got the chance to get out and I'm goin' to."

He had filled his can and rose, taking off his coat and throwing it on the ground. Picking up the knife and chisel he went back to where the bulrushes began and crushed in among them. Knapp, packing the other can, could hear the sound of his heavy movements, the hacking of the knife at the bulrush stalks and then the thud of falling earth. When he had filled his can he saw that there were two sacks left over. He took them up and, looking about, caught sight of a newspaper protruding from the pocket of Garland's coat. He pulled it out, calling as he did so:

"There's two sacks I can't get in. I'm goin' to put 'em in this here paper you got."

A grunt of acquiescence came from the bulrushes, the hacking of the knife, the thuds going on. Knapp unfolded the paper, set the sacks in it, and, gathering it about them, placed it on the top of his can. He heaved the whole up and crashed through the rushes to where Garland had already cleared a space and was digging a hole in the mud. When it was finished, the cans—the newspaper bundle on top—were lowered into it, and earth and roots replaced. No particular attempt was made at concealment; the cache was as secure against intrusion as if it were on the crest of the Sierra, and within the week they would be back to empty it. The box was filled with stones and sunk in the stream.

Then they rested, prone on the ground, at first talking a little. There was a question about the messenger; Knapp had shot and was casually confident he had only winged him. The matter seemed to give him no anxiety, and presently, his head burrowed into his arm, he fell asleep, a great, sprawled figure with the sun making his red hair shine like a copper helmet.

Garland lay on his back, his coat for a pillow, smoking a blackened pipe and thinking. He saw the sky lose its blue, and fade to a thin, whitish transparency, then flush to rose, bird specks skimming across it. He saw the tules grow dark, black walls flanking paths incredibly glossy, catching here and there a barring of golden cloud. He felt the breath of the marshes chill and salt-tainted, and watched the first star, white as a diamond, prick through the vault.

Then he rose and shook his partner, waking him with voluble profanity. The night had come, the dark that was to hide their stealthy exit. They went different ways; Knapp by a series of trails and planks to the south bank and thence across country, footing it through the night to his lair near Stockton. Garland would move north to friends of his up toward the mining camps along the Feather. They made a rendezvous for a night six days distant. Then they would carry away the money to places of safety which they went to prepare.

The sky was star-strewn as Garland's punt slipped away from the island. It was intensely still, a whisper of water round the moving prow, the sibilant dip of the paddle the only sounds. He could see the water as a pale, winding shimmer ahead, dotted with star reflections like small, scattered flowers. Once, rising to make sure of his course, he saw the tiny yellow light in a ranch house far away. He stood for a moment looking at it, and when he crouched again the light had kindled his imagination. Its spark glowed wide till it showed the ranch kitchen, windows open to the blue night, earth smells floating in, the table with its kerosene lamp, the rancher reading the paper, his dog sleeping at his feet, peaceful, unguarded, secure.

Conscious of distance to be traversed before he became a creature of wary instincts and watchful eyes, he let his thoughts have way. They slipped about and touched the future with a sense of ease, then veered to the past. Here they steadied, memories rising photographically distinct like a series of pictures, detached yet revealing an underlying thread of connection:

First it was his youth in the Southwest when he had been Tom Michaels, a miner, well paid, saving his wages. Then his marriage with Juana Ramirez, the half-breed girl at Deming, and the bit of land he had bought—with a mortgage to pay—in the glaring, green river valley. Glimpses of their life there, children and work—stupefying, tremendous work—to keep them going and to meet the interest; he had been a giant in those days.

And even so he hadn't been able to do it. Six years after they took possession they moved out, ruined. He remembered it as if it had been yesterday—the adobe house with its flat roof and strings of red peppers hanging on the walls, the cart piled high with furniture, Juana on the front seat and Pancha astride of the mule. Juana had grown old in those six years, fat and shapeless, but she had been dog-loyal, dog-loving, his woman. Never a word of complaint out of her—even when the two children died she had just covered her head with the blanket and sat by the hearth, stoical, dry-eyed, silent.

He could see now that it was his dream of making money—big money—that had been wrong. If he'd been content with a wage and a master he'd have done better by her, but from the start he'd wanted his freedom, balked at being roped and branded with the herd. That was why he drifted back to mining, not a steady job, though he could have got it, but as a prospector, leaving Arizona and moving to California. There were years of it; he knew the mineral belt from the Panamint mountains to the Kootenai country. Juana and Pancha plodded from town to town, seeing him at intervals, always expecting to hear he'd struck "the ledge," and be hardly able to scrape a living for them from the bottom of his pan.

One picture stood out clearer than the rest, ineffaceable, to be carried to his grave—the day he came back and heard that Juana was dead. He had left them at a place in Inyo, a scattering of houses on the edge of the desert. Pancha saw him coming, and her figure, racing to meet him in a blown flutter of cotton skirt, was as plain before his eyes as if she were running toward him now along the shining water path. She was twelve, brown as a nut, and scarecrow-thin, with a tangle of black hair, and narrow, dark eyes. He could recall the feel of her little hard hand inside his as she told him, excited at imparting such news, pushing the hair off her dirty face to see how he took it.

It had crushed the heart in him and some upholding principle of hope and resolution broke. He found a place for Pancha with Maria Lopez, the Mexican woman who ran the Buon Gusto restaurant at Bakersfield and agreed to look after the girl for pay. Then he went back to the open, not caring much, the springs of his soul gone dry. He had no energy for the old life and did other things, anything to make his own food and Pancha's keep—herded sheep, helped on the cattle ranges, tended store, hung on the fringes of the wilderness, saw men turn to savages and turned himself.

At long intervals he went down to the settlements and saw Pancha, growing into a gawky girl, headstrong, and with the wildness of her mother's people cropping out. She hated Maria Lopez and the work in the restaurant and wanted him to take her to the mountains. When she was sixteen a spell of illness laid him up and after that he had difficulty in getting work. Two months passed without a payment and when he finally got down to Bakersfield he found that Pancha had gone, run away with a traveling company of actors. Maria Lopez and he had a fight, raged at one another in mutual fury, and then he started out to find his girl, not knowing when he did what he would do with her.

She solved that problem; she insisted on staying with the actors. She liked the life, she could sing, they told her she had a future. She had fixed and settled everything, even to her name; she would retain that of Lopez, which she was already known by in Bakersfield. There was nothing for it but to let her have her way; a man without home, money or prospects has no authority. But the sense of his own failure, of the hopelessness of his desire to shelter and enrich her, fell on his conscience like a foot on a spark and crushed it out. He returned to the mountains, his hand against all men, already an outlaw, love for his own all that was left of the original man. That governed him, gave him the will to act, stimulated his brain, and lent his mind an unfailing cunning. The meeting with Knapp crystallized into a partnership, but when Garland the bandit rose on the horizon, no one, least of all Pancha, knew he was Michaels the miner.

He stood up in the boat and again reconnoitered; he was near the shore. The country slept under the stars, gray rollings of hills and black blotches of trees, very still in its somber repose. Dropping back to the seat, he plied the paddle with extraordinary softness, wary, listening, alert. Soon, in a week or two, if he could settle the sale, he would be on his way to San Francisco to tell Pancha he had sold his claim at last and had bought the ranch. Under his caution the pleasure of this thought pervaded him with an exquisite satisfaction. He could not forbear its indulgence and, leaning on the paddle, allowed himself a last, delightful vision—the ranch house piazza with Pancha—her make-up off—sitting on the steps at his feet.

That night he slept in the cowshed of an abandoned ranch. A billet of wood under his head, his repose was deep and dreamless, but in the dawn's light he woke, suddenly called out of slumber by a thought. It floated on the surface of his conciousness, vaguely disturbing, then took slow shape and he sat up feeling in the pockets of his coat. The paper was gone; Knapp saying he had taken it was not a dream. For a space he sat, coming to clearer recollection, his partner's voice calling, vaguely heard, its request unheeded in his preoccupation. He gave a mutter of relief, and dropping back settled himself into comfort. The paper was as safe there as in his own pocket and he'd have it again inside of a week. With the first light in his eyes, he lapsed off again for another hour.

CHAPTER III

MARQUIS DE LAFAYETTE

A FEW MILES BELOW where the stage was held up a branch road breaks from the main highway and cuts off at right angles across the plain. This is a ranchers' road. If you follow it southward you come to the region of vast holdings, acres of trees in parallel lines as straight as if laid with a tape measure, great, fawn-colored fields, avenues of palm and oleander leading to white houses where the balconies have striped awnings and people sit in cushioned wicker chairs.

The other end of it runs through lands of decreasing cultivation till—after it passes Tito Murano's cottage—it dips to the tules and that's the end of it. To be sure, a trail—a horse path—breaks away and makes a detour round the head of the marshes, but this is seldom used, a bog in winter and in summer riven with dried water-courses and overgrown with brambles. To get around the tules comfortably you have to strike farther in and that's a long way.

The last house before you get to Tito Murano's, which doesn't count, is the Burrage Ranch. In the white mansions among the fruit trees the Burrage Ranch doesn't count much either. It is old and small, fifty acres, a postage stamp of a ranch. There is no avenue to the house, which is close to the road behind a picket fence, and instead of encircling balconies and striped awnings, it has one small porch with a sagging top, over which climbs a rose that stretches long festoons to the gable. In its yard grow two majestic live oaks, hoary giants with silvered limbs reaching out in a thick-leaved canopy and casting a great spread of shade.

Old Man Burrage had had the ranch a long time as they reckon time in California. In his youth he had seen the great epoch in Virginia City, figured in it in a humble capacity, and emerged from its final *débâcle* with twenty thousand dollars. He should have emerged with more and that he didn't made him chary of mining. Peace and security exerted their appeal, and after looking about for a few reflective years, he had married the prettiest waitress in the Golden Nugget Hotel in Placerville and settled down to farming. He had settled and settled hard, settled like a barnacle, so firm and fast that he had never been able to pull himself loose. Peace he had found but also poverty. If the mineral vein was capricious, so were the elements, insect pests and the fruit market. Thirty years after he had bought the ranch he was still there and still poor with his wife Mary Ellen, his daughter Sadie and his son Mark.

Mark's advent had followed the decease of two older boys and his mother had proclaimed his preciousness by christening him Marquis de Lafayette. Her other sons had borne the undistinguished appellations of relatives, but this one, her consolation and her Benjamin, would be decked with the flower of her fancy. Of the original bearer of the name she knew nothing. Waiting on table at the Golden Nugget and later bearing children and helping on the ranch had not left her time for historical study. When her son, waking to the blight she had so innocently put upon him, asked her where she had found the name, she had answered, "In a book," but beyond that could give no data. When, unable to bear his shame, he had abbreviated it to "Mark D.L." she had been hurt.

Otherwise he had not disappointed her. When she had crowned him with a title she had felt that a high destiny awaited him and the event proved it. After a youth on the ranch, Mark, at sixteen, grew restive, at seventeen announced that he wanted an education and at eighteen packed his grip and went to work his way through Stanford University. Old Man Burrage made himself a bore at the crossroads store and the county fair telling how his boy was waiting on table down to Stanford and doing typewriting nights. Some boy, that!

When Mark came home on his vacations it was like the return of Ulysses after his ten years' wandering—they couldn't look at him enough, or get enough time to listen. His grammar was straightened out, his chin smooth, the freckles gone from his hands, and yet he was just the same—no fancy frills about him, Old Man Burrage bragged to his cronies. And then came the coping stone—he told them he was going to be a lawyer. Some of the neighbors laughed but others grew thoughtful and nodded commendingly. Even on the balconies of the white houses in the wicker chairs under the awnings Mark and his aspirations drew forth interested comment. Most of these people had known him since he was a shock-headed, barefoot kid, and when they saw him in his store clothes and heard his purified grammar, they realized that for youth in California belongs the phrase "the world is my oyster."

Now Mark had graduated and was studying in a large law office in San Francisco. He was paid twenty dollars a week, was twenty-four years old, rather silent, five-feet-ten and accounted good-looking. At the time this story opens he was spending his vacation—pushed on to the summer's end by a pressure of work in the office—on the ranch with his parents.

It was late afternoon, on the day following the holdup, and he was sitting in the barn doorway milking the brown cow. The doorway was shadowed, the blackness of the barn's interior behind it, the scent of clean hay drifting out and mingling with the scents of baked earth and tarweed that came from the heated fields. With his cheek against the cow's side he could see between the lower limbs of the oaks the country beyond, rust-colored and tan, streaked with blue shadows and the mottled blackness below the trees. Turning a little further he could look down the road with the eucalyptus tall on either side, the yellow path barred by their shade. From the house came a good smell of hot bread and a sound of voices—Mother and Sadie were getting ready for supper. At intervals Mother's face, red and round below her sleeked, gray hair, her spectacles up, her dress turned in at the neck, appeared at the window to take a refreshing peep at her boy milking the brown cow.

The milk sizzed and foamed in the pail and the milker, his forehead against the cow's warm pelt, watched it rise on the tin's side. It made a loud drumming which prevented his hearing a hail from the picket fence. The hail came again in a husky, dust-choked voice:

"Hello, can you give me a drink?"

This time Mark heard and wheeled on the stool. A tramp was leaning against the fence looking at him.

Tramps are too familiar in California for curiosity or interest, also they are unpopular. They have done dreadful things—lonely women in outlying farms have guns and dogs, the one loaded, the other cultivated in savagery against the visits of the hobo.

Mark rose unwelcoming, but the fellow did look miserable. He was gaunt and dirty, long ragged locks of hair falling below the brim of his torn straw hat, an unkempt straggle of beard growing up his cheeks. His clothes hung loose on his lean frame, and he looked all the same color, dust-brown, his hair, his shirt, his coat, even his face, the tan lying dark over a skin that was sallow. Only his eyes struck a different note. They were gray, very clear in the sun-burned face, the lids long and heavy. Their expression interested Mark; it was not the stone-hard, evil look of the outcast man, but one of an unashamed, smoldering resentment.

The same quality was in his manner. The request for water was neither fawningly nor piteously made. It was surly, a right churlishly demanded. Mark moved to the pump and filled the glass standing there. The tramp leaning on the pickets looked at him, his glance traveling morose over the muscular back and fine shoulders, the straight nape, the dark head with its crown of thick, coarse hair. As Mark advanced with the glass he continued his scrutiny, when, suddenly meeting the young man's eyes, his own shifted and he said in that husky voice, hoarse from a parched throat:

"It's the devil walking in the heat on these rotten dusty roads."

The other nodded and handed him the glass. He drained it, tilting his head till the sinews in his haggard throat showed below his beard. Then he handed it back with a muttered thanks.

"Been walking far?" said Mark.

The tramp moved away from the pickets, jerking his head toward the road behind him. For the first time Mark noticed that he had a basket on his arm, containing a folded blanket.

"From the fruit farms down there. I've been working my way up fruit picking. But it's a dog's job; better starve while you're about it. Thank you. So long."

It was evident he wanted no further parley, for he started off down the road. Mark stood looking after him. He noticed that he was tall and walked with a long stride, not the lazy shuffle of the hobo. Also he had caught a quality of education in the husky voice. Under its coarsened inflections there was an echo of something cultured, not fitting with his present appearance, a voice that might once have known very different conditions. Possibly a dangerous chap, Mark thought; had an ugly look, a secret, forbidding sort of face. When the educated kind dropped they were apt to fall further and come down harder than the others. He threw the glass into the bushes and went in to wash up. Before he was called to supper he had forgotten all about the man.

In the cool of the evening the Burrages sat on the porch, rather crowded for the space was small. Mark, on the bottom step, smoked a pipe and watched the eucalyptus leaves printed in pointed black groupings against the Prussian-blue sky. This was the time when the family, released from its labors, sat back comfortably and listened to the favored one while he told of the city by the sea. Old Man Burrage had a way of suddenly asking questions about people he had known in the brave days of the Comstock, some dead now, others trailing clouds of glory eastward this many years.

Tonight he was minded to hear about the children of George Alston whom Mark had met. Long ago in Virginia City Old Man Burrage had often seen George Alston, talked with him when he was manager of the Silver Queen and one of the big men of that age of giants. Mother piped up there—she wasn't going to be beaten. Many's the time she'd waited on George Alston when he and the others would come riding over the Sierras on their long-tailed horses—a bunch of them together galloping into Placerville like the Pony Express coming into Sacramento.

"And some of 'em," said the old woman, rocking in easeful reminiscence, "would be as fresh with me as if I'd given 'em encouragement. But George Alston, never—he'd treat me as respectful as if I was the first lady in the land. Halting behind to have a neighborly chat and the rest of them throwin' their money on the table and off through the dining room hollerin' for their horses."

Her son, on the lower step, stirred as if uncomfortable. These memories, once prone to rouse a tender amusement, now carried their secret sting.

"He was the real thing," the farmer gravely commented. "There wasn't many like him."

Sadie, who was not interested in a man dead ten years ago, pushed the conversation on to her own generation.

"His daughters are grown up. They must be young ladies now."

Mark answered:

"Yes—Miss Chrystie's just eighteen, came of age this summer. The other one's a few years older."

"Up in Virginia," said the farmer, "George Alston was a bachelor. Every woman was out with her lariat after him but he give 'em all the slip. And afterward, when he went back East to see his folks, a little girl in his home town got him—a girl a lot younger than him. She died after a few years."

There was regret in his tone, not so much for the untimely demise of the lady as for the fact that George Alston had not found his mate in California.

"What are they like?" said Sadie—"pretty?"

Mark had his back toward her. She could see the shape of it, pale in its light-colored shirt, against the dark filigree of shrubs at the bottom of the steps. His answer sounded indifferent between puffs of his pipe:

"Yes, I guess so. Miss Chrystie's a big, fine sort of girl, with yellow hair and lots of color. She's nearly as tall as I am. The other, Miss Lorry—well, she's small."

"They'd ought to have a heap of money," said the farmer. "But when he died I heard he hadn't cut up as rich as you'd think. Folks said he was too honest."

"They've got enough—four hundred thousand each."

"Well, well, well," said Mother with a lazy laugh, "that'd do me."

Her husband wouldn't have it.

"Lord, that's small for him," he mourned. "But I'm not surprised. He wouldn't 'a' stood for what some of the rest of 'em did."

"Is the house grand?" asked Sadie.

"I suppose it is; it's big enough, lots of bay windows and rooms and piazzas. It's on Pine Street, near town, with a garden round it full of palms and trees."

"Do they have parties there?"

"No—at least I never heard of any. They're quiet sort of girls, don't go out much. Just live there with an old lady—Mrs. Tisdale—some relative of their mother's."

Sadie was disappointed. Having been led to expect so much from these children of wealth, she felt cheated and was inclined to criticize. She rather grumbled about their being so quiet. Mother disagreed:

"It sounds as if they were nice and genteel. Not the flashy, fashionable kind. And their mother dying when they were so young—that makes a difference."

"It was Crowder got you acquainted with them?" said the old man.

Charlie Crowder was a college chum of Mark's who had spent several vacations on the ranch and who was regarded by the Burrages as a fount of wisdom. Mark from the steps said yes, Crowder had taken him to the house.

There was a pause after this, the parents sunk in gratified musings. The farmer, the simple, unaspiring male, saw no further than the fact of Mark a guest in George Alston's home, but Mother had far-reaching fancies, glimpsed future possibilities. It was she who broke the silence, observing casually as if all doors must be open to her brilliant son,

"I'm glad you know them, honey. There's no better companions for a young man making his way, than quiet, refined girls."

Sadie saw it as astonishing. She could hardly encompass the thought of her brother, a few years ago working on the ranch like a hired man, now moving in the glittering spheres that she read about in the Sunday edition of the *Sacramento Courier.*

"Do you go there often?" she asked.

"Oh, now and again. I haven't much time for calling."

It was Mark who turned the conversation, difficult at first. The farmer was tractable, but Mother and Sadie showed a tendency to cling to the Alston sisters. He finally diverted their attention by telling them about Pancha Lopez, the greaser girl, who was the new leading woman at the Albion Opera House, and a friend of Charlie Crowder's. Mother forgot the Alstons.

"You don't know her, do you, Mark?" she said uneasily.

"No, Mother, I've only seen her act."

The farmer stirred and rumbled warningly out of the darkness,

"And you don't want to, son. A hard-working boy don't want to waste his time lallygaggin' round with actresses."

When they dispersed for the night, Mother noticed that Mark was abstracted, almost as if he was depressed. No one else saw it; eyes and tongues were heavy at bedtime on the ranch. Sadie, dragging up the stairs to be awake tomorrow at sunrise, might have been depressed but she wasn't. And the farmer and his wife, creaking about in their stuffy room over the kitchen, their old bones stiff with fatigue, were elated.

A part of the attic, lighted by one window in the gable, had been Mark's den since he was eight. Here was the table with its hacked edge where he had done his "homework" when he went to the public school up the road, his shelf of books, the line of pegs for his clothes, the rifle his father had given him when he shot fifty rabbits in one month. He lit the lamp and looked about, his eyes seeing it as mean and unlovely, and his heart reproaching him that he should see it so.

He sat down by the table and tried to read, but the book fell to his knees and he stared, thought-tranced, at the pegs along the wall. What he thought of was the eldest Alston girl, Lorry, the one he had described as "small." Usually he did not permit himself to do this, but tonight the talk on the porch, his people's naive pleasure that he should know one so fine and far-removed, called up her image— dominant, imperious, not to be denied. With the lamplight gilding his brooding face, the back-growing crest of dark hair, the thick eyebrows, the resolute mouth, lip pressed on lip in an out-thrust curve, he sat motionless, seeing her against the background of her home.

Details of its wealth came to him, costly elegancies of her surroundings—the long parlor with its receding vista to a dining room where silver shone grandly, rich, still curtains, pictures, statues; the Chinese servants offering delicate food, coming at the touch of a bell, opening doors, carrying trays. It was not really as imposing as Mark thought. There were people who sniffed at the Alstons' way of living, in that queer, old-fashioned house far down town with the antiquated, lumbering furniture their father had bought when he married. But Mark had not the advantage of a comparative standard. Her setting gained its splendor not only from his inexperience, but by comparison with his own. He saw their two homes in contrast, just as he saw her in contrast with the other girls he had known, her fortune in contrast with his twenty dollars a week. It brought him a new, sharp pain, pain that he should have seen the difference, that he had acknowledged it, that what had once seemed good and fitting now looked poor and humble. He loved his people and hugged the love to him with a fierce loyalty, but it could not hide the fact that they were not as her people. It was the first jar to his glad confidence, the first blow in his proud fight for power and place, the first time the thought of his poverty had come with a humiliating sting. He was sore and angry with himself and would have liked to be angry with her. But he couldn't—she was so sweet!

CHAPTER IV

THE DERELICT

THE TRAMP WALKED DOWN the road, first on the grizzled grass, then, the earth under it baked to an iron hardness, back on the softened dust. He passed Tito Murano's cottage with dogs and chickens and little Muranos sporting about the kitchen door and then noticed a diminishing of trees and a sudden widening of the prospect. From here the road dwindled to a trail that sloped to the marsh which spread before him. He sat down on a bank by the roadside and looked at it.

Under the high, unsullied heavens it lay like an unrolled map, green-painted, divisions and subdivisions marked by the fine tracings of streams. His eye traveled down its length to where in a line, ruler-straight, it met the sky, then shifted to its upper end, a jagged point reaching to the hills. He had heard of it on the ranches where he had been picking fruit—"It's easy traveling till you reach the tules, but it's some pull round *them*." He gauged the distance round the point, and oaths, picturesque and fluent, came from him. He had sixteen dollars in the lining of his coat, and for days as he tramped and worked, he saw this hoard expended in San Francisco—a bath, clean linen, and a dinner, a dinner in a rôtisserie with a pint of red wine and a cigar. He saw no further than that—sixteen dollars' worth of comfort and good living.

Now he was like a child deprived of its candy. He ached with fatigue, his feet were blistered, his throat dry as a kiln. Throwing off his hat, he leaned forward, his elbows on his knees, and cursed the marsh as if it were a living thing, cursed it with a slow, unctuous zest, spat out upon it the venom and wrath that had accumulated within him.

Seeing him thus, his hat off, sullen indifference replaced by a malign animation, he was a very different being from the man who

23

had accosted Mark. A dangerous chap beyond doubt, dangerous from a dark soul and a stored power of malevolence. His face, vitalized with rage, was handsome; a narrow forehead, the hair receding from the temples, a high-bridged nose with wide-cut nostrils, lips thin and fine, moving flexibly as they muttered. It matched with what the voice had told Mark, was not the face of the brutalized hobo or low-bred vagrant, but beneath its hair and dirt showed as the mask of a man who might have fallen from high places. Even his curses went to prove it. They were not the dull profanities of the loafer, but were varied, colorful, imaginative, such curses as might come from one who had read and remembered.

Suddenly they stopped and his glance deflected, alert and apprehensive—his ear had caught a low crooning of song. It came from a small boy who, a little wooden boat in his hand, was advancing up the slope. This was Tito Murano, Junior, Tito's first-born, nine years old, softly footing it home after a joyous hour along the edge of the tules.

Tito's mother was Irish, but the Latin strain had flowered forth strong in her son. He was bronze-brown, with a black bullet head and eyes like shoe buttons. A pair of cotton trousers and a rag of shirt clothed him and his feet were bare and caked with mud. A happy day behind him and the prospect of supper made his heart light and he gave forth its joy in fresh, bird-sweet carolings.

He did not see the tramp and a sharp, "Hey, there, kid," made him halt, startled, gripping the treasured boat against his breast. Then he made out the man, and stood staring, poised to run.

"Is there any way of getting across this infernal place?" The tramp's hand swept the prospect.

Bashfulness held Tito speechless, and he stood rubbing one foot across the other.

The man's eyes narrowed with a curious, ugly look.

"Are you deaf?" he said very quietly.

A muttered negative came from the child. The question contained a quality of scorn that he felt and resented.

"I want to cross the marsh, get to the railway. What's the best way to go?"

Tito's arm made a sweeping gesture round the head of the tules.

"That. There's a trail. You go round."

"Good God—that's *miles*. How do people go, the people here, when they want to get to the other side?"

"That way." Tito repeated his gesture. "But they don't go often, and they mostly rides."

The man gave a groaning oath, picked up his hat, then cast it from him with fury, and, planting his elbows on his knees, dropped his forehead on his hands. Tito was sorry for him, and advanced charily, his heart full of sympathy.

"The duck shooters have laid planks," he murmured encouragingly.

The man raised his head.

"Planks—where?"

Tito indicated the marsh.

"All along. They lay 'em when they come to shoot and then they let 'em lay. Nobody don't ever go there 'cept the duck shooters."

"You mean I can get across by the planks?"

Tito forgot his bashfulness and drew nearer. He was emboldened by the thought that he could help the tramp, give assistance as man to man.

"*You* couldn't. It's all mud and water, and turns too, like you was goin' round in rings. But *I* could—I bin acrost, right over to the Ariel Club." He pointed to a small white square on the opposite side. "That's where. The railroad's a ways beyont that, but it ain't awful far."

The man looked and nodded, then smiled, a slight curling of his lip, a slight contraction of the skin round his eyes.

"If you show me the way I'll give you a quarter," he said, turning the smile on Tito.

Tito did not like the smile; it suggested a dog's lifted lip when contemplating battle. Also he had been forbidden to go into the marsh; some of the streams were deep, the mud treacherous. But a quarter had seldom crossed his palm. He saw himself spending it at the crossroads store, and, tucking his boat up under his arm, said manfully:

"All right—I'll get you over before sundown."

They started, the child running fleet-footed ahead, the man following with long strides. There was evidently a way and Tito knew it. His black head bobbed along in front, now a dark sphere glossed by the sunlight, now an inky silhouette against the white shine of water.

There were creeks to jump and pools to wade—the duck shooters' planks only spanned the deep places—and the way was hard.

Once the tramp stopped, surly-faced, and measured the distance to the Ariel Club house. It seemed but little nearer. He told Tito so, and the child, pausing to look back, cheered him with heartening phrases. But it was a hard pull, crushing through the dense growth, staggering on the slippery ooze, and he began to mutter his curses again. Tito, hearing them, made no reply, a little scared in the sun-swept loneliness with the swearing in his ears.

Finally the man, floundering on a bank of mud, slipped and fell to his knees. He groveled, his hands caked, and when he rose a fearful stream of profanity broke from him. Tito stopped, chilled, peering back between the rushes. If it had been a rancher or one of the boys he would have laughed. But he had no inclination to laugh at the staggering figure, with the haggard, sweat-beaded face and furious eyes.

"I said it was long, but we're gettin' there. We're halfway acrost now," his little pipe, mellow-sweet, was in strange contrast with what had come before.

"You're a liar, a damnable liar. You've led me into the middle of this—place that you don't know any more of than I do."

His eyes, ranging about in helpless desperation, saw, some distance beyond, a rise of dry ground. The sight appeared to divert him, and he stood looking at it. He had the appearance of having forgotten Tito, and the child, uneasy at this sudden stillness as he was ready to be at anything the tramp did, said with timid urgency:

"Say, come on. I got to get home for supper or I'll get licked."

For answer the man moved in an opposite direction, to where the stream widened. He saw there was deep water between him and the dry place, but he wanted to get there, rest, smoke, unroll his blanket and sleep. Tito's uneasiness increased.

"You're goin' the wrong way," he pleaded. "You can't get round there, it's all water."

Suddenly the man turned on him savagely. His brooding eyes widened and their look, a threatening glare, made the boy's heart quail.

"Get out," he shouted, "get out, I'm done with you. You're a fakir."

Tito retreated, crushing the rushes under his naked feet, his face extremely fearful.

"But I was takin' you. I sure was—"

"Get out. You don't know anything about it. You're a liar."

"I do. I was takin' you straight—and you promised me a quarter."

"To hell with you and your quarter. Didn't you hear me say get out?"

The thought of the quarter gave Tito a desperate courage; his voice rose in a protesting wail:

"But I done half already—you're halfway acrost. You'd oughter give me a dime. I've done more than a dime's worth."

The tramp, with a smothered ejaculation, bent and picked up a bit of iron, relic of some sportsman's passage. Tito saw the raised hand and ducked, hearing the missile hurtle over his head and plop into the water behind him. It frightened him, but not so much as the man's face. Like a small, terrified animal he bent and fled. The breaths came quick from his laboring breast, and as he ran, his head low, the rushes swaying together over his wake, sobs burst from him, not alone for fear, but for his lost quarter.

The sun was the dazzling core of a golden glow when he crept on to the dry ground, mud-soaked, tear-streaked, his wooden boat still in his hand. His terror was over and he padded home in deep thought, inventing a lie. For if his parents knew of his wanderings he would be beaten and sent to bed without supper.

The tramp picked his way round to the stream that separated him from the desired ground, slipped out of his clothes and, putting them in the basket, plunged in the current. On the opposite bank he stood up, a lean, shining shape, the sunlight gilding his wet body, till it looked like a statue of brass. The bath refreshed him; he would eat some fruit he had in his basket, take a smoke, and rest there for the night.

Still wet, he pulled on his clothes, stretched out, and drawing a pear from the basket began to eat it. As he did so his glance explored the place and brought up on a mark at the water's edge. It interested him, and still gnawing the pear, he crawled down to it—a footprint, large and as clearly impressed as if cast in plaster. Not far from it was a triangular indentation, its point driven deep—the mark of a boat's prow.

Both looked fresh, the uppressed outlines of mud crisp and flakey, which would happen quickly under such a sun. Among his fellow vagrants he had learned a good deal about the tules, one fact, corroborated by the child, that at this season no one ever disturbed their loneliness. Still squatting he glanced about—at the foot of the rush wall behind him were two burnt matches. Men had recently been there, come in a boat, and smoked; there were no traces of a fire.

To perceptions used to the open dealings of an unobservant honesty, it would have signified nothing. But to his, trained for duplicity, learned in the ways of a world where concealments were a part of life, it carried a meaning. His face took on an animal look of cunning, his movements became alert and stealthy. Rising to his feet, he moved about, staring, studying, saw other footprints and then a break in the rushes at the back. He went there, parted the broken spears and came on a space where some were cut away, the ground disturbed, and still moist.

Half an hour later, the sun, sending its last long shafts across the marsh, played on a strange picture—a tramp, white-faced, with trembling hands, and round him, on the ground, about his sprawled legs, falling from his shaking fingers, yellow in the yellow light, gold, gold, gold!

CHAPTER V

THE MARKED PARAGRAPH

THE FIRST HALF OF THE NIGHT he spent moving the money to the marshes' edge. Its weight was like the weight of millstones but disposed about him, in the basket, in the gunny sacks slung from his shoulders, in the newspaper carried in his hands, he dragged it across. When he reached the bank he fell like one dead. Outstretched beside his treasure he lay on his back and looked with half-closed eyes at the black vault and the cold satiric stars.

Before the dawn came he wrapped part of it in the paper and buried it among the sedge; the rest he put in his basket and his pockets. Early morning saw him, an inconspicuous, frowsy figure, slouching up to a way station on the line to Sacramento.

In the train he found a newspaper left by a departed traveler, and on its front page, featured with black headlines, the latest news of the Knapp and Garland holdup. After he had read it he sat very still. He knew what he had found and was relieved. It cleared the situation if it added to its danger. But he was intrigued by the difficulty of disposing of the money. To bank it was out of the question; he must rouse no curiosity and he could give no references. To leave it on the marshes' edge was impracticable. He had heard of men who kept their loot buried, but he feared the perils of a cache, to be dug and re-dug, ungettable, in a solitary place, hard to find and dangerous to visit. He must put it somewhere not too remote, secure against discovery, where he could come and go unnoticed and free from question. By the time the train reached Sacramento he had formulated a plan.

He knew the city well, had footed the streets of its slums before he went South. In a men's lodging house, kept by a Chinese, he engaged a room, left what gold he had there—he had to take his chance against theft—and in the afternoon took a down train to the marsh.

He was back with the rest of the money that night, buying a second-hand suitcase on his way from the depot. In this he packed it, still in the canvas sacks, the newspaper folded over it. He saw to it that the suitcase had a lock, and lead-heavy he laid it flat under the bed.

The next morning he rose, nerved to a day of action. He was out early, his objective the small, mean stores of the poorer quarter. In these he bought shoes, the coarse brogans of the workman, and a hat, a rusty, sweat-stained Stetson. A barber's shop in a basement was his next point of call. Here he was shaved and his hair cut. When he emerged into the light of day the tramp had disappeared. The ragged growth gone, the proud almost patrician character of his face was strikingly apparent. It matched so illy with his wretched clothes that passersby looked at him. He saw it and slunk along the walls, his hat on his brows, uneasily aware of the glances of women which usually warmed him like wine. At a secondhand dealer's, a dark den with coats and trousers hanging in layers about the entrance, he bought a suit of clothes and an overcoat. Carrying these in a bundle he went back to his room and put them on.

The transformation was now complete. He studied himself in the blotched and wavy mirror and nodded in grave approval. He might have been an artisan, a small clerk, or a traveling salesman routed through the country towns.

Half an hour later saw him at the desk of the Whatcheer House. This was a third-rate men's hotel, a decent enough place where the transient male population from the interior met the restless influx from the coast. Here floated in, lodged a space, then drifted out a tide of men, seekers of work, of pleasure, of change, of nothing at all. The majority were of the world's rovers impelled by an unquench-able wanderlust, but among them were the industrious and steady, quartered in the city or shifting to a new center of activity. He reg-istered as Harry Romaine of Vancouver and described himself as a traveling man who would use Sacramento as a base of operations. He took a room in the back—No. 19—said he would probably keep it all winter and paid a month's rent in advance.

By afternoon he had the money there and with it a chisel and hammer. It was intensely hot, the sun beating on the wall and slop-ing in through the one window. Complete silence from the rooms on either side reassured him, and in the scorching stillness he worked with a noiseless, capable speed. In one corner under the bed he pulled up the carpet and pried loose the boards. Some of the money went there, some below the pipes in the cupboard under the stationary washstand, the rest behind a piece of the baseboard.

Before he replaced the boards in the corner cache—the largest and least difficult to disturb—he glanced about for anything over-looked or forgotten for which the hole would be a convenient hid-ing-place. On the floor, outspread and crumpled, lay the newspaper. The outer sheets were brown and disintegrated from contact with the mud, but the two inner ones were whole and clean. Probably it would be better to take no chances and hide it; someone might notice it and wonder how it came to be in such a state. He picked it up, looked it over, and saw it was the *Sacramento Courier* of August 25. That would make it only three days old, the issue of the day before the holdup. If anything was needed to convince him that the cache was Knapp and Garland's this was it. He opened it on the table to fold, brushing out the creases, when suddenly his hand dropped and his glance became fixed. A marked paragraph had caught his attention.

The light was growing dim and he took the paper to the window. The paragraph was at the end of a column, was encircled by two curved pencil strokes, and on the edge of clean paper below it was written, also in pencil, "Hello, Panchita. Ain't you the wonder. Your best beau's proud of you."

He pulled a chair to the window, folded back the page and read the marked item. The column was headed "C. C.'s San Francisco Letter," was dated August 21, and was mainly concerned with social and business news of the coast city. That part of it outlined by the pencil strokes ran as follows:

> As to matters theatrical there's nothing new in sight, except that Pancha Lopez—our Pancha—made a hit this week in "The Zingara," the gypsy operetta produced on Sunday night at the Albion. I can't tell much about "The Zingara"—maybe it was good and maybe it wasn't. I couldn't reckon with anything but Pancha; she was the whole show. She's never done anything so well, was as dainty as a pink, as

brilliant as a humming bird, danced like a fairy, and sang—
well, she sang way beyond what she's led us to expect of her.
Can I say more? The public evidently agrees with me. The
S.R.O. sign has been out at the cozy little home of comic
opera ever since Sunday. C.C., who can't keep away from the
place, has seen so many dress shirt fronts and plush cloaks
that he's rubbed his eyes and wondered if he hasn't made a
mistake and it's the grand opera season come early with a
change of dates. But he hasn't. Pacific and Van Ness avenues
are beginning to understand that we've got a little song bird
right here in our midst that they can hear for half a dollar
and who gives them more for that than the Metropolitans
do for a V. Saluda, Pancha! Here's looking at you. Some day
the East is going to call you and you're going to make a little line of footsteps across the continent. But for our sakes
postpone it as long as you can. Remember that you belong
to us, that we discovered you and that we can't get on without you.

He read it twice and then studied the penciled words, "Hello,
Panchita! Ain't you the wonder. Your best beau's proud of you." In the
dying light he murmured them over as if their sound delighted him
and as he murmured a slight, sardonic smile broke out on his face.

His sense of humor, grim and cynical, was tickled. He, the picaroon, companion of rogues and small marauders, had seen many and
diverse love affairs. On the shady bypaths he had followed, edging
along the rim of the law, he had met all sorts of couples, men and wom-
en incomprehensibly attracted, ill-assorted, mysterious, picturesque.
This seemed to him one of the most piquant combinations he had ever
encountered—a bandit and a comic opera singer. It amused him vastly
and he crooned over the paper, grinning in the dusk. The fellow had evidently marked the item and written his congratulations, intending to
send it to her, then needed it to wrap round the money, and confident
in the security of his cache, left it there against his return. That thought
increased his amusement, and he laughed, a low, smothered chuckle.

It was dark and he rose and lit the lamp. Then he tore out the
piece of the paper and put it in the pocket of his suitcase. The rest he

folded and placed in the hole under the money. As he knelt, fitting the boards back, he thought of the singing woman, Pancha Lopez. The beloved of a highwayman, with a Spanish name, he pictured her as a dark, flashing creature, coarsely opulent and mature. It was evident that she too belonged to the world of rogues and social pirates, and he laughed again as he saw himself, swept back by a turn of fate, into the lives of the outlawed. He must see Pancha Lopez; she promised to be interesting.

CHAPTER VI

PANCHA

A WEEK LATER, AT ELEVEN at night, a large audience was
crowding out of the Albion Opera House. If you know San
Francisco—the San Francisco of before the fire—you will
remember the Albion. It stood on one of those thoroughfares that
slant from the main stem of Market Street near Lotta's Fountain.
That part of the city is of dubious repute; questionable back walls
look down on the alley that leads to the stage door, and after midnight there is much light of electricity and gas and much unholy
noise round its darkened bulk.

But that is not the Albion's fault. It did not plant itself in the
Tenderloin; it was the Tenderloin that grew. Since it first opened its
doors as a temple of light opera—fifty cents a seat and a constant
change of bill—its patrons have been, if not fashionable, always respectable. Smoking was permitted, also the serving of drinks—the
seat in front had a convenient shelf for the ladies' lemonade and
the gentleman's beer—but even so, no one could say that a strict
decorum did not prevail in the Albion's audiences even as it did in
the Albion's productions.

A young man with a cheerful, ugly face stood in a side aisle,
watching the crowd file out. He had a kindly blue eye, a merry thick-
lipped mouth, and blonde hair sleeked back across his crown, one
lock, detached from the rest, falling over his forehead. He had a way
of smoothing back this lock with his palm but it always fell down
again and he never seemed to resent it. Of all that pertained to his
outward appearance, he was indifferent. Not only his patience with
the recalcitrant lock, but his clothes showed it—dusty, carelessly fitting, his collar too large for his neck, his cravat squeezed up into a
tight sailor's knot and shifted to one side. He was Charlie Crowder,

not long graduated from Stanford and now a reporter on the *Despatch*, where he was regarded with interest as a promising young man.

His eye, exploring the crowd, was the journalist's, picking salient points. It noted fur collars and velvet wraps, the white gloss of shirt bosoms, women's hair, ridged with artificial ripples—more of that kind in the audience than he'd seen yet. "The Zingara" had made a hit; he'd just heard at the box office that they would extend the run through the autumn. It pleased him for it verified his prophecy on the first night and it was a bully good thing for Pancha.

He stepped out of a side entrance, edged through the throngs on the pavement, dove up an alley and reached the stage door. A single round lamp burned over it and already dark shapes were issuing forth, mostly women, Cinderellas returned to their dingy habiliments. There was a great chatter of feminine voices as they skirmished off, some in groups, some alone, some on the arms of men who emerged from the darkness with muttered greetings.

Crowder crossed the back of the large stage where supers were pulling scenery about; weights and ropes, forest edges, bits of sky and parlor ceilings, hanging in layers from the flies. The brick wall at the back was whitewashed and against it a line of men and girls passed scurrying to the exit, throwing remarks back and forth, laughing, pulling on their coats. Some of them hailed him and got a cheery word in reply. Then, skirting the wings, he turned down a passage and brought up at a door on which a small star was drawn in chalk. He knocked, and a woman's voice called from inside:

"Who is it?"

"Your faithful press agent."

The woman's voice answered:

"Enter Charlie, rear, smiling."

He opened the door, went in. The place was the Albion's best dressing room. It was small, with white-washed walls, and lighted by a gas jet inclosed in a wire shield. A mirror, its frame dotted with artificial flowers, bits of ribbon, notes and favors, surmounted the dressing table. This was a litter of paint pots, hair pins, toilet articles, powder rags, across which, like a pair of strayed snakes, lay two long braids of black hair. A powerful scent of cosmetics and stale perfumery mingled with the faint, thrilling breath of roses.

Seated in front of the glass in a soiled red satin kimono embroidered in storks, was Pancha Lopez, leading woman of the Albion. She was wiping off her make-up, a large jar of cold cream on the table before her, a grease rag in her hand. The kimono, falling richly, outlined a thin, lithe body, flat-backed, muscular and supple. The make-up still on her face turned her brown skin to a meerschaum pallor and the dusky brick-red of her cheeks to an unnatural rose. A long neck upheld a small, finely shaped head, the hair now drawn back and twisted in a tight knot to which the two long braids had been pinned. The Indian strain in her revealed itself in the flattened cheek-bones, the wide-cut, delicate nostrils and the small, high-set eyes as clearly black and white as if made of enamel. They were now outlined and elongated with lamp black which still clung to her lashes in flakes. She was twenty-two years old, and had been on the stage for six years.

After a glance over her shoulder and a flashing smile she returned to her work, pushing her hair still further off her forehead with one hand, and sweeping the greasy cloth over her face with the other.

"Well," said Crowder, standing beside her and looking at her reflection, "how's the baby-grand Patti tonight?"

"Fine!" She drew down her upper lip and slowly rubbed round her mouth, Crowder, as if fascinated, watching the process in the mirror. "Just sit down on something. Hang up my costume and take that chair if there isn't any other. I got to get this thing off before I can talk comfortably."

Her costume, a glittering heap of red and orange, lay across a chair, the pile surmounted by an open cardboard box whence the heads of roses protruded from tissue paper. He feared to touch that, and finding another chair against the wall, drew it to the side of the dressing table and sat down.

"Have you been in front?" she asked, rubbing along her jaw.

"Yes, it's packed. But I only came in just before the curtain. How was the house?"

She threw a radiant look at him.

"Ate it up, dearie. Couldn't get enough. Six encores for my Castanet song. Oh, Charlie," she dropped the hand with its rag to the edge of the table and looked at him, solemnly earnest, "you don't know how I feel—you don't know. It's hard to believe and yet it's true. I can see the future stretching up like a ladder, and me mounting, step by step, on rungs made of gold."

Pancha Lopez, unlettered, almost illiterate, child of the mountains and the ditches, wandering vagabond of the stage, would sometimes indulge in unexpected felicities of phrase. Her admirers said it was another expression of that "temperament" with which she was endowed. Crowder, who knew her better than most, set it down to the Indian blood. From that wild blend had come all that lifted her above her fellows, her flashes of deep intelligence, her instinct for beauty, her high-mettled, invincible spirit. He even maintained to his friend Mark Burrage—Mark was the only person he ever talked her over with—that it was the squaw in her which had kept her pure, made her something more than "a good girl," a proud virgin, self-sufficing, untamable, jealous of her honor as a vestal.

"That's what you ought to see," he said in answer to her serious eyes. "Haven't I always said it? Didn't I tell you so up there in Portland when we first met and you were doing a turn between six saxaphone players and a bunch of trained cockatoos?"

She nodded, laughing, and returned to her rubbing.

"You surely did, and fanned up the flame that was just a tiny spark then. Dear old press agent, I guess I'll have to change your name to the Bellows."

"A. 1. Have you read the last blast I've given out?" She shook her head and he thrust his hand into his overcoat pocket. "I've brought it along, though I thought your father might have sent it to you."

"Pa's in the mountains." Drawing down her upper lip she pressed on her cheeks with painted finger tips, scrutinizing her face in the mirror. "I haven't heard from him for weeks. He's off on the lode somewhere."

"Then he hasn't seen it. It's the best I've done yet, and it's true, every word."

He had drawn from his pocket a paper which he now opened. As he folded it back, Pancha took out her hairpins and shook down her hair. It extended to her shoulders, a thick, curly bush, through which she pulled the comb with short, quick sweeps.

"Read that," said the young man and handed her the paper. "*Sacramento Courier*—'C. C's San Francisco Letter.'"

She took it and read while he watched her with twinkling eyes. They were great pals, these two; had been since they met in Portland, five years ago. He was on his way to Stanford, and had seen her doing a singing and dancing act in a wretched vaudeville company. That vision of a girlhood, beset and embattled, the pitifulness of its acquired hardness, had called to his western chivalry and made him her champion. Ever since he had helped and encouraged, his belief and friendship a spur to the ruthless energy, the driving ambition, that had landed her in the Albion six months before.

As she read she began to smile, then squeals of delight broke from her.

"You old press agent!" she cried, hitting at him with the comb and still reading, and then: "You pet, you precious pet!"

She finished on a little cry and cast the paper to the floor.

"Oh, Charlie, oh, my good, *dear* Charlie!" Her face was suddenly stirred with an upswelling of emotion. No other man in her hard and sordid experience had been to her what Charlie Crowder had, never a lover, always a friend.

"Now, Pancha," he said pleadingly, "don't look at me like that or I'll burst into sobs."

She rose and, putting her hands on his shoulders, kissed him on the forehead with a sexless tenderness. Her eyes were wet and to hide it she turned to where her costume lay on the chair. Crowder had nothing to say; these bursts of gratitude from his friend made him embarrassed.

"Look," she cried suddenly and snatched up the box of roses, "even a Johnny at the stage door. That's going some," and thrusting her hand into the box, she plucked up by their heads a handful of blossoms. Their pure sweet breath flowed out on the coarse scents with which the small place reeked.

Crowder affected a shocked surprise.

"What's this? A lover at last and I kept in ignorance."

"This is his first appearance, not a yap till tonight. And look at the yap." She dropped the box and took out from under the paper a card which she held toward him, "Some style about that yap."

It was the square of pasteboard furnished by the florist. On it was written in a small, upright hand, "Let me offer you these roses, sweet as your voice, delicate as your art, and lovely as yourself. An admirer."

Crowder raised his eyebrows and widened his eyes in exaggerated amazement.

"Well, well, well! I must look into this. Who *is* the gentleman ?"

"I haven't a guess." She took the card and dwelt on it delightedly. "Ain't it stylish writing—scratchy and yet you can read it? And the words, they're almost poetry. I never got flowers before with a sentiment as swell as that."

"Don't you honest know who it is?" said Crowder, impressed by the flowery profusion of "the sentiment."

"Not me. Jake brought 'em in after the second curtain. They were left by a messenger boy. Whoever he is he certainly does things in a classy way. Maybe he's a newspaper man to write like that."

Crowder opined he was not. He could hardly imagine one of his fellows—even secure in his anonymity—permitting his pen such florid license.

"When you break through the dark secret let me know. Then I'll come round and cast my searchlight eye over him and see if he's a proper companion for little Panchita."

"No fear," she cried, throwing the card back in the box. "Little Panchita's got a searchlight eye of her own. Believe *me*, it's a good, trained, old eye. Now skiddoo. I've got to slip into my togs and then me for home and a glass of milk. If he comes to the surface with another gasp I'll tell you."

When he had gone she dropped the kimono and put on a blouse and skirt, both old and shabby. Her actions were quick and harmonious, no unnecessary moves made, the actions of one trained to an economy of time and labor. On a wall hook behind a curtain she hung her gypsy dress, touching it lightly, flicking off dust, settling the folds. Poverty had taught her this care, as ambition was teaching her a thrift that made her associates call her mean.

What they thought was a matter of indifference to her. Before she had reached the Albion she knew herself superior and had plans that stretched far. About these she was secret. Not one, not even her father, knew the amount of money she had saved, or that, when she had accumulated enough, she intended going East and to Europe. She felt her powers and dreamed of a future on stages far finer than the Albion's. Once she had thought her father could help her. Two years ago he had sold a prospect for four thousand dollars, but he had lost the money in an unlucky mining venture in Oregon. That ended all hopes of his assistance. Even if he did make another strike he needed what he got for himself; he was getting on, he wanted to buy a ranch and settle down. If she was to reach the summit of her desire—and she would reach it or die—she must do it herself. So she worked doggedly, nursed her voice, hoarded her earnings and said nothing.

She was ready to leave, her hat, a little black velvet toque, pulled down over her hair, a long shaggy ulster clothing her to the ankles. As she went to the dressing table to put out the light she saw her image in the glass and paused, eyeing it. So far her appearance had had no value for her save as a stage asset. Now she looked at herself with a new, critical interest. Behind the footlights she was another person, blossomed into an exotic brilliance, took on fire and beauty with the music and excitement. Might not a man seeing her there be disappointed when he met her as she really was? She studied her face intently, viewing it at different angles, judging it by the standards of her world. By these she found it wanting, and with a wistful sigh she stretched out her hand and turned off the light.

It was nearly midnight when she walked down the side streets that led to the car line which took her home. Overhead the fog hung, covering the city with a luminous rack which here and there parted, showing segments of dark, star-dotted sky. Passing men looked at her, some meeting a defiant stare, others a face so chastely unresponsive that they averted their eyes as if rebuked. On the car she took an outside seat, for she loved the swift passage through the night with the chill air on her face. The grip man knew her and smiled a greeting, and as she mounted the step she answered cheerily. Now and then as the car stopped he spoke to her, leaning over his lever, and she twisted round to reply, friendly, frank, intimate. Until she came to San Francisco his class was the best she had ever known.

It was part of her economy to live in the Mission. She had two rooms there in the old Vallejo Hotel, a hostelry once fashionable, now fallen on dreary days. It fronted on a wide street where new business buildings rose beside gabled houses, detached and disconsolate in the midst of withered lawns. The Vallejo was a connecting link between these samples of the new and the old. It belonged to the ornate bay-windowed period of the seventies. Each of its "front suites" had the same proud bulge, and its entrance steps were flanked by two pillars holding aloft ground glass globes upon which its name was painted in black. Tall buildings were unknown in those days; the Vallejo boasted only three stories and its architect had never dreamed of such an effete luxury as an elevator. Built on the filled-in ground of Mission Creek, it had developed a tendency to sag in the back, and when you walked down the oil-clothed hall to the baths, you were conscious of a list to starboard.

The Vallejo patrons did not mind these drawbacks, or if they did, thought of the low rates and were uncomplaining. All things considered, you got a good deal for your money. The place was quiet and respectable; even in its downfall it clung desperately to its traditions. It took no transients, required a certain standard of conduct in its lodgers, and still maintained a night clerk in the office of its musty front hall.

Pancha thought it quite regal. If it was a proud elevation for her to reign at the Albion, it was a corresponding one for her to have two rooms to herself in a real hotel. As she ascended the stairs—her apartment was on the second floor—she looked about her, taking in satisfactory details, the worn moquette carpet, the artificial palm on a pedestal in the corner, the high, gilt-topped mirror at the turn on the stairs. It all seemed to her what she would have called "refined"; she need never be ashamed to have a visitor come there.

In her parlor she lit the light and surveyed her surroundings with an increasing satisfaction. It was a startlingly ugly room, but she thought it a bower of elegance. What gave her authority on the stage, what had already lifted her above the mass, seemed to fall from her with her costume. That unwavering sense of beauty and grace, that instinctive taste which lent her performance poetry and distinction, left her at the wings. Now her eye dwelt, complacent, on the red plush chairs, the coarse lace curtains, the sofa pillows of etched leather and dissonant colors, the long mirror between the windows, and each and all received her approval. As she had thought on the stairs, she thought again—no one would be ashamed to receive a visitor, no matter how stylish, in such a room.

She put her roses in a vase and then fetched a bottle of milk from the window sill and a box of crackers from the bureau drawer. Setting these on the marble-topped table beside the droplight she sat and ate. It was too cold to take off her coat and from its pocket she drew the card that had come with the flowers. As she sipped and munched, the shadows of the room hovering on the light's circular edge, she read over the words, murmuring them low, her voice lingering on them caressingly.

It was the first knock at the door of her dreams, the first prismatic ray of romance that had penetrated the penumbra of brutal realities in which she had lived.

CHAPTER VII

THE PICAROON

THE ARGONAUT HOTEL—all San Franciscans will remember it—had, like the Vallejo, started life with high expectations and then declined. But not to so complete a downfall. Fashion had left it, but it still did a good business, was patronized by commercial travelers and old customers from the interior, and had a solid foundation of residentials, married couples beaten by the servant question and elderly men with no ties. Its position had been against it—on that end of Montgomery Street where the land begins to rise toward Telegraph Hill, with the city's made ground behind, and in front "the gore" where Dr. Coggeswell's statue used to stand. People who lived there were very loyal to it—not much style, but comfort, quiet and independence.

Three days before the events in the last chapter a man entered its office and asked for rooms. He was an impressive person, of the kind who usually went to the Palace or the St. Francis. Ned Murphy, the clerk, sized him up as an Easterner or maybe a foreigner. There was something foreign-looking about him—you couldn't just tell what; it might be the way he wore his hair, brushed back straight from his forehead, or an undemocratic haughtiness of bearing. He looked as if he was used to the best, and he acted that way; had to be shown four suites before he was satisfied and then took the most expensive, second floor front, two rooms and bath, and you could see he didn't think much of it. Ned Murphy lived up to him with an unbroken spirit, languidly whistled as he slid the register across the counter, looked up the hall with a bored air, and then winked at the bell boy holding the bags. But when the stranger had followed the boy up the stairs—the Argonaut had no elevator—he pulled the register round and eagerly read the entry—"Boyé Mayer, New York." A foreign name all right; you couldn't fool him.

He told the switchboard girl, who had been taking it all in from her desk, and she slid over to size up the signature. She thought he mightn't be foreign—just happened to have that sort of name—he didn't talk with any dialect. When the bell boy came back they questioned him, but he was grouchy—feller'd only given him a dime. And say, one of them suit cases was all battered and wore out, looked like the kind the hayseeds have when they come up from the country.

In his room the man went to the window, hitched back the lace curtains and threw up the sash. Life in the open had made these shut-in places stifling, and he drew in the air with a deep relish. Evening was falling, a belated fog drifting in, wreathing in soft whorls over the hills, feeling its way across their summits and through their hollows. It made the prospect depressing, everything enveloped in a universal, dense whiteness. He surveyed it, frowning—the looming shapes of the high land beyond, the line of one-story hovels sprawled on the gore. To the right the street slanted upward toward Telegraph Hill whence smaller streets would decline to the waterfront and the Barbary Coast. He knew that section well and smiled a little as he thought of it and of himself, a ragged vagrant, exploring its byways.

His thoughts stopped at that memory—the lowest point of his fall—hung there contemplative and then turned backward. They passed beyond his arrival in California, his days of decay before that, the first gradual disintegration, back over it all to the beginning.

Thirty-six years ago he had been born in New York, a few months after the arrival of his parents. They were Austrians, his father an officer in the Royal Hungarian Guards, his mother a dancer at the Grand Opera House in Vienna. When Captain Ruppert Heyderich, of a prosperous Viennese family, had, in a burst of passionate chivalry, married Kathi Mayer, end coryphée on the second row, he had deserted the army, his country and his world and fled to America. Captain Heyderich had not committed so radical a breach of honor and convention without something to do it on, and the early part of the romance had moved smoothly in a fitting environment. Their only child, Lothar, could distinctly recall days of affluence in an apartment on the Park. He had had a governess, he had worn velvet and furs.

Then a change came; the governess disappeared, also the velvet and furs, and they began moving. There was a period when to move was a feature of their existence, each habitat showing a decrease in size and splendor. Lothar was nine, a lanky boy with his hair worn *en brosse*, in baggy knickerbockers and turn-over white collars, when they were up on the West Side in six half-lighted rooms, with a sloppy Hungarian servant to do all the work. That was the time when his father taught languages and his mother dancing. But he went to a private school. Captain Heyderich never got over his European ideas.

Those lean years came to a sudden end; Captain Heyderich's mother died in Vienna and left him a snug little fortune. They moved once more, but this time it was a hopeful, jubilant move, also a long one—to Paris. They settled there blithely in an apartment on the Rue Victor Hugo, Lothar, placed at a Lycée, coming home for weekends. He remembered the apartment as ornate and over-furnished, voluble guests coming and going, a great many parties, his mother, elaborately dressed, always hurrying off to meet people in somebody's else house or hurrying home to meet them in her own. Several times Austrian relations visited them, and Lothar had a lively recollection of a fight one Sunday evening, when an uncle, a large, bearded man, had accused his mother of extravagance and she had flown into a temper and made a humiliating scene.

He was seventeen when his father died, and it was discovered that very little money was left. Some of the relations came from Vienna and there was a family conclave at which it was suggested to Lothar that he return to Vienna with them and become a member of the clan. Separation from his mother was a condition and he refused. He did this not so much from love of her as from fear of them. They represented a world of which he was already shy, of high standards, duties rigorously performed, pledges to thrift and labor. Life with Kathi was more to his taste. He loved its easy irresponsibility, its lack of routine, its recognition of amusement as a prime necessity. He delivered his dictum, his mother wept triumphant tears, and the relations departed washing their hands of him.

After that they went to London and Lothar made his first attempts at work. They were fitful; the grind of it irked him, the regular hours wore him to an ugly fretfulness. He tried journalism—could have made his place for he was clever—but was too unreliable, and dropped to a space writer, drifting from office to office. In his idle hours, which were many, he gambled. That was more to his taste, done in his own way, at his own time—no cramping restrictions to bind and stifle him. He was often lucky and developed a passion for it.

He was twenty-three when they returned to New York, Kathi having begged some more money from Vienna. She was already a worn, old witch of a woman, dressed gayly in remnants of past grandeur and always painting her face. She and her son held together in a partnership strained and rasping, but unbreakable, united by the mysterious tie of blood and a deep-rooted moral resemblance. They led a wandering life, following races, hanging on the fringes of migrating fashion, sometimes hiding from creditors, then reestablished by a fortunate coup. But in those days he was still careful to pick his steps along the edges of the law, just didn't go over though it was perilous balancing. When she died he was relieved and yet he grieved for her. He felt free, no longer subject to her complaints and bickerings, but in that freedom there was a chill, empty loneliness— no one was beside him in that gingerly picking of his steps.

It was when he was twenty-seven—not quite lost—that the news came from Vienna of an unexpected legacy. His uncle, dying at the summit of a successful career, had relented and left him fifty thousand dollars. He assured himself he would be careful—poverty had taught him—and at first he tried. But the habits of "the years that the locust had eaten" were too strong. Augmented by several successful speculations it lasted him for six years. At the end of that time he was ruined, worn in body, warped in mind, his mold finally set.

After that he ceased to pick his way along the edges of the law, he slipped over. He followed many lines of endeavor, knew the back waters and hinterlands of many cities, ceased to be Lothar Heyderich and was known by other names. It was in Chicago, the winter before this story begins, that an attack of pneumonia brought him to the public ward of a hospital. Before his discharge, a doctor—a man who had noticed and been interested in him—gave him a word of warning:

"A warm climate—no more lake breezes for you. If you stay here and keep on swinging round the circle it won't be long before you swing back here to us—swing back to stay. Do you get me?"

He did, his face gone gray at this sudden vision of the end of all things. The doctor, in pity for what he was now and evidently once had been, gave him his fare to California.

It had been hell there. The climate had done its work, he was well, but he had felt himself more a pariah than ever before. He had seemed like a fly crawling over a glass shield under which tempting dainties are clearly visible and maddeningly unattainable. A man wanted money in California—with money could lead the life, half vagabondage, half lazy luxury, that was meat to his longing. Never had he been in a place that allured him more and that held him more contemptuously at arm's length.

He had sunk to his lowest depth in this tantalizing paradise, tramped the streets of cattle towns, herded with outcasts lower than himself. In Los Angeles he had washed dishes in a cafeteria, in Fresno polished the brasses in a saloon. And all around him was plenty, an unheeding prodigal luxuriance, Nature rioting in a boundless generosity. Her message came to him from sky and earth, from sweep of flowered land, from embowered village and thronging town—that life was good, to savor it, plunge in it, live it to the full. At times he felt half mad, struggling to exist in the midst of this smiling abundance.

When he began that upward march through the state he had no purpose, his mind was empty as a dried nut, the terrible lethargy of the tramp was invading him. From down-drawn brows he looked, morose, at a world which refused him entrance, and across whose surface he would drift aimless as a leaf on the wind. Then, the strength regained by exercise and air, the few dollars made by fruit picking, gave a fillip to his languishing spirit and an objective point rose on his vision. He would go to San Francisco—something might turn up there—and with his hoarded money buy cleanliness and one good meal. It grew before him, desirable, dreamed of, longed for—the bath, the restaurant, the delicate food, the bottle of wine. He was obsessed by it; the deluge could follow.

The wind, blowing through the open casement, brought him back to the present. The night had fallen, the street below a misty rift, its lights smothered in swimming vapor. There was brightness about it, blotted and obscured but gayly intentioned, even the sheds on the gore sending out golden gushes that suffused the milky currents with a clouded glow. He lighted the gas and looked at his watch—nearly seven. He would go out and dine—that dinner at last—and afterward drop in at the Albion and see Pancha Lopez, "the bandit's girl."

CHAPTER VIII

THOSE GIRLS OF GEORGE'S

THE ALSTONS WERE FINISHING DINNER. From over the table, set with the glass and silver that George Alston had bought when he came down from Virginia City, the high, hard light of the chandelier fell on the three females who made up the family. It was devastating to Aunt Ellen Tisdale's gnarled old visage—she was over seventy and for several years now had given up all tiresome thought processes—but the girls were so smoothly skinned and firmly modeled that it only served to bring out the rounded freshness of their youthful faces.

The Alstons were conservative, clung to the ways of their parents. This was partly due to inheritance—mother and father were New Englanders—and partly to a reserved quality, a timid shyness, that marked Lorry who, as Aunt Ellen ceased to exert her thought processes and relapsed into a peaceful torpor, had assumed the reins of government. They conformed to none of those innovations which had come from a freer intercourse with the sophisticated East. The house remained as it had been in their mother's lifetime, the furniture was the same and stood in the same places, the table knew no modern enhancement of its solidly handsome fittings. Fong, the Chinese cook—he had been with George Alston before he married—ruled the kitchen and the two "second boys." No women servants were employed; women servants had not been a feature of domestic life in Bonanza days.

That was why the house was lit by chandeliers instead of lamps, that was why dinner was at half past six instead of seven, that was why George Alston's daughters had rather "dropped out." They would not move with the times, they would not be brought up to date. Friends of their mother's had tried to do it, rustled into the long drawing-room and masterfully attempted to assist and direct. But they had found Lorry unresponsive, listening but showing no desire to profit by the chance. They asked her to their houses—replenished, modern, object lessons to rich young girls—and hinted at a return of hospitalities. It had not been a success. She was disappointing, no snap, no go to her; the young men who sat beside her at dinner were bored, and the house on Pine Street had not opened its doors in reciprocal welcome. By the time she was twenty they shrugged their shoulders and gave her up—exactly like Minnie, only Minnie had always had George to push her along.

As the women friends of Minnie did their duty, the men friends of George—guardians of the estate—did theirs. They saw to it that the investments were gilt-edged, and the great ranch in Mexico that George had bought a few years before his death was run on a paying basis. At intervals they asked their wives with sudden fierceness if they had called on "those girls of George's," and the wives, who had forgotten all about it, looked pained and wanted to know the reason for such an unnecessary question. Within the week, impelled by a secret sense of guilt, the ladies called and in due course Lorry returned the visits. She suffered acutely in doing so, could think of nothing to say, was painfully conscious of her own dullness and the critical glances that wandered over her best clothes.

But she did not give much thought to herself. That she lacked charm, was the kind to be overlooked and left in corners, did not trouble her. Since her earliest memories—since the day Chrystie was born and her mother had died—she had had other people and other claims on her mind. Her first vivid recollection—terrible and ineffaceable—was of her father that day, catching her to him and sobbing with his face pressed against her baby shoulder. It seemed as if the impression made then had extended all through her life, turned her into a creature of poignant sympathies and an unassuagable longing to console and compensate. She had not been able to do that for him, but she had been able to love—break her box of ointment at his feet.

From that day the little child became the companion of the elderly man, her soft youth was molded to suit his saddened age, her deepest desire was a meeting of his wishes. Chrystie, whose birth had killed her mother, became their mutual joy, their shared passion.

Chrystie-worship was inaugurated by the side of the blue and white bassinet, the nursery was a shrine, the blooming baby an idol installed for their devotion. When George Alston died, Lorry, thirteen years old, had dedicated herself to the service, held herself committed to a continuance of the rites. He had left her Chrystie and she would fulfill the trust even as he would have wished.

Probably it was this enveloping idolatry that had made Christie so unlike parents and sister. She was neither retiring nor serious, but social and pleasure-loving, ready to dance through life as irresponsibly enjoying as a mote in a sunbeam. And now Lorry had wakened to the perplexed realization that it was her affair to provide the sunbeam and she did not know how to do it. They were rich, they had a fine house, but nothing ever happened there and it was evident that Chrystie wanted things to happen. It was a situation which Lorry had not foreseen and before which she quailed, feeling herself inadequate. That was why, at twenty-three, a little line had formed between her eyebrows and her glance dwelt anxiously on Chrystie as an obligation—her great obligation—that she was not discharging worthily.

The glare of the chandelier revealed the girls as singularly unlike—Lorry—her full name was Loretta—was slender and small with nut-brown hair and a pale, pure skin. The richest note of color in her face was the rose of her lips, clearly outlined and smoothly pink. She had "thrown back" to her New England forbears. On the elm-shaded streets of Vermont villages one often sees such girls, fragile, finely feminine, with no noticeable points except a delicate grace and serenely honest eyes.

Chrystie was all California's—tall, broad-shouldered, promising future opulence, her skin a warm cream deepening to shades of coral, her hair a blonde cloud, hanging misty round her brows. She was as unsubtle as a chromo, as fragrantly fresh as a newly wakened baby. Her hands, large, plump, with flexible broad-tipped fingers, were ivory-colored and satin-textured, and her teeth, narrow and slightly overlapping, would go down to the grave with her if she lived to be eighty. Two months before she had passed her eighteenth birthday and was now of age and in possession of more money than she knew how to spend. She was easily amused, overflowing with good nature and good spirits as a healthy puppy, but owing to her sheltered environment and slight contact with the world was, like her sister, shy with strangers.

The meal was drawing to its end when the doorbell rang.

"A visitor," said Chrystie, lifting her head like a young stag. Then she addressed the waiting Chinaman, "Lee, let Fong open the door, I want more coffee."

Lee went to fetch the coffee and direct Fong. Everybody in the house always did what Chrystie said.

Aunt Ellen laid her old, full-veined hand on the table and pushed her chair back.

"Maybe it isn't a visitor," she said, looking tentatively at Lorry—she hated visitors, for she had to sit up. "Do you expect someone?"

Lorry shook her head. She rarely expected anyone; evening callers were generally school friends of Chrystie's.

Fong, muttering, was heard to pass from the kitchen.

"I do hope," said Christie, "if it's some horrible bore Fong'll have sense enough to shut them in the reception room and give us a chance to escape."

Chrystie, like Aunt Ellen, was fond of going to bed early. She had tried to instruct Fong in an understanding of this, but Fong, having been trained in the hospitable ways of the past, could not be deflected into more modern channels.

In his spotless white, his pigtail wound round his head, his feet in thick-soled Chinese slippers, he passed up the hall to the front door. Another chandelier hung there but in this only one burner was lit. At five in winter and at six in summer Fong lit this as he had done for the last twenty-four years. No one, no matter what the argument, could make him light it any earlier, any later, or turn the cock at a lesser or greater angle.

The visitor was Mark Burrage, and seeing this Fong broke into smiles and friendly greeting:

"Good evening, Mist Bullage—Glad see you, Mist Bullage. Fine night, Mist Bullage."

Fong was an old man—just how old nobody knew. For thirty-five years he had served the Alstons, had been George Alston's China boy in Virginia City, and then followed him, faithful, silent, unquestioning to San Francisco. There he had been the factotum of his "boss's" bachelor establishment, and seen him through his brief period of married happiness. On the day when Minnie Alston's coffin had passed through the front door, he had carefully swept up the flower petals from the parlor carpet, his brown face inscrutable, his heart bleeding for his boss.

Now his devotion was centered on the girls; "Miss Lolly and Miss Clist," he called them. He ruled them and looked out for their welfare—refused to buy canvasbacks till they fell to the price he thought proper, economized on the kitchen gas, gave them costly presents on the New Year, and inquired into the character of every full-grown male who crossed their threshold.

Mark Burrage he liked, found out about him through the secret channels of information that make Chinatown one of the finest detective bureaus in the land, and set the seal of his approval on the young man's visits. He would no more have shown him into the reception room and gone to see if "Miss Lolly and Miss Clist" were receiving, than he would have permitted them to change the dinner hour.

"You bin away, Mist Bullage," he said, placing the card the young man gave him on the hall table—cards were only presented in the case of strangers.

"How did you know that?" Mark asked, surprised.

Fong's face suggested intense, almost childish amusement.

"I dunno—I hear some place—I forget."

"I've been up in Sacramento County with my people—maybe Crowder told you."

"Maybe—I not good memly, I get heap old man." He made a move for the parlor door, his face wrinkled with his innocent grin. "Miss Lolly and Miss Clist here; awful glad see you," and he threw the door open.

Mark took a deep breath and strode forward, pulling his cuffs over his hands, which at that moment seemed to him to emerge from his sleeves large and unlovely as two hams. The place always abashed him, its sober air of wealth, its effortless refinement, its dainty feminine atmosphere. No brutal male presence—one never thought of Chinese servants as men—seemed ever to have disturbed with a recurring, habitual foot its almost cloistral quietude. Now with memories of his own home fresh in his mind, dinner in the kitchen, the soiled tablecloth, the sizzling pans on the stove, he felt he had no place there and was an impostor. Their greeting increased his discomfort. They were so kind, so hospitable, making him come into the dining room and take a cup of coffee. It was an uprush of that angry loyalty, that determination to hold close to his own, which made him say as soon as he was seated,

"I've been home for two weeks."

"Home?" said Lorry gently.

And, "Where *is* your home?" came from Aunt Ellen, as if she had just recognized the fact that he must have one somewhere but had never thought about it before.

The sound of his voice, gruff as a day laborer's after these flute-sweet tones, increased his embarrassment. Nevertheless he determined that he would tell them about his home.

"Up in Sacramento County not far from the tules. My father's a rancher, has a little bit of land there."

"Yes, Charlie Crowder told us," said Lorry. She didn't seem to notice the "little bit of land," it was just as if he'd said four or five thousand acres and described a balconied house with striped awnings and cushioned chairs.

He cast a glance of gratitude toward her, met her eyes and dropped his own to his cup. There they encountered his hand, holding the coffee spoon, the little finger standing out from the others in a tricksy curve. With an inward curse he straightened it, sudden red dyeing his face to the temples. He began to hate himself and didn't know how to go on.

Chrystie unexpectedly came to the rescue.

"Sacramento County," she exclaimed with sudden animation, "not far from the tules! There was a holdup round there two or three weeks ago. I read it in the papers."

Aunt Ellen moved restlessly. She wanted to get to her chair in the drawing-room.

"Holdup?" she murmured. "They're always having holdups somewhere."

"Not like this," said Chrystie. "It was a good one—Knapp and Garland—and they shot Wells Fargo's messenger."

"It was while I was there," said Mark, "up toward the foothills above our ranch."

The young ladies were immensely interested. They wanted to hear all about it and moved into the parlor to be settled and comfortable. They tried to make Mark sit in a massive, gold-trimmed armchair, but he had his wits about him by this time and took a humbler seat beside Lorry. Aunt Ellen sank into her rocker with a sigh of achievement and Chrystie perched on the piano stool. Then he told them the story, forgetting his bashfulness under the spell of their attentive eyes.

"Why can't they catch them," said Chrystie, "if they know their names?"

He couldn't help laughing at that.

"Why, of course they have other names," Lorry explained. "They don't go about as Knapp and Garland."

"But people must see them," Chrystie insisted, "somebody must know what they look like."

Mark had to straighten it out for her.

"Their friends do—ranchers up in the hills, and their pals in the towns. But the sheriffs and the general public don't. When they're out for business they cover their faces, tie handkerchiefs or gunny sacks round them."

Chrystie shuddered delightedly.

"How awful they must be! I'd love to be held up just to see them."

Mark and Lorry looked at one another and smiled, as age and experience smile at the artlessness of youth. It was an interchange of mutual understanding, a flash of closer intimacy, and as such lifted the young man to sudden heights.

"Where do they put the money?" said Aunt Ellen, her thought processes, under the unusual stimulus of a conversation on bandits, stirred to energy.

"That's what we'd like to know, Mrs. Tisdale. They have a cache somewhere but nobody's been able to find it. I saw the sheriff before I left and *he* thinks it's up in the hills among the chaparral."

"Is the messenger dead?" asked Lorry.

"Oh, no—he's getting on all right. They don't shoot to kill, just put him out of business for the time being."

"That's merciful," Aunt Ellen announced in a sleepy voice.

Chrystie, finding no more delicious shudders in the subject, twirled round on the stool and began softly picking out notes on the piano. For a space Mark and Lorry talked—it was about the ranch near the tules—rather dull as it came to Chrystie through her picking. The young man kept looking at Lorry's face, then dropping his glance to the floor, abashed before the gentle attention of her eyes, fearful his own might say too much. He thought it was just her sweetness that made her ask about his people, but everything about Mark Burrage interested her. Had he guessed it he would have been as much surprised as she had she known that he thought her beautiful.

Presently Chrystie's notes took form and became a tinkling tune. She tried it over once then whirled round on the stool.

"There—I've got it! Listen. Isn't it just like it, Lorry?"

Lorry immediately ceased talking and listened while the tune ran a halting course through several bars.

"Like what?" she said. "I don't know what it's meant to be."

"Oh!" Chrystie groaned, then shook her head at Mark. "Trust your relations to take down your pride. Why, it's the Castanet song from 'The Zingara!' Tum-tum-tum, tum-tum-tum," and she began swaying her body in time, humming an air and banging out the accompaniment, "With my castanets, with my castanets.' That's exactly the way it goes only I don't know the words." She whirled again to Mark. "It's the most *delicious* thing! Have you seen it?"

He hadn't, and Chrystie sank together on the stool in reproachful surprise.

"Oh, Mr. Burrage, you *must* go. Don't lose a minute, this very night."

Lorry breathed an embarrassed "Chrystie!"

"I didn't mean that and he knows it. I mean the soonest night *after* tonight. We went yesterday and even Aunt Ellen loved it. Didn't you, Aunt Ellen?"

Aunt Ellen, startled from surreptitious slumber, gave an unnaturally loud assent to which Chrystie paid no attention.

"It's the new opera at the Albion and Pancha Lopez is—" She threw out her hands and looked at the ceiling, words inadequate.

"She's never done anything so good before," Lorry said.

"All in red and orange, and coins everywhere. Orange stockings and cute little red slippers, and two long braids of black hair. Oh, down to there," Chrystie thrust out her foot, her skirt drawn close over a stalwart leg, on which, just above the knee, she laid her finger tips. Her eyes on Mark were as unconscious as a baby's. "I don't think it's all her own, it's too long—I'll ask Charlie Crowder."

Aunt Ellen had not gone off again and to prove it said,

"How would he know?"

"Well he'd see it, wouldn't he? He'd see it when she took off her hat, all wound round her head, yards and yards of it. No, it's false, it was pinned on under that little cap thing. And after the second act when she came on to bow she carried a bunch of flowers—oh, that big," her arms outlined a wide ellipse, "the same colors as her dress, red carnations and some sort of yellowish flower I couldn't see plainly."

Mark, seeing some comment was expected of him, hazarded a safe,

"You don't say!"

"And just as she was going off"—Lorry took it up now—"she looked at someone in a box and smiled and—"

But Chrystie couldn't bear it. She leaned toward her sister imploringly.

"Now, Lorry, let me tell that—*you know* I noticed it first." Then to Mark, "She was close to the side where they go off and I was looking at her through the glasses, and I saw her just as plain give a sort of quick look into the box and then smile and point to the flowers. It was as if she said to the person in there, 'You see, I've got them.'"

"Who was in the box?"

Chrystie bounced exuberantly on the stool.

"That's the joke. None of us could see. Whoever he was he was far back, out of sight. It was awfully exciting to me for I simply adore Pancha Lopez and Charlie Crowder, who knows her so well, says she hasn't an admirer of any kind."

Aunt Ellen came to the surface with,

"Perhaps she's going to get one now."

And Lorry added,

"I hope, if she is, he'll be somebody nice. Mr. Crowder says she's had such a hard life and been so fine and brave all along."

Soon after that Mark left. There had been a time when the first move for departure was as trying as the ordeal of entrance, but he had got beyond that. Tonight he felt that he did it in quite an easy nonchalant way, the ladies, true to a gracious tradition, trailing after him into the hall. It was there that an unexpected blow fell; Chrystie, the *enfant terrible,* delivered it. Gliding about to the hummed refrain of the Castanet song her eye fell on his card. She picked it up and read it:

"Mark D.L. Burrage. What does D.L. stand for?"

It was Mark's habit, when this was asked, to square his shoulders, look the questioner in the eye, and say calmly, "Daniel Lawrence."

But now that fierce loyalty to his own, that chafed pride, that angry rebellion which this house and these girls roused in him, made him savagely truthful. A dark mahogany-red stained his face to the forehead and he looked at Chrystie with a lowering challenge.

"It stands for de Lafayette."

"De Lafayette!" she stared, amazed.

"Yes. My given name is Marquis de Lafayette."

There was a moment's pause. He saw Chrystie's face, blank, taking it in, then terrible rising questions began to show in her eyes. He went on, glaringly hostile, projecting his words at her as if she was a target and they were missiles:

"My mother liked the name. She thought it was unusual. It was she who gave it to me."

Chrystie's lips opened on a comment, also on laughter. He could see both coming and he braced himself, then Lorry's voice suddenly rose, quiet, unastonished, as if it was the most natural thing in the world to have such a name:

"What a fine thing for her to do! She admired Lafayette and called you after him. I think it was splendid of her."

Outside, in the darkness of the street, he could almost have wept, in rage with himself, in the smart of her kindness.

He wished his mother had been there, in that hall, in her old clothes. He would have hugged her to him, protested that his name was the crowning glory of his life. He would have liked to face them down, show them his pride in her, let them hear him tell her that whatever she had done was in his opinion right.

The place where he lived was not far, a lodging house on one of the steep streets that sloped to the city's hollow. As he swung down the hills he thought of the hour of work he had promised himself, looked forward to with relish. Now his enthusiasm was gone, extinguished like a spark trodden out by a haughty foot. All he had done looked suddenly trivial, his rise from a farm hand a petty achievement, he himself a rough, uncultured boor. What right had he at the house of Lorry Alston, breaking himself against unsurmountable barriers? In the beginning he had only thought to enthrone her as an ideal, lovely, remote, unaspired to. She would be a star fixed in his sky, object of his undesiring worship. But it had not been that way. The star had not changed but he had ceased to bow in contemplation—looked up, loved and longed.

The back wall of his dwelling rose above the trees and he saw the darkling panes of his own windows. Soon his lamplight would glow through them, and he would be in the armchair with his book and his pipe. The picture brought back a surge of his conquering spirit. Nothing he had set his hand to had beaten him yet. If he fought as he had fought for his education, was fighting now for his place, he could fight up to her side. There was no rival in sight; Crowder, who knew them well, had told him so. He could put out all his energies, do more than man had ever done before, climb, if not to her proud place, at least where he did not come as a beggar to a queen. Then, on his feet, the future clearing before him, he could go to her and try and win. He drew a deep breath and looked up at the stars, remote as she had seemed that evening. The lift of his passion swept him aloft on a wave of will and he murmured, "If she were there among you, I'd try and get to her and carry her away in my arms."

Meantime he would not go to her house any more—at least not for a long time. There was no good; he was not the man to sit round in parlors looking and acting like a fool. He could only work, blaze the trail, make the clearing, raise the homestead, and when it was ready go and tell her so.

CHAPTER IX

GREEK MEETS GREEK

ARLY ON THE EVENING when the Alstons had seen "The Zingara," Boyé Mayer walked up Kearney Street looking into florists' windows. A cigarette depended from his lip, his opened overcoat disclosed the glossy whiteness of a shield-like shirt bosom, his head was crowned by a shining top hat. He was altogether a noticeable and distinguished figure.

He had been twice to the Albion and was going again this evening, having already engaged the right-hand stage box. Now he was purporting to send Pancha Lopez a third floral tribute and with it reveal his identity. The two previous ones had been anonymous, but tonight her curiosity—roused to a high pitch, or he knew nothing of women—would be satisfied. She would not only know who her unknown admirer was, but she would see him sitting in stately solitude in the right-hand box.

She had been a great surprise. Where he had expected to find an overblown, coarse woman with the strident voice of the music hall and its banal vulgarities, he had seen a girl, young, spontaneous, full of a sparkling charm. He had heard enough singing to know that her voice, fresh and untrained, had promise, and that the spirited dash of her performance indicated no common gifts. Under any circumstances she would have interested him; how much more so now when he knew of her affiliation with a notorious outlaw! She was evidently a potent personality, lawless and daring. The situation appealed to his slyly malign humor, she confidently secure, he completely informed. It was a fitting sequel to the picaresque adventure and he anticipated much entertainment from meeting her, saw himself, with stealthy adroitness, worming his way toward her guilty secrets.

A florist's window, a bower of blossoms under the gush of electric lights, attracted him and he turned into the shop. The proprietor came forward, ingratiatingly polite, his welcoming words revealing white teeth and a foreign accent.

The gentleman wanted a large sheaf bouquet in two colors, red and orange—certainly, and a Gallic wave of the hand indicated a marble slab where flowers were ranged in funnel-shaped green vases. Looking over them, the gentleman lapsed into a French so perfect that the florist suggested Monsieur was of that nation, also his own. Monsieur neither admitted nor denied the charge, occupied over the flowers. He was very particular about them—perhaps the florist would understand better what he wanted when he knew they were for Miss Lopez at the Albion and were designed to match her gypsy dress.

Ah, perfectly—several vases were drawn forward—and over these the two men talked of Miss Lopez and her admirable performance.

"A true artist," the florist thought, "young, and without training as Monsieur can see. A Californian, a girl of the people, risen from nothing. But no doubt Monsieur has already heard her history."

Monsieur was a stranger, he knew little of the lady, and, apparently engrossed in his selection of the flowers, heard such facts in the career of Pancha Lopez as the public were allowed to know. The florist ended the biography with what should be—for the gentleman ordering so costly a bouquet—the most notable item—Miss Lopez was a girl of spotless reputation.

Monsieur looked surprised:

"Has no favored one, no lovers?"

The florist, combining a scarlet carnation with a sunset rose, shrugged his shoulders, treating the subject with the lively gravity of the Gaul:

"None, Monsieur. It is known that many men have paid their court, but no—good-day to you and out they go! She wants nobody—it is all work, work, work. A good, industrious girl, very unusual when one considers her beginnings. But being so, and with her talents, she will arrive. My God, it is certain."

Monsieur appeared no longer interested. He paid for his bouquet, which was to be sent to the stage door that evening, then wrote a message on a card. This time the card bore no "swell sentiment;" the words were frank and to the point:

Why can't I know you? I want to so much. I am alone here and a stranger. If you care to look me over and see if you think I'm worth meeting, I'll be in the right-hand stage box tonight.

BOYÉ MAYER,
Argonaut Hotel.

As he walked to the Albion he thought over what he had heard. It was very different from what he had expected to hear and increased his interest in her. He had given her credit for a high artistic intelligence, but evidently she possessed the other kind too. How else could she have spread an impression of herself so unlike what she really was? A deep, *rusée* girl! He began to be very keen to meet her and see which of the two would be the more expert in the duel of attack and parry.

The flowers and the note were delivered in the first entr'acte. With a sliding rush Pancha was back on the stage, her eye glued to the peephole in the curtain. What she saw held her tranced. Like Mark, her standards suffered from a limited experience. That the effective pose was studied, the handsome face hard and withered, the evening dress too showily elegant, escaped her. She had never—except on the covers of magazines—seen such a man.

The stage hands had to pull her away from the curtain and she went to her dressing room with her cheeks crimson under the rouge and her eyes like black diamonds. Upon his own stage, plumed, spurred and cloaked, romance had entered with the tread of the conqueror.

After the second gift of flowers her curiosity was as lively as Mayer had expected. But she was not going to show it, she was going to be cool and indifferent till he made himself known. Then she contemplated a guarded condescension, might agree to be met and even called upon; a man who wrote such sentiments and gave such bouquets should not be treated with too much disdain. But when she saw him, her surprise was so great that she forgot all her haughty intentions. Gratified vanity surged through her. At one moment she thrilled with the anticipation of meeting such a personage, and at the next drooped to fears that she might disappoint his fastidious taste.

That night she answered the letter, writing it over several times:

Mr. Boyé Mayer,

Dear Friend:

Thanks for the flowers. They're grand. I ain't ever before had such beautys espechully the ones that matched my dress. I looked you over and I don't think you're so bad, so if you still want to know me maybe you can. I live in the Vallejo Hotel on Balboa Street and if you'd give yourself the pleasure of calling I'll be there Tuesday at four.

Yours truly,

Miss Pancha Lopez.

P. S. Balboa Street is in the Mission.

The next evening she received his answer, thanking her for her kindness and saying he would come.

She prepared for him with sedulous care, not only her room and her clothes, but herself. She was determined she would comport herself creditably, would be equal to the occasion and fulfill the highest expectations. She was going to act like a lady—no one would ever suspect she had once waited on table in the Buon Gusto restaurant, or been a barefoot, miner's kid. As she put on her black velveteen skirt and best crimson crêpe blouse, she pledged herself to a wary refinement, laid the weight of it on her spirit. The only models she had to follow were the leading ladies of the road companies she had seen, and she impressed upon her mind details of manner from the heroines of "East Lynne" and "The Banker's Daughter."

When four o'clock struck she was seated by the center table, a book negligently held in one hand, her feet, in high-heeled, beaded slippers, neatly crossed, and a gold bracelet given her by her father on her arm. She took a last, inspecting glance round the room and found it entirely satisfactory. On the table beside her a battered metal tray held a bottle of native Chianti, two glasses and a box of cigarettes. In Pancha's world a visitor was always offered liquid refreshment and she had chosen the Chianti as less plebeian than beer and not so expensive as champagne. She had no acquaintance with either wine or cigarettes; her thrifty habits and care of her voice made her shun both.

Mayer recognized the room as a familiar type—he had been in many such in many lands. But the girl did not fit it. She looked to him very un-American, more like a Spaniard or a French midinette. There was nothing about her that suggested the stage, no make-up, none of its bold coquetry or crude allure. She was rather stiff and prim, watchful, he thought, and her face added to the impression. With its high cheek bones and dusky coloring he found it attractive, but also a baffling and noncommittal mask.

He was even more than she had anticipated. His deep bow over her hand, his deference, thrilled her as the Prince might have thrilled Cinderella. She was very careful of her manners, keeping to the weather, expressing herself with guarded brevity. A chill constraint threatened to blight the occasion, but Mayer, versed in the weaknesses of stage folk, directed the conversation to her performance in "The Zingara," for which he professed an ardent admiration.

"I was surprised by it, even after what I'd heard. I wonder if you know how good it is?"

Her color deepened.

"I try to make it good, I've been trying for six years."

He smiled.

"Six years! You must have begun when you were a child."

This was too much for Pancha. Her delight at his praise had been hard to suppress; now it burst all bonds. She forgot her refinement and the ladylike solemnity of her face gave place to a gamin smile.

"Oh, quit it. You can't hand me out that line of talk. I'm twenty-two and nobody believes it."

Then he laughed and the constraint was dissipated like a morning mist. They drew nearer to the table and Pancha offered the wine. To be polite she took a little herself and Mayer, controlling grimaces as he sipped, asked her about her career. She told him what she was willing to tell; nothing of her private life which she thought too shamefully sordid. It was a series of jumps from high spot to high spot in her gradual ascent. He noticed this and judged it as a story edited for the public, it tallied so accurately with what he had heard already from the florist. There was evidently a rubber stamp narrative for general circulation.

After she had concluded he made his first advance, lightly with an air of banter.

"And how does it come that in this long, lonely struggle you've stayed unmarried?"

A belated coquetry—Pancha climbing up had wasted no time on such unassisting arts—stirred in her. She tilted her head and shot a look at him from the sides of her eyes.

"I guess no one came along that filled the bill."

"Among all the men that must have come along?"

"Um-um," she stood her glass on the table, turning its stem with her long brown fingers.

"The lady must be hard to please."

"Maybe she is."

Her eyes rested on the ruby liquid in the glass. The lids were fringed with black lashes that grew straightly downward, making a semicircle of little, pointed dashes on each cheek. He could not decide whether she was embarrassed or slyly amused.

"Or perhaps she's just wedded to her art."

"That cuts some ice, I guess."

"Love is known to improve art. Haven't you ever heard that?"

"I shouldn't wonder. I've heard an awful lot about love."

"Only heard, never felt? Never responded to any of the swains that have been crowding round?"

"How do you know they've been crowding round?"

He leaned nearer, gently impressive:

"What I'm looking at tells me so."

She met his eyes charged with sentimental meaning, and burst into irrepressible laughter.

"Oh, *you*—shut up! I ain't used to such hot air. I'll have to open the windows and let in the cold."

It was not what he had expected and he felt rebuffed. Dropping back in his chair, he shrugged his shoulders.

"What can I say? It's not fair to let me come here and then muzzle me."

"Oh, I ain't going as far as that. But you don't have to talk to me that way. I'm the plain, sensible kind."

He shook his head, slowly, incredulously.

"No, I've got to contradict you. Lips can tell lies but eyes can't. You're a good many other things but you're not sensible."

"What other things?"

"Charming, fascinating, piquant, with a heart like a bright, glowing coal."

She threw back her head and let her laughter, rich and musical, float out on the room.

"Oh, listen to him! Wouldn't it make a dog laugh!" Then, swaying on her chair, she leaned toward him, grave but with her eyes twinkling. "Mr. Man, you can't read me for a cent. Right here," she touched her heart with a finger tip, "it's frozen hard. I keep it in cold storage."

"Hasn't it ever been taken out and thawed?"

"Never has and never will be."

She swayed away from him, keeping her glance on his. For a still second a strange seriousness, having no place in the scene, held them. She was conscious of perplexity in his face, he of something wistful and questioning in hers. She spoke first.

"You're very curious about me, Mr. Boyé Mayer?"

She ought not to have said that and it was his fault that she did. She was no mean adversary and that she had seen through his first tentatives proved them clumsy and annoyed him. He smiled, a smile not altogether pleasant, and rose.

"All men must be curious where you're concerned."

"Not as bad as you."

"Ah, well, I'm a child of nature. I don't hide my feelings. I'm curious and show it. Do you know what makes me so?"

She shook her head, anticipating flatteries. But he did not break into them as quickly as she had expected. Turning to where his hat lay he took it up, looked at it for a moment and then, with his gray eyes shifting to hers, said low, as if taking her into his confidence:

"I'm curious because you're interesting. I think you're the most interesting thing I've seen since I came to San Francisco."

This was even more than she had hoped for. An unfamiliar bashfulness made her look away from the gray eyes and stammer in rough deprecation:

"Oh, cut it out!"

"I never cut out the truth. But I'm going to cut out myself. It's time for me to be moving on. Good-by."

His hand was extended and she put hers into it, feeling the light pressure of his cool, dry fingers. She did not know what to say, wanted to ask him to come again, but feared, in her new self-consciousness, it wasn't the stylish thing to do.

"I'm real glad you called," was the nearest she dared.

He was at the door and turned, hopefully smiling.

"Are you?"

"Sure," she murmured.

"Then why don't you ask me to come again?"

"I thought that was up to you."

He again was unable to decide whether her coyness was an expression of embarrassment or an accomplished artfulness, but he inclined to the latter opinion.

"Right O! I'll come soon, in a few days. *Hasta mañana,* fair lady."

After the door had closed on him she stood sunk in thought, from which she emerged with a deep sigh. A slow, gradual smile curved her lips; she raised her head, looked about her, then moving to the mirror, halted in front of it. The day was drawing toward twilight, pale light falling in from the bay window and meeting the shadows in the back of the room. Her figure seemed to lie on the glass as if floating on a pool of darkness. The black skirt melted into it, but the crimson blouse and the warm pallor of the face and arms emerged in liquid clearness, richly defined, harmonious-ly glowing. She looked long, trying to see herself with his eyes, trying to know herself anew as pretty and bewitching.

Mayer walked home wondering. He was completely intrigued by her. Her performance in "The Zingara" had led him to expect a girl of much more poise and finish, and yet with all her rawness she was far from naïve. His own experience recognized hers; both had lived in the world's squalid byways; he could have talked to her in their language and she would have understood. But she was not of the women of such places, she had a clean, clear quality like a flame. Daring beyond doubt, wild and elusive, but untouched by what had touched the rest. He found it inexplicable, unless one granted her unusual capacity, unsuspected depths and a rare and seasoned astuteness. He had to come back to that and he was satisfied to do so. It would add zest to the duel which had just begun.

CHAPTER X

MICHAELS, THE MINER

S O DISTINGUISHED A FIGURE AS Boyé Mayer could not live long unnoticed in San Francisco. He had not been a month at the hotel before items about him appeared in the press. Mrs. Wesson, society reporter of the *Despatch*, after seeing him twice on Kearney Street, found out who he was and rustled into the Argonaut office for a word with Ned Murphy. Mr. Mayer was a wealthy gentleman from New York, but back of that Murphy guessed he was foreign, anyway the Frenchwoman who did his laundry and the Dutch tailor who pressed his clothes said he could talk their languages like he was born in the countries. He wasn't friendly, sort of distant; all he'd ever said to Murphy was that he was on the coast for his health and wanted to live very quiet to get back his strength after an illness.

It wasn't much but Mrs. Wesson made a paragraph out of it that neatly rounded off her column.

Even without the paragraphs he would not have been unheeded. Among the carelessly dressed men, bustling along the streets in jostling haste, he loomed immaculately clad, detached, splendidly idle amidst their vulgar activity. He had the air of unnoticing hauteur, unattainable by the American and therefore much prized. His clean-shaven, high-nosed face was held in a brooding abstraction, his well-shod foot seemed to press the pavement with disdain. Eating a solitary dinner at Jack's or Marchand's, he looked neither to the right nor the left. Beauty could stare and whisper and he never give it the compliment of a glance. Ladies who entertained began to inquire about him, asked their menkind to find out who he was, and if he was all right make his acquaintance and "bring him to the house."

He was not so solitary as he looked. Besides Pancha Lopez he had met other people. The wife of the manager of the Argonaut Hotel had asked him to a card party, found him "a delightful gentleman" and handed him on to her friends. They too had found him "a delightful gentleman" and the handing on had continued. He enjoyed it, slipping comfortably into the new environment—it was a change after the sinister years beyond the pale, and the horrible, outcast days. Also he did not confine himself to the small sociabilities to which he was handed on. There were many paths of profit and pleasure in the city by the Golden Gate and he explored any that offered entertainment—those that led to tables green as grass under the blaze of electric lights, those that led to the poker game behind Soledad Lanza's pink-fronted restaurant, those that led up alleys to dark, secretive doors, and that which led to Pancha's ugly sitting room.

He sought this one often and yet for all his persuasive cunning he found out nothing, got no further, surprised no admissions. He was drawn back there teased and wondering and went away again, piqued and baffled.

One evening, a month after her first meeting with him, Pancha, going home on the car, thought about her father. She felt guilty, for of late she had rather forgotten him and this was something new and blameworthy. Now she remembered how long it was since she had seen him and that his last letter had come over a month ago. It was a short scrawl from Downieville and had told her that the sale of his prospect hole—he had hoped to sell it sometime early in September—had fallen through. He had seemed down-hearted.

Despite the divergent lines of their lives a great tie of affection united them. They met only at long intervals—when he came into town for a night—and all correspondence between them was on his side as she never knew where he was. Even had he not lavished a rough tenderness upon her, the memory of pangs mutually suffered, of hardships mutually endured, would have bound her to him. He was the only person who had passed, closely allied, an intimate figure, through the full extent of her life. Though he was so much to her she never spoke of him, except to Charlie Crowder, her one friend, of whose discretion she was sure. This reticence was partly due to tenderness—the past and his place in it had their sacredness—and partly to the miner's own wish. As her star had risen it was he who had suggested the wisdom of "keeping him out." He thought it bad business; an opera singer's father—especially a father with a pick and a pan—had no advertising value and might be detrimental. When he put it that way she saw the sense of it—Pancha was always quick to see things from a business angle—and fell in with his wish. She was not unwilling to. It wasn't that she was ashamed of him, she cared too little for the world to be ashamed of anything, but she did not want him made a joke of in the wings or written up satirically in the theatrical column. When small road managers who had known her at the start came into town and asked where "Pancha's Pa" was, nobody knew anything about such a person, and they guessed "the old guy must have died."

Since she had lived at the Vallejo Hotel he had been there five times, always after dark. She had told Cushing, the night clerk, that Mr. Michaels was a relation of hers from the country and if he came when she was out to let him into her rooms.

As she drew up at the desk and asked for her key—it hung on a rack studded with little hooks—Cushing, drowsing with his feet on a chair, rose wearily, growling through a yawn:

"Mr. Michaels has came. He's been here about an hour. I done what you said and let him in."

She smothered an expression of joy, snatched the key and ran upstairs. Lovely—just as she was thinking of him! She let herself in anticipating a glad welcome and saw that he was lying on the sofa asleep.

The only light in the room was from the extension lamp on the table and by its shaded glow she stood looking at him. He was sleeping heavily, still wrapped in the old overcoat she knew so well, his coarse hands, with blackened finger nails, clasped on his breast. His face, relaxed in rest, looked worn, the forehead seamed with its one deep line, the eyes sunk below the grizzled brows. It came upon her with a shock that he seemed old and tired, and it hurt her. In a childish desire to bring him back to himself, have him assume his familiar aspect and stop her pain, she shook him by the shoulder, crying:

"Pa, Pa, wake up."

He woke with a violent start, his feet swung to the floor, his body hunched as if to spring, his glance wildly alive. Then it fell on her and the fierce alertness died out; his face softened into a smile, almost sheepish, and he rubbed his hand over his eyes.

"Lord, I was asleep," he muttered.

She kissed him, pulled him up, and with an arm round his back, steered him to an armchair, asking questions. His hand on her waist patted softly.

"Well, you ain't fattened up any," he said with a quizzical grin and side glance.

That made him look more like himself, but Pancha noticed that his movements were stiff.

"What's the matter?" she said sharply. "You ain't got the rheumatism again, have you?"

"Nup," he sank slowly into the chair. "But sometimes when I first move I sort 'er kink at the knees. Gets me in the morning, but I limber up all right."

She stood beside him, uneasily frowning.

"What are you goin' to do this winter when the rains begin? You can't run risks of being sick, and me not able to get to you."

"Sick—hell!" He shot a humorous look at her. "I ain't sick in God's own country—it's only down here. Why y'ain't all as stiff as stone images in this sea-damp beats me."

"Oh, it's the damp," she said, relieved.

"Course it's the damp. I wouldn't expect a rope dancer to live here and stay spry."

That was like Pa; her anxiety evaporated and she began to smile.

"Well, there's one person who does—yours truly. If you don't believe it, come to the Albion and see."

"There ain't another like you, hon. There's not your match from the Rockies to the Pacific."

"Oh, old blarney!" she cried, now joyous, and, giving him a pat on the shoulder, moved about collecting supper. "Sit tight there while I get you a bite. I've some olives that'll make you think you're back among the greasers."

The supper came from divers places—the window sill, the top bureau drawer, the closet shelf. Beer and sardines were its chief features, with black olives soaked in oil and garlic, cheese straws taken from a corset box, and ripe figs oozing through their paper bag.

They ate hungrily without ceremony, wiping their fingers on the towel she had spread for a cloth. As they munched they swapped their news—his failure at selling the ledge, her success in "The Zingara." He listened to that with avid attention.

"Can you stay and see me tomorrow night?" she asked.

He shook his head.

"'Fraid not. I got a date with a feller in Dutch Flat for tomorrow afternoon."

"About the prospect?"

"Yep—it's a chance and I got to jump at it."

"Why did it fall through before?"

He shoveled in a cracker spread with sardines before he answered.

"Oh, same old story—thought it didn't show up as big as they'd expected. You can't count on it, no more'n you can on the weather."

She smothered a sigh. The "prospect" and the "ledge" had been part of their life, lifting them to high hopes, dropping them to continual disappointment. She would have counseled him to give it all up, but that he now and then had had luck, especially in the last five years. She went back to herself.

"'The Zingara' has been a great thing for me. Everybody says so. If the next piece goes as big I'm going to strike for a raise. Wait till I show you," she jumped up, rubbing her oily fingers on the towel, "and you'll see why little Panchita's had to get an extra-sized hat."

She took from a side table a book—the actress's scrap album—and came back flirting its pages. At one she pressed it open and held it toward him, triumphantly pointing to a clipping. "There, from the *Sacramento Courier.*"

He gave a glance at the clipping and said:

"Oh, yes, *that.* Grand, ain't it?"

She was surprised.

"You've seen it. Why didn't you send it to me?"

"Who said I'd seen it?" He took the book from her, staring across it, suddenly combative. "Don't you run along so fast. Ain't you known if I had I'd have mailed it to you?"

"But how did you know about it?" she said, her surprise growing, for she saw he was moved.

"You're gettin' too darned quick." He pushed the book in among the dishes roughly, his irritation obvious.

"Ain't it possible I might have heard it? Might have met a feller that come up from Marysville who'd seen It and told me?"

"Yes, of course it is. You needn't get mad about it."

"Mad—who said I was mad?" He bent over the book, muttering like a storm in retreat. "I guess I ain't missed so many that when one does get by me you should throw it in my teeth."

She smoothed the top of his head with a placating hand and went back to her seat. Nibbling a ripe olive she watched him as he read. Her eyes were anxiously questioning. This too—anger at so small a thing—was unlike him.

When he had finished his annoyance was over; pride beamed from his face as if a light was lit behind it.

"I guess there ain't many of 'em get a write-up like that." He put the book aside and began a second attack on the supper. "Crowder's some friend. His little finger's worth more'n the whole kit and crew you've had danglin' round you since you started."

"You're right." She stretched her hand for a fig, spilling, bruised and bursting, from the torn bag. "There's a new one dangling."

With her father Pancha was always truthful. To the rest of the world she lied whenever she thought it necessary, never carelessly or prodigally, for to be fearless was part of her proud self-sufficiency. But as she had learned to fight, to battle her way up, to climb over her enemy, to wrest her chance from opposing forces, she had learned to lie when the occasion demanded. She was only entirely frank and entirely truthful with the one person whom she loved.

He put down his glass and looked at her, in sudden, fixed attention.

"What's that?"

"I've got a real, genuine, all-wool-yard-wide beau."

She leaned her elbows on the table, holding the fig to her mouth, her thin fingers manipulating the skin as she sucked the pulp. Her eyes were full of laughter.

"What do you mean?"

"Just what I'm telling you. You needn't look like I'd said he was a defaulting bank cashier, nor so surprised either. It ain't flattering to your only child."

Her father did not respond to her gayety.

"Look-a-here, Panchita," he began, but she stopped him, flapping a long hand.

"Cut it out, Pop. I know all that. You needn't come any stern parent business over me. *I'm* on. *I* know my way about. I ain't going to run my head into any noose, or tie any millstone round my neck. Don't you think by this time you can trust me?"

Her words seemed to reassure him. The bovine intensity of his gaze softened.

"You've had a heap of beaux," he said moodily.

"And kept every last one of 'em in their place, except for those I kicked out. And they got to their place; my kick landed them there."

"Who is he?"

Pancha returned to her fig, looking over its wilted skin for clinging tidbits.

"Named Mayer, a foreigner—at least he's born here, but he looks foreign and acts foreign; hands out the kind of talk you read in books. Awful high class."

"Treats you respectful?"

She gave him a withering glance.

"*Respectful!* Treats me like I'd faint if he spoke rough or break if he touched me. I ain't ever seen anything so choice. You said I was thin—it's keeping up such a dignified style that's worn me down."

This description was so unlike the bandit's idea of love-making that he became incredulous.

"How do you know he's a beau? Looks like to me he was just marking time."

She smiled, the secret smile of a woman who has seen the familiar signs. She had taken another fig and delicately breaking it open, eyed its crimson heart.

"He's jealous."

"Who of?"

"Nobody, anybody, everybody." She began to laugh, and putting her lips to the fruit, sucked, and then drew them away stained with its ruby juice. "He's always trying to draw me, find out if there isn't somebody I like. Pop, you'd laugh if you could hear him sniffing round the subject like a cat round the cream."

"What do you tell him?"

"*Me?*" She gave him a scornful cast of her eye. Her face was flushed, and with her crimsoned mouth and shining eyes she was for the moment beautiful. "I got my pride. I told him the truth at first, and when he wouldn't believe me—'Oh, no, there *must be* some-one'—I says to myself, 'All right, deary, have it your own way,' and I jolly him along now," she laughed with joyous memory. "I got him good and guessing, Pop."

The old man looked dissatisfied.

"I ain't much stuck on this, Panchita. What good are you goin' to get out of it?"

"Fun!" she cried, throwing the fig skin on the table. "Don't I deserve some after six years? If he wants to act like a fool that's his affair, and believe me, he's able to take care of himself. And so am I. No one knows that better than you do, deary."

He left soon after that. In his nomad life, with its long gaps of separation from her, it was easy for him to keep his movements con-cealed and caution had become a habit. So he had not told her that on his last visit to the city he had taken a room, instead of going to one of the men's hotels that dotted the Mission. It was in a battered, dingy house that crouched in shame-faced decay behind the shrubs and palms of a once jaunty garden. Mrs. Meeker, the landlady, was a respectable woman who had seen so complete an extinction of fortune that she asked nothing of her few lodgers but the rent in advance and a decent standard of sobriety. To the bandit it offered a seclusion so grateful that he had resolved to keep it, a hiding-place to which he could steal when the longing for his child would not be denied.

The house was not far from the Vallejo Hotel, on a cross street off one of the main avenues of traffic. As he rounded the corner he saw the black bushiness of its garden and then, barring the night sky, the skeleton of a new building. The sight gave him a disagree-able shock; anything that let more life and light into that secluded backwater was a menace. He approached, anxiously scanning it. It took the place of old rookeries, demolished in his absence, one side rising gaunt and high against Mrs. Meeker's. He leaned from the front steps and looked over the fence; the separation between the two walls was not more than two or three feet.

His room was on the top floor in the back, and gaining it, he jerked up the shade and looked out. Formerly a row of dreary yards extended to the houses in the rear. Now the frame of the new building filled them in, projecting in sketchy outline to the end of the lots. Disturbed he studied it—four stories, a hotel, apartments, or offices. Whatever it was it would be bad for him, bringing men so close to his lair.

He stood for some time gazing out, saw a late, lopsided moon swim into the sky and by its light the yard below develop a beauty of glistening leaves and fretted shadows. The windows of the houses beyond the fence shone bright, glazed with a pallid luster. Even Mrs. Meeker's stable, wherein she kept her horse and cart, the one relic saved from better days, stood out darkly picturesque amid the frosted silver of vines. He saw nothing of all this, only the black skeleton which would soon be astir with the life he shunned.

He drew down the shade and dropped heavily into a chair, his feet sprawled, his chin sunk on his breast. The single gas jet emitted a torn yellow flame that issued from the burner with a stuttering, ripping sound. The light gilded the bosses of his face, wax-smooth above the shadowed hollows, and it looked even older than it had in sleep. His spirit drooped in a somber exhaustion—he was so tired of it all, of the stealth, the watchfulness, the endless vigilance, the lack of rest. One more coup, one lucky haul, and he was done. Then there would be the ranch, peace, security, an honest ending, and Pancha, believing, never knowing.

CHAPTER XI

THE SOLID GOLD NUGGET

THE AUTUMN WAS DRAWING to an end and the winter season settling into its gait. Everybody was back in town, at least Mrs. Wesson said so in her column, where she also prophesied a program of festivities for the coming six months. This was reassuring as Mrs. Wesson was supposed to know, and anyway there were signs of it already—a first tentative outbreak of parties, little dinners cropping up here and there. People who did things were trailing back from Europe, bringing new clothes and ideas with which to abash the stay-at-homes. Big houses were opening and little houses that had been open all along were trying to pretend they had been shut. Furs were being hung on clothes lines and raincoats brought out of closets. Violets would soon be blooming around the roots of the live oaks and the Marin County hills be green. In short the San Francisco winter was at hand.

The Alston house had been cleaned and set in order from the cellar to the roof and in its dustless, shining spaciousness Lorry sat down and faced her duties. The time had come for her to act. Chrystie must take her place among her fellows, be set forth, garnished and launched as befitted the daughter of George Alston. It was an undertaking before which Lorry's spirit quailed, but it was part of the obligation she had assumed. Though she had accepted the idea, the translation from contemplation to action was slow. In fact she might have stayed contemplating had not a conversation one night with Chrystie nerved her to a desperate courage.

The girls occupied two adjoining rooms on the side of the house which overlooked the garden. Across the hall was their parents' room, exactly the same as it had been when Minnie Alston died there. Behind it were others, large, high-ceilinged, with vast beds and heavy curtains. These had been tenanted at long intervals, once by an uncle from the East, since deceased, and lately by the Barlow girls, Chrystie's friends from San Mateo. That had been quite an occasion. Chrystie talked of it as she did of going to the opera or on board the English man-of-war.

Lorry was sitting in front of the glass brushing her hair, when Chrystie, supposedly retired, came in fully dressed. She dropped onto the side of the bed, watching her sister, with her head tilted, her eye dreamily ruminant.

"What's the matter, dear?" said Lorry. "Why aren't you in bed?"

Chrystie yawned.

"I can't possibly imagine except that I don't want to be there," came through the yawn.

"Aren't you sleepy?"

"In a sort of way." She yawned again and stretched with a wide spread of arms. "I seem to be sleepy on the outside but it doesn't go down into my soul."

Lorry, drawing the comb through her long hair which fell in a shining sweep from her forehead to the chair seat, wanted this explained. But her sister vaguely shook her head and stared at the carpet, then, after a pause, murmured:

"I wish something would happen."

"What kind of thing?"

"Oh, just something—any old thing would be a change."

Lorry stopped combing.

"Do you mean that you're dull?" she asked. The worried gravity of her face did not fit the subject.

"That must be it." Chrystie raised her eyes and looked at the cornice, her red lips parted, her glance becoming animated. "Yes, of course, that's it—I'm dull. Why didn't I see it myself? You've put it before me in letters of fire—I'm dreadfully dull."

"What would you like to do?"

"Have some good times, lots of them. There aren't enough of them this way. We can't go to the theater too often or we'd get used to it, and I can't get the Barlows to come up here every week, they have such crowds of engagements."

She sighed at the memory of the Barlows' superior advantages and the sigh sounded like a groan of reproach in Lorry's ears. Innocently, unconsciously, unaccusingly, Chrystie was rubbing in the failure of her stewardship. She combed at the ends of her hair, her eyes blind to its burnished brightness.

"Would you like to have a party here?" she said in a solemn voice.

Chrystie's glance was diverted from the cornice, wide open and astonished.

"A party here, in *this* house?"

"Yes, it's big enough. There's plenty of room and we can afford it."

"But, Lorry"—the proposition was so startling that she could hardly believe it—"a *real* party?"

"Any kind of a party you want. We might have several. We could begin with a dinner; Fong can cook anything."

Chrystie, the idea accepted and held in dazzled contemplation, suddenly saw a flaw.

"But where would we get any men?"

"We know some and we could find some more."

"You talk as if you could find them scattered about on the ground the way they found nuggets in '49. Let's count our nuggets." She held up the spread fingers of a large white hand, bending one down with each name. "There's Charlie Crowder if he can get off, and his friend Robinson in the express company, and Roy Barlow, whom I know so well I could recite him in my sleep, and Mrs. Kirkham's grandnephew who looks like a child—and—and—good gracious, Lorry, is that *all* our nuggets?"

"We could have some of those young men whose mothers knew ours."

"You said you didn't like them."

"I know I did, but if you're going to give parties you have to have people you don't like to fill up."

"Um," Chrystie pondered, "I suppose you must. Oh, there's Marquis de Lafayette."

"Yes," said Lorry, "I thought of him."

Chrystie's eyes, bright with question, rested on her sister.

"You can't exactly call him a nugget."

"Why not?"

"Because he doesn't shine, darling."

This explanation appeared to strike its maker as a consummate witticism. She fell back on the bed in spasms of laughter.

Lorry looked annoyed.

"He's nicer than any of the others, I think."

"Of course he is, but he's been buried too long in the soil; he needs polishing." She rolled over on the bed in her laughter.

Lorry began to braid her hair, her face grave.

"I don't think things like that matter a bit, and I don't see at all what you're laughing at."

"I'm laughing at Marquis de Lafayette. I can't help it—something about his hands and his manners. They're so ponderously polite; maybe it's from waiting on table in the students' boarding house."

"I never knew you were a snob before, Chrystie."

"I guess I am. Isn't it awful? Oh, dear, I've laughed so much I've got a pain. It's perfectly true, I'm a snob. I like my nuggets all smooth and shiny with no knobs or bits of earth clinging to them."

Lorry's hair was done and she rose and approached her sister.

"You've spoiled my bed. Get off it and go."

But Chrystie would not move. With her face red and the tears of her laughter standing in her eyes she gazed at the serious one.

"Lorry, darling, you look so sweet in that wrapper with your hair slicked back. You look like somebody I know. Who is it? Oh, of course, the Blessed Damozel, leaning on the bar of Heaven, only it's the bar of the bed."

"Don't be silly, Chrystie. Get up."

"Never till I have your solemn, eternal, sworn-to promise."

"What promise?"

"To give that party."

"You have it—I said I'd do it and I will."

"And get nuggets for it?"

"Yes."

"All right, I'll go."

She sat up, rosy, disheveled, her hair hanging in a tousled mop from its loosened pins. Catching Lorry's hand, she squeezed it, looking up at her like an affectionate, drowsy child.

"Dear little Blessed Damozel, I love you a lot even though you are high-minded and think I'm a snob."

She had been in her room for some minutes, Lorry already in bed with a light at her elbow and a book in her hand, when she reappeared in the doorway. The pins were gone from her hair and it lay in a yellow tangle on her shoulders, bare and milk-white. Looking at her sister with round, shocked eyes, she said:

"It's just come to me how awful it is that two young, beautiful and aristocratic ladies should have to hunt so hard for nuggets. It's tragic, Lorry. It's *scandalous*," and she disappeared.

Lorry couldn't read after that. She put out the light and made plans in the dark.

The next day she rose, grimly determined, and girded herself for action. In the morning, giving Fong the orders, she told him she was going to have a dinner, and in the afternoon went to see Mrs. Kirkham.

Mrs. Kirkham had once been a friend of Minnie Alston's and she was the only one of that now diminishing group with whom Lorry felt at ease. Had the others known of the visit and its cause they would have thrown up their hands and said, "Just like that girl." Mrs. Kirkham was nobody now, the last person to go to for help in social matters. In the old days in Nevada her husband had been George Alston's paymaster, and she had held her head high and worn diamonds.

But that was ages ago. Long before the date of this story the high head had been lowered and the diamonds sold, all but those that encircled the miniature of her only baby, dead before the Con-Virginia slump. She lived in a little flat up toward the cemeteries, second floor, door to the left, and please press the push button. In her small parlor the pictures of the Bonanza Kings hung on the walls and she was wont, an old rheumatic figure in shiny black with the miniature pinned at her withered throat, to point to these and tell stories of the great Iliad of the Comstock.

She was very fond of Lorry and when she heard her predicament—a party to be given and not enough men—patted her hand and nodded understandingly. Times were changed—ah, if the girls had been in Virginia in the seventies! And after a brisk canter through her memories (she always had to have that) galloped back into the present and its needs. Lorry went home reassured and soothed. You could always count on Mrs. Kirkham's taking hold and helping you through.

The old lady was put on her mettle, flattered by the appeal, made to feel she was still a living force. Also she would have done anything in the world for Minnie's girls. She consulted with her niece, well married and socially aspiring if not yet installed in the citadel. It was a happy thought; the niece had the very thing, "a delightful gentleman," lately arrived in the city. So it fell out that Boyé Mayer, under the chaperonage of Mrs. Kirkham, was brought to call and asked to fill a seat at the formidable dinner.

Formidable was hardly a strong enough word. It advanced on Lorry like a darkling doom. Once she had set its machinery in motion it seemed to rush forward with a vengeful momentum. Everybody accepted but Charlie Crowder, who could not get off, and Mark Burrage, who wrote her a short, stiff note saying he "was unable to attend." For a space that made her oblivious to the larger, surrounding distress. It was a little private and particular sting for herself that concentrated her thoughts upon the hurt it left. After she read it her face had flushed, and she had dropped it into her desk snapping the lid down hard. If he didn't want to come he could stay away. Men didn't like her anyway; she knew it and she wasn't going to make any mistakes. Her concern in life was Chrystie and it was being pointed out to her that she wasn't supposed to have any other.

Finally the evening came and everything was ready. Fong's talents, after years of disuse, rose in the passion of the artist and produced a feast worthy of the past. A florist decorated the table and the lower floor. Mother's jewels were taken out of the safety deposit box, and Lorry and Chrystie, in French costumes with their hair dressed so that they looked like strangers, gazed upon each other in the embowered drawing-room realizing that they had brought it upon themselves and must see it through.

The start was far from promising; none of them seemed able to live up to it. Aunt Ellen kept following the strange waiters with suspicious eyes, then looking down the glittering table at Lorry like a worried dog. And Chrystie, who had been all blithe expectation up to the time she dressed, was suddenly shattered by nervousness, making detached, breathless remarks about the weather and then drinking copious draughts of water. As for Lorry, she felt herself so small and shriveled that her new dress hung on her in folds and her mouth was so dry she could hardly articulate.

It was awful. The guests seemed to feel the blight and wither under it, eating carefully as if fearing sounds of mastication might intrude on the long, recurring silences. There was a time when Lorry thought she couldn't bear it, had a distracted temptation to leap to her feet, say she was faint and rush from the place. Then came the turn in the tide—Mr. Mayer, the strange man Mrs. Kirkham had produced, did it. She had noticed that he alone seemed free from the prevailing discomfort, looked undisturbed and calm, glancing at the table, the guests, herself and Chrystie. But it was not until the fish that he started to talk. It was about the fish, but it branched away from the fish, radiated out from it to other fish, to the waters where the other fish swam, to the countries that gave on the waters, to the people who lived in the countries.

He woke them all up, held them entranced. Lorry couldn't be sure whether he really was so clever or seemed so by contrast with them, but she thought it was the latter. It didn't matter; nothing mattered except that he was making it go. And at first she had been loath to ask him! She hadn't liked him, thought he was too suavely elaborate, a sort of overdone imitation. Well, thank goodness she had, for he simply took the dinner which was settling down to a slow, sure death and made it come to life.

Presently they were all talking, to their partners, across the table, even to Aunt Ellen. The exhilarating sound of voices rose to a hum, then a concerted babble broken by laughter. It grew animated, it grew sparkling, it grew brilliant. Chrystie, with parted lips and glistening eyes, became as artlessly amusing as she was in the bosom of her family. She was delightful, her frank enjoyment a charming spectacle. Lorry, in that seat which so short a time before had seemed but one remove from the electric chair, now reigned as from a throne, proudly surveying the splendors of her table and the gladness of her guests.

When it was over, the last carriage wheels rumbling down the street, the girls stood in the hall and looked at one another. Aunt Ellen, creaking in her new silks, toiled up the stairs, an old, shaky hand on the balustrade.

"Come up, girls," she quavered; "you must be dead tired."

"Well," breathed Lorry with questioning eyes on her sister, "how was it?"

Chrystie jumped at her and folded her in a rapturous embrace.

"Oh, it was maddening, blissful, rip-roarious! Oh, Lorry, it was the grandest thing since the water came up to Montgomery street!"

"You *did* enjoy it, didn't you?"

"Enjoy it! Why, I never had such a galumptious time in my life. They all did. The Barlow girls are on their heads about it—they said so and I saw it."

"I think everybody had a good time."

"Of course they did. But, oh, didn't you nearly die at the beginning? I was sick. Honestly, Lorry, I felt something sinking in me down here, and my mouth getting all sideways. If it hadn't been for that man I'd have just slipped out of my seat under the table and died there at their feet."

"He saved it," said Lorry solemnly, as one might mention a doctor who had brought back from death a beloved relative.

The gas was out and they were mounting the stairs, arms entwined, warm young flesh on warm young flesh.

"Isn't he a thoroughbred, isn't he a gem!" Chrystie chanted. "I'd like to go to Mrs. Kirkham's tomorrow, climb up her front stairs on my knees and knock my forehead on the sill of her parlor door."

"Did you really like him? I think he's clever and entertaining but I wouldn't want him for a friend."

"I didn't think about him that way. I just sort of stood off and admired. He's the most *magnetic* thing!"

"Yes, I suppose he is, but—"

"There are no buts about it." Then in the voice of knowledge, "I'll tell you what he is, I'll put it in terms you can understand—he's the perfect specimen of the real, genuine, solid gold nugget."

CHAPTER XII

A KISS

A FTER THE DINNER Mayer walked downtown. He had been a good deal surprised, rather amused, and in the draw-ing-room afterward extremely bored. His amusement was sardonic. He grinned at the thought of himself in such company and wondered if it could have happened anywhere but California. Those two girls, rich and young, were apparently free to ask anybody into their house. It was curious, and he saw them similarly placed in Europe; they would have been guarded like the royal treasure, chiefly to keep such men as himself out.

The splendor of the entertainment had surprised him. He was becoming used to the Californian's prodigal display of flowers, but such a dinner, served to unappreciative youth, was something new. The whole affair had been a combination of an intelligent luxury and a rank crudity—food fit for kings set before boys and girls who had no more appreciation of its excellence than babies would have had. And the silver on the table, cumbrously magnificent, it was worth a small fortune.

Outside the humor of his own presence there, he had found the affair tedious, especially that last hour in the drawing-room. It was the sort of place that had always bored him even when he was young, governed by narrow, feminine standards, breathing a pon-derous respectability from every curtain fold. Neither of the girls had been attractive. The elder, the small, pale one, was a prim, stiff little thing. The other was nothing but a gawky child; fine color-ing—these Californians all had it—but with no charm or mystery. They were like the fruit, all run to size but without much flavor. He thought the elder girl had some intelligence; one would have to be on one's guard with her. He made a mental note of it, for he

intended going there again—it was the best meal he had eaten since
he left New York.

The night was warm and soft, a moon rising over the housetops.
He breathed deep of the balmy air, inhaling it gratefully. After such
a constrained three hours he felt the need of relaxation, of easy surroundings, of an expansion to his accustomed dimensions. Swinging
down the steep street between the dark gardens and flanking walls,
he surveyed the lights of the city's livelier center and thought of
something to do that would take the curse of the dinner off his spirit.

A half hour later Pancha, emerging from the alley that led to
the Albion's stage door, saw a tall, familiar shape approach from the
shadows. Her heart gave a jump, and as her hand was enfolded in
a strong, possessive grasp, she could not control the sudden quick-
ening of her breath.

"Oh, it's you! Gee, how you scared me," she said, to account for it.

He squeezed the hand, murmuring apologies, his vanity gratified, for he knew no man at the stage door would ever scare Pancha.

As it was so fine a night he suggested that she walk back to the
hotel and let him escort her, to which, with a glance at the moon,
and a sniff of the mellow air, she agreed.

So they fared forth, two dark figures, choosing quieter streets than
those she usually trod, the tapping of her high heels falling with a
smart regularity on the stillness held between the silver-washed walls.

They were rather silent, conversation broken by periods when
their mingled footfalls beat clear on the large, enfolding mutter of
the city sinking to sleep. It was his fault; heretofore he had been the
leader, conducting her by a crafty discursiveness toward those con-
fidences she so resolutely withheld. But tonight he did not want to
talk, trailing lazy steps beside her, casting thoughtful glances upward
at the vast, illumined sky. It made her nervous; there was something
of a deep, disturbing intimacy about it; not a sweet and soothing
intimacy, but portentous and agitating. She tried to be herself, laid
about for bright things to say and found she could pump up no
defiant buoyancy, her tongue clogged, her spirit oppressed by a dis-
integrating inner distress. It did not make matters any better when
he said in a dreamy tone:

"Why are you so quiet?"

"I've worked hard tonight. I'm tired and you're walking so fast."

He was immediately contrite, slackening his step, which in truth was very slow.

"Oh, Pancha, what a brute I am. Why didn't you tell me?" And he took her hand and tried to draw it through his arm.

But she resisted, pulling away from him almost pettishly, shrinking from his touch.

"No, no, let me alone. I like to walk by myself."

He drew back with a slight shrug, more amused than repulsed. Nevertheless he was rather sorry he had suggested the walk, he had never known her to be less entertaining.

"Always proud, always independent, always keeping her guard up." He cast a questioning side glance at her face, grave and pale by his shoulder. "You wild thing, can no one tame you?"

"Why do you say I'm wild?"

"Because you are. How long have I known you? Since early in September and I don't get any nearer. You still keep me guessing."

"About what?"

"About *what?*" He leaned down and spied at her profile. "About yourself."

"Oh, me!"

"Yes, you—what else? You're the most secretive little sphinx outside Egypt."

She did not answer for a moment. She had been secretive, but it was about the humble surroundings of her youth, those ignominious beginnings of hers. Of this she could not bring herself to tell, fearful that it would lower her in his esteem. She saw him, hearing of the Buon Gusto restaurant and the life along the desert, withdrawing from her in shocked repugnance. About other things—the stage, the lovers—she had been frank, almost confidential.

"I don't see why you say that," she protested; "I've told you any amount of stuff."

"But not everything. You know that, Pancha."

He was now so keen, like a dog with its nose to the scent, that he forgot her recent refusal and hooked his hand inside her arm. This time she did not draw away and they walked on, close-linked, alone in the moonlit street. Conscious of her reticences, ashamed of her lack of candor, and yet afraid to make damaging revelations, she said defensively:

"I've told you as much as I want to tell."

He seized on that, in his eagerness pressing her arm against his side, bending over her like a lover.

"Yes, but not all. And why not all? Why should you keep anything from me?"

"But why *should* I tell you?" she asked, her loitering step coming to a stop.

As the situation stood the question was a poser. He did not want to be her lover, had never intended it; his easy gallantry had meant nothing. But now, seeing her averted face, the eyes down-drooped, he could think of no reply that was not love-making. She stole a swift look at him, recognized his hesitation, and felt a stab, for it was the love-making answer she had expected. The mortified anger of the woman who has made a bid for tenderness and seen herself mistaken surged up in her.

She jerked her arm violently out of his grasp and walked forward at a swinging pace.

"What's the matter?" he said, chasing at her heels. "Are you angry?"

"I shouldn't wonder," she threw over her shoulder. "Being nagged at for fun doesn't appeal to me."

"But what do you mean?—I'm all at sea."

She suddenly brought up short, and wheeling, faced him, her face lowering, her breath quick:

"I'm the one to say that, for I don't get you, Boyé Mayer, I don't see what you're up to. But sometimes I think you've just come snooping round roe to find out something. You come and you go, always so curious, always wanting to know, pussy-footing round with your questions and your compliments. What's on your mind?"

Mayer found himself in an impasse. She knew him too well and she was too angry to be diverted with the temporizing lightness of their early acquaintance. There was only one thing to say to her, and—the cause of her excitement plain to his informed mind—it was not difficult to say.

"Pancha," he pleaded, "you don't understand."

"You bet I don't and I want to. I'd like to have it explained—I'd like to know what you hang round me for. Do you think I'm hiding something? Do you think I'm a criminal?"

"I think you're the most charming girl in the world," he protested.

She gave a smothered sound of rage and started off, faster than ever, down the street. This time he kept up with her, and rounding a corner the two lamps at the foot of the Vallejo's steps loomed up close at hand.

"Stop," he said. "Wait." He had no idea the hotel was so near, and surprised at the sight of it his voice became suddenly imperious and he seized her arm with a dominating grip. She tried to jerk it away, but he held it and drew her, stiff and averse, toward him.

"You foolish one," he whispered. "Why, don't you see? I hang around because I can't help it. I come because I can't stay away—I want to know about you because I'm jealous of every man that ever looked at you."

With the last word he threw his arm about her and snatched her close. Against him she suddenly relaxed, melted into a thing of yielding softness, while his lips touched a cheek like a burning rose petal.

The next moment she was gone. He had a glimpse of her on the Vallejo steps in swallow-swift silhouette and then heard the bang of the door.

In her room Pancha moved about mechanically, doing the accustomed things. She lighted the light, took off her hat and jacket, brought the milk from the window sill. Then, with the bottle on the table beside her, she sat down, her hands in her lap, her eyes on space. She was as motionless as a statue, save for the breaths that lifted her chest. She sat that way for a long time, her only movements a shifting of her blank gaze or a respiration deeper than the others. She saw nothing of what her glance rested on, heard none of the decreasing midnight sounds in the street or the house about her. An intensity of feeling had lifted her to a plane where the familiar and habitual had no more place than had premonitions and forebodings.

CHAPTER XIII

FOOLS IN THEIR FOLLY

"THE ZINGARA" HAD RUN its course and given place to "The Gray Lady," which had not pleased the public. The papers said the leading role did not show Miss Lopez off to the greatest advantage and the audiences thinned, for Miss Lopez had transformed the Albion from a house of light opera to a temple enshrining a star. The management, grumbling over their mistake, laid about for something that would give the star a chance to exhibit those qualities which had deflected so many dollars from the "Eastern attractions" to their own box office.

Charlie Crowder and Mark Burrage, walking together in the early night, turned into the Albion to have a look at the house and see Pancha in the last act. They stood in the back, surveying the rows of heads in a dark level, against the glaring picture of the stage, upon which, picked out by the spotlight, Pancha stood singing her final solo. Crowder's eye dropped from the solitary central figure to the audience and noted gaps in the lines, unusual in the Albion and predicting "The Gray Lady's" speedy demise. As the curtain fell he told Mark he was "going behind" for a word with his friend, she would need cheering up, and Mark, nodding, said he'd move along, he had work to do at home.

The floor of heads broke as though upheaved by an earthquake, and the house rose, rustling and murmurous, and began crowding into the aisles. The young man, leaning against the rail behind the last row, watched it, a dense, coagulated mass, animated by a single impulse and moving as a unit. Crowding up the aisle it looked like a thick dark serpent, uncoiling its slow length, writhing toward the exit, the faces turned toward him a pattern of pale dots on its back. Among them at first unnoticed by his vaguely roving glance were three he knew—the two Alston girls and Aunt Ellen.

It was always hot and stuffy in the Albion and Aunt Ellen had been uncomfortable and fussed about it, and Chrystie was disappointed that her favorite had not been able to make the performance a success. As they edged forward she explained to Lorry that it wasn't Pancha's fault, it was the sort of thing she didn't do as well as other things and she oughtn't to have been made to do it. Then, her eye ranging, she suddenly stopped and gave Lorry a dig with her elbow.

"There's Marquis de Lafayette. Do you see him?"

Lorry had, which did not prevent her from saying in a languid voice,

"Where?"

"Over there by the railing. You know he *is* good-looking, Lorry, when he's all by himself that way, not trying to be worthy of a college education."

"Um," said her sister. "It's fearfully hot in here."

"I don't see why we ever came," Aunt Ellen moaned.

They were near him now and he saw them. For a moment he stared, then gave a nod and reddened to his forehead.

"Oh, he's blushing!" Chrystie tittered as she returned the bow. "How perfectly sweet!"

The first sight of them had given Mark a shock as violent as if he had met them in an exploration of the South Pole or the heart of a tropical forest. It took him some minutes to recover, during which he stood rooted, only his head moving as he watched them borne into the foyer, there caught in merging side currents and carried toward the main entrance. It was not till they were almost at the door, Chrystie's high blonde crest glistening above lower and less splendid ones, that he came to life. He did it suddenly, with a sharp reaction, and started in impetuous pursuit. His first movement—a spirited rush—carried him into a family, a compact phalanx moving solidly upon the exit. He ran into someone, a child, stammered apologies, placated an irate mother, then craning his neck for his quarry, saw the high blonde head in the distance against the darkness of the street.

The check was more than physical. It caused a sudden uprush of his old timidity and he stood irresolute, in everybody's way, spying at the distant golden head. It seemed as if they had wanted to avoid him, they had gone so quickly, just bowed and been carried on—if only Chrystie would look back and smile. Standing on his toes, jostled and elbowed, he caught a glimpse of them, all three, outside the door. They appeared preoccupied, the two girls talking across Aunt Ellen, with no backward glances for a young man struggling to reach them—anyone could have seen they had forgotten his existence. With a set face he turned and made for the side exit. They had no use for him; he would go home to the place where he belonged.

The bitterness of this thought carried him through the side exit and there left him. Whatever they felt and however they acted, it was his duty to see them on the car. Boor! clod! goat! He could still catch them if he went round to the front, and he started to do it, facing the emerging throng, battling his way through. That was too slow; he backed out, turned into the street and ran, charging through streams that had broken from the main torrent and were trickling away in various directions. Rounding the corner he saw he was not too late. There, standing on the curb, were Aunt Ellen and Chrystie, conspicuous in their ornamental clothes, looking in the opposite direction up the street's animated vista. He followed their eyes and saw a sight that made him halt—Lorry, her satin-slippered feet stepping delicately along the grimy pavements, her pale skirts emerging from the rich sheath of her cloak. Beside her, responding to a beckoning hand, a carriage rattled down upon Chrystie and Aunt Ellen. They had a carriage and she had had to go and find it!

With a heart seared by flaming self-scorn, Mark turned and slunk away. He slid into the crowd's enveloping darkness as into a friendly shelter. He wanted to hide from them, crawl off unseen like the worm he was. This was the least violent term he applied to himself as he walked home, cursing under his breath, wondering if in the length and breadth of the land there lived a greater fool than he. There *was* a mitigating circumstance—he had never dreamed of their having a carriage. In his experience carriages, like clergymen, were only associated with weddings and funerals. He thought of it afterward in his room, but it didn't help much—in fact it only accentuated the difference between them. Girls who had carriages when they went to the Albion were not the kind for lawyers' clerks to dream of.

Inside the carriage, Aunt Ellen insisted on an understanding with the livery stable man:

"Running about in the mud in the middle of the night—it's ridiculous! Lorry, are your slippers spoiled?"

"No, Aunt Ellen. There isn't any mud."

"There might just as well have been. Any time in the winter there's liable to be mud. Will you see Crowley tomorrow and tell him we won't have any more drivers who go away and hide in side streets?"

"Yes, I'll tell him, but he wasn't hiding, he was only a little way from the entrance."

"Having no man in the family certainly *is* inconvenient," came from Chrystie, and then with sudden recollection: "What happened to Marquis de Lafayette? Why didn't he come and get it?"

"I don't know, I'm sure." Lorry was looking out of the window.

"Well, I must say if we ask him to our parties the least he can do is to find our hacks."

"I think so, too," said Aunt Ellen. "The young men of today seem to have forgotten their manners."

"Forgotten them!" echoed Chrystie. "You can't forget what you never had."

"Oh, do keep quiet," came unexpectedly from Lorry. "The heat in that place has given me a headache."

Then they were contrite, for Lorry almost never had anything, and their attentions and inquiries had to be endured most of the way home.

Crowder, contrary to his expectations, found Pancha in high good spirits. When a piece failed she was wont to display that exaggerated discouragement peculiar to the artist. Tonight, sitting in front of her mirror, she was as confident and smiling as she had been in the first week of "The Zingara."

"I'm glad to see you're taking it so well," he said. "It's pretty hard following on a big success."

"Oh, it's all in the day's work. You can't hit the bull's eye every time. The management are going to dig down into their barrel next week, hunting for another gypsy rôle. They want me again in my braids and my spangles. They liked my red and orange—Spanish colors for the Spanish girl."

She flashed her gleaming smile at him and he thought how remarkably well she was looking, getting handsomer every day. Her words recalled something he had wanted to ask her and had forgotten.

"Talking of red and orange, how about that anonymous guy that sent you the flowers? You remember, back in the autumn—a lot of roses with a motto he got out of a Christmas cracker?"

She had her comb in her hand and dropped it, leaning down to scratch round for it on the floor.

"Oh, *him*—he's just petered out."

"Did you find out who he was?"

Up to this Pancha had been nearly as truthful with Crowder as she was with her father. But now a time had come when she felt she must lie. That secret intimacy, growing daily dearer and more dangerous, could not be confessed. Crowder had been mentor as well as friend and she feared not only his curiosity but his disapproval. He would argue, plead, interfere. She disliked what she had to say, and as she righted herself, comb in hand, her face was flushed.

"Yes, a chap from the East. He just admired from afar and went his way."

"Oh, he's gone." Crowder was satisfied. "Seen your father lately?"

"No, but I had a letter to say he'd be down soon."

The color in her face deepened. She knew that her father would ask even more searching questions than Crowder and she was prepared to lie to him. Biting her lip at the thought, she looked down the long spray of lashes defined on her cheeks. Crowder stared at her, impressed anew by that suggestion of radiant enrichment in her appearance.

"I say, old girl," burst from him, "do you know you're looking something grand."

She raised her lids and let her glance rest on him, soft and deep. It was a strange look to come from Pancha's bold, defiant eyes.

"Am I?" she said gently. "I guess I'm happy, that's all."

"Well, it's powerful becoming, believe me. And why are you, especially with 'The Gray Lady' a frost?"

She rose, the red kimono falling straight about her lithe, narrow shape, then stretched, a slow spread of arms, languid and catlike. Pressing her hands on her eyes she said from smiling lips:

"Oh, there's no particular reason. It just happens so. I'm getting to feel sure of myself—that's what, I guess. Now run along, old son, I'm sleepy. 'The Gray Lady' does it to me as well as the audience. Good-night."

Crowder was not the only one who had noticed Pancha's improved looks and high spirits. Behind the scenes the failure of "The Gray Lady" had produced dejection and rasped tempers. She alone seemed to escape the prevailing gloom. She came in at night smiling, left a trail of notes behind her as she walked to her dressing room, and from there clear scales and mellow bars rose spasmodically as she dressed. Usually holding herself aloof, she was friendly, made jokes in the wings, chatted with the chorus, and when she left the old doorkeeper was warmed by her gay good-night.

Her confreres were puzzled; it was quite a new phase. They had not liked Miss Lopez at first; she gave herself airs and had a bad temper. Once she had slapped a chorus woman who had spoiled her exit; at a rehearsal she had been so rude to the tenor the stage manager had had to call her down and there had been a fight. Now they wondered and whispered—under circumstances conducive to ill-humor she was as sweet as honey dropping from the comb. They set it down to temperament; everybody from the start had seen she had it, and anyway there wasn't anything else to set it down to.

What they saw was only a gleam, a thin shining through of the glory within. It irradiated, permeated, illumined her, escaping in those smiles and words and snatches of song because she could not hold it in. As she had told Crowder, she was happy, and she had never been before. She came out of sleep to the warming sense of it. It stayed with her all day, fed on a note, a telephone message, a gift of flowers, fed on nothing but her own thoughts.

It was the happiness found in little of one who has been starved, nourished by trifles, tiny seeds flowering into growths that touched the sky. She did not see Mayer as often as formerly and when she did their talk was on other things than love. In fact he was rather shy of the subject, did not repeat his kiss, was more comrade than wooer. But he sought her, he had told her why and that was enough. What he had said she believed, not alone because it seemed the only reasonable explanation of his actions, but because she wanted to believe it. He had come, a nonchalant wayfarer, and grown to care, said at last the words she was longing to hear, and, hearing, she felt them true and was satisfied.

And then she had drifted, content to rest in the complete comfort of her belief. The moment was enough, and she stood on the summit of each one, swaying in blissful balance. Vaguely she knew she was moving on a final moment, on a momentous, ultimate decision, and she neither cared nor questioned. Like a sleepwalker she advanced, inevitably drawn, seeing a blurred dazzle at the path's end in which she would finally be absorbed.

Everything that had made her Pancha Lopez, familiar to herself, was gone. She was somebody else, somebody filled with a brimming gladness, with no room for any other feeling. Her old, hard self-sufficiency seemed a poor, bleak thing, her high head was lowered and gloried in its abasement. All the fierce, combative spirit of the past had vanished; even her work, heretofore her life, was executed automatically and pushed aside, an obstruction between herself and the sight and thought of Mayer. The laws that had ruled her conduct, the pride that had upheld her, melted like cobwebs before the sun. She lived to please a man she thought loved her and that she loved to the point where honor had become an empty word and self-respect transformed to self-surrender. Whatever he would ask of her she was ready to give. The Indian's blood prompted her to the squaw's impassioned submission, the outlaw's to a repudiation of the law and the law's restraints.

Early in January her father came down and when he asked her about Mayer she lied as she had to Crowder. She told him she still saw the man but that his devotion had lapsed, giving evidence of a languishing interest. When she saw her father's relief she had qualms, but her lover's voice on the phone, asking her to dine with him that night, dispersed them. All the lies in the world then didn't matter to Pancha.

So she drifted, not caring whither, only caring that she should see Mayer, listen to him, dwell on his face, try to catch his wish before it was spoken. Her outer envelope was the same, performed the same tasks, lived in the same routine, but a new creature, a being of fire, dwelt within it.

CHAPTER XIV

THE NIGHT RIDER

FEBRUARY HAD BEEN a month of tremendous rains. Days of downpour were succeeded by days of leaden skies and damp, brooding warmth, and then the clouds opened again and the downpour was renewed. Along the Mother Lode the rivers ran bank-high and the camps sat in lagoons, the sound of running water rising from the old flumes and ditches. Down every gully that cut the foothills came streams, loud-voiced and full of haste as they rushed under the wooden bridges.

It was a night toward the end of the month, no rain falling now, but the sky sagging low with a weight of cloud. An eye trained to such obscurity could have made out the landscape in looming degrees of darkness, masses rising against levels, the fields a shade lighter than the trees. These were discernible as huddlings and blots and caverned blacknesses into which the road dove and was lost. To the left the chaparral rose from the trail's edge in dense solidity, exhaling rich earth scents and the aromatic breath of pine and bay. The roadbed was torn to pieces, ruts knee-high; the stones, washed loose of soil, ringing to the blow of a moving hoof.

A rider, advancing slowly, had noticed this and with a jerk of his rein, directed his horse to the oozy grass along the side. Here, noiseless, man and beast passed, a moving blackness against stationary black, leaves and branches brushing against them. Neither heeded this; both were used to rough ways and night traveling and to each every foot of the road was familiar.

Under a roof of matted branches they drew up; the horse, the reins loose, stretched its neck, blowing softly from widened nostrils. The man took a match box from his pocket, struck a light and looked at his watch—it was close on ten. The flame, breaking out in a red spurt, gilded the limbs of the overarching trees, the glistening leaves, the horse's glossy neck and the man's face. It glowed beneath the brim of his hat like a portrait executed on a background of velvet varnished by the match's gleam—it was the face of Garland the outlaw.

His hand again on the rein sent its message and the horse padded softly on through the arch of trees to the open road. Had it been brighter Garland could have seen to the right rolling country, fields sprinkled with oak domes, falling away to the valley, to the left the chaparral's smothering thickness. Between them the road passed, a pale skein across the backs of the foothills, connecting camps and little towns. Farther on the Stanislaus River, rushing down from the Sierra, would crook its current, to run, swift and turbulent, beyond the screen of alders and willows.

The road ascended, and on a hillcrest he again halted and looked back, listening. Unimpeded by trees, the thick air holding all sound close to the earth, he could hear far-distant noises. The bark of a dog came clear—that was from Alec Porter's ranch on the slopes toward the valley. Facing ahead he caught, faint and thin, the roar of the Crystal Star's stamp mill. Over to the right—the road would loop down toward it at the next turning—was Columbus, gutted and dying slowly among its abandoned diggings.

He avoided this turn, taking a branch trail that slanted through the thicket, wet leaves slapping against him, the horse's hoofs sucking into the spongy turf. It was still and dark, the air drenched with the odors of mossed roots and pungent leaves. When he emerged, the lights of Columbus shone below, a small sprinkling of yellow dots gathered about the central brightness of the Magnolia Saloon. The night was so still he could hear the voices of roysterers straggling home.

Presently the rushing weight of the Stanislaus River swept along the nearby bank. He could hear the rustle of its current, the wash of its waves sucking and nosing on the stones; feel the breath of its swollen tide chilled by mountain snows. It was up to the alder bushes, nearly flood high, cutting him off from a detour he had hoped to make—he would have to ride through San Marco. He put a spur to his horse and took it boldly, hoping the mud would dull the sound of his passage. The cabins and shacks that fringed the town were dark but in the main street there were lights, from the ground floor of the Mountain Hotel where he caught a glimpse of shirt-sleeved men playing cards, from the Pioneer Saloon, whence the jingling notes of a piano issued. There was less mud than he had expected and the thud of his flying hoofs was flung from wall to wall and called out a burst of barking dogs, and a startled face behind a drawn curtain in a red-lit cabin window.

Then away into the darkness—round Chinese Crossing, under the eaves of the spreading plant of the Northern Light, up a hill and down on the other side through a tunnel of trees to the Stanislaus Ferry. As he passed into their hollow he could hear the thunder of the Lizzie J's stamps across the river, beating gigantic on the silence, shaking the night.

The stream showed a flat space between bulwarked hills, one yellow spot—the light in the ferryman's window—shining like an eye unwinking and vigilant. Garland's hail was answered from within the shack, and the ferryman came out, a dog at his heels, a lantern in his hand. There was a short conference, and the lantern, throwing golden gleams on the ground, swung toward the flat boat, the horse following, his steps, precise and careful, ringing hollow on the wooden boards.

They slid out into the current, the boat vibrating to the buffets of little waves, the dog running from side to side, barking excitedly. The ferryman, the lantern lifted, took a look at his passenger.

"Mighty wet weather we're having," he said.

"Terrible. Don't ever remember it worse."

The light of the lantern fell on the horse's mud-caked legs.

"Looks as if you'd rid quite a ways."

"From this side of Jackson."

"That's some ride. Guess y'ain't met many folks."

"Not many. Staying indoors this weather, all that can."

"Belong round here?"

"No—back up toward the Feather."

They were in midstream, the scow advancing with a tremulous motion, spray springing across its low edges and showering the men. The dog, who had come to a standstill, his forepaws on the gunnel, his face toward Garland, suddenly broke into a furious barking. Garland shifted in his saddle.

"What's got your dog?" he said gruffly. "He ain't afraid, is he?"

"Afraid? Don't know the meanin' of the word. Don't mind him—it's his way; lived so long with me he acts sort of notional. Some days he'll bark like now at a passenger and then again he won't take no notice. Just somethin' about you, can't tell what, but he scents somethin' that makes him act unfriendly."

"What do you suppose it is?" growled the other.

The ferryman laughed.

"Oh, you can't ever tell about them animals—they got a thinkin' outfit of their own. Goin' far?"

"To Angels."

"Well, hope you'll get there all right. Sort of black weather to be traveling specially if you got money on you. Knapp and Garland's bound to get busy soon."

It was the passenger's turn to laugh.

"I'm not the sort they're after. It's big business for them. Ever seen 'em?"

"Search me. I guess mebbe I've taken 'em acrost, but how was I to know?"

The scow bumped against its landing and man and horse embarked. There was an interchange of rough good-nights, interrupted by the dog's frenzied barking. As the boat pulled out into the stream, the ferryman called back above the noise of the water:

"Looks like he had somethin' on you. I ain't ever seen him act so ugly before." Then to the dog, "Quit that, Tim, or I'll bust your jaw."

Garland mounted the slope. The sound of the river behind him was drowned by the roar of the Lizzie J's mill. Its rampart-like wall towered above him, cut by the orange squares of windows, the thunder of its stamps, a giant's feet crushing out the gold, pounding tremendous on the nocturnal solitude. As the horse snorted upward, digging its hoofs among the loosened stones, he looked up at it. Millions had been made there; millions were still making. Men in distant cities were being enriched by the golden grains beaten free by those giant feet. Once he had thought that he, too, might ravish the earth's treasure, become as they were by honest labor.

An unexpected surge of depression suddenly rose upon him. He set it down to the barking of the dog, for, after the manner of those who lead the lonely lives of the outlawed, he was superstitious. He believed in signs and portents, lucky streaks, the superior instinct of animals, and as he rode he brooded uneasily. Did it simply mean menace, or had the brute known him for what he was and tried to warn his master?

He muttered an oath and told himself, as he had done often of late, that he was growing old. Time and disappointment were wearing on the nerve that had once been unbreakable. In the past he had seen his path going unimpeded to its goal; now he recognized the possibility of failure, saw obstructions, crept cautious where he had formerly strode undismayed, hesitated where he had once leaped. He jerked himself upright and expelled his breath in an angry snort. This was no time for such musings. At Sheeps Bar, ten miles farther on, he was to meet Knapp and plan for the holdup of the stage that tomorrow night would carry treasure to the Cimarroon Mine at North Fork.

It was after midnight when the few faint lights of Sheeps Bar came into view. The place was small, a main street flanked by frame houses, a wooden arcade jutting over the sagging sidewalk. Sleep held it; blank windowpanes looked over the arcade's roof, the one bright spot the oblong of light that shone from the transom over the door of the Planters Hotel. Mindful of dogs he kept to the soft earth near the sidewalk, shooting glances left and right. But Sheeps Bar was dead; there was not a stir of life as he passed, not the click of a latch, not a face at door or window.

Beyond the arcade the town broke into a scattering of detached houses. The last of these, a one-story cabin staggering to its fall on the edge of a stream, sent forth a pale ray from a wide, uncurtained window. Across the pane, painted in blue, were the words "Hop Sing, Chinese Restaurant," and within the light of a kerosene lamp showed a bare whitewashed room set forth in tables and having at one end a small counter and cash register. On the window ledge stood a platter of tomales and a pile of oranges.

Garland drew up, listened, then dropped off his horse and led it toward the hovel. Before he reached it a side door opened and a head was thrust out. A whispered hail passed and the owner of the head emerged—a Chinaman, shadow-thin and shadow-noiseless. He slipped through the wet grass and with an "All 'ighty, boss," that might have been a murmur of the stirred leaves, took the horse and disappeared with it toward a rear shed.

Garland went to the cabin. The room which he entered opened into the restaurant and was the Chinaman's den. Its only furniture was a bunk with a coil of dirty blankets, a chair and table, on which stood an adding machine, the balls running on wires. Near it was the ink well and bamboo pen and small squares of paper covered with Chinese characters. One door led into the restaurant and another into the kitchen. In this room, lit by a wall lamp, its window giving on a tangled growth of shrubs, sat Knapp sprawled before the stove.

Their greetings were brief, and drawing up to the table they began the plans for the next night's work. Through the window the air came cool and moist, fighting with the odors of cooking and the rank, stifling Chinese smell. On the silence without rose the horses' soft whinnyings to one another and then the Chinaman's returning passage through the grass and the rasp of the closing door. He put a bottle and glasses before the men, slipped speechless into the restaurant, and returned, an animated shadow, with the lamp in his hand. This he set on the table in his own room, and sitting before it, began moving the balls in the adding machine. Upon the low voices in the kitchen, the dry click of the shifted balls broke in sharp staccato, followed by pauses when, with a hand as delicate as a woman's, he traced the Chinese characters on the paper.

It was he who heard first. His hand, raised to move a line of the balls, hung suspended, his eyes riveted in an agate-bright stare on the wall opposite. He half rose; his meager body stiffened as if the muscles had suddenly become steel; his face turned in wild question to the room beyond. He was up and had hissed a terrified, "Look out, boss, someone come!" when a rending blow fell on the door.

For a breath there was stillness, then pandemonium—a sudden burst of action following on a moment of paralysis, an explosion of sound and movement. It all came together—the breaking in of the door, the rat-like rush of the men, the crash of falling furniture, of shivered glass, of dark, scrambling figures, and the blinding flash of a revolver. The Chinaman's face, ape-like in its terror, showed above the blankets of his bunk, Knapp lay on the ground caught by the falling table, and in the window jagged edges of glass and a trail of blood on the sill showed the way Garland had gone. In the doorway the sheriff stood with his leveled revolver, while the voices and trampling of men came from the shrubs outside.

CHAPTER XV

THE LAST DINNER

I T WAS DEPRESSING WEATHER, rain, rain, and then again rain. For two weeks now, off and on, people had looked out through windows lashed with fine spears or glazed with watery skins which endlessly slipped down the pane. Muddy pools collected and spread across the street, the cars that drove through them sending the water in fan-like spurts from their wheels. Down the high, cobbled hills rivulets felt their way and grass sprouted between the granite blocks. A gray wall shut in the city, which showed dimly under the downpour, gardens blossoming, roof shining beyond roof, wet wall dripping on wet wall.

From his parlor window in the Argonaut Hotel, Boyé Mayer looked down on the street's swimming length, and then up at the sky's leaden pall. It was not raining now but there was no knowing when it might begin again. He yawned and stretched, then looked at his watch—half-past four. What should he do for the rest of the afternoon?

Several times during the last month this problem of time to be passed had presented itself. The rain had cut him off from stately promenades on the sunny side of the street and the diversions of San Francisco had grown stale from familiarity. The bloom of his adventure was tarnished; he was becoming used to riches, and comfort had lost its first, fine, careless rapture. It was not that he was actually bored, but he saw, as things were going, he might eventually become so, especially if the rain continued. So far, the green tables and Pancha had held off this undesired state, but like all attractive pastimes both had their dangers. His luck at the green tables had been so bad that he had resolved to give them up, and that made the menace of boredom loom larger. Life in San Francisco in the height of the wet

season, with cards denied him and Pancha only to be visited occa-
sionally, was not what it had promised to be.

He had thought of leaving, going to the South, and then decided against it. There were several reasons why it was better for
him to stay. One was the money in Sacramento. This had become
an intruding matter of worry and indecision. It was not only that
the store was so greatly diminished—his losses had made astonishing inroads in it—but he feared its discovery and he hated his trips
there. He always spent a night in the place, on a stone-hard bed in a
dirty, unaired room, and in his shabby clothes was forced to patron-
ize cheap eating houses where the fare sickened him. He managed
it very adroitly, carrying in his old suitcase the hat, coat, shoes and
tie he had bought in Sacramento, changing into them in the men's
washroom in the Sacramento depot, and emerging therefrom the
Harry Romaine who rented room 19 in the Whatcheer House.

Of course there was danger of detection, and faced by this and
the memory of his discomfort on the train down, he told himself
he would certainly move the money. But back in the Argonaut Hotel his resolution weakened. Where would he move it to? He could
bank it in San Francisco, but here again there were perils, of a kind
he dreaded even more than the Sacramento trips. There was that
question of references, and he feared the eyes of men, honest men,
business men. He kept away from them; they were shrewd, bitterly
hostile to such as he. So he invariably slipped back into a state where
he said he must do something, waited until he had only a few dollars
left, then, cursing and groaning, pulled the old clothes out of his
trunk, packed his battered suitcase and told Ned Murphy he was
going into the interior "on business."

But outside all these lesser boredoms and anxieties there was
another bigger than all the rest and growing every day: After the
money was gone, what?

It was a question that, in the past, he would have sheered away
from as a horse shies from an obstacle intruding on a pleasant road.
But time had taught him many things—the picaroon was becoming far-sighted; the grasshopper had learned of the ant. The spring
of his youth was gone; the renewal of the old struggle too horrible
to contemplate. And he would have to contemplate it or decide on

something to forestall it. That was what he had been thinking about for the past week, shut up in his hotel room, his hands deep in his pockets, his eyes morosely fixed on space.

At the Alston dinner an idea had germinated in his mind. It was only a seed at first, then it began to grow and had now assumed a definite shape. At first he had toyed with it, viewed it from different angles as something fantastic and irrelevant, but nevertheless having a piquancy of its own. Then his ill-luck and that necessary facing of the situation made him regard it more closely, compelled him to award it a serious consideration. He did not like it; it had almost no point of appeal; it was not the sort of thing, had chance been kinder, he would ever have contemplated. But it was inescapable, the angel with the flaming sword planted in his path.

Reluctant, with dragging feet, he had gone to call on the Alston girls. There had been several visits before that in return for continued hospitalities; but this was the first of what might be called a second series, the first after the acceptance of his idea. It had driven him to it, hounded him on like Orestes hounded by the furies. When he got there he saw behind the hounding the hand of fate, for instead of finding both sisters at home or both sisters out, he found Chrystie in and alone. She had talked bashfully, a shy-eyed novice with blush-rose cheeks and fingers feeling cold in the pressure of farewell. The hand of fate pointed to her. If it had been the other sister the hand would have pointed in vain. From the start he had felt the fundamental thing in Lorry—character, brain, vision, whatever you like to call it—upon which his flatteries and blandishments would have been fruitless, arrows falling blunted against a glittering armor. But this child, this blushing, perturbed, unformed creature, as soft and fiberless as a skein of her own hair, was fruit for his plucking.

That was his idea.

He had brooded on it all the week, hearing the rain drumming on the roof outside, smoking countless cigarettes, harassed, balky and beaten. He thought of it now, his hands deep in his pockets, his chest hollowed, his sullen eyes surveying the hill opposite, up which a cable car crawled like a large wet beetle. He watched the car till it dipped over the summit and there was nothing to see but the two shining rails, and the glistening roofs and the shrouded distance. It was like his idea, inexpressibly dreary, a forlorn, monotonous, gray shutting out what once had been a bright, engaging prospect.

He looked again at his watch—not yet half past five—at least an hour to pass before dinner. The green tables began to call, and he turned from the window to the dusk of the room, tempted and restless. He must do something or he would answer the call, and he searched his resources for a diversion at once enlivening and inexpensive. The search brought up on Pancha. She and her mysteries were always amusing; her love flattered him; blues and boredom died in her presence. Dangerous she could be, but dangerous he would not let her be—his was the master mind, cold, self-governing, and self-sure. One more swing around the circle with Pancha and then good-by. Soon he "would give his bridle rein a shake beside the river shore." At that he laughed—"river shore" aptly described San Francisco under present conditions—and laughing went to the telephone and called her up. He caught her at rehearsal and made a rendezvous for dinner in the banquet room at Solari's.

Solari's was a small Italian restaurant in the business quarter which had gained fame by the patronage of the local illuminati known to press and public as "Bohemians." They foregathered nightly there, the plate glass window giving a view of them, conspicuously herded at a large central table, to interested passersby. To the right of the window was a door, giving on a narrow staircase which led up to the second floor and what Solari called his "banquet room." Here on state occasions the Bohemians entertained celebrities, secretly fretted by the absence of their accustomed audience. They had decorated the walls with samples of their art, and when Eastern visitors came to Solari's, they were always taken up there, and expected to say that San Francisco reminded them of Paris. Mayer liked the place and had dined there several times with Pancha, always in the banquet room. There were newspaper men among the Bohemians who would have found material in the simultaneous appearance of the picturesque Mr. Mayer and the Albion's star.

He had ordered the dinner, had the fire lighted and the table spread when she came. She had run up the stairs and was out of breath, bringing in a whiff of the night's fresh dampness, and childishly glad to be there. She made no attempt to hide it, laughing as she slid out of her coat and tossed her hat on a chair. With her feet in their worn, high-heeled shoes held out to the fire, her hands rosily transparent against the blaze, she filled the room with a new magic and charm, sent waves of well-being through it. They warmed and lifted Mayer from his worries, and he was nearly as glad that he had asked her to come as she was to obey his summons. In his relief that she was able to dissipate his gloom, he forgot his caution and laughed with her, the laugh of the lover rejoicing in the sight of his lady.

The dinner was good and they were merry over it. Under the shaded light above the table he could see her color fluctuate and the quick droop of her eyes as they met his, and these evidences of his power added to his enjoyment. The inhibition he had put upon himself was for the time lifted, and he spoke softly, caressingly, words that made the rose in her cheeks burn deeper and her voice tremble in its low response. Always keener in his chase of money than of women, his cold blood was warmed and he permitted himself to grow tender, safe in the thought that this would be their last dinner.

At seven she had to go, frankly reluctant, making no pretense to hide her disinclination. She rose and went to where her coat lay over a chair, but he was before her, and snatching it up held it spread for her enveloping. With her arms outstretched she slid into it, then felt him suddenly clasp her. Weakened, like a body from which the strength has fled, she drooped against him, her head fallen back on his shoulder. He leaned his cheek against hers, rubbing it softly, then bending lower till he found her lips.

Out of his arms she steadied herself with a hand on the mantel-piece, the room blurred, no breath left her for speech. For a moment the place was noiseless save for the small, friendly sounds of the fire. Then she asked the woman's eternal question,

"Do you love me?"

"What do you think?" he said, surprised to hear his voice shaken and husky.

"Oh, Boyé," she cried and turned on him, clasping her hands against her heart, a figure of tragic intensity, "is it true? Do you mean it?"

He nodded, silent because he was not sure of what to say.

"It's not a lie? It's not just to get me because I'm Pancha Lopez who's never had a lover?"

"My dear girl!" he gave his foreign shrug. "Why all this unbelief?"

"Because it's natural, because I can't help it. I want to trust, I want to believe—but I'm afraid, I'm afraid of being hurt." She raised her clasped hands and covered her face with them. From behind their shield her voice came muffled and broken, "I couldn't stand that. I've never cared before, I never thought I would—anyway not like this. It's come and got me—it's got me down to the depths of my heart."

"Why, Pancha," he said, exceedingly uneasy, sorry now he'd asked her, sorry he'd come. "What's the sense of talking that way—don't be so tragic. This isn't the stage of the Albion."

"No, it's not." She dropped her hands and faced him. "It's real life—it's *my* real life. It's the first I've ever had." And suddenly she went to him, caught his arm, and pressing against it looked with impassioned eyes into his.

"Do you love me—not just to flirt and pay compliments, but truly—to want me more than any woman in the world? Tell me the truth."

Her eyes held his, against his arm he could feel the beating of her heart. Just at that moment the truth was the last thing he could tell.

"Little fool," he said softly, "I love you more than you deserve."

Her breath came with a sob; she drooped her head and, resting her face against his shoulder, was still.

Over her head he looked at the fire, with his free hand gently caressing her arm. He did not want to say any more. What he wanted was to get away, slide out of range of her eyes and her questions. It was his own fault that the interview had developed in a manner undesired and unintended, but that did not make him any the less anxious to end it. Presently she lifted her head and drew back from him. Stealing a look at her, he saw she was pale and that her eyes were wet. She put her fingers on them, pressing on the lids, her lips set close, her breast shaken.

In dread of another emotional outburst he looked at his watch and said in a brisk, matter-of-fact tone,

"Look here, young woman, this is awfully jolly, but I don't want to be the means of making trouble for you at the Albion. Won't you be late?"

She started and came to life, throwing a bewildered glance about her for her hat.

"Yes, I'd forgotten. I must hurry. It takes me an hour to make up."

Immensely relieved, he handed her the hat, saw her put it on with indifferent pulls and pats, and followed her to the door. At the top of the stairs he pushed by her with a laughing,

"Here, let me go first. It's my job to lead."

She drew aside, and as he passed her he caught her eyes, lighted with a soul-deep tenderness, the woman's look of surrender. Then as he descended a step below her, she leaned down and brushed her cheek along his shoulder, a touch light as the passage of a bird's wing.

"It's my job to follow where you lead," she whispered.

They went down the narrow staircase crowded close together, arm against arm, silent. In the doorway she turned to him.

"Don't come with me. I want to be alone. I want to understand what's happened to me. You can think of me going through the streets and saying over and over, 'I'm happy, I'm happy, I'm happy—' And you can think it's because of you I'm saying it."

She was gone, a small, dark figure, flitting away against the glistening splotches of light that broke on the street's wet vista.

Not knowing what else to do, Mayer walked home. He was angry with everything—with Pancha, with himself, with life. He thought of her without pity, savage toward her because he had to put her away from him. Joy came to him with outstretched hands, and he had to turn his back on it; it made him furious. He was exasperated with himself because so much of his money was gone, and he had to do what he didn't want to do. The money instead of making things easier had messed them into an enraging tangle. Life always went against him—he saw the past as governed by a malevolent fate whose business had been a continual creating of pitfalls for his unwary feet.

One thing was certain, he must have done with Pancha. Fortunately for him, it would not be hard. He would give his bridle rein a shake beside the river shore, and let the fact that he had gone sink into her, not in a break of brutal suddenness, but by slow, illuminating degrees. For if he was to carry out his idea—and there was nothing else to be done—there must be no entanglements with such as Pancha. He must be foot-loose and free, no woman clinging to that shaken bridle rein with passionate, restraining hands.

Cross and dispirited he entered the hotel and mounted to his room. He was beginning to hate it, its hideous hotel furniture, the memory of hours of ennui spent there. Against his doorsill the evening paper lay, and picking it up he let himself in and lighted the gas. On the mantel the small nickel clock seemed to start out at him, insolently proclaiming the hour, half past seven. He groaned in desperation and cast the paper on the table. It had been folded once over, and as it struck the marble, fell open. Across the front page in glaring black letters he read the words,

"Knapp, the bandit, caught at Sheeps Bar."

CHAPTER XVI

THROUGH A GLASS DARKLY

THAT NIGHT MAYER COULD NOT SLEEP. He kept assuring himself there was nothing to fear, yet he did fear. Dark possibilities rose on his imagination—in his excitement at finding the treasure he might have left something, some betraying mark or object. Was there any way in which the bandits could have obtained a clew to his identity; could they have guessed, or discovered by some underground channel of espionage, that he was the man who had robbed them? Over and over he told himself it was impossible, but he could not lift from his spirit a dread that made him toss in restless torment. With the daylight, his nerves steadied, and a perusal of the morning papers still further calmed him. Only one man had been caught—Knapp. Garland had broken through the window, and with the darkness and his knowledge of the country to aid him, had made his escape. The sheriff's bullet had not done its work; no man seriously wounded could have eluded the speed and vigilance of the pursuit. A posse was now out beating the hills, but with the long stretch of night in his favor he had slipped through their fingers and was safe somewhere in the chaparral or the mountains beyond. If his friends could not help him, a force more implacable than sheriff or deputy would bring him to justice: hunger.

The paper minutely described Knapp—young, thirty he said, a giant in strength, and apparently simple and dull-witted. The game up, he accepted the situation stoically and was ready to tell all he knew. Then followed a summary of his career, his meeting with Garland six years before and their joint activities. Of his partner's life where it did not touch his he had no information to give. They met up at intervals, planned their raids, executed them and then separated. He knew of Garland by no other name, had no knowledge

112

of his habitats or of what friends he had among the ranchers and townspeople. His description of the elder man was meager; all he seemed sure of was that Garland had once been a miner, that he wanted to quit "the road," and that he was middle-aged, somewhere around forty-five or it might be even fifty. Hop Sing, the Chinaman, was equally in the dark as to the man who, the papers decided, had been the brains of the combination. The restaurant keeper had merely been a humble instrument in his strong and unscrupulous hand.

So far there was no mention of the cache in the tules. The reporters, spilled out in the damp discomfort of the county seat, were filling their columns with anything they could scrape together, but it was still too early for them to have scraped more than the obvious, surface facts. Mayer would have to wait. As he sat at the table, picking at his breakfast, his mind darkly disturbed, he wondered if he had not better get out, and then called himself a fool. He was secure, absolutely secure. The man of the two who had had some capacity had escaped, and if he had had the capacity of Napoleon how could he possibly have anything to say that would involve Boyé Mayer?

So he soothed himself and, braced by a cup of coffee and a cold bath, began to feel at ease. But he decided to keep to his room till he knew more. If anything should happen he could break away quickly and he felt safer under cover. Now, more than ever, he feared the eyes of honest men.

He had reached this decision when he suddenly remembered Pancha. The thought of her came with an impact, causing him to stiffen and give forth a low ejaculation. His mind ran with lightning speed over what he had been reading, then flashed back to her. Was this man, this hulking country Hercules, her "best beau," or was it the other one, Garland, the one who had the brains, and who was old? It was more likely Knapp. He could have come to the city, seen her play, been inspired by a passion that made him daring, been her choice till Mayer had come and conquered.

Her place in the affair, overlooked in the first shock of his own alarms, rose before him, formidable and threatening. A desire to see her, deeper than any he had yet experienced, seized him. Her guard would be down; with all her sly skill she could not deceive him now. She would be frightened, she was in danger, she would betray herself. Even if she had long ceased to care for the man, she might have some fears for him, and how much more fears for herself? As he realized the perils of her position, a faint, slow smile curved his lips. It was not of derision but of a cynical comprehension. He saw her scared to the soul, scared of discovery as Knapp's girl, who was aware of his business, who kept tab on his comings and goings. For all anyone knew some of that money of hers, so thriftily hoarded, might be part of the bandit's unlawful gains.

"Whew!" he breathed out. "She must be frozen to the marrow!"

But he did not dare go to her till he was more certain of how he himself stood.

The next day was Sunday, and on the *Despatch's* front page appeared Knapp's picture and his story of the rifled cache. Licking along his dry lips with a leathern tongue, Mayer read it and then cast the paper on the floor and sank back in his chair in a collapse of relief. Neither man had had any suspicion of the identity of the robber; all they knew was that their hiding place had been discovered and the treasure stolen.

He was safe, safer than he had ever felt before. As the tramp, only two people had seen him near the marshes, a child and a boy in a ranch yard. Even if either of them should remember and speak of him in relation to the theft, was there a human being who would connect that tramp with Boyé Mayer, gentleman of leisure, in California for his health? He raised his eyes and encountered his reflection in the mirror. Gathering himself into an upright posture, he studied it, aristocratic, cold, immeasurably superior; then, closing his eyes, he called up the image of himself as he had been when he crossed the tules. No one, unless gifted with second sight, could have recognized the one in the other. Dropping back in his chair, he raised his glance to the floriated cement molding on the ceiling, from which the chandelier depended, feeling as if borne by a peaceful current into a shining, sunlit sea.

There was a performance at the Albion on Sunday night, but no rehearsal, and in the gray of the afternoon he went across town to see Pancha.

He found her in a litter of dressmaking—lengths of material, old costumes, bits of stage jewelry, patterns, gold lace, were outspread on chairs, hung from the table, lay in bright rich heaps on the floor. The shabby room, glowing with the lights on lustrous fabrics, the gloss of crumpled silks, the glints and sweeps and sparklings of color, looked as if in the process of transformation at the touch of a magician's wand. In the midst of it—the enchanted princess still waiting for the wand's touch—sat Pancha, in a faded blouse and patched skirt, sewing. Part of her transformation was accomplished when she saw Mayer. If her clothes remained the same, the radiance of her face was as complete as if the spell was lifted and she found herself again a princess encountering her long-lost prince.

His first glance fell away startled from that radiant face. There was nothing on it or behind it but joy. He pressed a hand soft and clinging, encircled a body that trembled under his arm and in which he could feel the thudding of a suddenly leaping heart. Her eyes, searching his, shone with a deep, pervasive happiness. She was nothing but glad, quiveringly, passionately glad, moving in his embrace toward a chair, babbling breathless greetings; she had not expected him, she was surprised, she was—and the words trailed off, her face hidden against his arm.

It was far from what he had expected and he was thankful for that moment when she stopped looking at him and he could master his surprise. It nearly flooded up again when he saw the paper, news sheet on top, in a pile by the sofa where it had evidently been thrown as she lay reading.

Presently he was in the armchair and she was moving about clearing things away in a futile, incapable manner, darting like a perturbed bird for a piece of silk, then dropping it and making a dive for a coil of chiffon, which she pressed half into a drawer and left hanging over the edge in a misty trail. As she moved, she continued her broken babblings—excuses for the room's disorder, costumes for the new piece to be made, all the time flashing looks at him, watchful, humble, adoring, ready to come at his summons of word or hand. Finally, the materials thrown into hiding places, the dresses heaped on the sofa, she came toward him—a lithe, feline stealing across the carpet—and slipped down on the floor at his feet.

"Well," he said, "what's the news?"

"There isn't any, except that I'm glad to see you."

She curled her legs under her tailor-fashion, and looked up at him.

"Nothing's happened to disturb the even tenor of your way?"

"Only rehearsals for the new piece and they don't bother me now. That's all that ever happens to me, except for a gentleman caller now and again."

She caught his eye, and, her hands clasped round one knee, swayed gently, laughing in pure joy. He did not join in, adjusting his thoughts to this new puzzle. Leaning against the chair back, the afternoon light yellow on his high, receding temples and the backward brush of his hair, his look was that of a fond, rather absent-minded amusement such as one awards to the antics of a playful child. To anyone watching him his lack of response would have suggested a preoccupation in more pregnant matters. Receiving no answer, she went on:

"Only one gentleman caller, one sole alone gentleman, named Mayer, who, I think, likes to come here." She paused, but again there was no answer and she finished, addressing the carpet, "Or maybe I just imagine it, and he only comes dull Sunday afternoons when there's nowhere else to go."

"Oh, silly, unbelieving child!" came his voice, slightly distrait it is true, but containing sufficient of the lover's chiding tenderness to fill her with delight.

But this was not what had brought him. The interview started, it was his business now or never to solve the enigma. He stirred in his chair and, raising a languid hand, pointed to the paper.

"I see you've been reading the *Despatch*."

"Um–um—this morning."

"Very good story, that one on the front page, about the bandit chap."

"Knapp? Yes, bully. They've got him at last. It was exciting, wasn't it? Like a novel. I don't often read the papers, but I did read that."

She gave no evidence, either of agitation, or of any especial interest. Unclasping her hands from about her knee, she turned a gold bracelet that hung loose on her wrist, watching the light slide on its surface. Her face was gently unconcerned, serene, almost pensive. The man's eyes explored it, searched, scanned it for a betraying sign.

"Did you notice his picture? A pretty hard-looking customer."

She nodded, absently looking at the bracelet.

"He sure was, but they're not all as bad as that. Once down at Bakersfield I saw a bandit. They caught him near a place where I lived and the sheriff brought him in there. He looked like a rough sort of rancher, nothing dangerous about him."

The expression of pensiveness deepened, increased by a sudden, disturbing thought. Would she tell him about Bakersfield and the horrible life there with Maria Lopez?

The temptation to be frank with him, to have no secrets, to let him know her as she was, assailed her. She resolved upon it, drew a deep breath and said,

"I never told you that I once lived in Bakersfield."

"There are lots of things you never told me. They seem to think the other fellow—what's his name—Garland—has really made his escape."

The confession died on her lips. She was glad of it; she would tell him later, some other time, he was too engrossed in the bandits now.

"I guess that's right. He's got up in the hills where there are ranchers that'll help him."

"Would any rancher dare to help him now—wouldn't they be afraid to?"

"Not his kind. Country people aren't as dull as you'd think. I've seen a lot of them, when I was a kid and lived round in small places. They act sort of dumb, but some of them are awful smart behind it."

"Probably get their share of the loot."

"Sure. That would be the natural thing to keep them quiet, wouldn't it?"

Mayer murmured an assent and drew himself to the edge of his chair.

"I'd hate to be one of them the way things stand now! The law, when it gets busy, has a pretty long arm."

"I guess it has," she agreed, toying with the bracelet.

"Anyone who has had any sort of dealings, been a friend or a confederate of either of those fellows, is in a desperately ugly position."

She nodded. He leaned still further forward, his elbows on his knees, his glance riveted on her.

"Suppose either of them had a wife or a sweetheart—and it's probable they have—*that's* the person the authorities will be after."

"Yes," she dropped the bracelet and looked away from him, her expression dreamy, "it would be. They'll start right in to hunt for them. If they got them, what would they do to them?"

"Do?" He suddenly stretched an index finger at her, pointing into her face. "If they find a woman or a girl who's had any acquaintance or intimacy with either Knapp or Garland they'll land her in jail so quick she won't have time to think. Jail, young woman, and after that the third degree. And if she's stood in with them—well, it'll be jail for a home till she's served her term."

She pondered for a moment, then said softly,

"It wouldn't matter if she loved him."

"Jail wouldn't matter?"

Her glance had been fastened in meditation on the shadows of the room. Now it shifted to him, rapt and luminous. She raised herself to her knees and laid a hand on his shoulder.

"Nothing would matter if he was her man. It would be great to stand by him and suffer for him. It would be happiness to go to jail for him, to die for him. There'd be only one thing that she'd be thinking about—that would make her glad to do it—to know that he loved her, Boyé."

Eye holding eye, she drew him closer till her black-fringed lids lowered and her face, held up to his, offered itself—a symbol of a fuller gift.

Gathering her in his arms, he rose and drew her to her feet. Pressed against him, shaken by the beating of the heart that leaped at his touch, she again breathed the eternal question, "Do you love me"—words that come from under-layers of doubt in the despairingly impassioned.

He reassured her as the unloving man does, lying to get away, soothing with kisses, eager to break loose from arms that are unwelcome and yet tempt. He played his part like a true lover and at the door was genuinely stirred when he saw there were tears in her eyes. He had not guessed she could be so tender, that her hard exterior hid such depths of sweetness. His parting embrace might have deceived a more love-learned woman, and he left her with a slight, unwonted sense of shame in his heart.

Away from her, where he could think, he pushed the shame aside as he was ready to push her. The fire she had kindled in him died; the woman he had clasped and kissed ceased to figure as a being to desire and became an enigma to solve.

The fate of the bandits had touched no vulnerable spot in her. She had been unmoved by it. Even did she adore Mayer so ardently and completely that his presence was an anodyne for every other thought, she would have shown, she *must* have shown, some disturbance. He had known women who lived so utterly in the moment that the past lost its reality, was as dissevered from the present as though it had never existed. Was she one of these? Could her relation—whatever it was—with either of the outlaws have been so erased from her consciousness that she could talk of his danger with a face as unconcerned as the one she had presented to Mayer's vigilant eye?

It was impossible. There would have been a betrayal, a quiver of memory, a flash of apprehension—And suddenly, gripped by conviction, he stopped in the street and stood staring down its length.

Night was coming, the gray spotted with lamps. Each globe a sphere of pinkish yellow, they stretched before him in a line that marched into a distance of mingled lights and more accentuated shadows. He looked along them as if they were bearing his thoughts back over the past, every globe a station in the retrospect, stage by stage advancing him toward a final point of certainty.

She didn't know!

It formed in a sentence, detached and exclamatory, in his mind, and he stood staring at the lamps, people jostling him and some of them turning to look back.

Now that he had guessed it everything became clear. It was like a piece of machinery suddenly supplied with a lacking wheel which moved it to instant action. He walked forward, seeing all the disconnected elements take their places, seeing the whole, harmonious, intelligently related and extremely simple. That was what had led him astray. He was not used to simple solutions; intricate byways, complex turnings and doublings, were what he was trained to. Working along the familiar lines, he had overlooked what should have been easily discerned.

The man loved her, wanted to stand well with her and had deceived her as to his occupation. And it was the older one—Knapp's picture had been in the paper, she had seen it and it had meant nothing to her. So it was Garland, the chap with the brains, on toward fifty—but these mountain men with their outdoor life and unspent energies held their youth long. His imagination, stirred to unwonted activity, pictured him, an outcast, hunted and hiding in the mountain wilderness. As he had smiled at the thought of Pancha's terrors, he smiled now, and again it was a curving of the lips that had no humor behind it. It was the bitter smile of an understanding that has no sympathy and yet has power to comprehend.

As for himself, he was out of it, the mystery was solved and he could go his way in peace of mind. It was a fortunate ending, come just in time. There was no need now for any more folly or philandering. They were cut off short, romance snipped by Fate's shears, a full stop put at the last word of the sentence. He had no fears of Pancha, she knew too much to make trouble, and anyway there was nothing for her to make trouble about. He had treated her with a consideration that was nothing short of chivalrous. Even if there had been anyone belonging to her to take him to task he could defend his conduct as that of a Sir Galahad—and there wasn't anyone.

He felt brisk, light, mettlesome. Troubles that had threatened were dispersed; the future lay fair before him. Relieved of all encumbering obstacles, it extended in clear perspective toward his idea. With keen, contemplative eye he viewed it at the end of the vista, calculating his distance, gathering his powers to cover it in a swift dash, sure of his success.

CHAPTER XVII

THE WOLF IN SHEEP'S CLOTHING

ONE AFTERNOON, A WEEK LATER, Chrystie Alston was crossing Union Square Plaza. It was beautiful weather, the kind that comes to San Francisco after long spells of rain. Across the bay the distances were deep-hued and crystal-clear, the hills clean-edged against a turquoise sky. Green slopes showed below the dense olive of eucalyptus woods and around the shore were the white clusterings of little towns. Where the water filled in the end of a street's vista it was like an insert of blue enameling, and from the city's high places Mount Diavolo could be seen, a pointed gem, surmounting in final sharpness the hill's carven skyline.

Chrystie felt the exhilaration of the air and the sun, and walked with a bounding, long-limbed swing. She was a glad and prosperous figure, silk skirts swept by scintillant lights eddying back from the curves of her hips, glossy new furs lying soft on her shoulders, and on her bosom—a spot of purple—a bunch of violets. Her eyes were as clear as the sky, and her hair, pressed down by the edge of a French hat, hung in a misty golden tangle to her brows. No one needed to be told she was rich and carefree. Her expensive clothes revealed the former, her buoyant step and happy expression, the latter condition.

She was halfway across the Plaza when her progress suffered a check. There was a drop in her swift faring, a poised moment of indecision. During the halt her face lost its blithe serenity, showed a faltering uncertainty, then stiffened into resolution. Inside her muff her hands gripped, inside her bodice her heart jumped. Both these evidences of agitation were hidden and that gave her confidence. Assuming an air of nonchalance she moved forward, her gait slackened, her eyes abstractedly shifting from the sky to the shrubs.

Boyé Mayer, advancing up the path, saw she had seen him and drew near, watchfully amused. Almost abreast of him she directed her glance from the shrubs to his face. Surprise at the encounter was conveyed by a slight lifting of her brows, pleasure and greeting by a smile and inclination of the head. Then she would have passed on, but he came to a stop in front of her.

"Oh, don't go by as if you didn't want to speak to me," he said, and pressed a hand that slid warm out of the new muff.

Standing thus in the remorseless sunshine she was really very handsome, her skin flawless, her lips as red and smooth as cherries. And yet in spite of such fineness of finish there was no magic about her, no allure, no subtlety. Achieving graceful greetings he inwardly deplored it, noting as he spoke how shy she was and how she sought to hide it under a crude sprightliness. There was a shyness full of charm, a graceful gaucherie delightful to watch as the gambolings of young animals. But Chrystie was too conscious of herself and of him to be anything but awkward and constrained.

She was going shopping, but when he claimed a moment—just a moment, he saw her so seldom—went to the bench he indicated and dropped down on it. Here, a little breathless, sitting very upright, her burnished skirts falling deep-folded to the ground, she tried to assume the worldly lightness of tone befitting a lady of her looks in such an encounter.

"Do you often go this way, through the Plaza?" he asked after they had disposed of the fine weather.

"Yes, quite often. When it's a nice day like this I always walk downtown, and it's shorter going through here."

"It's odd I haven't met you before. This is my regular beat, across here about three and then out toward the Park."

"That's a long walk," Chrystie said. "You must like exercise."

"I do, but I also like taking little rests on the way. That is, when I meet a lady"—his eye swept her, respectfully admiring—"who looks like a goddess dressed by Worth."

She moved in her flashing silks, making them rustle.

"Oh, Mr. Mayer, how silly," was the best she could offer in response.

"Silly! But why?" His shoulders went up with that foreignness Chrystie thought so bewitching. "Why is it silly to say what's true?"

"But you know it's not—it's just—er—" She wanted to retort with the witty brilliance that the occasion demanded, and what she said was, "It's just hot air and you oughtn't to."

Then she felt her failure so acutely that she blushed, and to hide it buried her chin in her fur and sniffed at the violets on her breast.

His voice came, close to her ear, very kind, as if he hadn't noticed the blush,

"Well, then, I'll express it differently. I'll say you're just charming. Will that do?"

"I don't think I am. It sounds like someone smaller. I'm too big to be charming."

That made him laugh, a jolly ringing note.

"Whatever *you* think you are, *I* think you're the most delightful person in San Francisco."

The silks rustled again. Chrystie lifted her eyes from the violets to the bench opposite from which two Italian women were watching with deep interest this coquetting of the lordlings.

"Now you're making fun of me," she said, like a wounded child.

"Oh, dear lady," it was he who was wounded, misunderstood, hurt, "how unkind and how untrue. Could I make fun of anyone I admired, I respected, I—er—thought as much of as I do of you?"

She looked down at her muff. Just for a moment he thought her shyness was quite winning.

"I don't know—I don't know you well enough. But you've been everywhere and seen everything, and I must seem so—so—sort of stupid and like a kid. I don't know what you think, but I know that's the way I feel when I'm with you."

The Italian women were aware of a slight movement on the part of the aristocratic gentleman which suggested an intention of laying his hand upon that of the golden-haired lady. Then he evidently thought better of it, and his hand dropped to the head of his cane. The golden-haired lady had seen it, too, and affrighted slid her own into the shelter of her muff. With down-drooped head she heard the cultured accents of the only perfect nugget she had ever met murmur reproachfully.

"Now it's *you* who are making fun of *me*. Why, *I'm* the one who feels stupid and tongue-tied. I'm the one who comes away from you abashed and embarrassed. And why, do you suppose? Because I feel I've been with someone who's so much finer than all the others. Not the pert, smart girl of dinners and dances, but someone genuine and sincere and sweet"—his glance touched the bunch of violets— "as sweet as those violets you're wearing."

Chrystie experienced a feeling of astonishment, mixed with an uplifting exaltation. Staring before her she struggled to adjust the familiar sense of her shortcomings with this revelation of herself as a creature of compelling charm. She was so thrilled she forgot her pose and murmured incredulously,

"Really?"

"Very really. Why are you so modest, little Miss Alston?"

"I didn't know I was."

"Wonderfully so—amazingly so. But perhaps it's part of you. It is so sometimes with a beautiful woman."

"Beautiful? Oh, no, Mr. Mayer."

"Oh, yes, Miss Alston."

Chrystie began to feel as if she was coming to life after a long period of deadness. She had a consciousness of sudden growth, of expanding and outflowering, of bursting into glowing bloom. A smile that she tried to repress broke out on her lips, the repression causing it to be one-sided, which gave it piquancy. She was invaded by a heady sense of exhilaration and a new confidence, daring, almost reckless. It made it possible for her to quell a rush of embarrassment and lead the conversation like a woman of the world:

"You're mistaken about my being modest. Everybody who knows me well says I'm spoiled."

"Who's spoiled you?"

"Lorry and Aunt Ellen and Fong."

She gave him a quick side glance, met his eyes, and they both laughed, a light-hearted mingling of treble and bass.

The Italian women breathed deeply on their bench, aware that the interchanged glances and chimed laughter had advanced the romance on its happy way.

"Three people can't do any serious spoiling—there should be at least four. Who's Fong?"

"Our Chinaman; he's been with us for centuries."

"Let me make the fourth. Put me on the list."

"I think you've put yourself there without being invited. Since we sat down you've done nothing but pay me compliments."

"Never mind that. Here's a sensible suggestion: I'll judge myself if you're spoiled and if I think you are I won't pay you one more. Isn't that fair?"

"I think so."

"Very well. Of course I must know you better, have a talk with you before I can be sure. How can we arrange that? Ah—I have it! Some bright afternoon like this we might take a walk together."

"Yes, we could do that."

"We might go to the park—it's wonderful there on days like this."

She nodded and said slowly,

"And we could take Lorry."

"To be sure, if she'd care to come."

There was a slight pause and he saw by her profile there was doubt in her mind.

"I don't know about her caring. Lorry doesn't like walking much."

"Then why ask her to do it?"

She stroked her muff, evidently discomfited.

"Well, you see, it's this way, I don't think Lorry'd like me to go with you alone."

"But why?" He drew himself up from the bench's back, his tone surprised, slightly offended. "Surely having invited me to her house, she could have no objection to my going for a stroll with you?"

"No, no—" Her discomfort was obvious now. "It isn't *you*. It's just that father was very particular and Lorry always tries to do what he would have liked."

"My dear young lady, your father's been dead a good many years. Things have changed since then; the customs of his day are not the customs of ours. Of course I wouldn't suggest that you go counter to your sister's wishes, but"—he turned away from her, huffy, head high, a gentleman flouted in his pride—"it's rather absurd from my point of view. Oh, well, we'll say no more about it."

Chrystie was distracted. It was not only the humiliation of appearing out of date and provincial; it was something much worse than that. She saw Boyé Mayer retiring in majestic indignation and not coming back, leaving her at this first real blossoming of their friendship because Lorry had ideas that the rest of the world had abandoned with hoop skirts and chignons.

"Why, why," she stammered, alarm pushing her to the recklessness of the desperate, "couldn't we go and not tell her? It's—it's—just a prejudice of Lorry's—no one else feels that way. The Barlow girls, who've been very strictly brought up, go walking and even go to the theater with"—she was going to say "their nuggets" and then changed with a gasp to—"the men their mother asks to her parties."

So Chrystie, guileless and subjugated, assisted in the development of the Idea. She made an engagement to meet Mr. Mayer four days later in the Plaza and go with him to see the orchids in the park greenhouse. The Holy Spirit orchid was in bloom and she had never seen it. A flower with such a name as the Holy Spirit seemed to Chrystie in some way to shed an element of propriety if not righteousness over the adventure.

It was when they were sauntering toward the end of the Plaza that a woman, coming up a side street, saw them. She was about to cross when her eye, ranging over the green lawns, brought up on them and she stopped, one foot advanced, its heel knocking softly against the curbstone. As the two tall figures moved her glance followed them, her head slowly turning. She watched them cross the intersection of the streets, lights chasing each other up and down the lady's waving skirt and gilding the web of golden hair; she watched them pass by a show window, its glassy surface holding their bright reflections; she watched their farewells at the door of a large shop which finally absorbed the lady. Then she faced about, and walked toward the Albion, where a rehearsal was awaiting her.

That afternoon a week had passed since Pancha had seen her lover.

During the first three days of it she experienced a still and perfect peace. She did not want to see him; she had reached a point of complete assurance and was glad to wait there, rest in the joy that had come to her, dwell, awed, on its wonderfulness. In her short periods of leisure she sat motionless, recalling lovely moments, living them over, sometimes asking herself why he cared for her, then throwing the question aside—that he did was all that concerned her now.

On the fourth day her serenity was disturbed very slightly, but she could not banish a faint, intruding surprise that she had not heard from him. She tried to smother it by a return to her old interests, but her work had lost its power to engross and she went through it mechanically without enthusiasm. By the fifth her mental state had changed. She would not admit that she was uneasy, but in spite of her efforts a queer, upsetting restlessness invaded her. Everything was all right, she knew it, but she seemed to be dodging a shadow that fell thinly across the brightness. That evening she played badly, missed a cue and had no snap. She realized it, saw it in the faces of her fellows, and knew she must do better or there would be complaints.

On the way home she argued it out with herself. She was thinking too much of Mayer—worrying about nothing—and it was interfering with her work. She oughtn't to be such a fool, but her place at the Albion was important, and a word from him—a line or a phone message—would tone her up, and she would go on even better than before. At an "all night" drug store she bought a box of pink notepaper and a sachet, and before she went to bed put the scented envelope in the box and covered them both with a sofa pillow to draw out the perfume.

In the morning, after sniffing delicately at the paper, which exhaled a powerful smell of musk, she sat at her table and wrote him a letter. She made several drafts before she attained the tone, jocose and tender, that would save her pride and draw from him the line that was to dissipate her foolish fancies.

DEAREST BOYÉ:

No one has knocked at my door for nearly six days now. Not even sent me a telephone message. But I'm not complaining as maybe the caller may have a lot of things to keep him busy. But I would like a word just so I won't forget you. I don't want to do that but you know these stage dames do have sort of tricky memories. So it might be a good idea to give mine a jolt. A post card will do it and a letter do it better, and I guess yourself would do it best of all.

Thine,
PANCHITA.

The next morning his answer came and she forgot that she ever had been uneasy. The world shone, the air was as intoxicating as wine, the sun a benediction. She kissed the letter and pinned it in her blouse, where it lay against her heart, from which it had lifted all care. The second floor of the Vallejo rang to her singing, warbling runs and high, crystal notes, gushes of melody, and tones clear as a bird's held exultingly. People passing stopped to listen, looking up at the open windows. And yet it was far from a love letter:

DEAR PANCHA:

What a brute I must seem. I've been out of town, that's all. I have to go every now and then—business I'm meditating in the interior. I forgot to tell you about it, but it will take up a good deal of my time from now on. I won't be able to see you as often as I'd like, but as soon as I have a spare moment there'll be a knock at your door, or someone waiting in the alley to the stage entrance. Until then *au revoir,* or in your own beautiful language, *hasta mañana,*

B.

If she had seen Mayer and the blonde lady before the receipt of this missive her alarms would have increased. But the letter with one violent push had sent her to the top of the golden moment again. She was poised there firmly; it would take more than the sight of Mayer in casual confab with a woman to dislodge her. He knew many people, went to many places; she was proud of his social progress. So undisturbed was she that as she walked to the theatre she smiled to herself, a sly, soft smile. How surprised the lady would be if she knew that the shabby girl unnoticed on the curb was Boyé Mayer's choice—the Rosamund of his bower, the inmate of his secret garden.

CHAPTER XVIII

OUTLAWED

THE NIGHT AND THE CHAPARRAL had made Garland's escape possible. In those first moments, breaking through the thicket with the shots and shouts of his pursuers at his back, his mind had held nothing but a frantic fear. A thing of gaping mouth and strained eyes, he had groped and rushed, torn between branches, splashed through streams, a menaced animal possessed by an animal's instinct for flight.

Then a bullet, tearing the leaves above his head, had pulled his scattered faculties together. He dropped and lay, crawled forward in a moist darkness, rose and made a slantwise dart across the hill's face, crouching as a bullet struck into a nearby trunk. Pausing to listen, he could hear the voices of his pursuers flung back and forth, sound against sound, broken, clamorous, the baying of the pack. Against the ground, trickle of water and stir of leaves soft around him, he lay for a second, the breaths coming in rending gasps from his lungs.

By a series of doublings and loops, he gained the summit and here rose and looked down. The voices were fainter, the trampling among the branches was drifting toward the right. The lights of the town showed a central cluster with a scattering of bright, disconnected particles as if a fiery thing had fallen and burst, sending sparks in every direction. Some of them moved, a train of dancing dots, lanterns carried on the run—the town was roused for the man hunt.

He went on, down from the crest and then up; the voices died and he was alone in the vast, enmuffling dark.

For the time safe, he allowed himself a rest, flat on his back under a pine, breathing through open mouth. It was then that he was aware of a wet warmth on his neck, and feeling of it with clumsy fingers remembered the shot that had followed the breaking of the door. One inch to the left and he would have been a dead man. As it was, it was only a surface tear through the flesh and he sopped at it with his bandanna, muttering and wiping his fingers on the moss.

Presently he moved on again, one with the woodland creatures in their night prowls. He could hear them, cracklings of twigs under their furtive feet, scurrying retreats before his heavier human tread. Once he stopped at a cry, a shriek tearing open the silence as the lightning tears the cope of the sky. He knew it well, had heard it often by his camp fire in his old prospecting days—the yell of a California lion in the mountains beyond. The night was drawing toward its last deep hours when he came to a straight uprearing of rock, a ledge, broken and heaved upward in some ancient earth-throe. He felt along its face, glazed by water films, close-curtained by shrubs and ferns, found an opening and crawled in.

There he stayed for a week; saw the sun rise over the sea of pines, wheel across the sky, drop behind the rock whence its last glow painted every tree top with a golden varnish. Then came evening, long and still, a great rush of color to the west, birds winging their way homeward, shadows slanting blue over the slopes, brimming purple in the hollows. Then night with its majestic silence and its large, serene stars. He lay in the cave mouth looking at them, his thoughts ranging far. Sometimes they went back to the past and he remembered the deep blue nights in Arizona, the white glare of the days. He could see the walls of his ranch house, with the peppers in red bunches, Juana in her calico wrapper and Pancha playing in the shade. He rose, cursing, sopped his bandanna in the water trickling from the rock and put it on his wound. It hurt and made him feverish, a prey to such harassing memories.

With a piece of cord he found in his pocket he made a trap—a noose suspended from a bent sapling—and caught a rabbit. This kept him in food for two days, then setting it again he broke the cord, and driven by hunger went forth, revolver in hand. He saw fresh deer tracks, and was lucky enough to find his quarry, steal close and shoot it. His hunger made him reckless and he lit a fire, roasting the meat on planted sticks. But the birds came and wheeled about overhead and the specks of moving birds in the sky can be seen from afar.

His forces restored by nourishment he grew restless. The loneliness of the place oppressed him and he wanted to hear of Knapp. Knapp had been caught and Knapp would talk and he burned to know what Knapp would say of him. He was sure the man knew little; he had foreseen such a catastrophe and been as secret as the grave, but Knapp might have picked up something. Anyway he wanted to know just how he stood. Food, his greatest need, supplied, his next was news, someone to tell him, or a newspaper.

The people who stood in with him were scattered far. Up beyond Angels the Garcias were his friends, and over to the left, on the bend of the river near Pine Flat, Old Man Haley, reputed cracked and a survivor of the great days of the lode, had been his confederate from the start. But Haley's shack was too near Pine Flat, and now with a reward probably offered, he feared the Garcias—greasers, father and son, not to be trusted. The wisest course was to lie low and keep to himself, anyway till he knew more.

So he tracked across the country from landmark to landmark, a cave, an abandoned tunnel, the shell of a ruined cabin. He left the foothills and went back toward the mountain spurs where ridge rises beyond ridge, and at the bottom of ravines rivers lie like yellow threads. Nature held him aloof, an atom leaving no mark upon it, an intruder on its musing self-engrossment. He moved, secure and solitary, seeing no living thing but the game he shot and the hawk hanging poised in the blue. Sometimes he sat for hours watching its winged shadow float over the tree tops.

Finally he knew he would have to return to the settlements, for his store of cartridges was almost exhausted. He tried to hoard them, eking out his deer meat with roots and berries till body and nerve began to weaken. That decided him and he started back, eating only just enough to give him strength to get there. He was nearly spent when he found himself once more among the chaparral's low growth, looking down on the brown and green fields.

There was a ranch below him whose acres stretched like a patterned cloth along the hill's slant. The house, white-painted, stood in the midst of cultivated land which he would have to cross to reach it. But driven by hunger he stole down, his way marked by a swaying in the close-packed foliage. He could see the smoke rising in a blue skein from its chimney and at night its windows break out in bright squares. He drew close enough to watch the men go off to their work and the women move, sunbonneted, about the yard.

The second day, faint and desperate, he ventured; it was mid-morning, the men away in the fields till noon. There was not a sound when he reached the house, skirted the rear, and walked round to the side where a balcony ran the length of the building. Chairs stood here and evidences of sewing, work baskets, spools and scissors, and a tumbled heap of material. On the step lay a newspaper and he was stretching his hand for it when he heard the voices of women.

Through an open door he saw them—two—standing in front of a mirror, one with her back toward him, in a blouse of pink that she was pulling into a waistband. The other watched her, pins in her mouth, a tape measure over her arm. Both were absorbed, the one in her reflection in the glass, the other in the pink blouse. He trod on the step with a heavy foot and muttered a gruff "Say, lady."

The women flashed round and he saw them to be middle-aged and young—a mother and daughter evidently. The elder with a quick, defensive movement walked to the doorway and stood there, blocking it. He heard the younger exclaim, "A tramp!" and then she came forward, squeezing in beside her mother. Hostility and appre-hension were on both their faces.

"What do you want here?" said the elder sharply.

"Somethin' to eat," he answered, trying to make his hoarse tones mild; "I bin on the tramp for days."

"No, no, go off," she cried, waving him away.

"I'm starved," he pleaded. "Any bones or scraps'll do me."

They eyed him, still apprehensive, but evidently impressed by his appearance.

"Honest to God it's true," he said, snatching at his advantage. "Can't you see it by the looks of me?"

The girl, thrusting her hand through her mother's arm and drawing her back, answered,

"All right. Go round to the kitchen."

With the words she banged the door and he heard the click of the lock, then their scurrying steps, bangs of other doors and their receding voices. In a twinkling he grabbed the paper, thrust it into his coat pocket, and slouched round to the kitchen door.

"Stay out there," called the mother from within. "I'll give you food, but I don't want no tramp tracking up my kitchen."

He could see them cutting bread and chunks of meat, flurried and he knew frightened. Leaning against a chair was a rifle, placed where he could see it. He could have smiled at it had he not been so bound and cramped with fear. As they cut they interchanged low-toned remarks, and once the elder looked at him frowningly over her shoulder.

"Why ain't you workin'? A big, husky man like you?" she asked.

"I'm calcalatin' to find work at Sonora, but I have to have the strength to git there. I've had a bad spell of ague."

The girl raised her eyes to him and compassion softened them. As she went back to her bread-cutting he heard her murmur,

"I guess that's straight. He sure has an awful peaked look."

It was she who gave him the food, rolled in a piece of newspaper. Standing in the doorway, she held it out to him and said, smiling,

"There, it's a good lunch. I hope it'll brace you up so you can get to Sonora all right. I believe you're tellin' the truth and I wish you luck."

He grunted his thanks and made off, shambling across the yard and out into the sun-flooded fields. He had to cross them to get out of range behind a hill spur before he turned into the woods. As he walked, feeling their eyes boring into his back, conscious of himself as hugely conspicuous in the untenanted landscape, he opened the paper and ate ravenously, tearing at the bread and meat.

He was far afield before he dared to rest and look at the paper. It was part of the Sunday edition of the *Stockton Expositor*, and in it he read of the approaching trial of Knapp. Both Danny Leonard and Jim Bailey had identified him by his hands and his size as the man who had wounded the messenger, and Knapp had admitted it. The paper predicted a life sentence for him. Then it went on to Garland, who was still at large. Various people were sure they had seen him. A saloon keeper on the outskirts of Placerville was ready to swear that a mounted man, who had stopped at his place one night for a drink, was the fugitive outlaw. If this evidence was reliable Garland was moving toward his old stamping ground, the camps along the Feather, where it was said he had friends.

His relief was intense, for it was evident Knapp had had little to say of him, and his hunters were on the wrong trail. Food cravings appeased, his anxieties temporarily at rest, he was easier than he had been since the night at Sheeps Bar. Curled under a thicket of madrone he slept like a log and woke in the morning, his energies primed, his brain alert, thinking of Pancha.

There were two things that had to be done—get a letter to her and replenish his store of cartridges. If too long a time passed without news of him, she would grow anxious, might talk, might betray suspicious facts or draw inferences herself. A word from him, dispatched from a camp along the lode, would quiet her. So he must gird his loins for the perilous venture of a break into the open under the eyes of men.

Up beyond Angels, slumbering amid its rotting placers and abandoned ditches, lies the old camp of Farleys. In times past it was a stop on the way to the Calaveras Big Trees, but after the railroad diverted the traffic to the Mariposa Group, Farleys was left to pursue its tranquil way undisturbed by stage or tourist. Still it remains, if stagnant, self-respecting, has a hotel, a post office and a street of stores, along which the human flotsam and jetsam of the mineral belt may drift without exciting comment. A derelict could pass along its wooden sidewalk, drop a letter in the post box, even buy a box of cartridges without attracting notice. And even if he should be noticed, Farleys was sleepy and a good way from anywhere. Warnings sent from there would not be acted upon too quickly. A man could catch the eye of Farleys, wake its suspicions and get away while it was talking things over and starting the machinery for his arrest.

This was the place he decided on and forthwith moved toward. He had four cartridges and if game was plentiful and his aim good he might make Farleys and still have one or maybe two left.

But it took longer than he calculated, swollen rivers blocking his path, luck going against him. Three of his cartridges were expended on a deer before he brought it down and the rains came back, blinding and torrential. Forced to make detours because of the unfordable streams he lost his way and spent precious hours groping about in pine forests, dark as twilight, their boughs bent to the onslaught of the storm. Crossing a watercourse he fell and his matches were soaked, and that night, crouched against a tree trunk, a creature less protected than the beasts who had their shelters, he sucked the raw meat.

The next day his misfortunes reached a climax when he used his last bullet on a rabbit and missed it. He went on for twelve hours, and in the darkness under a mass of dripping bracken began to think of Farleys less as a place of peril than as a refuge, even though known for what he was. But he pushed that thought away as other men push temptation and tried to sleep under his saturated tent. In the morning he was on the trail with the first light, staggering a little, squinting down the columned aisles for open ground whence he could look out and get his bearings.

It was late in the afternoon, dusk at hand, when he saw the light of a clearing. He hastened, staring ahead, stood for a stunned second, then leaped behind a tree, muscles tight, the dull confusion of his brain gone. Looming high through the gray of the twilight, balconied, many-windowed, was a large white building. Outhouses sprawled at one side, a weed-grown drive curved to its front steps, down the slant of its roof the rain ran, spouting from broken gutters and lashing the shutters that blinded its tiers of windows.

The first shock over, he stole cat-soft from trunk to trunk, studying it. There were no lights, no smoke from the chimneys, no sign of habitation. A loosened shutter on the ground floor banged furiously, calling out echoes from the solitude. He circled the back of it, round by the outbuildings, a lot of them, one like a stable—all silent. Then made his way to the side with its deep, first-floor veranda and was creeping toward the front when he ran into something—a circular construction covered with a rough bark and topped by a balustrade.

One look at it and he gave a smothered exclamation and ran back among the trees. The light was almost gone, but there was enough to show a line of enormous shafts towering into a remote blackness. Like reddish monoliths they reared themselves in a receding file, silence about their feet, their crests far aloft moaning under the wind. In the encroaching darkness they showed like the pillars of a temple reared by some primordial race of giants, their foliage a roof that seemed to touch the low sky. He knew where he was now—the Calaveras Big Trees. The house was the old hotel, once a point of pilgrimage, long since fallen from popularity and left to gradual decay. In summer a few travelers found their way there, but at this season the spot was in as complete a solitude as it had been when the first gringoes came and stood in silent awe.

He broke his way in by the window with the loosened shutter and passed through the dimness of long rooms, bare and chilly, his steps loud on the uncarpeted floors. The place was damp and had the musty smell of a house long unaired and unoccupied. The double doors into the dining room were jammed and he had to wrench them open; in the pantry a windowpane was broken and the rain had seeped in. Here, on a three-legged table, he found a calendar and remembered hearing that the hotel had been opened during the previous summer, but that, business being bad, the proprietor had closed it after a few weeks.

In the kitchen he found signs of this period of habitation. On a shelf in a cupboard, hidden by a debris of paper and empty boxes, he came upon two cans evidently overlooked. He took them to the window, threw back the shutter, and saw they contained tomatoes and cherries. This heartened him to new efforts and he began a search through the dirty desolation of the room. He was rewarded by finding a half-filled match box, a few sticks of split wood and in the bottom of a coal bunker in the passage enough coal to make at least one good fire.

Before he started it he closed the shutter tight, then, groping in the dusk, filled the big range with paper and wood and set a match to it. It flickered, caught, snapped cheerily, light flickering along the walls, shining between the bars. He poured on the coal, opened all the draughts, saw the iron grow slowly red and felt the grateful warmth. With his knife he cut open the tomato can, heated its contents in a leaky saucepan, and, taking it to the sink, spooned it up with a piece of wood. The cherries were his dessert.

After that he peeled off his outer clothes and lay on the floor in front of the range. It threw out a violent heat, but not too much for him; he luxuriated, basked in it, delighting in the rosy patches that grew on the stove's rusty surface, the bright droppings from its grate. Holding his stiff feet out to it, he cooked himself, stretching and turning like a cat. Finally, he lay quiet, his hands clasped behind his head, his eyes touching points that the red light played upon, and listened to the rain. The building shook to its buffets; it swept like feeling fingers across the windows, drummed on the low roofs of the outhouses, ran in a spattering rush along the balcony. The sound of it soothed him like a lullaby, and with the banging of the unfastened shutter loud in his ears he slept the sleep of the just.

The next morning, with the daylight to help him, he extended his search and found a few spoonfuls of tea in a glass preserve jar, a handful of moldy potatoes in a gunny-sack and in a shed back of the kitchen a pile of cut wood. He breakfasted royally, finishing the remains of the cherries, built the fire up high and hot, and started to explore the house.

It was as empty as a shell, room opening out of room, half lighted, bare and dismal. There was nothing to be got out of it and he was back on his way to the warmth of the kitchen when he thought of the broken-legged table in the pantry. Propping this up against the window ledge, a drawer fell from it, scattering sheets of paper and envelopes on the floor. He stood staring at them, lying round his feet, fallen there as if from heaven to supply his last and now greatest need. With an upturned box for a seat, the stub of pencil he always carried sharpened to a pin point by his knife, he steadied the table on the windowsill, and sat down to write to Pancha. He wrote the word "Farleys" at the top of the sheet, as he knew she would see the Farleys postmark, but the date he omitted:

My deary Panchita: *Farleys*

Here's the old man writing to you from Farleys. Sort of small dead place, but there's business moving round it, so I got washed up here for a few days. I ain't had anything that's good yet, but there's a feller that looks like he might nibble, and take it from me my hooks are out. Anyways if he does I'll let you know. Plenty lot of rain, but I've been comfortable right along. Got a good room here and swell grub. And don't you worry about my roomatiz. All you want to know is I ain't got it. I can't give you no address, as I'm moving on soon, Wednesday maybe. But I'll drop you a line from somewheres as soon as I got anything to say. You want to remember I'm all right and as happy as I ever am when I ain't with my best girl. This leaves me in good health, which I hope it finds you.

YOUR BEST BEAU.

The rain lasted that day, but on the next the sun rose on a world washed clean, woodland-scented, fresh and beautiful. The time had come for him to dare. At nightfall he started, a young moon to guide him, followed a road ankle high in ruts and mud, and at dawn crept into an alder thicket for rest and sleep. It was nine, the day well started, when he walked into Farleys.

The little town was up and about its business, windows open, housewives sweeping front steps. The air was redolent of pine balsam, the sun licking up the water in hollows on the sidewalks, the distances colored a transparent blue. Outside the saloon the barkeeper was patting his dog, women in sunbonnets with string bags on their arms were on their way to the general store, men were bringing out chairs and placing them with pondering calculation the right distance from the hitching bar.

He bought his stamp and posted his letter, the man inside the window offering comments on the weather. Then he had to face the length of the street; he had been there before and knew the hardware store was at its other end. As he traversed it the heads of the men—already settled in their chairs for the day—turned hopefully at the sound of his masculine tread. It might be someone who would stand a drink, and even if it wasn't, staring at a passerby was something to do. To run such a gauntlet required all his fortitude, and as he walked under the battery of eyes the sweat gathered on his face and his heart thumped in his throat.

The clerk at the hardware store was reading a paper. When he went for the cartridges he left it on the counter and the fugitive saw the heading of a column, "Garland still eludes justice." As he waited he read it, turning from it to take his package and then back to it as the clerk made change. They were hunting in the Feather country. A blacksmith beyond Auburn swore he knew the outlaw and had seen him, mounted on a bay horse, ride past his shop a week before at sunset. The clerk held out the change, and Garland, reading, nodded toward the counter. He was afraid to extend his hand, knowing that it shook, and presently, dropping the paper, scooped up the money with a curved palm.

"Looks like Garland was goin' to give 'em the slip after all," said the clerk.

"Um—looks that way, but I wouldn't bank on it. If he's lyin' low in one of them camps up the Feather he's liable to be seen. There's folks there that knows him it says here and you can't always trust your friends. Fine weather we're havin' after the rain. So long."

When he came out into the street he was nerved for a last, desperate venture. He went to the general store and bought a stock of provisions: bread, sugar, bacon, coffee and tobacco. The salesman was inclined to be friendly and asked him questions, and he explained himself as a prospector in the hills, cut off by the recent rains. He got away from there as quickly as he could, dropped down a side path and made for the woods and "home."

That evening he went out and lay under the giant trees, and smoked his first pipe for weeks. The sunset gleamed through the foliage in fiery spots, here and there piercing it with a long ray of light which slanted across the red trunks. From the forest recesses twilight spread in stealthy advance, and looking up he could see bits of the sky, scatterings of pink through the darkening green. It was intensely quiet, not a stir of wind, not a bird note, or leaf rustle. The place was held in that mysterious silence which broods over the Californian country and suggests a hushed and ominous attention. It is as if nature were aware of some impending event, imminent and portentous, and waited in tranced expectancy. The outlaw felt it, and moved, disquieted, setting his oppression down to loneliness.

One afternoon a week later, while standing at the kitchen window, he saw a figure dart across an opening between the trees. It went so swiftly that he was aware of it only as a dash of darkness, the passage of a shadow, but It left a moving wake in the ferns and grasses. With his heart high and smothering, he felt for his revolver and crept through the rooms to the broken window on the veranda. If he was caught he would die game, fight from this citadel till his last cartridge was gone. His eyes to a crack in the shutter he looked out—no one was there. The vista of the forest stretched back as free of human presence as in the days before man had roamed its solemn corridors.

Then he saw it again; the tightness of his muscles relaxed, and the hand holding the revolver dropped to his side. It was a child, a boy; there were two of them. He watched them move, foot balanced before foot, wary eyes on the house, emerge from behind a trunk and flee to the shelter of the next one. They were little fellows, eight or perhaps ten, in overalls and ragged hats, scared and yet adventurous, creeping cautiously nearer.

It was easy to guess what they were and what had brought them: ranch children who had seen the smoke of his fire, and, knowing the hotel to be empty, had come to discover who was there. The game was up—they might have been round the place for hours, for days. He suddenly threw open the shutters and roared at them, an unexpected and fearful challenge. A moment of paralyzed terror was followed by a wild rush, the bracken breaking under their flying feet. After they had passed from his sight he could hear the swish and crashing of their frantic flight. Two boys, so frightened, would not take long to reach home and gasp out their story.

He left on their heels, window and door flapping behind him, the fire red in the range.

Two days later he found cover in a deserted tunnel back in the hills. Its timbers sagged with the weight of the years, the yellow mound of its dump was hidden under a mantle of green. Even its mouth, once a black hole in the hillside verdure, was curtained by a veil of creepers. There was game and there was water and there he stayed. At first he rested, then idle and inert lay among the ferns on the top of the dump, staring at the distance, squinting up at the sky, deadened with the weight of the interminable, empty days.

CHAPTER XIX

HALF TRUTHS AND INFERENCES

C HRYSTIE HAD DEVELOPED a liking for long walks. As she was a person of a lazy habit Lorry inquired about it and received the answer that walking was the easiest way to keep down your weight. This was a satisfactory explanation, for Chrystie was of the ebullient, early-spreading Californian type, and an extending acquaintance among girls of her age might readily awake a dormant vanity. So the walks passed unchallenged.

But, beside an unwonted attention to her looks, Lorry noticed that her sister was changing. Quite suddenly she seemed to have emerged from childhood, blossomed into a grown-up phase. She was losing her irrelevant high spirits, bubbled much less frequently, sometimes sat in silence for half an hour at a time. Then there were moments when her glance was fixed and pondering, as if her thoughts ranged afar. The new interest in her appearance extended from her figure to her clothes. She spent so much money on them that Lorry spoke to her about it and was answered with mutinous irritation. Why shouldn't she have pretty things like the other girls? What was the sense of hoarding up their money like misers? Lorry could do it if she liked; she was going to get some good out of hers.

Lorry saw the change as the result of a widening social experience—she had tried to find amusement, the proper surroundings of her age and station, for Chrystie and she had succeeded. Gayeties had grown out of that first, agitating dinner till they now moved through quite a little round of parties. Under this new excitement Chrystie was acquiring poise, also fluctuations of spirit and temper. Lorry supposed it was natural—you couldn't stay up late when you weren't used to it and be as easy-going and good-humored as when you went to bed every night at ten.

Lorry might have seen deeper, but her attention was diverted. For the first time in her life she was thinking a good deal about her own affairs. What she felt was kept very secret, but even if it hadn't been there was no one to notice, certainly not Chrystie, nor Aunt Ellen. The only other person near enough to notice was Fong, and it wasn't Fong's place to help—at least to help in an open way.

One morning in the kitchen, when he and "Miss Lolly" were making the menu for a new dinner, he had said,

"Mist Bullage come this time?"

"Miss Lolly," with a faint access of color and an eye sliding from Fong's to the back porch, had answered,

"No, I'm not asking Mr. Burrage to this one, Fong."

"Why not ask Mist Bullage?" Fong had persisted, slightly reproving.

"Because I've asked him several times and he hasn't come."

That was in the old Bonanza manner. One answered a Chinaman like Fong truthfully and frankly as man to man.

"He come this time. You lite him nice letter."

"No, I don't want to, I've enough without him. It's all made up."

"I no see why—plenty big loom, plenty good dinner. Velly nice boy, good boy, best boy ever come to my boss's house."

"Now, Fong, don't get side-tracked. I didn't come to talk to you about the people, I came to talk about the food."

Fong looked at her, gently inquiring, "You no like Mist Bullage, Miss Lolly?"

"Of course I like him. Won't you please attend to what I'm saying?"

"Then you ask him and I make awful swell dinner—same like I make for your Pa when General Grant eat here."

When Fong had a fixed idea that way there was no use arguing with him; one rose with a resigned air and left the kitchen. As Lorry passed through the pantry door he called after her, amiable but determined,

"All samey Mist Bullage no come I won't make bird nest ice cleam with pink eggs."

No one but Fong bothered about Mr. Burrage's absence. After the evening at the Albion Chrystie set him down as "hopeless," and when he refused two dinner invitations, said they ought to have asked him to wait on the table and then he would have accepted. To this gibe Lorry made no answer, but that night before the mirror in her own room, she addressed her reflection with bitterness:

"Why should any man like me? I'm not pretty, I'm not clever, I'm as slow as a snail." She saw tears rise in her eyes and finished ruthlessly, "I'm such a fool that I cry about a man who's done everything but say straight out, 'I don't care for you, you bore me, do leave me alone.'"

So Lorry, nursing her hidden wound, was forgetful of her stewardship.

It was a pity, for there were times when Chrystie, caught in a contrite mood and questioned, would have told. Such times generally came when she was preparing for one of her walks. At these moments her adventure had a way of suddenly losing its glamour and appearing as a shabby and underhand performance. Before she saw Mayer she often hesitated, a prey to a chill distaste, sometimes even questioning her love for him. After she saw him things were different. She came away filled with a bridling vanity, feeling herself a siren, a queen of men. Helen of Troy, seeing brave blood spilled for her possession, was not more satisfied of her worth than Chrystie after an hour's talk with Boyé Mayer.

It was the certainty of Lorry's disapproval that made secrecy necessary. He soon realized that Lorry was the governing force, the loved and feared dictator. But he was a cunning wooer. He put no ban upon confession—if Chrystie wanted to tell he was the last person to stop it. And having placed the responsibility in her hands, he wove closer round the little fly the parti-colored web of illusion. He made her feel the thrill of the clandestine, the romance of stolen meetings, see herself not as a green, affrighted girl, but a woman queening it over her own destiny, fit mate for him in eagle flight above the hum-drum multitude.

But the moments when her conscience pricked still recurred. She was particularly oppressed one afternoon as she sat in her room waiting for the clock to strike three. At half past she was to meet Mayer in the plaza, opposite the Greek Church. She had no time for a long walk that day—an engagement for tea claimed her at five—so he had suggested the plaza. No one they knew ever went there, and a visit to the Greek Church would be interesting.

Her hat and furs lay ready on the bed and she sat in the long wicker chair by the window, one hand supporting her chin, while her eyes rested somberly on the fig tree in the garden. She was reluctant to go; she did not know why, except that just then, waiting for the clock to strike, she had had an eerie sort of fear of Mayer. She told herself it was because he was so clever, so superior to any man she had ever known. But she wished she could tell Lorry, say boldly, "Lorry, Mr. Mayer is in love with me"—she wished she could dare.

At that moment Lorry appeared in the doorway between the two rooms.

"Hello," she said. "How serious you look."

"I'm thinking," said Chrystie, studying the fig tree.

"Are you going out?" The things on the bed had caught her eye.

"Um—presently."

"So soon? You're not asked to the Forsythe's till five and it's not three yet."

"I *could* be going somewhere else first."

"Oh—where?"

"Somewhere out of this house—that's the main thing. Since the furnace was put in it's like a Turkish bath."

"You're going for a walk?" Lorry went to the bed and picked up the hat. It was a new one with a French maker's name in the crown. "You oughtn't to hack this hat about, Chrystie. I wouldn't wear it when I went for a walk."

"Do you think it would be better to wear it in the house? Having bought it I must wear it somewhere."

Lorry, laughing, put on the hat and looked at herself in the glass. There was a moment's pause, then the chair creaked under a movement of Chrystie's, and her voice came very quiet.

"Lorry, do you like Boyé Mayer?"

Lorry, studying the effect of the hat, did not answer with any special interest. The Perfect Nugget had lost all novelty for her. He came to the house now and then, was a help in their entertainments, and was always considerate and polite—that was all.

"No, not much," she murmured.

"Why not?"

"It's hard to say exactly—just something." She placed her hand over a rakish green paradise plume to see if its elimination would be an improvement.

"But if you don't like a person you ought to have a reason."

"You don't always. It's just a feeling, an instinct like dogs have. I've an instinct against Mr. Mayer—he's not the real thing."

Chrystie sat forward in the chair.

"That's exactly what I'd say he was, and everybody else says so, too."

"On the outside—yes, I didn't mean that. I meant deep down. I don't think he's real straight through—it's all varnish and glitter. Of course I don't mind his coming here the way he does; we don't see him often and he's amusing and pleasant. But I wouldn't like him to be on a friendly footing. In fact he never could be—I wouldn't let him."

It was the voice of authority. Chrystie felt its finality, and guided by her own inner distress and the hopelessness of revolt, said sharply:

"And yet you wouldn't mind Mark Burrage being on a friendly footing."

"Mark Burrage!" There was something ludicrous in Lorry's face, full of surprise under the overpowering hat. "What has Mark Burrage to do with it?"

Chrystie climbed somewhat lumberingly out of the chair. Her movements were dignified, her tone sarcastic.

"Oh, nothing, nothing. Only if Mr. Mayer is so far below your standard I'm wondering where Mr. Burrage comes in." She stretched a long arm and snatched the hat. "Excuse me," she said with brusque politeness, setting it on her own head and turning to the glass, "but I really must be going. Only a salamander could live comfortably in this house."

Lorry was startled. Her sister's face, deeply flushed, showed an intense irritation.

"I don't understand you. You can't make a comparison between those two men. They're as different as black and white."

"They certainly are," said Chrystie, driving a long pin through the hat. "Or chalk and cheese, or brass and gold, or whatever else stands for the real thing and the imitation."

"What's the matter with you, Chrystie? Are you angry?"

"Me?" She gave a glance from under her lifted arm. "Why should I be angry?"

"I don't know but—" An alarming thought seized Lorry, and she moved nearer. It was preposterous, but after all girls took strange fancies, and Chrystie was no longer a child. "You don't *care* for Boyé Mayer, do you?"

It was the propitious moment, but Chrystie was now as far from telling as if she had taken an oath of silence. What Lorry had already said was enough, and the tone in which she asked the question was the finishing touch. If she thought her sister had fallen in love with Fong, she couldn't have appeared more shocked and incredulous.

"Care for him?" said Chrystie, pulling out the bureau drawer and clawing about in it for her gloves. "Well, I care for him in some ways, and then I don't care for him in other ways."

"I don't mean that, I mean *really* care."

"Do you mean, am I *in love* with him?"

Her eye on Lorry was steady and questioning, also slightly scornful. Lorry was abashed by it; she felt that she ought not to have asked, and in confusion stammered, "Yes."

Chrystie moved to the bed and threw on her furs. Her ill-humor was gone, though she was still a little scornful and rather grandly forbearing. Her manner suggested that she could condone this in Lorry owing to her relationship and the honesty of her intention.

"Dearest Lorry, you talk like an old maid in a musical comedy. In love with him? How I wish I could be! At my age every self-respecting girl ought to be in love—they always are in books. But try as I will, I can't seem to manage it. I guess I've got a heart of stone or perhaps it's been left out of me entirely. Good-by, the heartless wonder's going for her walk."

She ended on a laugh, a little strident, and crossed the room, perfume shaken from her brilliant clothes. Outside the door she broke into a song that rose above her scudding flight down the stairs.

Lorry's momentary uneasiness died. Chrystie, as a woman of ruses and deceptions, was a thing she could not at this stage accept.

They met in the plaza and saw the Greek Church and then sat on a bench under a tree and talked. They were so secure in the little park's isolation that they gave their surroundings no attention. That was why a woman crossing it was able to draw near, stand for a watching moment, skirt the back of their bench, and pass on unnoticed. She was the same woman who had seen them at that earlier meeting in Union Square.

During that month the new operetta at the Albion had been put on and had fallen flat. There was a good deal of speculation as to the cause of the failure, and it was rumored that the management set it down to Miss Lopez. She had slighted her work of late, been careless and indifferent. Nobody knew what was the matter with her. She scorned the idea of ill health, but she looked worn out and several times had given vent to savage and unreasonable bursts of temper. She was too valuable a woman to quarrel with, and when the head of the enterprise suggested a rest—a week or two in the country—she rejected the idea with an angry repudiation of illness or fatigue.

Crowder was there on the first night and went away disturbed. He had never seen her give so poor a performance; all her fire was gone, she was mechanical, almost listless. Her public was loyal though puzzled, and the papers stood by her, but "What's happened to Pancha Lopez? How she *has* gone off!" was a current phrase where men and women gathered. Behind the scenes her mates whispered, some jealously observant, others more kindly, concerned and wondering. Gossip of a love affair was bandied about, but died for lack of confirmation. She had been seen with no one, the methodical routine of her days remained unchanged.

For her the month had been the most wretched of her life. Never in the hard past had she passed through anything as devastating. Those trials she had known how to meet; this was all new, finding her without defense, naked to unexpected attack. Belief and dread had alternated in her, ravaged and laid her waste. After the manner of impassioned women she would not see, clung to hope, had days, after a letter or a message from Mayer, when she had almost ascended to the top of the golden moment again. Then there was silence, a note of hers unanswered, and she fell, sinking into darkling depths. Once or twice, waking in the night or waiting for his knock, she had sudden flashes of clear sight. These left her in a frozen stillness, staring with wide eyes, frightened of herself.

The process of enlightenment had been gradual. Mayer wanted no scenes, no annoying explanations; there was to be no violent moment of severance. To accomplish his withdrawal gracefully, he put himself to some trouble. After that first letter he waylaid her at the stage door one night, and walked part of the way home with her. He had been kind, friendly, brotherly—a completely changed Mayer. She felt it and refused to understand, walking at his side, trying to be the old, merry Pancha.

It was at this time that she received her father's letter from Farleys. Weeks had passed since she had heard from him, and when she saw his writing on the envelope she realized that she had almost forgotten him. The thought left her cold, but when she read the homely phrases she was moved. In a moment of extended vision she saw the parents' tragedy—the love that lives for the child's happiness and is powerless to create it. He would have died for her and she would have thrust him aside, pushed him pleading from her path, to follow a man a few months before a stranger.

After that she endured a week without a word from Mayer, and then, unable to sleep or work, telephoned to his hotel. In answer to her question the switchboard girl said Mr. Mayer had not been out of town at all for the last two weeks. She asked to speak with him and heard his voice, sharp and cold. He couldn't talk freely over the wire; he would rather she didn't call him up; his out-of-town business had been postponed, that was all.

"Why are you mad with me?" she breathed, trying to make her voice steady.

"I am not," came the answer. "Please don't be fanciful. And *don't* call me up here, I don't like it. I'll be around as soon as I can, but I've a lot to do, as I've already told you several times. Good-by."

She had sent the call from a telephone booth, and carefully, with a slow precision, she hung up the receiver. A feeling of despair, a stifling anguish, seized her and she began to cry. Shut into the hot, small place, she broke into rending sobs, her head bent, her hands gripped, rocking back and forth. Small, choked sounds, whines and cries came from her, and fearful of being heard, she pressed her hands against her mouth, looking up, looking down, an animal distracted in its unfamiliar pain.

The following day he wrote to her, excused himself, said he had been worried on business matters and sent her flowers. She buoyed herself up and once more tried to believe, but her will had been weakened. From lower layers of consciousness the truth was forcing its way to recognition, yet she still ignored it. Realization of her state if she admitted it made her afraid and her fight had the fierceness of a struggle for life. It was only in the night—awake in the dumb dark—that she could not escape it. Then, staring at the pale square of the window, she heard her voice whispering:

"What will I do? What will become of me?"

In all her miserable imaginings and self-queries the thought that she had been supplanted had no place. Mayer had often spoken to her of his social diversions and no woman had ever figured in them. The paragraphs which still appeared about him touched on no feminine influences. It was her fault; she had been weighed in the balance and found wanting. Had she not always wondered that he should have cared for her? On close acquaintance he had found her to be what she was—common, uneducated, impossible. At first she had tried to hide it and then it had come out and he had been repelled. It was not till the afternoon, aimlessly walking to ease her pain, when she saw him again with the blonde-haired girl, that the thought of another woman entered her mind.

That night Crowder, after watching the last act from the back of the house, resolved to see her and find out what was wrong. He had been talking to the manager in the foyer and the man's sulky discontent alarmed him. If Pancha didn't buck up she'd lose her job.

She was at the dressing table in her red kimono when he came in. The grease was nearly all off and with her front hair drawn back from her forehead, her face had a curiously bare, haggard look. As he entered she glanced up, not smiling, and saw the knowledge of her failure in his eyes.

For a moment she looked at him, grave and sad, confessing it. The expression caught at his heart, and he had nothing to say, turning away from her to look for a chair.

She picked up the rag and went on wiping her face.

"Well," she said in a brisk voice, "I wasn't on the job tonight, was I?"

Reassured by her tone, he sat down and faced her.

"No, you weren't. It wasn't a good performance, Panchita. I've always told you the truth and I've got to go on doing it."

"Go ahead, you're not telling me anything I don't know. I've got my finger on the pulse of this house. I know every rise and fall of its temperature. But I can't always be up in G, can I?"

"No, but you can't stay down at zero too long."

"It was as bad as that, was it?"

"Yes, it was bad."

She dropped her hand to the edge of the dressing table and looked at it. Her face, with the hair strained back, the rouge gone, looked withered and yellow. Crowder eyed it anxiously.

"Say, Panchita, you're sick."

"Sick? Forget it! I never was better in my life."

"Then why are you off your work—why do you act as if you didn't care?"

"Can't I have a part I hate? Can't I get weary of this old joint with its smoke and its beer? God!" She began to pull the pins out of her hair and fling them on the dresser. "I'm human—I've got my ups and downs—and you keep forgetting it."

"That's just what I'm not forgetting."

"Stop talking about me—I'm sick of it," she cried, and snatching up the comb began tearing it through her hair.

"It's nerves," said Crowder. "Everything shows it. The way you're combing your hair does."

"If you don't let me alone I'll put you out—all of you nagging and picking at me; a saint couldn't stand it!" Crowder rose, but she whirled round on him, the comb held out in an arresting hand. "No, don't go yet. I'll give you another chance. I want to ask you something. I saw a woman the other day and I want to know who she is—at least I don't really want to know, but she'll do as well as anything else to change the subject. Tall with yellow sort of dolly hair and a dolly face. Dark purple dress with black velvet edges, lynx furs and a curly brimmed hat with a green paradise plume falling over one side."

Crowder's face wrinkled with a grin.

"Well, that's funny! You might have asked me forty others and I'd not have known. But thanks to your vivid description I *can* tell you—I saw her yesterday afternoon in those very togs. It's the youngest Alston girl."

"Who's she?"

"One of the two daughters of George Alston. They're orphans, live in a big house on Pine Street. The one you saw was Chrystie. What do you want to know about her?"

Pancha, gathering her hair in one hand, began to whisk it round into a knot. Her head was down bent.

"I don't know—just curiosity. She's sort of stunning looking. Did you ever meet her?"

Crowder smiled.

"I know them well—have for over a year. Awfully nice girls—the best kind."

Pancha lifted her head, her face sharp with interest.

"What's she like?"

He considered, the smile softened to an amused indulgence.

"Oh, just a great big baby, good-natured and jolly. Everybody likes her—you couldn't help it if you tried. She's so simple and sweet, accepts the whole world as if it was her friend. Her money hasn't spoiled her a bit."

"Money—she has money?"

"To burn, my dear. She's rich."

Pancha took up a hand glass and turning her back to him studied her profile in the mirror. It did not occur to Crowder that he never before had seen her do such a thing.

"Rich, is she?" she murmured. "How rich?"

"Something like four hundred thousand dollars; her father was one of the Virginia City crowd. Chrystie's just come into her part of the roll. Eighteen years old and an heiress—that's a good beginning."

"Um—must be a queer feeling. I guess the men are around the honey thick as flies."

Crowder screwed up his eyes considering.

"No, they're not—not yet anyhow. Until this winter the girls lived so retired—didn't know many people, kept to themselves. Now they've broken out and I suppose it's only a matter of time before the flies gather, and if you asked me I'd say they'd gather thickest round Chrystie. She hasn't as much character or brains as

Lorry, but she's prettier and jollier, and after all that's what most men like."

"It certainly is, especially with four hundred thousand thrown in for good measure."

The hand holding the glass dropped to her lap. She sat still for a moment, then without turning told him to go; she was tired and wanted to get home. It did not even strike him as odd that she never looked at him, just flapped a hand over her shoulder and dismissed him with a short "Good-night."

When he had gone she sat as he had left her, the mirror still in her lap. The gas jet flamed in its wire cage, and so silent was the room that a mouse crept out from behind the baseboard, spied about, then made a scurrying dart across the floor. Her eye caught it, slid after it, and she moved, putting the glass carefully on the dresser. The palms of her hands were wet with perspiration and she rubbed them on the skirt of her kimono and rose stiffly, resting for a moment against the back of her chair. She had a sick feeling, a sensation as if her heart were dissolving, as if the room looked unfamiliar and much larger than usual. When she put on her clothes she did it slowly, her fingers fumbling stupidly at buttons and hooks, her mouth a little open as if breathing was difficult.

CHAPTER XX

MARK PAYS A CALL

MARK BURRAGE SAW THE WINTER pass and only went once to the Alstons and then they were not at home. He had refused three invitations to the house and after the ignominious event at the Albion received no more. When he allowed himself to think of that humiliating evening he did not wonder.

But, outside of his work, he allowed himself very little thinking. All winter he had concentrated on his job with ferocious energy. The older men in the office had a noticing eye on him. "That fellow Burrage has got the right stuff in him, he'll make good," they said among themselves. The younger ones, sons of rich fathers who had squeezed them into places in the big firm, regarded his efforts with indulgent surprise. They liked him, called him "Old Mark," and were a little patronizing in their friendliness: "He was just the sort who'd be a grind. Those ranch chaps who had to get up at four in the morning and feed the 'horgs' were the devil to work when they came down to the city. Even law was a cinch after the 'horgs.'"

Sometimes at night—his endeavor relaxed for a pondering moment—he studied the future. The outlook might have daunted a less resolute spirit. A great gap yawned between the present and the time when he could go to Lorry Alston and say, "Let me take care of you; I can do it now." But he figured it out, bridged the gap, knew what one man had done another man could do. He reckoned on leaving the office next year and setting up for himself, and grim-visaged, mouth set to a straight line, he calculated on the chances of the fight. Its difficulties braced him to new zeal and in the strain and stress of the struggle his youthful awkwardness wore away, giving place to a youthful sternness.

No one guessed his hopes and high aspiration, not even his friend Crowder. When Crowder rallied him about this treatment of the Alstons he had been short and offhand—didn't care for society, hadn't time to waste going round being polite. He left upon Crowder the impression that the Alston girls did not interest him any more than any other girls. "Old Mark isn't a lady's man," was the way Crowder excused him to Chrystie. Of course Chrystie laughed and said she had no illusions about that, but whatever kind of a man he was he ought to take some notice of them, no matter how dull and deadly they were. Crowder, realizing his own responsibility—it was he who had taken Mark to the Alston house—was kind but firm.

"It's up to you to go and see those girls. It's not the decent thing to drop out without a reason. They've gone out of their way to be civil to you, and you know, old chap, they're *ladies*"

Mark grunted, and frowning as at a disagreeable duty said he'd go.

It took him some weeks to get there. Twice he started, circled the house, and tramped off over the hills. The third time he got as far as the front gate, weakened and turned away. After long abstinence the thought of meeting Lorry's eyes, touching her hand, created a condition of turmoil that made him a coward; that, while he longed to enter, drew him back like a sinner from the scene of his temptation. Then an evening came when, his jaw set, his heart thumping like a steam piston, he put on his best blue serge suit, his new gray overcoat, even a pair of mocha gloves, and went forth with a face as hard as a stone.

Fong opened the door, saw who it was and broke into a joyful grin.

"Mist Bullage! Come in, Mist Bullage. No see you for heap long time, Mist Bullage."

"I've been busy," said the visitor. "Hadn't much time to come around."

Fong helped him off with the gray overcoat.

"You work awful hard, Mist Bullage. Too hard, not good. You come here and have good time. Lots of fun here now. You come."

He moved to hang the coat on the hatrack, and, as he adjusted it, turned and shot a sharp look over his shoulder at the young man.

"All men who come now not like you, Mist Bullage."

There was something of mystery, an odd suggestion of withheld meaning, in the old servant's manner that made Mark smile.

"How are they different—better or worse?"

Fong passed him, going to the drawing-room door. His hand on the knob, he turned, his voice low, his slit eyes craftily knowing.

"Ally samey not so good. I take care Miss Lolly and Miss Clist—*I* look out. *You* all 'ight, *you* come." He threw open the door with a flourish and called in loud, glad tones, "Miss Lolly, Miss Clist, one velly good fliend come—Mist Bullage."

At the end of the long room Mark was aware of a small group whence issued a murmur of talk. At his name the sound ceased, there was a rising of graceful feminine forms which floated toward him, leaving a masculine figure in silhouette against the lighted background of the dining room. He was confused as he made his greetings, touched and dropped Lorry's hand, tried to find an answer for Chrystie's challenging welcome. Then he switched off to Aunt Ellen in her rocker, groping at knitting that was sliding off her lap, and finally was introduced to the man who stood waiting, his hands on the back of his chair.

At the first glance, while Lorry's voice murmured their names, Mark disliked him. He would have done so even if he had not been a guest at the Alstons, complacently at home there, even if he had not been in evening dress, correct in every detail, even if the hands resting on the chair back had not shown manicured nails that made his own look coarse and stubby. The face and each feature, the high-bridged, haughty nose, the eyes cold and indolent under their long lids, the thin, close line of the mouth—separately and in combination—struck him as objectionable and repellent. He bowed stiffly, not extending his hand, substituting for the Westerner's "Pleased to meet you," a gruff "How d'ye do, Mr. Mayer."

Before the introduction, Mayer, watching Mark greeting the girls, knew he had seen him before but could not remember where. The young man in his neat, well fitting clothes, his country tan given place to the pallor of study and late hours, was a very different person from the boy in shirt sleeves and overalls of the ranch yard. But his voice increased Mayer's vague sense of former encounter and with it came a faint feeling of disquiet. Memory connected this fellow with something unpleasant. As Mark turned to him it grew into uneasiness. Where before had he met those eyes, dark blue, looking with an inquiring directness straight into his?

They sank into chairs, everyone except Aunt Ellen, seized by an inner discomfort which showed itself in a chilled constraint. Mayer, combing over his recollections, the teasing disquiet increasing with every moment, was too disturbed for speech. The sight of Lorry had paralyzed what little capacity for small talk Mark had. She looked changed, more unapproachable than ever in a new exquisiteness. It was only a more fashionable way of doing her hair and a becoming dress, but the young man saw it as a growing splendor, removing her to still remoter distances. She herself was so nervous that she kept looking helplessly at Chrystie, hoping that that irrepressible being would burst into her old-time sprightliness. But Chrystie had her own reasons for being oppressed. The presence of Mayer, paying no more attention to her than he did to Aunt Ellen, and the memory of him making love to her on park benches, gave her a feeling of dishonesty that weighed like lead.

It looked as if it was going to be a repetition of one of those evenings in the past before they had "known how to do things," when Fong caused a diversion by appearing from the dining room bearing a tray.

To regale evening visitors with refreshments had been the fashion in Fong's youth, so in his old age the habit still persisted. He entered with his friendly grin and set the tray on a table beside Lorry. On it stood decanters of red and white wine, glasses, a pyramid of fruit and a cake covered with varicolored frosting.

Nobody wanted anything to eat, but they turned to the tray with the eagerness of shipwrecked mariners to an oyster bed. Even Aunt Ellen became animated, and looking at Mark over her glasses said:

"Have you been away, Mr. Burrage?"

No, Mr. Burrage had been in town, very busy, and, the hungriest of all the mariners, he turned to the tray and helped Lorry pour out the wine. The ladies would take none, so the filled glass was held out to Mayer.

"Claret!" he said, leaning forward to offer the glass.

As he did so he was aware of a slight, curious expression in the face he had disliked. The eyelids twitched, the upper lip drew down tight over the teeth, the nostrils widened. It was a sudden contraction and then flexing of the muscles, an involuntary grimace, gone almost as soon as it had come. With murmured thanks, Mayer stretched his hand and took the wine.

It had all come back with the offered glass. A glance shot round the little group showed him that no one had noticed; they were cutting and handing about the cake. He refused a piece and found his stiffened lips could smile, but he was afraid of his voice, and sipped slowly, forcing the wine down the contracted passage of his throat. Then he stole a look at Mark, clumsily steering a way between the chairs to Aunt Ellen who wanted some grapes. The fellow hadn't guessed—hadn't the faintest suspicion—it was incredible that he should have. It was all right but—he raised his hand to his cravat, felt of it, then slipped a finger inside his collar and drew it away from his neck.

Through a blurred whirl of thought he could hear Aunt Ellen's voice.

"I've wanted to see you for a long time, Mr. Burrage. You come from that part of the country and I thought you'd know."

Then Mark's voice:

"Know what, Mrs. Tisdale?"

"About that Knapp man's story. Didn't you tell us your ranch was up near the tules where those bandits buried the gold?"

Lorry explained.

"Aunt Ellen's been so excited about that story, she couldn't talk of anything else."

"And why not?" said Aunt Ellen. "It's a very unusual performance. Two sets of thieves, one stealing the money and burying it and another coming along and finding it."

Chrystie, diverted from her private worries by this exciting subject, bounced round toward Mark with something of her old explosiveness.

"Why, you were up there at the time—the first time I mean. Don't you remember you told us that evening when you were here. And you said people thought the bandits had a cache in the chaparral. Why didn't any of you think of the tules?"

"Stupid, I guess," said Mark. "Not a soul thought of them. And it was an A1 hiding-place. Besides the duck shooters, nobody ever goes there."

"But somebody *did* go there," came from Aunt Ellen with a knowing nod.

They laughed at that, even Mr. Mayer, who appeared only languidly interested, his eyes on the film of wine in the bottom of his glass.

"Who do you suppose it could have been?" asked Chrystie.

"A duck shooter, probably." This was Mr. Mayer's first contribution to the subject.

Mark was exceedingly pleased to be able to correct this silent and supercilious person.

"No, it couldn't have been. The duck season doesn't open till September fifteen, and Knapp said when they went back in six days the cache was empty." He turned to Chrystie. "I've often wondered if it could have been a man I saw that afternoon."

As on that earlier visit his knowledge of the holdup had made him an attractive center, so once again he saw the girls turn expectant eyes on him, Aunt Ellen forget her grapes, and even the strange man's glance shift from the wineglass and rest, attentive, on his face.

"It was a tramp. He stopped late that afternoon at my father's ranch which gives on the road and asked for a drink of water. I gave it to him and watched him go off in the direction of the trail that leads to the tules. Of course it would have been an unusual thing for him to have tried to get across them, but he might have done it and stumbled on the cache."

"Could he have—isn't it all water?" Lorry asked.

"There's a good deal of solid land and here and there planks laid across the deeper streams. There *is* a sort of trail if you happen to know it and a tramp might. It's part of his business to be familiar with the short cuts and easiest ways round."

"What was he like?" said Chrystie.

"A miserable looking fellow—most of them are—all brown and dusty with a straggly beard. There was one thing about him that I noticed, his voice. It was like an educated man's—a sort of echo of better days."

Aunt Ellen found this very absorbing and she and Chrystie had questions to ask. Fong's entrance for the tray prevented Lorry from joining in. As the Chinaman leaned down to take it, she whispered to him to open a window, the room was hot. Her eye, touching Mr. Mayer, had noticed that he had drawn out his handkerchief and wiped his forehead which shone with a thin beading of perspiration. No one heard the order, and Fong, after opening the window, carried the tray into the dining room and left it on the table. When Lorry turned to the others, Mark had proved to Aunt Ellen that the gentleman tramp was a recognized variety of the species, and Chrystie had taken up the thread.

"Did your people up there know anything about him? Did they think he was the man?"

"None of them saw him. After Knapp's story came out I wrote up and asked them but no one round there remembered him."

"Would you know him again if you saw him?"

"If I saw him in the same clothes I would, but"—he smiled into Chrystie's eager face—"I'm not likely to do that. If it's he, he's got twelve thousand dollars and I guess he's spent some of it on a shave and a new suit."

Here Mr. Mayer, moving softly, turned to where the tray had stood. It was gone, and, gracefully apologetic, he rose—he wanted to put down his glass and get a drink of water. His exit from the group put a temporary stop to the conversation, chairs were in the way, and Aunt Ellen let her grapes fall on the floor. Mark, scrabbling for them, saw Lorry rise and press an electric bell on the wall; she had remembered there was no water on the tray. Mayer, moving to the dining room, did not see her, and called back over his shoulder:

"Your American rooms are a little too warm for a person used to the cold storage atmosphere of houses abroad."

He said it well, better than he thought he could, for he was stifled by a sudden loud pounding of his heart. To hide his face and steady himself with a draught of wine was what he wanted. A moment alone, a moment to get a grip on his nerves, would be enough. With his back toward them he leaned against the table and lifted a decanter in his shaking hand. As he did so, Fong entered through a door just opposite.

"Water for Mr. Mayer, Fong," came Lorry's voice from the room beyond.

The voice and Fong's appearance, coming simultaneously, abrupt and unexpected, made Mayer give a violent start. His hand jerked upward, sending the wine in a scattering spray over the cloth. Fong made no move for the water, but stood looking from the crimson stain to the man's face.

"You sick, Mist Mayer?" he said.

The strained tension snapped. With an eye if steel-cold fury on the servant the man broke into a low, almost whispered, cursing. The words ran out of his mouth, fluent, rapid, in an unpremeditated rush. They were as picturesque and malignantly savage as those with which he had cursed the tules; and suddenly they stopped, checked by the Chinaman's expression. It was neither angry or alarmed, but intently observant, the eyes unblinking—an imperturbable, sphinx-like face against which the flood of rage broke, leaving no mark.

Mayer took up the half-filled glass and drained it, the servant watching him with the same quiet scrutiny. He longed to plant his fist in the middle of that unrevealing mask, but instead tried to laugh, muttered an explanation about feeling ill, and slid a five-dollar gold piece across the table.

To his intense relief Fong picked it up, dropped it into the pocket of his blouse, and without a word turned and left the room.

No one had noticed the little scene. When Mayer came back the group was on its feet, Mark having made a move to go.

There were handshakes and good-nights, and Burrage and Lorry moved forward up the long room. Aunt Ellen took the opportunity of slipping through a side door that led to the hall, and Chrystie and her lover faced each other among the empty chairs.

With his eye on the receding backs of the other couple, Mayer said, hardly moving his lips:

"When can I see you again? Tomorrow at the Greek Church at four?"

She demurred as she constantly did. At each station in the clandestine courtship he had the same struggle with the same faltering uncertainty. But, after tonight, the time for humoring her moods was past. What he had endured during the last hour showed in a haggard intensity of expression, a subdued, fierce urgence of manner. Chrystie looked at him and looked away, almost afraid of him.

He was staring at her with an avid waiting as if ready to drag the answer out of her lips. She fluttered like a bird under the snake's hypnotic eye.

"I can't," she whispered; "I'm going out with Lorry."

"Then when?"

"Oh, Boyé, I don't know—I have so many things to do."

He had difficulty in pinning her down to a date, but finally succeeded five days off. In his low-toned insistence he used a lover's language, terms of endearment, tender phrases, but her timorous reluctance roused a passion of rage in him. He would have liked to shake her; he would have liked to swear at her as he had at Fong.

CHAPTER XXI

A WOMAN SCORNED

FTER THE CONVERSATION with Crowder, Pancha was very quiet for several days. She spoke only the necessary word, came and went with feline softness, performed her duties with the precision of a mechanism. Her stillness had a curious quality of detachment; she seemed held in a spell, her eye, suddenly encountered, blank and vacant; even her voice was toneless. She reacted to nothing that went on around her.

All her vitality had withdrawn to feed the inner flame. Under that dead exterior fires blazed so high and hot that the shell containing them was empty of all else. They had burned away pride and reason and conscience; they were burning to explosive outbreak. The girl had no consciousness of it; she only felt their torment and with the last remnant of her will tried to hide her anguish. Then came a day when the shell cracked and the fires burst through.

Unable to bear her own thoughts, weakened by two sleepless nights, she telephoned to the Argonaut Hotel and said she wanted to speak to Mr. Mayer. The switchboard girl answered that he was in and asked for her name. On Pancha's refusal to give it, the girl had crisply replied that Mr. Mayer had left orders no one was to speak with him unless he knew the name. Pancha gave it and waited. Presently the answer came—"Very sorry, Mr. Mayer doesn't seem to be there—thought he was in, but I guess I was wrong."

This falsehood, contemptuously transparent, act of final dismissal, was the blow that broke the shell and let the fire loose. Such shreds of pride and self-respect as remained to the wretched girl were shriveled. She put on her hat and coat, and tying a thick veil over her face, went across town to the Argonaut Hotel.

162

It was the day after Mayer had met Mark at the Alstons'. He too had not slept, had had a horrible, harassing night. All day he had sat in his rooms going over the scene, recalling the young man's face, assuring himself of its unconsciousness. But he was upset, jarred, his security gone. Luxury had corroded his already wasted and overdrawn forces; the habits of idleness weakened his power to resist. One fact stood out in his mind—he must carry the courtship with Chrystie to its conclusion, and arrange for their elopement. Sprawled in the armchair or pacing off the space from the bedroom door to the window he planned it. One or two more interviews with her would bring her to the point of consent, then they would slip away to Nevada; he would marry her there and they would go on to New York. It ought not to take more than a week, at the longest ten days. If he had had any other woman to deal with—not this spiritless fool of a girl—he could manage it in a much shorter time. All he had to do was to make a last trip to Sacramento and get what was left of the money and that could be done in a day.

A knock at the door made him start. Any sound would have made him start in the state he was in, and a knock called up nightmare visions of Burrage, police officers, Lorry Alston—there was no end to his alarms. Then he reassured himself—a package or the room boy with towels—and called out "Come in."

At the first glance he did not know who it was. Like a woman in a novel a female, closely veiled, entered without greeting and closed the door. When she raised the veil and he saw it was Pancha Lopez he was at once relieved and exasperated. Her manner did not tend to remove his irritation. Leaning against the table, her face very white, she looked at him without speaking. Had not the sight of her just then been extremely unwelcome, the melodrama of the whole thing—the veil, the pallid face, the dramatic silence—would have amused him. As it was he looked anything but amused, rising from the armchair, his brows drawn together in an ugly frown.

"What on earth brings you here?" was his greeting.

"You," she answered.

Her voice, husky and breathless, matched the rest of the crazy performance. He saw an impending scene, and under his anger had a feeling of grievance. This was more than he deserved. He gave her an ironical bow.

"That's very flattering, I'm sure, and I'm highly honored. But, my dear Pancha, pardon me if I say I don't like it. It's not my custom to see ladies up here."

"Don't talk like that to me, Boyé," she said, the huskiness of her tone deepening. "Don't put on style and act like you didn't know me. We're past that."

He shrugged.

"Answer for yourself, Pancha. Believe me, I'm not at all past conforming to the usages of civilized people." He had moved back to the fireplace, and leaning against the mantel waited for her to reply. As she did not do so, he said, "Let me repeat, I don't like your coming here."

Her eyes, level and fixed, were disconcerting. To avoid them he turned to the mantel and took up a cigarette and matches lying there.

"Then why don't you come to see me?" she said.

"Teh—Teh!" He put the cigarette between his teeth and struck the match on the shelf. "Haven't I told you I'm busy?"

"Yes, you've *told* me that."

"Well?"

"You've told me lies."

"Thank you." He was occupied lighting the cigarette.

"Why, when I telephoned an hour ago and gave my name, did you say you were out?"

He affected an air of forbearance.

"Because I happened to be out."

"Boyé, that's another lie."

He threw the match into the fireplace and turned his eyes on her full of a steely dislike.

"Look here, Pancha. You've bothered me a lot lately, calling me up, nagging at me about things I couldn't help. I'm not the kind of man that likes that; I'm not the kind that stands it. I've been a friend of yours and hope to stay so, but—"

She cut him off, her voice trembling with passion.

"*Friend*—you a friend! *You* who do nothing but put me off with lies—who are trying to shake me, throw me away like an old shoe!"

Her restraint was gone. With her shoulders raised and her chin thrust forward, the thing she had been, and still was—child of the lower depths, bred in its ways—was revealed to him. It made him afraid of her, seeing possibilities he had not grasped before. What he had thought to be harmless and powerless might become one more menacing element in the dangers that surrounded him. His natural caution put a check upon his anger. He tried to speak with a soothing good humor.

"Now, my dear girl, don't talk like that. It's not true in the first place, it's stupid in the second, and in the third it only tends to make bad feeling between us that there's no cause for."

"Oh, yes, there's cause, lots of cause."

He found her steady eyes more discomfiting than ever, and looking at his cigarette said:

"Panchita, you're not yourself. You're overworked and overwrought, imagining things that don't exist. Instead of standing there slanging me you ought to go home and take a rest."

She paid no attention to this suggestion, but suddenly, moving nearer, said:

"What did you do it for, Boyé?"

"Do what?"

"Make love to me—make me think you loved me. Why did you come? Why did you say what you did? Why did you kiss me? Why, when you saw the way I felt, did you keep on? What good was it to you?"

To gain a moment's time, and to hide his face from her haggard gaze, he turned and put the cigarette carefully on the stand of the matchsafe. He found it difficult to keep the soothing note in his voice.

"Why—why—why? I don't see any need for these questions? What *did* I do? A kiss! What's that? And you talk as if I'd ceased to care for you. Of course I haven't. I always will. I don't know anyone I think more of than I do of you. That's why I want you to go. You don't look well, and as I told you before, it's not the right thing for you to be here."

She was beside him and he laid his hand on her arm, gentle and persuasive. She snatched the arm away, and with a small, feeble fist struck him in the chest and gasped out an epithet of the people.

For a still moment they stood looking at one another. Both faces showed that bitterest of antagonisms—the hate of one-time lovers. She saw it in his and it increased her desperation, he in her's, and in the uprush of his anger he forgot his fear. She spoke first, her voice low, her breathing loud on the room's stillness.

"You could fool me once, but it's too late now. There's no coming over me any more with soft talk."

"Then I'll not try it. Take it from me straight. I've come to the end of my patience. I've had enough of you and your exactions."

"Oh, you needn't tell me *that*," she cried. "I know it, and I know why. I know the secret of *your* change of heart, Mr. Boyé Mayer."

She saw the alarm in his face, the sudden arrested attention.

"What are you talking about?" he said, too startled to feign indifference.

"Oh, you thought no one was on," she cried, backing away from him, "but *I* was. I've been for the past month. Four hundred thousand dollars! Think of it, Boyé! You're getting on in the world. Some difference between that and an actress at the Albion."

If Pancha had still cherished a hope that she might have been mistaken, the sight of Mayer's rage would have extinguished it. He made a step toward her, hard-eyed, pale as she was.

"You're mad. That's what's the matter with you. I might have known it when you came. Now go—I don't want any lunatics here."

She stood her ground and tried to laugh, a horrible sound.

"You don't even like me to know that. Won't even share a secret with me—me, the friend that you care for so much."

"Go!" he thundered and pointed to the door.

"Not till I hear more, I'm curious. Is it just the money, or would you like the lady even if she hadn't any?"

Exasperated beyond reason he made a pounce at her and caught her by the arm. This time his grasp was too strong for her to shake off. His fingers closed on the slender stem and closing shook it.

"Since you won't go, I'll have to help you," he breathed in his fury.

She squirmed in his grip, trying to pull his fingers away with her free hand, and in this humiliating fashion felt herself drawn toward the door. It was the last consummate insult, his superior strength triumphing. If he had loosed her she would have gone, but anything he did she was bound to resist, most of all his hand upon her. That, once the completest comfort, was now the crowning ignominy.

As he pushed her, short sentences of savage hostility flashed between them, sparks struck from a mutual hate. Hers betrayed the rude beginnings she had tried to hide, his the falseness of his surface finish. It was as if for the first time they had established a real understanding. At grips, filled with fury, they attained a sudden intimacy, the hidden self of each at last plain to the other.

The scene was interrupted in an unexpected and ridiculous manner—the telephone rang. As the bell whirred he stopped irresolute, his fingers tight on her arm. Then, as it rang again, he looked at her with a sort of enraged helplessness, and made a movement to draw her to the phone. An outsider would have laughed, but the two protagonists were beyond comedy, and glared at one another in dumb defiance. Finally, the bell filling the room with its clamor, there was nothing for it but to answer. With grim lips and a murderous eye on his opponent, Mayer dropped her arm, and going to the phone, took down the receiver. From the other end, plaintive and apologetic, came Chrystie's voice.

Pancha retreated to the door, opened it and came to a halt on the sill. Out of the corner of his eye he was aware of her watching him, a baleful figure. He feared to employ the tenderness of tone necessary in his conversations with Chrystie, and as he listened and made out that she wanted to break her next engagement, he turned and fastened a gorgon's glance on the woman in the doorway, jerking his head in a gesture of dismissal.

She answered it with ominous quiet, "When I've finished. I've just one more thing to say."

In desperation he turned to the mouthpiece and said as softly as he dared:

"Wait a minute. The window's open and I can't hear. I must shut it," then put the receiver against his chest and muttered:

"Do you want me to kill you?"

"Not yet—after I get square you can. I won't care then what you do. But I've got to get square and I'm going to. There's Indian in me and that's the blood that doesn't forget. And there's something else you don't know—yes, there *was* something I never told you. I've someone to fight my fights and hit my enemies, and if I can't get you, they can. Watch out and see."

She retreated, closing the door. Mayer had to resume his conversation with the blood drumming in his ears, uplift Chrystie's flagging spirit, and shift their engagement to another day. When it was over he fell on the sofa, limp and exhausted. He lay there till dinner time, thinking over what Pancha had said, and what she could do, assuring himself it was only bluff, the impotent threatenings of a discarded woman. He felt certain that the champion she had alluded to was her one-time admirer, the bandit. This being the case, there was nothing to be feared from him, in hiding in the wilderness. It would be many a day before he'd venture forth. But the girl herself, full of venom, burning with the sense of her wrongs, was a new factor in the perils of his position. Stronger now than ever was this conviction that he must hurry his schemes to their climax.

CHAPTER XXII

THEREBY HANGS A TALE

THAT SAME EVENING the audience at the Albion had a disappointment. At half past eight the manager appeared before the curtain and said that Miss Lopez was ill and could not appear. As they all knew, she had been an unremitting worker, had given them of her best, and in her love of her art and her public had worn herself out and suffered a nervous breakdown. A week or two of rest would restore her, and meantime her place would be taken by Miss Lottie Vere.

The audience, not knowing what was expected of them, applauded and then looked at one another in aggrieved surprise. They felt rather peevish, for they had come to regard Pancha Lopez as a permanent institution devised for their amusement. They no more expected her to fail them than the clock in the Ferry Tower to be wrong. Charlie Crowder heard it at the *Despatch* office next morning—Mrs. Wesson, who picked up local news like a wireless, met him on the stairs and told him.

"I'm glad she's given in at last," said the good-natured society reporter. "She's been running down hill for the past month, and if she'd kept on much longer she'd have run to the place where you jump off."

That afternoon Crowder went round to see her. There was no use phoning, the Vallejo was still in that archaic stage where the only telephone was in the lower hall and guests were called to it by the clerk. Besides, you never could tell about a girl like Pancha; she was half a savage, liable to lie curled up in a corner and never think of a doctor.

He found her on the sofa in her sitting-room, a box of crackers and a bottle of milk on the table, a ragged Navajo blanket over her feet. When she saw who it was she sat up with a cry of welcome, her wrapper falling loose from her brown neck. She looked very ill, her eyes dark-circled and sunken in her wasted face.

He sat beside her on the sofa's edge—she was so thin there was plenty of room—and taking her hand held it while he tried to hide the concern that seized him. After the first sentence of greeting she fell back on the crumpled pillow, and lay still, the little flicker of animation dying out.

"Well, well, Panchita," he said, patting her hand, a kindly awkward figure hunched up in his big overcoat; "this is something new for you."

She made an agreeing movement with her head, her glance resting where it fell, too languid to move.

"I seem to be all in," she murmured.

"Just played out?"

"Looks that way."

"I didn't know till this morning—Mrs. Wesson told me. How did it happen?"

"I don't know, I got all weak. It was last night."

"At the theater?"

"No, here, in my room. I kept feeling worse and worse, but I thought I could pull through. And then I knew I couldn't and I got down to the phone some way and told them. And then I came back here and—I don't know—I sort of broke to pieces."

As she completed the sentence tears suddenly welled into her eyes and began to run, unchecked, in shining drops down her cheeks. She drew her hand from Crowder's and turning on her side placed it and its fellow over her face and wept, a river of tears that came softly without sobs. Crowder was overwhelmed. He had never thought his friend could be so broken, never had imagined her weak as other women, bereft of her gallant pride.

"Oh, Pancha," he said, unutterably distressed, "you poor girl! I'm so sorry, I'm so awfully sorry." He crooned over her in his rough man's tenderness, stroking her hair. "You've worked yourself to the bone. You ought to have given in sooner, you've kept it up too long."

Her voice came smothered through the shielding hands:

"It's not that, Charlie, it's not that."

This surprised him exceedingly. That any other cause than over-work could so reduce her had never occurred to him. Had she some ailment—some hidden suffering—preying on her? He thought of the Indian's stoicism and was filled with apprehension.

"Well, then, what is it?" he asked. "Are you ill?"

She moved her head in silent negation.

"But if it isn't work, it must be something. A girl as strong as you doesn't collapse without a reason."

She dropped her hands and sat up. Her face was brought on a level with his, the swollen eyes blinking through tears, the mouth twisted and pitiful.

"It's pain, it's pain, Charlie," she quavered.

"Then you *are* sick," he said, now thoroughly alarmed.

"No—it's not my body, it's my heart. It's here." She clasped her hands over her heart, and suddenly closing her eyes rocked back and forth. "A little while ago I was so happy. I never was like that before—every minute of the day lovely. And then it was all changed, it all ended. I couldn't believe it. I wouldn't believe it. I kept saying 'it'll come all right, nothing so awful could happen to anyone.' But it could—it did. And it's that that's made me this way—to be so full of joy and then to have it snatched away. It's too much, Charlie. Even I couldn't stand it—I who once thought nothing could beat me."

Crowder had had a wide experience in exhibitions of human suffering, but he had never seen anything quite like this. Tenderness was not what was needed, and, his eyes stern on her working face, he said with quiet authority:

"Pancha, I don't get what this means. Now, like a good girl, tell me. I've got to know."

Then and there, without more urging, she told him.

She told her story truthfully as far as she went, but she did not go to the end. All the preceding night, the interview with Mayer, had repeated itself in her memory, bitten itself in in every brutal detail. Hate trailed after it a longing to repay in kind and she saw herself impotent. The threat of her father's championship, snatched at in blind rage, she knew meant nothing, the boast of "getting square" was empty. Subtlety was her only weapon and now in her confession to Crowder she employed it. What she told of Mayer's conduct was true, but she did not tell what to her was a mitigating circumstance—the counter-attraction of Chrystie. The lure of money was to this child of poverty an excuse for her lover's desertion. Even Crowder, her friend, might condone a transfer of affection from Pancha Lopez to the daughter of George Alston. So the young man, hearing the story ended, saw Mayer as Pancha intended him to—a blackguard, breaking a girl's heart for pastime.

"The dog!" he muttered. "The cur! Why didn't you tell me? I'd have sized him up for you."

"I believed him, I thought it was true. And I was afraid you'd interfere—tell me it was all wrong."

The young man shifted his eyes from her face and stifled a comment. It was no time now to reproach her. There was a moment's silence and then she broke out into the query, put so often to herself, put to Mayer, tormenting and inexplicable.

"Why did he do it—why did he begin it? It was he who came, sought me out, gave me flowers. He'd come whenever I'd let him— and he was so interested, couldn't hear enough about me. There wasn't any little thing in my life he didn't want to know. Every man who'd ever come near me he'd want me to tell him about, he'd just *hound* me to tell him. What made him do it? Was it all a fake from the beginning, and if it was did he do it just for sport?"

Crowder had no answer for these plaints. He was deeply moved, shocked and indignant, more than he let her see. "An ugly business, a d——d ugly business," he growled, his honest face overcast with sympathy, his hand, big and not over clean, lying on hers.

"Never mind, old girl," he said; "we'll pull you out, we'll get you on your feet again. We've got to do that before we turn our attention to him. I guess he's got a weak spot and I'll find it before I'm done. Who is he, anyway—where does he come from—what's he doing here? He's too d——d reserved to come out well in the wash. You keep still and leave the rest to me. I'm not your old pal for nothing."

But his encouragement met with no response. Her heart unburdened, she lapsed into apathy and dropped back on the pillow, her spurt of energy over.

He lighted the light and tried to make her eat, but she pushed away the glass of milk he offered and begged him to let her be. So there was nothing for it but to make her as comfortable as he could, draw the table to her side, straighten the Navajo blanket and get another pillow from the bedroom. Tomorrow morning he would send in a doctor and on his way out stop at the office and leave a message for the chambermaid to look in on her during the evening. She answered his good-by with a nod and a slight, twisted smile, the first he had seen on her face.

"Lord!" he thought as he closed the door, "she looks half dead. How I'd like to get my hooks into that man!"

Downstairs he gave the clerk instructions and left a tip for the chambermaid—a doctor would come in the morning and he would look in himself in the course of the day. She was to want for nothing; if there was any expense he'd be responsible. On the way up the street he bought fruit, magazines and the evening papers and ordered them sent to her.

The next morning he found time to drop into the Argonaut Hotel for a chat with Ned Murphy. The chat, touching lightly on the business of the place, drifted without effort to Mr. Mayer, always to Ned Murphy, an engaging topic. Crowder went away not much the wiser. Mayer, if a little offish, was as satisfactory a guest as any hotel could ask for—paid his bill weekly, always in gold, gave no trouble, and lived pretty quiet and retired, only now and then going to the country on business. What the business was Ned Murphy didn't know—he'd been off five times now, leaving in the morning and coming back the next day. But he wasn't the kind to talk—you couldn't get next him. It was evident that Ned Murphy took a sort of proprietary pride in the stately unapproachableness of the star lodger.

In the shank of the afternoon, Crowder, at work in the city room, was called to the phone. The person speaking was Mark Burrage and his communication was mysterious and urgent. The night before, in a curious and unexpected manner, he had received some information of a deeply interesting nature upon which he wanted to consult Crowder. Would Crowder meet him at Philip's Rotisserie that evening at seven and arrange to come to his room afterward for an hour? The matter was important, and Crowder must hustle and fix it if it could be done. Crowder said it could, and, shut off from further parley by an abrupt "So long," was left wondering.

CHAPTER XXIII

THE CHINESE CHAIN

WHAT MARK HAD HEARD was, as he had said, interesting. It had been imparted in an interview as startling as it was unexpected, which had taken place in his room the evening before.

He was sitting by the table reading, the radiance of a green drop-light falling over the litter of papers and across his shoulder to the page of his book. The room, at the back of the house, had been chosen as much for its quiet as its low rent. A few of his own possessions relieved the ugliness of its mean furnishings, and it had acquired from his occupancy a lived-in, comfortable look. Two windows at the back framing the night sky were open, and the soft April air flowed in upon an atmosphere, smoke-thickened and heated with the lamplight.

Interruptions were unusual—a call to the telephone in the lower hall, a rare visitor, Crowder or a college friend. This was why, when a knock fell on the door, he looked up, surprised. It was an unusual knock, soft and low, not like the landlady's irritated summons, or Crowder's brusque rat-tat. In answer to his "Come in," the door swung slowly back and in the aperture appeared Fong.

He wore the Chinaman's outdoor costume, the dark, loose upper garment fastening tight round the base of the throat, the short, wide trousers, and on his head a black felt hat. Under the brim of this his face wore an expression of hesitating inquiry as if he were not sure of his reception.

"Why, hello!" said Mark, dropping his book in surprise; "it's Fong!"

The old man, his hand on the doorknob, spoke with apologetic gentleness.

"I want see you, Mist Bullage—you no mind if I come in? I want see you and talk storlies with you."

"First-rate, come ahead in and take a seat."

Closing the door noiselessly Fong moved soft-footed to a chair beside the table. Here, taking off his hat and putting it in his lap, he fixed a look on Burrage that might have been the deep gaze of a sage or the vacant one of a child. The green-shaded lamp sent a bright, downward gush of light over his legs, its mellowed upper glow shining on his forehead, high and bare to his crown. He had the curious, sexless appearance of elderly Chinamen; might have been, with his tapering hands, flowing coat, and hairless face, an old, monkey-like woman.

"Well," said Mark, stretching a hand for his pipe, thinking his visitor had come to pay a friendly call, "I'm glad to see you, Fong, and I'm ready to talk all the storlies you want. So fire away."

Fong considered, studying his hat, then said slowly:

"You velly good man, Mist Bullage, and you lawyer. You know what to do—I dunno no one same likey you. Miss Lolly and Miss Clist two young ladies—not their business. And Missy Ellen"—he paused for a second and gave a faint sigh—"Missy Ellen velly fine old lady, but no sense. My old boss's fliends most all dead, new lawyers take care of his money. They say to me, 'Get out, old Chinaman!' But you don't say that. So I come to you."

Mark's hand, extended to the tobacco jar at his elbow, fell to the chair arm; the easy good humor of his expression changed to attention.

"Oh, you've come for advice. I'll be glad to help you any way I can. Let's hear the trouble."

Again the Chinaman considered, fingering delicately at his hat-brim.

"My old boss awful good to me. He die and no more men in the house. I take care my boss's children—I care all ways I can. Old Chinaman can't do much but I watch out. And one man come that I no likey. I know you good boy, I know all the lest good boys, but Mist Mayer bad man."

"Mayer!" exclaimed Mark. "The man I met there the other night?"

"Ally samey him."

"What do you mean by 'bad'?"

"I come tell you tonight."

"You know something definite against him?"

"Yes. I find out. I try long time—one, two months—and bimeby I get him. Then he not come for a while and I say maybe he not come any more and I keep my mouth shut. But when you there last time he come again and I go tell what I know."

"You've found out something that makes you think he isn't a fit person to have in the house ?"

"Yes—I go velly careful, no one know but Chinamen. Two Chinamen help me—one Chinaman get another Chinaman and we catch on. I no tell Miss Lolly, she too young; I come tell you."

Mark leaned forward, his elbows on his knees.

"Say, Fong, I'm a little mixed up about this. Suppose you go to the beginning and give me the whole thing. If you and this chain of China boys have got something on Mayer I want to hear it. I'm not surprised that you think him a 'bad man,' but I want to know why you do."

What Fong told cannot be given in his own words, recited in his pidgin English, broken by cautions of secrecy and digressions as to the impracticability of enlightening his young ladies. It was a story only to be comprehended by one familiar with his peculiar phraseology, and understanding the complex mental processes and intricate methods of his race. Condensed and translated, it amounted to this:

From the first he had doubted and distrusted Mayer. In his dog-like loyalty to his "old boss," his love for the children that he regarded as his charge, he had personally studied and, through the subterranean lines of information in Chinatown, inquired into the character and standing of every man that entered the house. Sometimes when Mayer was there, he had stood behind the dining-room door and listened to the conversation in the parlor. The more he saw of the man the more his distrust grew. Asked why, he could give no reason; he either had no power to put his intuition into words, or—what is more probable—did not care to do so.

Two months before the present date a friend of his, member of the same tong, was made cook in the Argonaut Hotel. This gave him the opportunity to set in action one of those secret systems of espionage at which the Oriental is proficient. The cook, confined to his kitchen, became a communicating link between Fong and Jim, the room boy who attended to Mayer's apartment. Jim, evidently paid for his services and described as "an awful smart boy," was instructed to watch Mayer and note anything which might throw light on his character and manner of life.

To an unsuspecting eye the result of Jim's investigations would have seemed insignificant. That Mayer gambled and had lost heavily the three men already knew from the gossip of Chinatown. The room boy's information was confined to small points of personal habit and behavior. Among Mayer's effects, concealed in the back of his closet, was a worn and decrepit suitcase which he always carried when he went on his business trips. These trips occurred at intervals of about six weeks, and in his casual allusions to them to Ned Murphy and Jim himself he had never mentioned their objective point.

It was his habit to breakfast in his room, the meal being brought up on a tray by Jim and being paid for in cash each morning. For two and sometimes three days before the trips, Mayer always signed a receipt for the breakfast, but on his return he again paid in cash. Through a bellboy, who had admitted Jim to a patronizing intimacy, the astute Oriental had extended his field of observation. One of this boy's duties was to carry the mail to the rooms of the guests. For some weeks after his arrival Mayer had received almost no mail. After that letters had come for him, but all had borne the local postmark. The boy never remembered to have seen a letter for Mayer from New York, the city entered on the register as his home. Through this boy Jim had also gleaned the information that Mayer invariably paid his room rent in coin. He had heard Ned Murphy comment on the fact.

From this scanty data Fong and his associates drew certain conclusions. Mayer had no bank account, but he had plenty of money. Besides his way of living, his losses at gambling proved it. His funds ran low before his journeys out of town, suggesting that these journeys were visits to some source of supply. Arrived thus far they decided to extend their spying. The next time Mayer left the city Jim was paid to follow him. The room boy waited for the familiar signs, and when one morning Mayer told him to bring a check slip for his breakfast, went to the housekeeper and asked for a leave of absence to visit a sick "cousin." The following day Jim sat in the common coach, Mayer in the Pullman, of the Overland train.

Alighting at Sacramento the Chinaman followed his quarry into the depot and saw him enter the washroom, presently to emerge dressed in clothes he had never seen, though his study of Mayer's wardrobe had been meticulously thorough. He noted every detail—unshined, brown, low shoes, an overcoat faded across the shoulders, a Stetson hat with a sweat-stained band, no collar and a flashy tie. He did not think that anyone, unless on the watch as he was, would have recognized Mayer thus garbed.

From there he had trailed the man to the Whatcheer House. Dodging about outside the window he watched him register at the desk, then disappear in the back of the office. A few minutes later Jim went in and asked the clerk for a job. This functionary, sweeping him with a careless cast of his eye, said they had no work for a Chinaman and went back to his papers. During the moment of colloquy Jim had looked at the last entry in the register open before him. Later he had written it down and Fong handed the slip of paper to Mark. On it, in the clear round hand of the Chinaman who goes to night school, was written "Harry Romaine, Vancouver."

This brought Fong to the end of his discoveries. Having come upon a matter so much more momentous than he had expected, he was baffled and had brought his perplexities to a higher court. His Oriental subtlety had done its part and he was now prepared to let the Occidental go on from where he had left off. Mark inwardly thanked heaven that the old man had come to him. It insured secrecy, meant a carrying of the investigation to a climax and put him in a position where he could feel himself of use to Lorry. If to the Chinaman George Alston's house was a place set apart and sacred, it was to her undeclared lover a shrine to be kept free at any cost from such an intruder as Mayer. It did not occur to him as strange that Fong should have chosen him to carry on the good work. In the astonished indignation that the story had aroused he saw nothing but the fact that a soiled and sinister presence had entered the home of a girl, young, ignorant and peculiarly unprotected. Neither he nor Fong felt the almost comic unusualness of the situation—an infrequent guest called upon by an old retainer to help run to earth another guest. As they sat side by side at the table each saw only the fundamental thing—from separate angles the interests of both converged to the same central point.

At this stage Mark was unwilling to offer advice. They must know more first, and to that end he told Fong to bring Jim to his room the following night at eight. Meantime he would think it over and work out some plan. The next day he sent the phone message to Crowder and that night told him the story over dinner at Philip's Rôtisserie.

It threw Crowder into tense excitement; he became the journalist on the scent of a sensation. He was so carried away by its possibilities that he forgot Pancha's part in the unfolding drama. It was not till they were walking to Mark's lodging that he remembered and stopped short, exclaiming:

"By Ginger, I'd forgotten! Another county heard from; it's coming in from all sides."

So Pancha's experience was added to the case against Mayer, and breasting the hills, the young men talked it over, Crowder leaping to quick conclusions, impulsive, imagination running riot, Mark more judicial, confining himself to what facts they had, warning against hasty judgments. The talk finally veered to the Alston's and Mark had a question to ask that he had not liked to put to Fong. He moved to it warily—did Mayer go to the Alston house often, was he a constant visitor?

"Well, I don't know how constant, but I do know he goes. I've met him there a few times."

"He hasn't been after either of them—his name hasn't been connected with theirs?"

"Oh, no—nothing like that. He's just one of the bunch that drops in. I was jollying Chrystie about him the other night and she seemed to dismiss him in an offhand sort of fashion."

"He oughtn't to go at all. He oughtn't to be allowed inside their doors."

"Right, old son. But there's no good scaring them till we know more. He can't do them any harm."

"Harm, no. But a blackguard like that calling on those girls—it's sickening."

"Right again, and if we get anything on him it's up to us to keep them out of the limelight. It won't be hard. He only went to their house now and again as he went to lots of others. If this Chinese story pans out as promising as it looks, then we can put Lorry wise and tell her to hang out the 'not at home' sign when Mr. Mayer comes around. But we don't want to do that till we've good and ample reason. Lorry's the kind that always wants a reason—especially when it comes to turning down someone she knows. No good upsetting the girl till we've got something positive to tell her."

Mark agreed grudgingly and then they left the Alston sisters, to work out the best method of discovering what took Boyé Mayer to Sacramento and what he did there.

Jim proved to be a young, and as Fong had said, "awful smart boy." Smuggled into the country in his childhood, he spoke excellent English, interspersed with slang. He repeated his story with a Chinaman's unimaginative exactness, not a detail changed, omitted or overemphasized. The young men were impressed by him, intelligent, imperturbable and self-reliant, a man admirably fitted to put in execution the move they had decided on. This turned on his ability to insinuate himself into the Whatcheer House and by direct observation find out the nature of the business that required an alias and a disguise.

Jim said it could easily be done. By the payment of a small sum—five dollars—he could induce the present room boy in the Whatcheer House to feign illness, and be installed as a substitute. The custom among Chinese servants when sick to fill the vacancy they leave with a friend or "cousin" is familiar to all Californians. The housewife, finding a strange boy in her kitchen and asking where he comes from, receives the calm reply that the old boy is sick, and the present incumbent has been called upon to take his place. Mayer's last visit to Sacramento had been made three weeks previously. Arguing from past data this would place the next one at two or three weeks from the present time. But, during the last few days, Jim had noticed a change in the man. He had kept to his room, been irritable and preoccupied, had asked for a railway guide and been seen by Jim in close study of it. To wait till he made his next trip meant running the risk of missing him. It would be wiser to go to Sacramento and be on the spot, even if the time so spent ran to weeks. The room boy could easily be fixed—another five dollars would do that.

So it was settled. The young men, pooling their resources, would pay Jim's expenses, ten dollars for the room boy, and a bonus of fifty. If he brought back important information this would be raised to a hundred. When he came back he was to communicate with Fong, who in turn would communicate with Mark, and a date for meeting be set. It was now Monday; arrangements for his temporary absence from the Argonaut Hotel could be made the next morning, and he would leave for Sacramento in the afternoon.

CHAPTER XXIV

LOVERS AND LADIES

MAYER WAS PUTTING HIS affairs in order, preparatory to flight. A final interview with Chrystie would place him where he wanted to be, and that would be followed by a visit to Sacramento and a withdrawal of what remained of his money. He had a little over two thousand dollars left, enough to get them to New York and keep them there for a month or so in a good hotel. Before this would be expended he would have gained so complete an ascendancy over her that the control of her fortune would be in his hands. Payment of a gambling debt of three hundred and fifty dollars—owed him now for some weeks—had been promised on the following Monday. He would go to Sacramento on Saturday or Sunday, get this money on his return and then all would be ready for his exit.

He went over it point by point, scanning it closely, viewing it in its full extent, weighing, studying, determined that no detail should be overlooked. Outwardly his serenity was unruffled; his veiled eye showed its customary cool indifference, his manner its ironical suavity. Inwardly he was taut as a racer, his toe to the line, waiting for the starting signal. There were moments, pacing up and down his room, when he felt chilled by freezing air currents, as if icebergs might have suddenly floated down Montgomery Street and come to anchor opposite the hotel.

There were so many unexpected menaces—the man Burrage that he might run against anywhere, Pancha, a jealous virago—nobody knew what a woman in that state mightn't do—and Chrystie herself. In the high tension of his nerves she was indescribably irritating, full of moods, preyed upon by gnawings of conscience. He had already given her an outline of his plan, tentatively suggested it—you had

182

to suggest things tentatively to Chrystie—drawn lightly a romantic picture of their flight on the Overland to Reno.

They were to leave on Tuesday night, reaching Reno the next morning and there alighting for the marriage. He had chosen the night train as the least conspicuous. Chrystie could be shut up in a stateroom and he on guard outside where he could keep his eye on the door—it was more like a kidnaping than an elopement. At other times he might have laughed, but he was far from laughing now. It wasn't someone else's distressing predicament, it was his own.

When he had explained it he had met with one of those maddening stupidities of hers that strained his forbearance to the breaking point. How could she get away without Lorry knowing—Lorry always knew where she went? She was miserable over it, sitting close against his shoulder on a bench opposite the Greek Church.

"How about going for a few days to your friends, the Barlows, at San Mateo?" he had said, his hand folded tight on hers.

"The Barlows!" she exclaimed. "The Barlows haven't asked me."

That was the sort of thing she was always saying and he had to answer with patient softness.

"I know that, dear one, but why can't you tell Lorry that they have. They're going to have a dance and a house party and they want you to come on Tuesday and stay over till, say Thursday or Friday."

She cogitated, looking very troubled. He was becoming used to the expression, it invariably followed his promptings to falsehood.

"I suppose I could," she murmured.

He pressed the hand tenderly.

"I don't want to urge you to do anything you don't like, but I don't see what else there is for it. It's not really our fault that we have to run away—it's Lorry's. You've said yourself that she'd make objections, not to our way of doing things, but to me."

Chrystie nodded.

"She would. I'd have a fight to marry you anyway."

No one was in sight and he raised the gloved hand and pressed it to his lips. Dropping it he purred:

"We don't want any fights. We don't want our joy marred by bickerings and interference."

Chrystie agreed to that and then muttered in gloomy repudiation of Lorry's prejudices:

"I don't see why she feels that way about you. Nobody else does."

"We won't bother about that. She doesn't have to love me. Perhaps later I'll be able to prove to her that her brother-in-law isn't such a bad chap after all." He shifted a little closer, flicking up with a possessive finger a strand of golden hair that had fallen across her cheek, and murmuring his instructions into the shell pink ear his hand brushed. "You tell her you've had an invitation from the Barlows to come down on Tuesday and stay till Friday. Say they're going to have a party. That being the case you'll take a good-sized trunk. Give the order yourself to the expressman and tell him to send it to the ferry and when you get there check it to Reno. Then you leave the house in time to catch the late afternoon train to San Mateo and as soon as you get out of sight order your driver to take you to the ferry. You'd better cross at once and do what waiting you'll have on the Oakland side."

"You'll be there?" she said, stirring uneasily.

"Yes, but I won't speak to you."

"Oh, dear"—it was almost a wail—"how I wish we could be married at home like Christians!"

"My darling, my darling, don't make it any harder for me. You never wanted anything in your life as much as I want to take your hand and call you mine before the eyes of the whole world. But it's impossible—you yourself were the first to say so. We don't want a family row, a scandal, all in the papers. Love mustn't be dragged through that sort of ignominy."

She thought so, too; she always agreed with him when he talked of love. But he had to come down to earth and the Barlows, finding it necessary to instruct her even in such small matters as how she was to get the letter from them. She was simply to tell Lorry such a letter had come and she had answered it, accepting the invitation. It was perfectly simple—didn't she see?

She saw, her head drooped, telling Lorry about that letter which was never to arrive and that answer which was never to be written, bringing back the old, sick qualms. There had to be more inspiring talk of love before she was brought up to the point where he dared to leave her, felt his influence strong enough to last till the next meeting. He wondered irascibly if all home-bred, nice young girls were such fools and realized why he'd never liked them.

That same afternoon Lorry had a visitor. While Chrystie was walking home, poised on the edge of the great exploit, at one moment seeing the tumult left by her flight, at the next that flight, wing and wing, through the golden future with her eagle mate, Lorry was sitting in the drawing-room talking to Mark Burrage.

He had not told Crowder that he was going, had not decided to go till the morning after he had seen Crowder and the two Chinamen. When they had gone he had sat pondering, and that question which he had not liked to ask Fong and which he had only tentatively put to his friend, rose, insistent, demanding a more informed answer. Was this man—more than objectionable, probably criminal—paying court to Lorry? It was a horrible idea, that haunted him throughout the night. He recalled Mayer's manner to her the evening of his visit, and hers to him. Not that he thought she could have been attracted to the man; she was too fine, her instincts too true. But on the other hand she was young, so unlearned in the world's ways, so liable to be duped through her own innocence. His thoughts swung like a pendulum from point of torment to point of torment and in the morning he rose, determined on the visit. It was to satisfy himself and if possible drop a hint of warning. He never thought of Chrystie. She was a child and on that evening Mayer had treated her as such, paying her only the scanty meed of attention that politeness demanded.

When he started for the house he had entered on a new phase in his relation to her. He was no longer the humble visitor, overawed by her riches, but someone whose business it was to watch over and take care of her. It bridged the gulf between them, swept away artificial distinctions. He forgot himself, his awkwardness, how he impressed her. These once important considerations ceased to exist and a man, concerned about a woman, feeling his obligations to look after her, emerged from the hobbledehoy that had once been Marquis de Lafayette Barrage.

She saw the change at the first glance. It was in his face, in his manner, no longer diffident, assured, almost commanding. Their positions were transformed, she less a fine lady, queening it amid the evidences of her wealth, than a girl, lonely and uncared for, he the dominating, masculine presence that her life had lacked. The woman in her, slowly unfolding in secret potency, felt his ascendancy and bloomed into fuller being. They were conscious of the constraint and shyness that had been between them giving place to a gracious ease, of having suddenly experienced a harmonious adjustment that had come about without effort or intention.

Over the smooth, sweet sense of it they talked on indifferent matter, items of local importance, small social doings, the Metropolitan Opera Company which was to open its season on the following Monday night. It was wonderful how interesting everything was, how they passed from subject to subject. They had so much to say that the shadows were rising in the distant end of the room before Mark came to the real matter of moment. It was proof of the change in him that he did not grope and blunder to it but brought it forward with one abrupt question.

"Who is Mr. Mayer that I met here the other night?"

"Well—he's just Mr. Mayer—a man from the East who's in California for his health. That's all I know about him, except that he lived a long time in Europe when he was a boy and a young man."

"How did you come to meet him?"

"Through Mrs. Kirkham, an old friend of Mother's. She brought him here and then we asked him to dinner." She paused, but the young man, his eyes on the ground, making no comment, she concluded with, "Did you think he was interesting?"

He raised his glance to hers and said:

"No—I didn't like him."

Lorry leaned from her chair, her eyebrows lifted, her expression mischievously confidential.

"Then we have one taste in common—neither do I."

She was surprised to see Mark flush, and his gaze widen to a piercing fixity. She thought her plain speaking had offended him and hastened to excuse it:

"I know that isn't a nice thing to say about a guest in your house, and I don't say it to everybody—only to you. Are you shocked?"

"No, I'm relieved. But I couldn't think you would like him."

"Why? All the other girls do."

"You're not like the other girls. You're—" He stopped abruptly, again dropped his eyes and said, "He's no good—he's a fake."

"There!" She was quite eager in her agreement. "That's just the impression he gives me. I felt it the first time I saw him."

"Then why do you have him here?"

The note of reprimand was unconscious, but to the young girl it was plain and her heart thrilled in response to its authority.

"We needed an extra man for our dinner—the dinner that you refused to come to."

She laughed at him in roguish triumph, and it was indescribably charming. He joined in, shame-faced, mumbling something about his work.

"So you see, Mr. Burrage," she said, "in a sort of way it was your fault."

"It's not my fault that he keeps on coming."

"No, I guess that's mine. I ask him and he has to pay a call. He's *very* polite about that."

She laughed again, delighted at this second chance, but now he did not join in. Instead he became gravely urgent, much more so than so slight a matter demanded.

"But look here, Miss Alston, what's the sense of doing that? What's the sense of having a person round you don't like?"

She gave a deprecating shrug.

"Oh, well, it's not as bad as all that. I have really nothing against him; he's always entertaining and pleasant and makes things go off well. It's just my own feeling; I have no reason. I can't discriminate against him because of that."

Mark was silent. It was hateful to him to hear her blaming herself, offering excuses for the truth of her instinct. But he had agreed with Crowder not to tell her, and anyway he had satisfied himself as to her sentiments—she was proof against Mayer's poisonous charm. At this stage he could enlighten her no further; all that now remained for him to do was to give her a hint of that guardianship to which he was pledged.

"It's a big responsibility for you, running a place like this, letting the right people in and keeping the wrong ones out."

"It is, and I don't suppose I do it very well. It was all so new and I was so green."

"Well, it's not a girl's job. You ought to have a watch dog. How would I answer?"

She smiled.

"What would you do—bay on the front steps every time Mr. Mayer came?"

"That's right—show my teeth so he couldn't get at the bell. But, joking apart, I'd like you to look upon me that way—I mean if you ever wanted anyone to consult with. You're just two girls—you might need a man's help—things come up."

The smile died from her lips. She was surprised, gratefully, sweetly surprised.

"Oh, Mr. Burrage, that's very kind of you."

"No, it's not. The kindness would be on your side, the way it has been right along. I'd think a lot of it if you'd let me feel that if you wanted help or advice, or anything of that kind, you'd ask it of me."

Had she looked at him the impassioned earnestness of his face would have increased her surprise. But she was looking at the tassel on the chair arm, drawing its strands slowly through her fingers.

"Perhaps I will some day," she murmured.

"Honest—not hesitate to send for me if you ever think I could be of any service to you? Will you promise?"

A woman more experienced, more quick in a perception of surface indications, might have guessed a weightier matter than the young man's words implied. Lorry took them as they were, feeling only the heart behind them.

"Yes, I'll promise," she said.

"Then it's a pact between us. I'll know if you ever want me you'll call on me. And I'll come; I'll come, no matter where I am."

The room was growing dim, dusk stealing out from its corners into the space near the long windows where they sat. Their figures, solid and dark in the larger solidity of the two armchairs, were motionless, and in the pause following his words, neither stirred or spoke. It was a silence without embarrassment or constraint, a moment of arrested external cognizances. Each felt the other as close, suddenly glimpsed intimate and real, a flash of finer vision that for an instant held them in subtle communion. Then it passed and they were saying good-by, moving together into the hall. Fong had not yet lighted the gas and it was very dim there;

Mark had to grope for his hat on the stand. He touched her hand in fare-well, hardly conscious of the physical contact, heard his own mechanical words and her reply. Then the door opened, shut and he was gone.

Lorry went upstairs to her own room. Her being was permeated with an inner content, radiating like light from a center of peace. She closed her eyes to better feel the comfort of it, to rest upon its infinite assurance. She had no desire to know whence it rose, did not even ask herself if he loved her. From a state of dull distress she had suddenly come into a consciousness of perfect well-being, leaving behind her a past where she had been troubled and lonely. Their paths, wandering and uncertain, had met, converging on some higher level, where they stood together in a deep, enfolding security.

She was still motionless in the gathering dusk when Chrystie en-tered the room beyond, filling it with silken rustlings and the tapping of high heels. Lorry did not know she was there till she came to the open door and looked in.

"Oh, Lorry, is that you? What are you doing sitting like Patience in a rocking chair?"

"I don't know—thinking, dreaming."

Chrystie withdrew with mutterings; could be heard moving about. Suddenly she exclaimed, "It's a glorious afternoon," and then shut a drawer with a bang. Presently two short, sharp rings sounded from the hall below and following them her voice rose high and animated:

"That's the mail. I'll go and see if there's anything exciting."

Lorry heard her turbulent descent of the stairs and came back to a realization of her environment. In a few minutes Chrystie was in her room again, a little breathless from her race up the long flight.

"There're only two letters," she called. "One for you and one for me."

Lorry was not interested in letters and made no response, and af-ter a pause heard her sister's voice, raised in the same vivacious note:

"Mine's from Lilly Barlow. She wants me to come down on Tuesday and stay over till Friday. They're having a dance."

"A dance—oh, that'll be lovely. When is it to be?"

"Tuesday night. I'm to go down on the evening train and they'll meet me with the motor."

"I'm so glad—you always have a good time there."

Lorry appeared in the doorway. The room was nearly dark, the last blue light slanting in through the uncurtained window. By its faint illumination she saw Chrystie's face in the mirror, glum and unsmiling. It was not the expression with which the youngest Miss Alston generally greeted calls to festivals.

"What's the matter, Chrystie?" she said. "Don't you want to go?"

The girl wheeled round sharply.

"Of course I do. Why shouldn't I? Did you ever know me not want to go to a dance?"

"Then you'd better write and accept at once. They're probably putting up other people and they'll want to know if you're coming."

"I'll do it tonight. There's no such desperate hurry; I can phone down. There's your letter on the bureau."

She threw herself on the bed, a long, formless shape in the shadowy corner. She lay there without speaking as Lorry took her letter to the window and read it. It was from Mrs. Kirkham; a friend had sent her a box for the opera on Tuesday night and she invited both girls. It would be a great occasion, everybody was going, Caruso was to sing. Lorry looked up from it, quite dismayed; it was too bad that Chrystie would miss it. But Chrystie from the darkness of the bed said she didn't care; she'd rather dance than hear Caruso, or any other singing man—music bored her anyhow. Lorry left her and went into her own room to write an acceptance for herself and regrets for her sister.

At nine that night Mark was sitting by his table, his book on his knee, his eyes on the smoke wreaths that lay across the air in light layers, when his dreams were broken by a knock on his door. It was his landlady with a telegram:

Mother very sick. Pneumonia. Come at once.

SADIE.

There was a train for Stockton in half an hour, and he could make the distance between the town and the ranch by horse or stage. He made a race for it and at the station, finding himself a few minutes ahead, took a call for Crowder at the *Despatch* office and caught him. In a few words he told him what had happened, that he didn't know how long he might be away and that if news came from Jim before his return to let him know. Crowder promised.

CHAPTER XXV

WHAT JIM SAW

THE NEXT MORNING CROWDER sent a letter to Fong advising him of Mark's departure. Should Jim get back from Sacramento within the next few days he was to communicate with Crowder at the *Despatch* office. The young man had no expectation of early news, but he was going to run no risks with what promised to be a sensation. His journalist's instincts were aroused, and he was resolved to keep for his own paper and his own *kudos* the most picturesque story that had ever come his way. He went about his work, restless and impatient, seeing the story on the *Despatch's* front page and himself made the star reporter of the staff.

He had not long to wait. On Monday morning he was called from the city room to the telephone. Through the transmitter came the soft and even voice of Jim; he had returned from Sacramento the night before, and if it was convenient for Mr. Crowder could see him that afternoon at two in Portsmouth Square. Mr. Crowder would make it convenient, and Jim's good-by hummed gently along the wire.

The small plaza—a bit of the multicolored East embedded in the new, drab West—was a place where Orient and Occident touched hands. There Chinese mothers sat on the benches watching their children playing at their feet, and Chinese fathers carried babies, little bunched-up, fat things with round faces and glistening onyx eyes. Sons of the Orient, bent on business, passed along the paths, exchanging greetings in a sing-song of nasal voices, cues braided with rose-colored silk swinging to their knees. Above the vivid green of the grass and the dark flat branches of cypress trees, the back of Chinatown rose, alien and exotic: railings touched with gold and red, lanterns, round and crimson or oblong with pale, skin-like coverings, on the window ledges blue and white bowls upholding sheaves of lilies, the rich emblazonry of signs, the thick gilded arabesques of a restaurant's screened balconies.

Crowder found his man standing by the pedestal on which the good ship *Bonaventure* spreads its shining sails before the winds of romance. A quiet hail and they were strolling side by side to a bench sheltered by a growth of laurel.

Mayer had appeared at the Whatcheer House the day before at noon. Jim, crossing the back of the office, had seen him enter, and loitering heard him tell the clerk that he would give up his room that afternoon as his base had shifted to Oregon. Then he had gone upstairs, and Jim had followed him and seen him go into No. 19, the last door at the end of the hall on the left-hand side.

The hall was empty and very quiet. It was the lunch hour, a time at which the place was deserted. Arming himself with a duster Jim had stolen down the passage to No. 19. Standing by the door he could hear Mayer walking about inside, and then a sound as if he was moving the furniture. With the duster held ready for use Jim had looked through the keyhole and seen Mayer with a chisel in his hand, the bed behind him drawn out from the wall to the middle of the room.

Emboldened by the hall's silence, Jim had continued to watch. He saw Mayer go to the corner where the bed had stood, lift the carpet and the boards below it and take from beneath them two canvas sacks. From these he shook a stream of gold coins—more than a thousand dollars, maybe two. He let them lie there while he put back the sacks, replaced the boards and carpet and pushed the bed into its corner. Then he gathered up the money, rolling some of it in a piece of linen, which he packed in his suitcase, and putting the rest in a money belt about his waist. After that he took up his hat and Jim slipped away to a broom closet at the upper end of the hall.

From here the Chinaman saw his quarry come out of the room and go down the stairs. At the desk Mayer stopped, told the clerk he had vacated No. 19, but would wait in the office for a while as his train was not due to leave till the afternoon. From the stairhead Jim watched him take a seat by the window, and, the suitcase at his feet, pick up a paper and begin to read.

It was a rule of the Whatcheer House that a vacated room was subjected to a "thorough cleaning." Translated this meant a run over the floor with a carpet sweeper and a change of sheets. The door of No. 19 had been left unlocked, and while Mayer sat in the office conning the paper, Jim with the necessary rags and brooms was putting No. 19 in shape for the next tenant. An inside bolt on the door made him secure against interruption, and the bed drawn to the middle of the floor was part of the traditional rite. Carpet and boards came up easily; his cache empty Mayer had not troubled to renail them. In the space between the rafters and the flooring Jim had found no more money, only a bunch of canvas sacks, and a dirty newspaper. With the Chinaman's meticulous carefulness he had brought these back to his employers; in proof of which he laid a small, neatly tied package on Crowder's knee. For the rest his work was done. He had paid the Whatcheer room boy and seen him reinstated, had followed Mayer to the depot, viewed his transformation there, and ridden with him on the night train back to San Francisco.

To Crowder's commending words he murmured a smiling deprecation. What concerned him most was his "prize money," which was promised on Mark's return. Then, nodding sagely to the young man's cautioning of secrecy, he rose, and uninterested, imperturbably enigmatic and bland, passed out of sight around the laurels.

Crowder, on the bench, slipped down to a comfortable angle and thought. There was no doubt now—but what the devil did it mean? A concealed hoard hidden under the floor of a men's lodging house—that could only be stolen money. Where had he stolen it from? Was he some kind of gentleman burglar, such as plays and novels had been built around? It was a plausible explanation. He looked the part so well; lots of swagger and side, and the whole thing a trifle overdone. *What* a story! Crowder licked his lips over it, seeing it splashed across the front page. At that moment the parcel Jim had given him slipped off his knee to the ground.

He had forgotten it, and a little shamefaced—for your true detective studies the details before formulating his theory—picked it up and opened it. Inside a newspaper, its outer sheets mud-stained and torn, were six small bags of white canvas, marked with a stenciled "W. F. & Co." Crowder sat erect and brushed back his pendent lock of hair. He knew what the stenciled letters stood for as well as he knew his own initials. Then he spread out the paper. It was the *Sacramento Courier* of August 25. From the top of a column the heading of his own San Francisco letter faced him, the bottom part torn away. But that did not interest him. It was the date that held his eye—August 25—that was last summer—August 25, Wells Fargo— he muttered it over, staring at the paper, his glance glassily fixed in the intensity of his mental endeavor.

Round date and name his memory circled, drawing toward a focus, curving closer and closer, coming nearer in decreasing spirals, finally falling on it. With the pounce a broken sentence fell from his lips: "The tules! Knapp and Garland!"

For the first moment of startled realization he was so surprised that he could not see how Mayer was implicated. Then his mind leaped the gap from the holdup in August to that picturesque narrative still fresh in the public mind—Knapp's story of the robbed cache. The recollection came with an impact that held him breathless; incidents, details, dates, marshaling themselves in a corroborating sequence. When he saw it clear, unrolled before his mental vision in a series of events, neatly fitting, accurately dovetailed, he sat up looking stupidly about him like a person emerging from sleep.

He had work to do at the office, but on the way there stopped at the Express Company for a word with Robinson, one of the clerks, whom he knew. He wanted information of any losses by theft or accident sustained by the company since the middle of the preceding August. Robinson promised to look up the subject and let him know before the closing hour. At six Crowder was summoned to one of the telephone booths in the city room. Robinson had inquired: during the time specified Wells Fargo and Company had suffered but one loss. This was on the twenty-sixth of August, when Knapp and Garland had held up the Rocky Bar stage and taken thousand dollars in coin consigned to the Greenhide Mine at Antelope.

It was Crowder's habit to dine at Philip's Rôtisserie at half past six. They liked him at Philip's. Madame at her desk, fat and gray-haired, with a bunch of pink roses at one elbow and a sleeping cat at the other, always had time for a chat with "Monsieur Crowdare."

Even Philip himself, in his chef's cap and apron, would emerge from the kitchen and confer with the favored guest. But tonight "Monsieur Crowdare" had no words for anyone. He did no more than nod to Madame, and Gaston, the waiter, afterward told her he had hardly looked at the menu—just said bring anything, he didn't care what. Madame was quite worried over it, hoped "*le cher garçon*" wasn't sick, and comforted herself by thinking he might be in love.

Never before in his cheery existence had Crowder been so excited. Over his unsavory dinner he studied the situation, planning his course. He was resolved on one point—to keep the rights of discovery for the *Despatch*. He could manage this, making it a condition when he laid his knowledge before the Express Company people. That would be his next move, and he ought to do it soon; Mayer's withdrawal of the money might indicate an intention of disappearing. He would go to Wells Fargo and tell them what he had found out, asking in return that the results of their investigation should be given to him for first publication in the *Despatch*.

It was a pity Mark wasn't there—he didn't like acting without Mark. But matters were moving too quickly now to take any chances. There was no telephone at the ranch, or he could have called up long-distance, and a telegram, to be intelligible, would have to be too explicit. He would write to Mark tomorrow, or perhaps the next day—after he had seen the Express people.

To be secret as the grave was the charge Crowder laid upon himself, but he longed to let loose some of the ferment that seethed within him, and in his longing remembered the one person to whom he dared go—Pancha. Hers were the legitimate ears to receive the racy tale. She was not only to be trusted—a pal as reliable as a man—but it would cure her of her infatuation, effectually crush out the passion that had devastated her.

CHAPTER XXVI

PANCHA WRITES A LETTER

ANCHA HAD BEEN MUCH ALONE. Crowder had seen her several times, the doctor had come, the chambermaid, one or two of her confreres from the theater. But there had been long, dreary hours when she had lain motionless, looking at the walls and thinking of her wrongs. She had gone over and over the old ground, trodden the weary round like a squirrel in a cage, asked herself the same questions and searched, tormented, for their answers. As the days passed the weight of her grievance grew, and her sick soul yearned to hit back at the man who had so wantonly wounded her.

Gradually, from the turmoil an idea of retaliation was churned into being. It did not reach the point of action till Monday evening. Then it rose before her imperious, a vengeance, subtle and if not complete, at least as satisfying as anything could be to her sore heart. It was that expression of futile anger and poisoned musings, an anonymous letter. She wrote it on the pink note paper which she had bought to write to Mayer on. It ran as follows:

DEAR LADY:

This letter is to warn you. It comes from a person friendly to you and who wants to put you wise to something you ought to know. It's about Boyé Mayer, him that goes to your house and is after your sister. Maybe you don't know that, but *I* do—it's truth what I'm telling you every word. He's no good. Not the kind to go round with your kind. It's your sister's money he wants. If she had none he'd not trouble to meet her in the plaza opposite the Greek Church. Watch out for him—don't let her go with him.

Don't let her marry him or you'll curse the day. I know him
well and I know he's bad right through.

Wishing you well,

From a Friend.

She had written the letter to Lorry as the elder sister, whose
name she had seen in the papers and whom Crowder had described
as the intelligent one with brains and character. Her woman's instinct
told her that her charges might have no weight with the younger
girl, under the spell of those cajoleries and blandishments whose
power she knew so well. With the letter in her hand she crept out
to the stairhead and called to the clerk in the office below. Gushing
had not come on duty yet, and it was the day man who answered
her summons. She asked him to post the letter that night, and he
promised to do so. The lives of the group of which this story tells
were drawing in to a point of fusion. In the centripetal movement
this insignificant incident had its importance. The man forgot his
promise, and it was not till the next day at lunch that he thought of
the letter, posting it on his way back to the hotel.

In her room again, Pancha dropped on the sofa, and lay still. The
exertion had taxed her strength and she felt sick and tremulous. But
she thought of what she had done with a grim relish, savored like a
burning morsel on her tongue, the bitter-sweet of revenge.

Here an hour later Crowder found her. She was glad to see him,
and told him she was better, but the doctor would not let her get up yet.

"And even if he would," she said, "I don't want to. I'm that weak,
Charlie, you can't think. It's as if the thing that made me alive was
gone, and I was just the same as dead."

Crowder thought he understood his friend Pancha even as he
did his friend Mark. That she could have complexities and reservations beyond his simple ken had never occurred to him. What he
saw on the surface was what she was, and being so, the news he was
bringing would be as a tonic to her broken spirit.

"You'll not stay that way long, Panchita," he said. "You'll be on
the job soon now. And what I've come to tell you will help on the
good work. I've got a story for you that'll straighten out all the creases and bring you up on your feet better than a steam derrick would."

"What is it?" She did not seem especially interested, her glance listless, her hand lying languid where he had dropped it.

"It's about Mayer."

He was rewarded by seeing her shift her head on the pillow that she might command him with a vivid, bird-bright eye.

"What about him?"

"Every thing, my dear. We've got him coming and going. We've got him dead to rights. He's a rogue and a thief."

With her hands spread flat on either side of her she raised herself to a sitting posture. Her face, framed in its bush of hair, had a look of strained, almost wild, inquiry.

"Thief!" she exclaimed.

"Yes. It's a honeycooler of a story. Burst out all of a sudden like a night blooming cereus. But before I say a word you've got to promise on everything you hold sacred that you won't breathe a word of it."

"I promise."

"It's only for a little while. It'll be public property in a day or two—Thursday or Friday maybe."

"I'm on. How is he a thief?"

Crowder told her. The story was clear in his head by this time, and he told it well, with the journalist's sense of its drama. As he spoke she drew up her knees and clasping her hands round them sat rigid, now and then as she met his eyes, raised to hers to see if she had caught a point, nodding and breathing a low, "I see—Go on."

When he had finished he looked at her with challenging triumph.

"Well—isn't it all I said it was?"

Already she showed the effect of it. There was color in her face, a dusky red on the high cheek bones.

"Yes—more. I didn't think—" She stopped and swallowed, her throat dry.

"Did you have the least idea, did he ever say a word to suggest he had anything as juicy as that in the background?"

"No. I can't remember all in a minute. But he never said much about himself; he was always asking about me." She paused, fixedly staring; then her glance, razor-sharp, swerved to the young man. "Will he go to jail?"

"You bet he will. I'm not sure on just what count, but they'll find one that'll fit his case. He's as much a thief as either Knapp or Garland. He knew it wasn't Captain Kidd's treasure; he saw the papers. He can't play the baby act about being ignorant. The way he hid his loot proves that."

"Yes," she murmured. "He's a thief all right. He's bad every way."

"That's what I wanted you to see. That's why I told you. You can't go on caring now."

"No." Her voice was very low. "It puts the lid on that."

"You can thank God on your bended knees he threw you down."

"Oh, yes," she rocked her head slightly from side to side with an air of morose defiance, "I *can*."

"*Do* you?" said the young man, leaning closer and looking into her face.

He was satisfied by what he saw. For a moment the old pride flamed up, a spark in the black glance, a haughty straightening of the neck.

"A common thief like him for my lover? Say, you know me, Charlie. I'd have killed myself, or maybe I'd have killed him."

Crowder had what he would have called "a hunch" that this might be true. From his heart he exclaimed:

"Gee, I'm glad it's turned out the way it has!"

"So am I. Only I'm sorry for one thing. It's *you* that have caught him, not *me*."

Crowder laughed.

"You Indian!" he said. "You red, revengeful devil!"

"Oh, I'm *that!*" she answered, with biting emphasis. "When I get a blow I want to give one. I don't turn the other cheek; I strike back—with a knife if I have one handy."

"Well, don't you bother about knives now. The hitting's going to be done for you. All you have to do is to sit still, like a perfect lady, and say nothing."

"Um." She paused, mused an instant, and then said: "You're sure you can't be mistaken?"

"Positive. Funny, isn't it? It was the paper that gave me the lead. Sort of poetic justice his being landed by that—the paper that had the article about you in it."

She looked at him, struck with a sudden idea:

"Perhaps it was that article that made him come to see me in the beginning."

Crowder smiled.

"I guess he wasn't bothering about articles just then. He'd used it to wrap the money in. It was all muddy and ragged, the lower half of the letter gone—the piece about you—got torn out by accident I guess. As I see it he happened to have the paper and when he got the sacks out of the ground, put some of 'em in it. Then when he was in the Whatcheer House he stuffed it in the hole under the floor. It was the handiest way to get rid of it."

Soon after that Crowder left, feeling that he had done a good work. The news had had the effect he had hoped it would. She was a different girl. The last glimpse of her, sitting in that same attitude with her hands clasped round her knees, showed her revitalized, alive once more, with something of the old brown and red vividness in her face.

When he had gone she remembered her letter. It was of no use now. She would have liked to recall it, but it was too late; the clock on the table marked eleven. Through the fitful sleep of her uneasy night it came back, invested by the magnifying power of dreams with a fantastic malignity; in waking moments showing as a bit of spite, dwindled to nothing before the forces gathering for Mayer's destruction.

CHAPTER XXVII

BAD NEWS

O LD MAN HALEY'S SHACK stood back from a branch road that wound down from Antelope across the foothills to Pine Flat. Commercial travelers, staging it from camp to camp, could see his roof over the trees, and sometimes the driver would point to it with his whip and tell how the old man—a survival of the early days—lived there alone cultivating his vegetable patch. In the last four or five years people said he had gone "nutty," had taken to wandering down the stream beds with his pickax and pan, but he was a harmless old body and seemed able to get along. He said he had a son somewhere who sent him money now and again, and he always had enough to keep himself in groceries and tobacco, which he bought at the general store in Pine Flat. Maybe you'd see him straying along, sort o' kind and simple, with his pick over his shoulder, smilin' up at the folks in the stage.

On that Sunday when Mayer had made his last trip to Sacramento Old Man Haley had risen with the sun. While the rest of the world was slumbering on its pillow he was out among his vegetables, hoe in hand.

It was one of those mornings that deck with a splendor of blue and gold the foothill spring. The air was balmy, the sky a fleckless vault, where bird shapes floated on aerial currents or sped in jubilant flight. From the chaparral came the scents of sun-warmed foliage, the pungent odor of bay, the aromatic breath of pine, and the sweet, frail perfume of the chaparral flower. This flecked the hillside with its powdery blossom, a white blur among the glittering enamel of madrona leaves.

Old Man Haley, an ancient figure in his rusty overalls, paused in his labor to survey the sea of green from which he had wrested his garden. His eye traveled slowly, for he loved it, and had grown to regard it as his own. Leaning on his hoe he looked upward over its tufted density and suddenly his glance lost its complacent vagueness and became sharp and fixed. Through the close-packed vegetation a zigzag movement descended as if a fissure of earth disturbance was stirring along the roots. After a moment's scrutiny he turned and sent a look, singularly alert, over the shack and the road beyond. Then, pursing his lips, he emitted a whistled bar of bird notes.

The commotion in the chaparral stopped, and from it rose a wild figure. It looked more ape than man, hairy, bearded to the cheekbones, sunken-eyed and staggering. It started forward at a run, branches crashing under its blundering feet, and as it came it sent up a hoarse cry for food.

Some years before Old Man Haley had built a woodshed behind the cabin. When he bought the planks he had told "the boys" in Pine Flat that he was getting too old to forage for his wood in winter, and was going to cut it in summer, and have it handy when the rains came. He had built the shed well and lined it with tar paper. Adventurous youngsters, going past one day, had peeped in and seen a blanket spread over the stacked logs as if the old man might have been sleeping there; which, being reported, was set down to his craziness.

Here Garland now hid, ate like a famished wolf, and slept. Then when night came, and all wayfarers were safe indoors, stole to the shack, and with only the red eye of the stove to light their conference, exchanged the news with his confederate. Hunger had driven him back to the settlements; four days before his last cartridge had been spent, and he had lived since then on berries and roots. Old Man Haley, squatting in the rocking-chair made from a barrel, whispered cheering intelligence: they'd about given up the hunt, thought he had died in the chaparral. Someone had seen birds circling round a spot off toward the hills behind Angels.

The next day when Garland told his intention of moving on to San Francisco, the old man was uneasy. He was the only associate of the bandit who knew of the daughter there, and he urged patience and caution. He was even averse to taking a letter to her when he went into Pine Flat for supplies. The post office was the resort of loungers. If they saw Old Man Haley coming in to mail a letter, they'd get curious; you couldn't tell but what they might wrastle with him and grab the letter. In a day or two maybe he could get into Mormons Landing, where he wasn't so well known, and mail it there. To placate Garland he promised him a paper; the man at the store would give him one.

When he came back in the rosy end of the evening he was exultant. A woman, hearing him ask the storekeeper for a paper, had told him to stop at her house and she would give him a roll of them. There they were, a big bundle, and not local ones, but the *San Francisco Despatch* almost to date. He left Garland in the woodshed, reading by the light that fell in through the open door, and went to the shack to cook supper.

Presently a reek of blue smoke was issuing from the crook of pipe above the roof, and wood was crackling in the stove. Old Man Haley, mindful of his guest's dignities and claims upon himself, set about the preparation of a goodly meal, part drawn from his own garden, part from the packages he had carried back from Pine Flat. He was engrossed in it, when, through the sizzling of frying grease, he heard the sound of footsteps and the doorway was darkened by Garland's bulk. In his hand he held a paper, and even the age-dimmed eyes of the old man could see the pallid agitation of his face.

"My daughter!" he cried, shaking the paper at Haley. "She's sick in Francisco—I seen it here! I got to go!"

There was no arguing with him, and Old Man Haley knew it. He helped to the full extent of his capacity, set food before the man, and urged him to eat, dissuaded him from a move till after nightfall, and provided him with money taken from a hiding-place behind the stove.

Then together they worked out his route to the coast. The first stage would be from there to the Dormer Ranch where he had friends. They'd victual him and give him clothes, for even Garland, reckless with anxiety, did not dare show himself in the open as he now was, a figure to catch the attention of the most unsuspicious. He would have to keep to the woods and the trails till he got to Dormer's, and it would be a long hike—all that night and part of the next day. They would give him a mount and he could strike across country and tap the railroad at some point below Sacramento, making San Francisco that night.

The dark had settled, clearly deep, when he left. There were stars in the sky, only a few, very large and far apart, and by their light he could see the road between the black embankment of shrubs. It was extremely still as he stole down from the shack, Old Man Haley watching from the doorway. It continued very still as he struck into his stride, no sound coming from the detailless darkness. Its quiet suggested that same tense expectancy, that breathless waiting, he had noticed under the big trees.

CHAPTER XXVIII

CHRYSTIE SEES THE DAWN

NO SHADOW OF IMPENDING DISASTER fell across Mayer's path. On the Monday morning he rose feeling more confident, lighter in heart, than he had done since he met Burrage. It had been a relief to put an end to the Sacramento business; Chrystie had been amenable to his suggestion; the weather was fine; his affairs were moving smoothly to their climax. As he dressed he expanded his chest with calisthenic exercises and even warbled a little French song.

He was out by ten—an early hour for him—and he fared along the street pleasantly aware of the exhilarating sunshine, the blueness of the bay, the tang of salty freshness in the air. The hours till lunch were to be spent in completing the arrangements for the flight. At the railway office he bought the two passage tickets to Reno, his own section and Chrystie's stateroom, and even the amount of money he had to disburse did not diminish his sense of a prospering good fortune.

From there he went to the office of the man who owed him the gambling debt and encountered a check. The gentleman had gone to the country on Friday and would not be back till Wednesday morning at ten. A politely positive clerk assured him no letter or message had been left for Mr. Mayer, and a telegram received that morning had shown his employer to be far afield on the Macleod River.

Mayer left the office with a set, yellowish face. The disappointment would have irritated him at any time; now coming unexpected on his eased assurance it enraged him. For an hour he paced the streets trying to decide what to do. Of course he could go and leave the money, write a letter to have it sent after him. But he doubted whether his creditor would do it, and he needed every cent he could

get. His plan of conquest of Chrystie included a luxurious background, a wealth of costly detail. He did not see himself winning
her to complete subjugation without a plentiful spending fund. He
had told her they would go North from Reno and travel eastward by
the Canadian Pacific, stopping at points of interest along the road.
He imagined his courtship progressing in grandiose suites of rooms
wherein were served delicate meals, his generous largesse to obse-
quious hirelings adding to her dazzled approval. He had to have that
money; he couldn't go without it; he had set it aside to deck with
fitting ceremonial the conquering bridal tour.

He stopped at a telegraph office and wrote her a note telling her
to meet him that afternoon at three in the old place opposite the
Greek Church. This he sent by messenger and then he pondered a
rearrangement of his plans. He would only have to shift their departure on a few hours—say till Wednesday noon. He had heard at the
railway office there was a slow local for Reno at midday. They could
take this, and though it was a day train there would be little chance
of their being noticed, as the denizens of Chrystie's world and his
own always traveled by the faster Overland Flyer.

As he saw her approaching across the plaza his uneasy eye discerned from afar the fact that she was perturbed. Her face was anxious, her long swinging step even more rapid than usual. And, "Oh,
Boyé!" she grasped as they met and their hands clasped. "Has anything happened?"

It was not a propitious frame of mind, and he drew one of her
hands through his arm, pressing the fingers against his side as they
walked toward the familiar bench. There gently, very gently, he acquainted her with the version of the situation he had rehearsed: a
business matter—she wouldn't understand—but something of a
good deal of importance had unfortunately been postponed from
that afternoon till Wednesday morning. It was extremely annoying—in fact, maddening, but he didn't see how it was to be avoided.
She looked horrified.

"Then what are we to do—put it off?"

"Yes, until Wednesday at noon. There's a slow train we can get.
There's no use waiting till evening."

She turned on him aghast.

"But the Barlows? What am I to do about them? I've told Lorry I was going there on Tuesday."

"Darling girl, that's very simple. You've had a letter to say they don't want you till Wednesday."

"But, Boyé," she sat erect, staring distressfully at him, "I've told Lorry the party was on Tuesday night. That's what they've asked me for. Now how can I say they don't want me?"

He bit his lip to keep down his anger. Why had he allowed her to do *anything*—why hadn't he written it all down in words of one syllable?

"We'll have to think of some reason for a change in their plans. Why couldn't they have postponed the party?"

"Even if they did they wouldn't postpone *me*. I go there often, they're old friends, it doesn't matter when I come."

Her voice had a quavering note, new to him, and extremely alarming.

"Dearest, don't get worked up over it," he said tenderly.

"Worked up!" she exclaimed. "Wouldn't any girl be worked up? It's *awful* for a person in my position to elope. It's all very well for you who just go and come as you please, but for me—I believe if I was in prison I could get out easier."

He caught her hand and pressed it between his own.

"Of course, it's hard for you. No one knows that better than I, and that you should do it makes me love you more—if that's possible." He raised the hand to his lips, kissed it softly and dropped it. "I know how you can manage—it's as easy as possible. Say you have a headache, a splitting headache, and can't take the railway trip, but rather than disappoint them you'll go down the next day."

She drew her hand out of his, and said in a stubborn voice:

"No. I don't want to."

"Why? Now why, darling? What's wrong about that?"

"I won't tell any more lies to Lorry."

He looked at her, and saw her flushed, mutinous, tears standing in her eyes.

"But, dearest—"

She cut him off, her voice suddenly breaking:

"I can't do it. I didn't know it was going to be so dreadful. But I can't look at Lorry and tell her any more lies. I *wont*. It makes me sick. It's asking too much, Boyé. There's something hateful about it."

Her underlip quivered, drew in like a child's. With a shaking hand she began fumbling about her belt for her handkerchief.

"Sometimes I feel as if I was doing wrong," she faltered. "I love you, I've told you so—but—but—Lorry's not like anybody else—anyway to me. And to keep on telling her what isn't true makes me feel—like—like—a *yellow dog!*"

The last words came on a breaking sob, and the handkerchief went up to her face. Mayer was frightened. A quick glance round the plaza showed him no one was in sight, and he threw him arm about her and drew the weeping head down to his shoulder. Though the green paradise plume was in the way and his fear of passersby acute, he was still sufficiently master of himself to soothe with words of beguiling sweetness.

While he did it, his free hand holding the paradise plume out of his face, his eye nervously ranging the prospect, his mind ran over ways to meet the difficulty. By the time Chrystie had conquered her tears, and, with a creaking of tight-drawn silks, was sitting upright again, he had hit on a solution and was ready to broach it.

"Well, then, we'll rule out any more lies as you call them. You won't have to say another word to Lorry. We can go on just as we'd planned."

"How?" she asked, in a stopped-up voice, dabbing at her eyes with the handkerchief.

"You can leave on Tuesday afternoon at the same time and go to a hotel."

"A hotel!" She stopped dabbing, extremely surprised, as if he had suggested going to something she had never heard of before.

"Yes, not one of the big ones; a quiet place where you're not liable to run into anyone who may recognize you. I know of the very thing, not long opened, in the Mission. You leave for the train as you intended, but instead of going to the ferry, you go there. I'll take the rooms for you. All you'll have to do will be to write your name in the book—say, Miss Brown—and go up to your apartment. Order your dinner up there and your breakfast the next morning. I'll have a cab sent round for you at half-past eleven that'll take you straight to the ferry, and I'll send your tickets and trunk check to your rooms before that. There'll be nothing for you to do but cross on the boat and go into your stateroom on the train."

This was all very smooth and clear. It was proof of Chrystie's unpractical trend of thought that her comment was an uneasy,

"A hotel in the Mission?"

"Yes, a new place, very quiet and decent. I heard of it from some people who are living there. I'll not come to see you, but I'll phone over in the evening and find out how you're getting on. And the next morning I'll be on the platform at Oakland, watching out for you."

"But you won't speak to me?"

"Not then. In the train we might meet—just accidentally run into one another. And you'll say, 'Why, there's Mr. Mayer! How odd. How d'ye do, Mr. Mayer.'" He bowed with a mincing imitation of Chrystie's best society manner. "'I didn't expect to see *you* here.'"

She laughed delightedly, nestling against his shoulder.

"Will that be all? Can I say any more?"

"Not much. It will be only a greeting as we pass each other: 'So glad to see you, Miss Alston. Going up to Reno for a short stay. See you in town soon again, I hope.' And then you to your stateroom and me in my section, both of us looking out of the window as if we were bored."

They both laughed, lovers again. He was as relieved as she was. After all it might turn out the better plan. He could keep his eye on her, watch for signs of distress or mutiny and be ready with the comforting word. He had to take some risk, and it was better to take that of being seen than that of leaving her a prey to her own disinte-grating musings. Chrystie thought it was a great deal better than the other way. She saw herself in the train, conscious of him, knowing he was there, and pretending not to care. She felt uplifted on the wings of romance, heard the air around her stirred by the beating of those rainbow pinions.

The thrill of it lasted until dinner, then began to die away. Her home and the familiar surroundings pressed upon her attention like live things insisting on recognition. The trivial talk round the table took on the poignancy of matters already in the past. The night before Fong, on his way back from Chinatown, had found a deserted kitten and brought it home announcing his intention to adopt it and call it George Washington. Lorry and Aunt Ellen made merry over it, but Chrystie couldn't. The kitten would grow from youth to maturity, and she not be there to see. It took its place in her mind as something belonging to a vanished phase, having the cherished value of a memory.

Finally, Lorry noticed her silence, and wanted to know if anything was the matter. She was pale and had hardly eaten a bite. Aunt Ellen arraigned the Spring as a malign influence, and suggested quinine. Chrystie snapped at her, and said she wouldn't take quinine if she was dying. Thus warned away, Lorry and Aunt Ellen left her alone and made Summer plans together. Lake Tahoe for July and August was taking shape in Lorry's mind. July and August! Where would *she* be? Boyé had said something about Europe, and at the time it had seemed to her the *ultima Thule* of her dreams. Now it looked as far away as the moon and as inhospitable.

The inner excitement of the next day carried her over qualms and yearnings—the beating of the rainbow pinions was again in her ears.

In the morning she went to the bank and drew five hundred dollars. She must have some money of her own, and when she reached New York she would want clothes. It was unfortunate that while she was making holes in her trunk to pack it, Lorry should have come in and seen more than half of it stacked on the bureau. That necessitated more lies, and Chrystie told them with desperation. It was to pay people, of course, milliners and dressmakers—she owed a lot, and as she was passing the bank she'd drawn it in a lump.

Lorry was disapproving—her sister's carelessness about money always shocked her—and offered to take charge of it till Chrystie came back. There had to be another crop of lies, and Chrystie's face was beaded with perspiration, her voice shaking, as she bent over her trunk. She'd lock it in her desk, it would be all right—and please go away and don't bother—the expressman might be here any minute now.

She had a hope that Lorry would go out in the afternoon, and she could get away unobserved, but the faithful sister persisted in staying to see her off. That was dreadful. Bag in hand, a lace veil—to be lowered later—pushed back across her hat, she had tried to get the good-by over in the hall, but Lorry had followed her out to the steps. There in the revealing daylight the elder sister's smiles had died away, and scrutinizing the face under the jaunty hat, she had said sharply:

"Is anything the matter, Chrystie? You know, you look quite ill. Are you sure you feel well?"

It brought up a crowding line of memories—Lorry concerned, vigilant, always watching over her with that anxious tenderness. A surge of emotion rose in the girl and she snatched her sister to her, kissed her with a sudden passion, then ran.

"Good-by, good-by," she called out as she flew down the steps to the waiting carriage.

Her eyes were blinded, and she was afraid to look back for fear Lorry might see the tears. She waved a hand, then crouched in the corner of the seat and spied out of the little rear window. She could see Lorry on the top step watching the carriage, her face grave, her brows low-drawn in a frown.

The thrill came back when she dismissed the cab at the door of the hotel. As she walked up the entrance hall it was as if she was walking into the first chapter of a novel—a novel of which she was the heroine. And as Boyé had said, it was all very easy—she was expected, everything was ready. A bellboy snatched her bag, and the elevator whisked her up to her rooms, suite 38, third floor rear.

They seemed to her very uninviting; a parlor with crimson plush furniture, smelling of varnish and opening into a bedroom. The blinds were down, and when the boy had left she went to the window and threw it up, letting light and air into the stuffy, unfriendly place. That was better and she leaned out, breathing in the balmy freshness, catching a whiff from gardens blooming bravely between the crowding walls.

She stayed there for some time, staring about, to the left where the bay shone blue beyond the roofs, to the right where on the flanks of the Mission hills she could see the city's distant outposts, white dottings of houses, and here and there the gleam of a tin roof touched by the low sun. The nearby prospect was not attractive—

what one might expect in the Mission. Only a narrow crevice separated the hotel wall from the next house, whose yard stretched below her, crossed with clothes lines, the plants and shrubs showing a pale green, elongated growth in their efforts to reach the sunlight. Her down-drooped glance ranged over it with disfavor, and she idly wondered what kind of people lived there. It had once been a sort of detached villa; she could trace the remains of walks and flower beds, and the shed in the back had a broken weather vane on the roof—it must have been a stable.

She leaned out on her folded arms till the flare of sunset blazed on the westward windows, then sank through a burning decline into grayness and the night. The fiery windows grew blank and chains of lamps marked the lines of the streets. Then she turned back to the room, dark behind her, yawning like a cavern. She lighted the lights and sat in a stiff-backed rocking-chair, the hard white radiance beating on her from a cluster of electric bulbs close against the ceiling as if they had been shot up there by an explosion. It was half-past six, but she did not feel at all hungry. She felt—with a smothered exclamation she jumped up, ran to the telephone and ordered her dinner.

At eight o'clock Mayer's voice on the phone brought back a slight, faint echo of the thrill. What he said was matter-of-fact and colorless—he had warned her that it would be—just if she was comfortable and everything Was all right. She tried to answer it with debonair brevity; show the right spirit, bold and undismayed, of the dauntless woman to the companion of her daring.

Then came the slow undrawing of the night, the noises of the house dying down, car bells and auto horns less frequent in the streets below. The bedroom was at the back of the building, with windows that looked across a paved court to the rear walls of houses. There were lights in many of them, glimpses of bright interiors, people chatting in friendly groups. The sight brought a stabbing memory of the drawing-room at home, and in the dark she undressed and slipped into bed.

But sleep would not come—her mind would not obey her; slipped and slid away from her direction like an animal racing for its goal. At home at this hour the door between her room and Lorry's would be open and they would be calling back and forth to one an-

other as they made ready for bed. They had done that as far back as
she could remember, back to the time when there had been a nurse
in her room and Lorry had worn her hair in braids. She lay still, almost breathless, her eyes fixed on the yellow oblong of the transom,
recalling Lorry in those days, in stiff white skirts and a wide silk sash,
very grave, a little woman even then. She groaned and turned over in
the bed, digging her head into the pillow and closing her eyes.

After an hour or two she rose and put on her wrapper and slippers. The turmoil within her was so intense that she could not keep
still, and prowled, a tall, swathed form, from one room to the other.
It seemed then that there never had been a thrill—nothing but this
repulsion, this repudiation, nothing but a desire to be back where she
belonged. She fought it, less for love of Mayer than for shame at her
own backsliding. She saw herself a coward, lacking the courage to take
her life boldly, renouncing the man who had her promise. That held
her closer to her resolve than any other consideration; her troth was
plighted. Could she now—the wedding ring almost on her finger—
turn and run crying for home like a child frightened of the dark?

But she didn't want to, she didn't want to! She seemed to see
Mayer with a new clearness; glimpsed, to her own dread, his compelling power. He was her master, someone she feared, someone who
could make her at one moment feel proud and glad, and at another
small and trivial and apologetic. A majestic figure, a woman built
on the grand plan, poor Chrystie paced through the silent rooms,
weeping like a lost baby.

When the dawn began to grow pale she went to the bedroom
window and pulled up the blinds. Like a place of dreams the city
slowly grew into solidity through the spectral light. It was as gray as
her mood, all color subdued, walls and roofs and chimneys an even
monochrome, above them in the sky an increasing, thin, white luster.
The air stole in chill as the prospect and from the street beyond rose
the sound of a footfall, enormously distinct, echoing prodigiously,
as if it was the only footfall left in the world and the sound of the
others—refused individual existence—had concentrated in that one
to give it volume.

Chrystie drew up a chair and sat down. There with swollen eyes
and leaden heart she waited for the day.

CHAPTER XXIX

LORRY SEES THE DAWN

C HRYSTIE'S MANNER ON HER departure had disturbed Lorry. As she dressed for the opera that night she pondered on it, and back from it to the change she had noticed in the girl of late. She hadn't been like the old, easy-going Chrystie; her indolent evenness of mood had given place to a mercurial flightiness, her gay good-humor been broken by flashes of temper and morose silences.

Rustling into her new white dress Lorry reproached herself. She should have paid more attention to it. If Chrystie wasn't well or something was troubling her she should have found out what it was. She had been negligent, engrossed in her own affairs—thinking of a man, dreaming like a lovesick girl. That admission made her blush, and seeing her face in the mirror, the cheeks pink-tinted, the eyes darkly glowing, she could not refrain from looking at it. She was not so bad, dressed up that way with a diamond spray in her hair, and her shoulders white above the crystal trimming of her bodice. And so—just for a moment—she again forgot Chrystie, wondering, as she eyed the comely reflection, if Mark would be at the opera.

But when she was finished and had called in Aunt Ellen to look her over, the discomforting sense of duties shirked came back. As she slowly turned under Aunt Ellen's inspecting gaze and drooped her shoulders for the blue velvet cloak that the old lady held out, her thoughts were full of self-accusal. On the stairway they took the form of a solemn vow to pledge herself anew to the accustomed watchful care. In the cab they crystallized into a definite resolution: as soon as Chrystie came back from the Barlows' she would have an old-time, intimate talk with her and find out if anything really was the matter with the child.

214

At the opera it was so exciting and so wonderful that everything else was wiped out of her mind. In the front of the box she sat—its sole ornament—against a background of Mrs. Kirkham's contemporaries, withered and sere in contrast with her lily-pure freshness. In the entr'actes the hostess recalled the opera house in its heyday when the Bonanza Kings occupied their boxes with the Bonanza Queens beside them, when everyone was rich, and all the women wore diamonds. The old ladies cackled over their memories, their heads together, forgetful of "Minnie's girl," who swept the house with her lorgnon searching for a familiar face.

Mrs. Kirkham was going to make a night of it, and afterward took her party to Zinkand's for supper. Here, too, it was very exciting, too much claiming one's attention for private worries to intrude. The opera crowd came thronging in, women in beautiful clothes, men one's father had known, youths who had come to one's house. Some of the ladies who had been Minnie Alston's friends stopped to have a word with Lorry and then swept on making murmurous comment to their escorts—the Alston girls were coming out of their shells, beginning at last to take their places; it was a pity they went about with fossils of the Stone Age like Mrs. Kirkham, but they had a queer, old-fashioned streak in them—ah, there's a vacant table!

It was past midnight when Mrs. Kirkham dropped Lorry at her door and rolled off with the rest of her cargo. The joy of the evening was still with the girl as she entered the hall. She stood there for a moment, pulling off her gloves and looking about with the prudent eye of a proprietor. In its roving her glance fell on a letter in the card tray. It was addressed to her and had evidently come after she had left. Standing under the single gas jet that was all Fong's thrifty spirit would permit, she opened it.

Anonymous and written in an unknown hand it struck upon her receptive mood with a staggering shock.

It came, a bolt from the blue, but a bolt that fell precise on a spot ready to accept it. It was like a sign following her troubled premonitions, an answer to her anxious queries. If its author had known just how Miss Alston's thoughts had been engaged, she could not have aimed her missile better or timed it more accurately.

During the first moment she saw nothing but the central fact—the concealed love affair of which the writer thought she was cognizant. Her mind accepted that instantaneously, corroborating memories coming quick to her call. They flashed across her mental vision, vivid and detached like slides in a magic lantern—glimpses of Chrystie in her unfamiliar brooding and her flushed elation, and the walks, the long walks, from which she returned withdrawn and curiously silent—the silence of enraptured retrospect.

Then quick, leaping upon her, came the recollection of Chrystie's departure that afternoon—the clinging embrace, the rush down the steps, the absence of her face at the carriage window. Lorry gave a moan and her hands rose, clutched against her heart. It was proof of how her lonely life had molded her that in this moment of piercing alarm, she thought of no help, of no outside assistance to which she could appeal. She had always been the leader, acted on her own initiative, and the will to do so now held her taut, sending her mind forces out, clutching and groping for her course. It came in a low-breathed whisper of, "The Barlows," and she ran to the telephone, an old-fashioned wall instrument behind the stairs. As she flew toward it another magic lantern picture flashed into being—Chrystie boring down into her trunk and the pile of money on the bureau. That forced a sound out of her—a sharp, groaned note—as if expelled from her body by the impact of a blow.

She tried to give the Barlows' number clearly and quietly and found her voice broken by gasping breaths. There was a period of agonized waiting, then a drowsy "central" saying she couldn't raise the number, and Lorry trying to be calm, trying to be reasonable—it *must* be raised, it was important, they were asleep that was all. *Ring—ring—*ring till someone answers.

It seemed hours before Roy Barlow's voice, sleepy and cross, came growling along the wire:

"What the devil's the matter? Who is it?"

Then her answer and her question: Was Chrystie there?

That smoothed out the crossness and woke him up. He became suddenly alert:

"Chrystie? Here—with us?"

"Yes—staying over till Friday. Went down this afternoon."

"No. *She's* not here. What makes you think she is?"

She did not know what to say; the instinct to protect her sister was part of her being, strong in a moral menace as a physical. She fumbled out an explanation—she'd been out of town and in her absence Chrystie had gone to the country without leaving word where. It was all right of course, she was a fool to bother about it, but she couldn't rest till she knew where the girl had gone. It was probably either to the Spencers or the Joneses; they'd been teasing her to visit them all winter. Roy, now wide-awake, showed a tendency to ask questions, but she cut him off, swamped his curiosity in apologies and good-bys and hung up the receiver.

She was almost certain now, and again she stood pressing down her terrors, urging her faculties to intelligent action. She did not let them slip from her guidance; held them close as dogs to the trail. A moment of rigid immobility and she had whirled back to the telephone and called up a near-by livery stable. This answered promptly and she ordered a cab sent round at once.

While she waited she tried to keep steady and think clearly. Prominent in her mind was the necessity not to move rashly, not to do anything that would react on Chrystie. There might yet be a mistake—a blessed, unforseen mistake. She clung to the idea as those about a deathbed cling to the hope that a miracle may supervene and save their loved one. There *was* a possibility that Chrystie had gone on some mysterious adventure of her own, was playing a trick, was doing anything but eloping with a man that no one had ever thought she cared for. The only way to find out whether Mayer had any part in her disappearance was to go directly to him.

She sat stiffly in the cab holding her hands tight-clenched to control their trembling. Her whole being seemed to tremble like a substance strained to the point of a perpetual vibration. She was not conscious of it; was only conscious of her will stretching out like a tangible thing, grasping at a fleeing Chrystie and dragging her back. And under that lay a substratum of anguish—that it was *her* fault, *her* fault. The wheels repeated the words in their rhythmic rotation; the horse's hoofs hammered them out on the pavement.

The night clerk at the Argonaut Hotel, drowsing behind his desk, sat up with a start when he saw her. Ladies in such gala array were rare at The Argonaut at any hour, much more so at long past midnight. That this one was agitated even the sleepy clerk could see. Her face was nearly as white as the dress showing between the loosened fronts of her cloak. The voice in which she asked if Mr. Mayer was there was a husky undertone. The clerk, scrambling to his feet, said yes, as far as he knew Mr. Mayer was in his room. He had come in about ten and hadn't gone out since.

A change took place in her expression; the strained look relaxed and the white neck, showing between the cloak edges, lifted with a caught breath.

"Where is he?" she said, and before the man could answer had turned and swept toward the stairs.

"Second floor—two doors from the stairs on your right—No. 8," he called, and watched her as she ran, her skirts lifted, the rich cloak drooping about her form as it slanted forward in the rush of her ascent.

Mayer was still up and sitting at his desk. Everything was progressing satisfactorily. An excellent dinner had exerted its comforting influence and the telephone message to Chrystie had shown her to be reassuringly uncomplaining and tranquil. Elated by a heady sense of approaching success he had packed his trunk in the bedroom and then come back to the parlor and added up his resources and coming expenses. He had calculated what these would be with businesslike thoroughness, his mind, under the process of addition and subtraction, cogitating on a distribution of funds that would at once husband them and yield him the means of impressing his bride. Through the word "jewelry" he had drawn his pen, substituting "candy and flowers," and was leaning back in gratified contemplation when a knock fell on the door. He rose to his feet, frightened, for the first moment inclined to make no answer. Then knowing that the light through the transom would betray his presence, he called, "Come in."

Lorry Alston, in evening dress, pale-faced and alone, entered.

His surprise and alarm were overwhelming. With the pen still in his hand he stood speechless, staring at her, and had she faced him then and there with her knowledge of the facts, admission might have dropped, in scared amaze, from his lips.

But the sight of him, peacefully employed in his own apartment, when she had suspected him of being somewhere else, nefariously engaged in running away with her sister, had so relieved her, that, in that first moment of encounter, she was silent. Bewilderment, verging toward apology, kept her on the threshold. Then the memory of the letter sent her over it, brought back the realization that even if he was here by himself he must know something of Chrystie's whereabouts.

Closing the door behind her she said:

"Mr. Mayer, I'm looking for my sister."

If that told him that she did not know where Chrystie was, it also told that she connected him with the girl's absence. He controlled his alarm and drew his shaken faculties into order.

"Looking for your sister!" he repeated. "Looking for her *here?*"

"Yes." She advanced a step, her eyes sternly fixed on him. He did not like the look, there was question and accusation in it, but he was able to inject a dignified surprise into his answer.

"I don't understand you, Miss Alston. Why should you come to *me* at this hour to find your sister?"

He did it well, wounded pride, hostility under unjust suspicion, strong in his voice.

"Chrystie's gone," she answered. "She told me she was going to friends, and I find she isn't there. She deceived me and I had reason—I heard something tonight that made me think—" She stopped. It was horrible to state to this man, now frankly abhorred, what she suspected. There was a slight pause while he waited with an air of cold forbearance.

"Well," he said at length, "would it be too much trouble to tell me what you think?"

She had to say it:

"That she had gone to you."

"To *me?*" He was incredulous, astounded.

"Yes. Had run away with you."

"What reason had you for thinking such a thing?"

She made a step forward, ignoring the question.

"She isn't here—I can see that—but where is she?"

"How should I know?"

"Because you must know something about her, because you *do* know. Chrystie of herself wouldn't tell me lies; someone's made her do it, *you've* made her do it."

"Really, Miss Alston—"

But she wouldn't give him time to finish.

"Mr. Mayer, you've got to tell me where she is. I won't leave here till you do."

He had always felt and disliked a quality of cool reasonableness in this girl. Now he saw a fighting courage, a thing he had never guessed under that gentle exterior, and he liked it even less. Had he followed his inclination he would have treated her with the rough brutality he had awarded Pancha, but he had to keep his balance and discover how much she knew.

"Miss Alston, we're at cross-purposes. We'd come to a better understanding if I knew what you're talking about. You spoke of finding out something tonight. If you'll tell me what it is I'll be able to answer you more intelligently."

She thrust her hand into her belt, drew out a folded paper and handed it to him.

"*That.* I found it when I came back from the opera."

He recognized the writing at once, and before he was halfway through his rage against Pancha was boiling. When he had finished he could not trust his voice, and staring at the paper, he heard her say:

"I've known for some time Chrystie was troubled and not herself, and this afternoon when I saw her go I *knew* something was wrong. She looked ill; she could hardly speak to me. And then *that* came, and I telephoned to the Barlows'—the place she was going. She wasn't there, they'd never asked her, never expected her. She's gone somewhere—disappeared." She raised her voice, hard, threatening, her face angrily accusing, "Where is she, Mr. Mayer? Where is she?"

He knew it all now, and his knowledge made him master.

"Miss Alston, I'm very sorry about this—"

"Oh. don't talk that way!" she cried, pointing at the letter. "What does *that* mean?"

"I think I can explain. You've given yourself a lot of unnecessary trouble and taken this thing," he scornfully dropped the letter on the table, "altogether too seriously. Sit down and let me straighten it out."

He pointed to the rocker, but she did not move, keeping her eyes with their fierce steadiness on his face.

"How *could* I take it too seriously?" she said.

"Why"—he smiled in good-natured derision—"what is it? An anonymous letter, evidently by the wording and the writing the work of an uneducated person. It's perfectly true that I've seen your sister several times on the streets, and once I *did* happen upon her when she was taking a walk in the plaza by the Greek Church. But there's nothing unusual about that—I've met and talked with many other ladies in the same way. The writer of that rubbish evidently saw us in the plaza and decided—to use his own language—that he'd have some fun with us, or rather with me. The whole thing—the expression, the tone—indicates a vulgar, malicious mind. Don't give it another thought, it's unworthy of your consideration."

He saw he had made an impression. Her eyes left him and she stood gazing fixedly into space, evidently pondering his explanation. In a pleasantly persuasive tone he added:

"You know that I've not been a constant visitor at your house. You've seen my attitude to your sister."

She made no reply to that, muttering low as if to herself:

"Why should anyone write such a letter without a reason?"

"Ah, my dear lady, why are there mischief makers in the world? I'm awfully sorry; I feel responsible, for the person who'd do such a thing is more likely to be known by me than by you. It's probably some servant I've forgotten to tip or by accident given a plugged quarter."

There was a pause, then she turned to him and said:

"But where's Chrystie?"

He came closer, comforting, very friendly:

"Since you ask me I'd set this down as a prank. She's full of high spirits—only a child yet. She's gone somewhere, to some friend's house, is playing a joke on you. Isn't that possible?"

"Yes, possible." She had already found this straw herself, but grasped it anew, pushed forward by him.

He went on, his words sounding the note of masculine reason and reassurance.

"You'll probably hear from her tomorrow, and you'll laugh together over your fears of tonight. But if you take my advice, don't say anything outside, don't tell anyone. You're liable to set the gossips talking, and you never know when they'll stop. They might make it very unpleasant for you both. Miss Chrystie doesn't want her schoolgirl tricks magnified into scandals."

She nodded, brows drawn low, her teeth set on her underlip. If he had convinced her of his innocence he saw he had not killed her anxieties.

"Is there any way I can help you?" he hazarded.

She shook her head. She had the appearance of having suddenly become oblivious to him—not finding him a culprit, she had brushed him aside as negligible.

"Then you'll go home and give up troubling about it?"

"I'll go home," she said, and with a deep sigh seemed to come back to the moment and his presence. Moving to the table she picked up the letter. Now that he was at ease, her face in its harassed care touched a vulnerable spot. He was sorry for her.

"Don't take it so to heart, Miss Alston. I'm convinced it's going to turn out all right."

She gave him a sharp, startled look.

"Of course it is. If I thought it wasn't would I be standing here doing nothing?"

She walked to the door, the small punctilio of good-bys ignored as she had ignored all thought of strangeness in being in that place at that hour.

"I wish I could do something to ease your mind," he said, watching her receding back.

"You can't," she answered and opened the door.

"Have you a trap—something to take you home?"

She passed through the doorway, throwing over her shoulder:

"Yes, I've a cab—it's been waiting."

In spite of his success he had, for a moment, a crestfallen sense of feeling small and contemptible. He watched her walk down the hall and then went to the window and saw her emerge from the street door, and enter the cab waiting at the curb.

Alone, faced by this new complication, the sting of her disparaging indifference was forgotten. There was no sleep for him that night, and lighting a cigarette he paced the room. He would have to

let the gambling debt go; there could be no delay now. By the afternoon of the next day Lorry would be in a state where one could not
tell what she might do. He would have to leave on the morning train,
call up Chrystie at seven, go out and change the tickets, and meet
her at Oakland. In the sudden concentrating of perils, the elopement
was gradually losing its surreptitious character and becoming an affair openly conducted under the public eye. But there was no other
course. Even if they were seen on the train they would reach Reno
without interference, and once there he would find a clergyman and
have the marriage ceremony performed at once. After that it didn't
matter—he trusted in his power over Chrystie. In the back of his
mind rose a discomforting thought of an eventual "squaring things"
with Lorry, but he pushed it aside. Future difficulties had no place in
the present and its desperate urgencies. The thought of Pancha also
intruded, and on that he hung, for a moment, his face evil with a
thwarted rage, his hands instinctively bent into talons. Had he dared
he would like to have gone to her and—but he pushed that aside too
and went back to his plans and his pacings.

Lorry went home convinced of Mayer's ignorance. Finding
him at the hotel had done half, his arguments and manner the rest.
And during the drive back his explanation of Chrystie's disappearance had retained a consoling plausibility. She held to it fiercely,
conned it over, tried to force herself to see the girl impishly bent on
a foolish practical joke.

But when she was in her own room, the blank silence of the
house about her, it fell from her and left her defenseless against
growing fears. It was impossible to believe it—utterly foreign to
Chrystie's temperament. She racked her memory for occasions in
the past when her sister had indulged in such cruel teasing and
not one came to her mind. No—she wouldn't have done it, she
couldn't—something more than a joke had made Chrystie lie to
her. A sumptuous figure in her glistening dress, she moved about,
rose and sat, jerked back the curtains, picked up and dropped the
silver ornaments on the bureau. Her lips were dry, her heart contracted with a sickening dread; never in all the calls made upon her
had there been anything like this; finding her without resources,
reducing her to an anguished helplessness.

If in the morning there was no word from Chrystie she would have to do something and she could not think what this should be. Mayer had not needed to warn her against giving her sister up to the tongue of gossip. The most guileless of girls living in San Francisco would learn that lesson early. But what could she do? To whom could she go for help and advice? She thought of her mother's friends, the guardians of the estate, and repudiated them with a smothered sound of scorn. They wouldn't care; would let it get into the papers; would probably suggest the police. And would she not herself—if Chrystie did not come back or write—have to go to the police?

That brought her to a standstill, and with both hands she pressed on her forehead pushing back her hair, sending tormented looks about her. If there was only someone who would understand, someone she could trust, someone—she dropped her hands, her eyes widening, fixed and startled, as a name rose to her lips and fell whispered on the stillness. It came without search or expectation, seemed impelled from her by her inward stress, found utterance before she knew she had thought of him. A deep breath heaved her chest, her head drooped backward, her eyelids closing in a relief as intense, as ineffably comforting, as the cessation of an unbearable pain.

She stood rigid, the light falling bright on her upturned face, still as a marble mask. For a moment she felt bodiless, her containing shell dissolved, nothing left of her but her longing for him. Like an audible cry or the grasp of her hand drawing him to her, it went out from her, imperious, an appeal and a summons. Again she whispered his name; but she heard it only as the repetition of a solace and a solution, was not aware of forces tapped in lower wells of being.

After that she felt curiously calmed, her wild restlessness gone, her nightmare terrors assuaged. If she did not hear from Chrystie by midday she would call him up at his office and ask him to come to her. She seemed to have found in the thought of him not only a staff to uphold, but wisdom to guide.

She drew the curtains and saw the first thin glimmering of dawn, pearl-faint in the sky, pearl-pale on the garden. The crystal trimmings of her bodice gave a responsive gleam, and looking down she was aware of her gala array. She slipped out of it, put on a morning dress, and denuded her hair of its shining ornament. It seemed long ago, in another life, that she had sat in Mrs. Kirkham's box, rejoicing in her costly trappings, glad to be admired.

Then she pulled a chair to the window and sat there waiting for the light to come. It crept ghostly over the garden, trees and plants taking form, the walks and lawns, a vagueness of dark patches and lighter windings, emerging in gradual definiteness. The sky above the next house grew a lucid gray, then a luminous mother-of-pearl. She could see the glistening of dew, its beaded hoar upon cobwebs and grassy borders. There was no footstep here to disturb the silence; the dawn stole into being in a deep and breathless quietude.

CHAPTER XXX

MARK SEES THE DAWN

THAT SAME TUESDAY AFTERNOON Mark sat in the doorway of the cowshed looking at the road.

It was the first period of rest and ease he had had since his arrival. He had found the household disorganized, his father hovering, frantic, round the sick bed, and Sadie distractedly distributing her energies between her mother's room and the kitchen. It was he who had driven over to Stockton and brought back a nurse, insisted on the doctor staying in the house and made him a shakedown in the parlor. When things began to look better he had turned his hand to the farm work and labored through the week's accumulation, while the old man sat beside his wife's pillow, his chin sunk on his breast.

Today the tension had relaxed, for the doctor said Mother was going to pull through. An hour ago he had packed his kit and driven off to his own house up the valley, not to be back till tomorrow. It was very peaceful in the yard, the warm, sleepy air full of the droning of insect life which ran like a thin accompaniment under a low crooning of song from the kitchen where Sadie was straightening up. On the front porch, the farmer, his feet on the railing, his hat on his nose, was sunk in the depths of a recuperating sleep.

Astride the milking stool Mark looked dreamily at the familiar prospect, the black carpet of shade under the live oak, the bright bits of sky between its boughs, beyond the brilliant vividness of the landscape. This was crossed by the tall trunks of the eucalyptus trees, all ragged bark and pendulous foliage, the road striped with their shadows. He looked down its length, then back along the line of the picket fence, his glance slowly traveling and finally halting at a place just opposite.

Here his imagination suddenly restored a picture from the past—the tramp asking for water. His senses, dormant and unobserving, permitted the memory to attain a lifelike accuracy and the figure was presented to his inward eye with photographic clearness. Very still in the interest of this unprovoked recollection, he saw again the haggard face with its lowering expression, and remembered Chrystie's question about recognizing the man.

He felt now that he could, even in other clothes and a different setting. The eyes were unmistakable. He recalled them distinctly—a very clear gray as if they might have had a thin crystal glaze like a watch face. The lids were long and heavy, the look sliding out from under them coldly sullen.

As he pictured them—looking surlily into his—a conviction rose upon him that he had seen them since then, somewhere recently. They were not as morose as they had been that first time, had some vague association with smiles and pleasantness. He was puzzled, for he could only seem to get them without surroundings, without even a face, detached from all setting like a cat's eyes gleaming from the dark. Unable to link them to anything definite he concluded he had dreamed of them. But the explanation was not entirely satisfactory; he was left with a tormenting sense of their importance, that they were connected with something that he ought to remember.

He shook himself and rose from the stool—no good wasting time chasing such elusive fancies. The tramp had brought to his mind the money found in the tules and he decided to walk up the road and try to locate the spot described to him that morning by Sadie.

On the hillock, where eight months earlier Mayer had sat and cursed the marshes, he came to a stand, his glance ranging over the long, green floor. By Sadie's directions he set the place about midway between where he stood and the white square of the Ariel Club house. If it *was* the tramp he had gone across from there, which would argue a knowledge of the complicated system of paths and planks. It was improbable—from his childhood he could remember the hoboes footing it doggedly round the head of the tules.

His thoughts were broken into by a voice hailing him, a fresh, reed-sweet pipe.

"Hello, Mark—what you doin' there?"

It was Tito Murano returning from the Swede man's ranch up the trail, with a basket of eggs for his mother. Tito had become something of a hero in the neighborhood. In the preceding autumn he had developed typhoid, nearly died, and been sent to a relative in the higher land of the foothill fruit farms. From there he had only recently returned with the *réclame* of one who has adventured far and seen strange lands. Barelegged, his few rags flapping round his thin brown body, he charged forward at a run, holding the egg basket out at arm's length. His face was wreathed in happy smiles, for the encounter filled him with delight. Mark was his idol and this was the first time he had seen him.

They sat side by side on the knoll and Tito told of his wanderings. At times he spit to show his growth in grace, and after studying the long sprawl of Mark's legs disposed his own in as close an imitation as their length would permit. It was when his story was over and the conversation showed a tendency to languish that Mark said:

"I was just looking out over there and trying to locate the place where the bandits had their cache."

Tito raised a grubby hand and pointed.

"Right away beyont where you see the water shinin'. It's a sort of island—I was out there after I come back but the hole was all washed away and filled up."

"*You* were out there? Do you know the way?"

Tito spit calmly, almost contemptuously.

"*Me?* I bin often—there ain't a trail I don't know. I could lead you straight acrost. I took a tramp wonct; anyways I would have took him if he'd let me."

"A tramp!" Mark straightened up. "When?"

The episode of the tramp had almost faded from Tito's mind. What still lingered was not the memory of his fear but the way he had been swindled. Now in company with one who always understood and never scolded, he was filled with a desire to tell it and gain a tardy sympathy. He screwed up his eyes in an effort to answer accurately.

"I guess it was last fall. Yes, it was, just before school commenced. I wouldn't 'a done it—Pop'd have licked me if he'd 'a known—but he promised me a quarter."

"Who promised you a quarter?"

"Him—the tramp. And I was doin' it, but he got awful mean, swore somethin' fierce and said I didn't know. And how was he to tell and us only halfway acrost?"

"You mean you only took him halfway?"

"It was all he'd let me," said Tito, on the defensive. "I tolt him it was all right, but he just stood up there cursin' me. And then he got to throwin' things, almost had me here"—he put his hand against his ear—"like he was plumb crazy. But I guess he wasn't, for he wouldn't give me the quarter."

"Did you leave him there?"

"Sure I did. I run, I was scairt. Pop and Mom'd always be tellin' me to have nothin' to do with tramps. And it was awful lonesome out there and him swearin' and firin' rocks."

Tito did not receive that immediate consolation he had looked for. His friend was silent; a side glance showed him studying the tules with meditative eyes. For a moment the little boy had a dreary feeling that his confidence was going to be rewarded by a reprimand, then Mark said:

"Do you remember what the man looked like?"

"Awful poor with long whiskers all sort 'er stragglin' round. He'd a straw hat and a basket and eyes on him like he was sleepy."

Again Mark made no response, and Tito, feeling that he had not grasped the full depths of the tragedy, piped up plaintively:

"I'd 'a stood the swearin' and I could 'a dodged the rocks if he'd given me the quarter. But I couldn't get it off him—not even a dime."

That had a good effect, much better than Tito's highest hopes had anticipated.

"Well, he treated you mean, old man. And, take it from me—don't you go showing the way to any more tramps. They're the kind to let alone. As for the quarter I guess that's due with interest. Here it is." And a half dollar was laid on Tito's knee.

At the first glance he could hardly believe it, then seeing it immovable, a gleaming disk of promise, his face flushed deep in the uprush of his joy. He took it, weighed it on his palm, wanted to study it, but instead slipped it mannishly into the pocket of his blouse. His education had not included a training in manners, so he said nothing, just straightened up and sent a slanting look into Mark's face. It was an eloquent look, beaming, jubilant, a shining thanks.

They walked back together, or rather Mark walked and Tito circled round him, curvetting in bridling ecstasy. Mrs. Murano's temper being historic, Mark took the egg basket, and Tito, all fears of accident removed, abandoned himself to the pure joys of the imagination. He became at once a horse and his rider, pranced, backed, took mincing sidesteps and long, spirited rushes; at one moment was all steed, mettlesome and wild; at the next all man, calling, gruff-voiced, in quelling authority.

Mark, the eggs safe, was thoughtful. So it must have been the tramp as he had suspected. But the eyes—he could not shake off that haunting fancy of a second encounter. All the way home his mind hovered round them, strained for a clearer vision, seemed at moments on the edge of illumination, then lost it all.

That night in his room under the eaves he did not sleep till late. The house sank early into the deep repose following emotional stress, the nurse's lamp brightening one window in its black bulk. Outside the night brooded, deep and calm, with whispers in the great oak's foliage, open field and wooded slope pale and dark under the light of stars. Mark, his hands clasped behind his head, looked at the blue space of the window and dreamed of Lorry. He saw her in various guises, a procession of Lorrys passing across the blue background. Then he saw her as she had been the last time and that Lorry had not passed with the rest of the procession. She had lingered, reluctant to follow the fleeting, unapproachable others, had seemed to draw nearer to him, almost with her hands out, almost with a shining question in her eyes. Holding that picture of her in his heart he finally fell asleep.

Some hours later he woke with the sound of her voice in his ears. She was calling him—"Mark, Mark," a clear, thin cry, imploring and urgent. He sat up answering, heard his own voice suddenly fill the silence loud and startling, "Lorry," and then again lower, "Lorry." For a moment he had no idea where he was, then the starlight through the open window showed him the familiar outlines, and, looking stupidly about, he repeated, dazed, certain he had heard her, "Lorry, where are you?"

The silence of the house, the large outer silence enfolding it, answered him.

He was fully awake now and rose. The reality of the cry in its tenuous, piercing importunity, grew as his mind cleared. He could not believe but that he had heard it, that she might not be somewhere near calling to him in distress. He opened the door and looked into the hall—not a sound. At the foot of the stairs the light from his mother's room fell across the darkness in a golden slant. He turned and went to the window. His awakening had been so startling, his sense of revelation so acute, that for the moment he had no consciousness of prohibiting conditions. When he looked out of the window he would have felt no surprise if he had seen Lorry below gazing up at him.

After that he stood for a space realizing the fact. He had had no dream, the voice had come to him from her, a summons from the depths of some dire necessity. He knew it as well as if he had heard her say so, as if she *had* been outside the window calling him to come. He knew she was beset, needed him, that her soul had cried to his and in its passionate urgency had broken through material limitations.

He struck a match and consulted his watch—a quarter to four. Then, as he dressed and threw some clothes into a bag, he thought over the quickest route to the city. A stage line to Stockton crossed the valley eight miles to the south. By making a rapid hike he could catch the down stage and be in San Francisco before midday. He scrawled a few lines to Sadie, stood the note up across the face of the clock, and, his shoes in his hand, stole down the stairs and out of the house.

The country slept under the hush that comes before the dawn. There was not a rustle in the roadside trees, a whisper in the grass. Farmhouse and mansion showed in forms of opaque black, muffled in black foliage and backed by a blue-black horizon. Above the heavens spread, vast and far removed, paved with stars and mottlings of star dust. The sparkling dome, pricked with white points and blotted with milky stains, diffused a high, aerial luster, palely clear above the land's dense darkness. Mark looked up at it, unaware of its splendors, mind and glance raised in an instinctive appeal to some remote source of strength in those illumined heights.

As his glance fell back to the road he suddenly knew where he had seen the eyes. There was no jar of recognition, no startled uncertainty. He saw them looking at him from the face of Boyé Mayer, standing in Lorry's drawing-room with his hands resting on the back of a chair.

He stopped dead, staring ahead. Lorry's summons, the tramp, the man in evening dress against the background of the rich room— all these drew to a single point. What their connection was he could not guess, was only aware of them as related, and, accepting that, forged forward at a swinging stride. The beat of his feet fell rhythmic on the dust; his breath came deep-drawn and even; his eyes pierced the dark ahead, fixed on landmarks to be passed, goals to be gained, stations to leave behind him in his race to the woman who had called.

Unnoted by him a pale edge of light stole along the east, throwing out the high, crumpled line of the Sierra. The landscape developed from nebulous shadows and enfoldings to hill slopes, tree domes, the clustered groupings of barns. A stir passed, frail and delicate, over the earth's face, a light tentative trembling in the leaves, a quiver through the grain. Birds made sleepy twitterings; the chink of running water came from hidden stream beds; plowed fields showed the striping of furrows on which the dew glistened in a silvery crust. The day was at hand.

CHAPTER XXXI

REVELATION

WHILE LORRY WAS STILL QUEENING IT in the front of Mrs. Kirkham's box, while Chrystie was tossing in her strange bed, while Boyé Mayer was packing his trunk, while Mark was thinking of Lorry in his room under the eaves, Garland, one of the actors in this drama now drawing to its climax, stood against the chain of a ferry boat bumping its way into the Market Street slip.

He was over it first, racing up the gangway and along the echoing passage to the street. People growled as he elbowed them, plowed a passage through their slow-moving ranks, and ran for the wheeling lights of the trolleys. He made a dash for one, leaped on its step, and holding to an upright, stood, breathing quickly, as the car clanged its way up the great thoroughfare. He had to change by the Call Building, and his heart was hammering on his ribs as he dropped off the second car at the corner of Pancha's street.

Up its dim perspective he could see the two ground glass globes at the Vallejo's steps. He wanted to run but did not dare—the habits of the hunted still held—and he walked as fast as he could, sending his glance ahead for her windows. When he saw light gleaming from them his head drooped in a spasm of relief. All the way down the fear that she might be in a hospital—a public place dangerous for him to visit—had tortured him.

Cushing, behind the desk, yawning over the evening paper, roused at the sight of him and showed a desire to talk. At the sentence that "Miss Lopez was gettin' along all right," the visitor moved off to the stairs. He again wanted to run but he felt Cushing's eyes on his back and made a sober ascent till the turn of the landing hid him; then he rushed. At her door he knocked and heard her voice, low and querulous:

"Who is it now?"

"The old man," he whispered, his mouth to the crack. It was opened by her and he had her in his arms.

Joy at the sight and feel of her, the knowledge that she was not as he had pictured in desperate case, made him speechless. He could only press her against him, hold her off and look into her face, his own working, broken words of love and pity coming from him. His unusual display of emotion affected her, deeply stirred on her own account, and she clung to him, weak tears running down her cheeks, caressing him with hands that said what her shaking lips could not utter.

He supported her to the sofa and laid her there, covering her, soothing her, his concern finding expression in low, crooning sounds such as women make over their sick babies. When she was quieted he drew the armchair up beside her, and, his hand stroking hers, asked about her illness. He had read in the paper that it was a nervous collapse caused by overwork, and he chided her gently.

"What did you keep on for when you were so tuckered out? Why didn't you let up on it sooner? You could 'a stood the expense, and if you didn't want to use your own money what's the matter with mine?"

"I didn't want to stop," she murmured. "Every day I kept thinking I'd be all right."

"Oh, hon, that don't show good sense. How can I keep up my lick if I can't trust you better? You've pretty near finished me. I come on it in a paper up there in the hills-God, I didn't know what struck me. It's tore me to pieces."

His look bore testimony to his words. He was old, seamed with lines, fallen away from his robust sturdiness. She suddenly seemed unable to bear all this weight of pitifulness—his, hers, the world's outside them. At first she had resolved to keep the real cause of her illness secret. But now his devastated look, his pathetic tenderness, shattered her. She was a child again, longing to creep into the arms that would have held her against all harm, droop on the rough breast where she had always found sympathy. As the truth had come out under Growder's kindness, the truth came again. But this time there were no reservations; the rich girl took her place in the story. Others might see in that a mitigating circumstance but not the man who valued her above all girls, rich or poor.

Garland listened closely, hardly once interrupting her. When she finished his rage broke and she was frightened. Years had passed since she had seen him aroused and now his lowering face, darkened with passion, his choked words, brought back memories of him raging tremendously in old dead battles with miner and cattleman.

"Pa, Pa," she cried, stretching her hands toward him, "what's the use—what can you do? It's finished and over; getting mad and cursing won't make it any better."

But he cursed, flinging the chair from him, rumbling out his wrath, beyond the bounds of reason.

"Don't talk so," she implored and slid off the sofa to her feet. "They'll hear you in the next room. I can't afford to let this get around."

For the first time in her knowledge of him he was deaf to the claims of her welfare.

"Who is this fancy gentleman?" he cried. "Where is he?"

"Oh, why did I tell you?" she wailed. "What got into me to tell you! I can't fight with you—I won't let you go to him. There's no use—it's all over, it's done, it's ended. *Can't* you see?"

He made no answer and she went to him, catching at his arm and shoulder, staring, desperately pleading, into his face.

"You talk like a fool," he said, pushing her away. "This is my job. Where is he?"

As she had said, she was unable to fight with him. Her enfeebled body was empty of all resistant force. Now, as she clung to him, she felt its sickly weakness, its drained energies. She wanted peace, the sofa again, the swaying walls to steady, the angry man to be her father, quiet in the armchair. She forgot her promise to Crowder, her pledged word, everything, but that there was a way to end the racking scene. Holding to the hand that thrust her aside she said softly:

"There's a punishment coming to him that's better than anything *you* can give."

His glance shifted to hers, arrested.

"What you mean?"

"He's done something worse than the way he's treated me—something the law can get him for."

"What?"

"Sit down quiet here and I'll tell you."

She pointed to the overturned chair and made a step toward the sofa. He remained motionless, watching her with somberly doubting eyes.

"It's true," she said; "every word. It comes from Charlie Crowder. When you hear it you'll see, and you'll see too that you'll only mix things up by butting in. They're getting their net ready for him, and they'll have him in it before the week's out."

This time the words had their effect. He picked up the chair and brought it to the sofa. She sat there erect, her legs curled up beside her, and told him the story of Boyé Mayer and the stolen money.

The light was behind him and against it she saw him as a formless shape, the high, rounded back of the chair projecting above his head. The silence with which he listened she set down to interest, and feeling that she had gained his attention, that his wrath was appeased by this unexpected retribution, her own interest grew and the narrative flowed from her lips, fluent, complete, full of enlightening detail.

Once or twice at the start he had stirred, the rickety chair creaking under his weight. Then, slouched against its back, he had settled into absolute stillness. To anyone not seeing him, it might have seemed that the girl was talking to herself, pauses that she made for comment passed in silence, questions she now and then put remained unanswered. Peering at him she made him out, a brooding mass, his chin sunk into his collar, his hands clasped over his waist, his eyes fixed on the floor.

When she was done he stayed thus for a moment apparently so buried in thought that he could not rouse himself.

"Well," she said, surprised at his silence, "isn't it true what I said? Hasn't fate rounded things up for him?"

The chair creaked as he moved, heavily as if with an effort. He laid his hands on the arms and drew himself forward.

"Yes," he muttered, "it sounds pretty straight."

"Would anything you could do beat that?"

He sat humped together looking at the floor, his powerful, gnarled hands gripping at the chair arms. She could see the top of his head with a bald place showing through the thick, low-lying grizzle of hair.

"Nup," he said, "I guess not."

He heaved himself up and walked across the room to the window.

"It's as hot as hell in here," he growled as he fumbled at the sash.

"Hot!" she exclaimed. "Why, it's cold. What's the matter with you?"

"It's these barred-up city places; they knock me out. I smother in 'em." He threw back the window and stood in the opening. "I'll shut it in a minute."

She pulled up the Navajo blanket and cowering under it said with vengeful zest:

"I guess there won't be a more surprised person in this burg than Mr. Boyé Mayer when they come after him."

"Do you know when they're calculatin' to do it?"

"Thursday or Friday. Charlie said he was going to give the Express people his information some time tomorrow and after they'd fixed things he'd spring the story in the *Despatch*."

"If he gives it in tomorrow they'll have him by evening."

"I don't think they'll be in any rush. Mr. Mayer's not going to skip; he's too busy with his courting."

There was no reply, and pulling the blanket higher, for the night air struck cold, she went on in her embittered self-torment:

"I wanted to give him a jolt myself and I tried, but I might as well have stayed out. You and me show up pretty small when the law gets busy. That's the time for us to lie low and watch. And he thinking himself so safe, drawing out all the money. Maybe it was to buy her presents or get his wedding clothes. I'd like—"

The voice from the window interrupted her.

"That paper—the one he had under the floor—Crowder said a piece was tore out?"

"Yes, part of his correspondence letter—the last paragraph about me. Don't you remember it? It was that one after 'The Zingara' started, way back in August. I showed it to you here one evening. I thought maybe Mayer had read it and that was what brought him to see me—got him sort of curious. But Charlie thinks he wasn't bothering about papers just then. He had it on him and used it to wrap up the money and that piece got torn out someway by accident."

"Um—looks that way."

The current of air was chilling the room, and Pancha, shivering under the blanket, protested.

"Say, Pa, aren't you going to shut that window? It's letting in an awful draught." He made no movement to do so, and, surprised at his indifference to her comfort, she said uneasily, "You ain't got a fever, have you?"

"Let me alone," he muttered. "Didn't I tell you these het-up rooms knock me out."

She was silent—a quality in his voice, a husky thinness as if its vigor was pinching out, made her anxious. He was worn to the bone, the shade of himself. She slid her feet to the floor, and throwing off the blanket said:

"Looks like to me something is the matter with you. The room ain't hot."

"Oh, forget it. For God's sake, quit this talk about me."

He closed the window and turned to her. As he advanced the lamp's glare fell full on him and she saw his face glistening with perspiration and darkened with unnatural hollows. In that one moment, played upon by the revealing side light, it was like the face of a skeleton and she rose with a frightened cry.

"Pop! You *are* sick. You look like you were dead."

She made a step toward him and before her advance he stopped, bristling, fierce, like a bear confronted by a hunter.

"You let me alone. You're crazy—sit down. Ain't I gone through enough without you pickin' on me about how I *look?*"

She shrank back, scared by his violence.

"But I can't help it. The room's like ice and you're sweating. I saw it on your forehead."

He almost roared.

"And supposin' I am? Ain't I given you a reason? Sweating? A Chihuahua dog 'ud sweat in this d——d place. It's like a smelting furnace." With a stiff, uncertain hand he felt in his pocket, drew out a bandanna and ran it over his face. "God, you'd think there was nothin' in the world but the way I *look!* I hiked down from the hills on the run to see you and you nag at me till I'm almost sorry I come."

That was too much for her. The tears, ready to flow at a word, poured out of her eyes, and she held out her arms to him, piteously crying:

"Oh, don't say that. Don't scold at me. I wouldn't say it if I didn't care. What would I do if you got sick—what would I do if I lost you? You're all I have and I'm so lonesome."

He ran to her, clasped her close, laid his cheek on her head as she leaned against him feebly weeping. And what he said made it all right—it was his fault, he was ugly, but it was because of what she'd told him. That had riled him all up. Didn't she know every hurt that came to her made him mad as a she-bear when they're after its cub?

"Will you be back tomorrow?" she said when he started to go.

"Yes, in the morning. Eight be too early?"

"No—but—" her eyes were wistful, her hands reluctant to loose his. "Will you have to leave the city soon?"

"I guess so, honey."

"Tomorrow?"

"Maybe—but we'll get a line on that in the morning."

"I wish you could stay, just for one day," she pleaded.

"I'll tell you then. What you want to do now is rest. Sleep tight and don't worry no more. It's going to be all right."

He gave her a kiss and from the doorway a farewell nod and smile.

CHAPTER XXXII

THE VOICE IN THE NIGHT

W HEN GARLAND PASSED THROUGH the lobby the hall clock showed him it was after midnight. Cushing, roused from a nap, looked up at the sound of his step, and asked how Miss Lopez was. "Gettin' on first rate," he called back cheerily as he opened the door and went out.

His immediate desire was for silence and seclusion—a place where he could recover from the stunned condition in which Pancha's story had left him. Before he could act on it he would have to get back to a clearness where coordinated thought was possible. He walked down the street in the direction of his old lodgings; he had a latch-key and could get to his room without being heard. On the way he found himself skirting the open space of South Park, an oval of darkness, light-touched at intervals and encircled by a looming wall of houses. Here and there on benches huddled figures sat, formless and immovable, less like human beings than ghosts come back in the depths of night to find themselves denied an entrance into life, and drooping disconsolate. His footsteps sounded abnormally loud, thrown back from the houses, buffeted between their frowning fronts, as if they were maliciously determined to reveal his presence, wanted him to know that they too were leagued against him. He stumbled over the sidewalk's coping to the grass and stole to a bench under the shade of a tree.

There he burrowed upward toward the light through the avalanche that had fallen on him.

At first there was only a gleam of it, a central glow. About this his thoughts circled like May flies round a lamp, irresistibly attracted and seemingly as purposeless.

"Hello, Panchita! Ain't you the wonder. Your best beau's proud of you"—that was the glow. He saw the words traced at the end of the column, saw a hand tearing the piece out, saw into the mind that directed the hand, knew its conviction of the paper's value.

It was some time before he could get away from it; divert his mental energies to this night, the hour and its necessities, and the next day, the formidable day, now so close at hand.

From a clock tower nearby two strokes chimed out, dropping separate and rounded on the silence. They dropped on him like tangible things, calling him to action. He sat up, his brain-clouds dispersed, and thought. Any information of the lost bandit would gain clemency for Mayer, and Mayer had a clew. Knapp would remember the paper taken from his partner's coat and buried with the money. That would lead them to Pancha. Years before in Siskiyou he had witnessed the cross-examination of a girl, daughter of an absconding murderer, and the scene in the crowded courtroom of the wild mountain town rose in his memory, with Pancha as the central figure. They would badger and break her down as they had the murderer's daughter. She would know everything. There would be no secrets from her any more.

In an uprush of despair his life unrolled before him, all, it now seemed, progressing to this climax. Step by step he had advanced on it, builded up to it as if it were the goal of his desire. Wanting to keep her in ignorance he had created a situation that had worked out worse for her than for him. He could fly, leave her to face it alone, enlightenment come with shame and ignominy. It wasn't fair, it wasn't human. If it had only been himself that he had ruined he wouldn't have cared, he would have been glad to end the whole thing. But under the broken law of his conduct he had held to the greater law of his love. It was that he would sacrifice; be untrue to what had sustained him as his one ideal. He could have cried to the heavens that to let her know him for what he was, was a retribution too great for his sins. Death would have been a release but he could not die. He must live and make one final fight to preserve the belief that was his life's sole apology.

That determination toughened him, his despair past, and wrestling with the problem he came upon its solution and with it his punishment.

He would tell the man, give him warning and let him go. There was plenty of time; the authorities were not yet informed; no one was on the watch. Mayer could leave the city that morning and make the Mexican border by night. It was the only way out and it dragged his penance with it—Pancha unavenged, the enemy rewarded, the prison doors set wide for the flight of their mutual despoiler.

Three strokes chimed out and he rose, trying to step lightly with feet that felt heavy as lead. It was very silent, as if the night and the brooding city were at one in that conspiracy to impress him with a sense of their hostility. The houses were still malignly watchful, again took up and tossed about his footsteps, echoed them from wall to wall till he wondered doors did not open, people did not come. On the main street he shrank by shop window and closed doorway, gliding blackly across a gush of light, slipping, a moving darkness, against the deeper darkness of shuttered lower stories. He had it almost to himself—a policeman lounging on a corner, a reveler reeling by with indignant mutterings, one or two night workers footing it homeward to rest and bed.

At the door of a drugstore he stopped and looked in. A frowsy woman was talking across the counter to a clerk whose bald head shone, glossy as ivory, above the gray fatigue of his face. In a corner was a telephone booth. Garland opened the door, then started as a bell jangled stridently and the bald-headed man craned his neck and the woman whisked round.

"Telephone," he muttered, tentative on the sill.

The clerk, too listless for words, jerked his head toward the booth and then handed the woman a package. As Garland entered the booth he heard her dragging step cross the floor and the bell jangle on her exit.

While he waited he struggled for a closer control on the rage that possessed him. He had decided what he would say and he cleared his throat for a free passage of the words that were to carry deliverance to one he longed to kill. He had expected a wait—the man, confidant in his security, would be sleeping—but almost on top of his request for Mr. Mayer came a voice, wide-awake and incisive:

"Hello, who is it?"

His answer was very low, the deep tones hoarse despite his effort.

"Is this Mr. Boyé Mayer?"

"Yes. What do you want? Who are you?"

The voice fitted his conception of the man, hard, commanding, with something sharply imperious in its cultivated accents. He thought he detected fear in it.

"It don't matter who I am. I got somethin' to say to you that matters. It's time for you to skip."

There was a momentary pause, then the word was repeated, seemed to be ejected quickly as if delivered on a rising breath:

"Skip?"

"Yes—get out. You've got time—till tomorrow afternoon. They'll be lookin' for you then."

Again there was that slight pause. When the voice answered, trepidation was plain in it.

"Who's looking for me? What are you talking about ?"

It was Garland's turn to pause. For a considering moment he sought his words, then he gave them in short, telegraphic sentences:

"End of August. The tules—opposite the Ariel Club. Twelve thousand. Whatcheer House, Sacramento. Harry Romaine."

The pause was longer, then the voice came breathless, shaken:

"What in hell do you mean by this gibberish?"

"I guess that's all right. You don't need to play any baby business. You know now and *I* know, and by tomorrow evening the Express company and the police'll know."

A stammering of oaths came along the wire, a burst of maledictions, interspersed by threats. Garland cut into it with:

"That don't help any. You ain't got time to waste that way. You want to make the Mexican border by tomorrow night and to do that you got to go quick."

The man's anger seemed to rise to a pitch of furious incoherence. His words, shot out in a storm of passion and fear, were transmitted in a stuttering jumble of sound, from which phrases broke, here and there rising into clearness. Garland caught one: "Who's turned you loose on this? Who's behind it?" and the restraint he had put on himself gave way. He laid his hand on the shelf before him as something to seize and wrenched at it.

"If *I* was there you'd know—I'd make it plain. And maybe you guess. You thought you'd struck someone who was helpless. But she could pay you back and she *has*."

He stopped, realizing what he was saying. Through the singing of the blood in his ears the answering words came as an unintelligible mutter. With an unsteady hand he hung up the receiver, his breath beating in loud gasps on the stillness that had so suddenly fallen on the small, walled-in place. For a space he sat crouched in the chair, trying to subdue the pounding of his heart, the shaking of his limbs. Then, stealthily, like a guilty thing, he opened the door and came out. From above a line of bottles on the prescription desk the clerk's bald head gleamed, his eyes dodging between them.

"It's all right," Garland muttered; "I'm through," and shambled to the door with its jangling bell.

In his room at Mrs. Meeker's he threw himself dressed on the bed. The shade was up and through the window he could see the long flank of the new building and above it a section of sky. He kept his eyes on the night-blue strip and as he lay there his spirit, all spring gone, sank from depths to depths. He saw nothing before him but the life of the outlaw, and, mind and body taxed beyond their powers, he longed for death.

Presently he slept, sprawled on the wretched bed, the light of the dawn revealing the tragedy of his ravaged face.

CHAPTER XXXIII

THE MORNING THAT CAME

WHEN THE VOICE HAD CEASED Mayer stood transfixed at the phone, seeing nothing. He fumbled the receiver back into its hook and, wheeling, propped himself against the wall, his mouth slack, his eyelids drooped in sickly feebleness. The final shock, succeeding the long strain, came like a blow on the head leaving destruction.

He got to a chair and dropped into it, sweat-bathed, feeling as if cold airs were blowing on his damp skin. Sunk against the back, his legs stretched before him, his arms hanging over the sides, he lay shattered. His mind tried to focus on what he had heard and fell back impotent, eddying downward through darkling depths like a drowning swimmer. A vast weakness invaded him, turning his joints to water, giving him a sensation of nausea, draining his strength till he felt incapable of moving his eyes, which stared glassily at the toes of his shoes.

Presently this passed; he raised his glance and encountered the clock face on the mantelpiece. He held to it like a hand that was dragging him out of an abyss; watched it grow from a circular object to a white dial crossed by black hands and edged by a ring of numerals. The hour marked slowly penetrated to his consciousness—a quarter to four. He drew himself up and looked about; saw his notes on the desk, his hat on the table, the matchsafe with a cigarette stump lying on its saucer. They were like memorials from another state of existence, things that connected him with a plane of being that he had left long ago. He had a vision of himself in that distant past, packing his trunk, making brisk, satisfactory jottings on a sheet of hotel paper, standing on the hearth looking into Lorry Alston's angry eyes.

Groaning, he dropped his head into his hands, rocking on the chair, only half aroused. He was aware of poignant misery without the force to combat it, and knowing he must act could only remember. Irrelevant pictures, disconnected, having no point, chased across his brain—the saloon in Fresno where he had cleaned the brasses, and, jostling it, Chrystie's face, just before she had wept, puckered like a baby's. He saw the tules in the low sun, the green ranks, the gold-glazed streams, Mark Burrage coming down the long drawing-room eyeing him from under thick brows, Lorry's hand with its sparkle of rings holding out the letter.

That last picture shook him out of his torpor. He lifted his head and knew his surroundings for what they were—four walls threatening to close in on him. The necessity to go loomed suddenly insistent, became the obsessing matter, and he staggered to his feet. Flight suggested disguise and he went to the bedroom and clawed about in the bottom of the cupboard for the old suitcase which held the clothes he had worn on his Sacramento trips. As he pulled it out he remembered the side entrance of the hotel accessible by a staircase at the end of the hall; he could slip out unseen. There would be early trains, locals, going south; an express to be caught somewhere down the line. By the next night he could be across the Mexican border. It was the logical place, the only place—he knew it himself and the voice had said so.

The Voice! Obliterated by the mental chaos it had caused, whelmed in the succeeding rush of fear, it now rose to recognition—a portentous fact. He stood stunned, the suitcase dangling from his hands, immovable in aghast wonder as if it had just come to his ears. A voice without a personality, a voice behind which he could envisage no body, a voice of warning dropping out of the unknown, dropping doom!

His surface faculties were now obedient to his direction and automatically responded to the necessity for haste. As he went about collecting his clothes, tearing up letters, opening drawers, he ransacked his brain for a clew to the man's identity, tried to rehear the voice and catch a familiar echo, went back and forth over the words. And in the fevered restoration of them, the last sentences, "You thought you'd struck someone who was helpless. But she could pay you back and she has," brought light in an illuminating flash. "Pancha," he whispered, "Pancha," and stood rooted, recalling, searching the past, linking the known with the deduced.

The man was the bandit, the old lover, the one he had supplanted, the one who had written the message on the paper. He had heard she was sick—come to see her—and she had told him, called upon him to avenge her as she said she would. And the man—he couldn't—his hands were tied. If Mayer had the paper—and the cache showed it was gone—Mayer could direct the pursuit to Pancha and to Pancha's "best beau." So, fact marshaled behind fact, he drew to the truth, grasped it, knew why he had been warned and by whom.

Pancha had found out somehow—but he did not linger on that; his mind wasted no time filling profitless gaps. Fiercely alive now it only saw what counted. He turned and looked out of the window, a glance in her direction. She had made good, kept her word, beaten him. The feeble thing, the scorned thing, that he had kicked out of his path, had risen and destroyed him. He stood for a still moment looking toward where she was, triumphant, waiting for his arrest, and he muttered, his gray face horrible.

Soon afterward he was ready, the old hat and coat on, the suitcase packed. There was a look about for forgotten details and he attended to them with swift competence. The papers on the desk—those expense accounts—were crammed into his pockets, the shades drawn up, the bed rumpled for the room boy's eye in the morning. Then a last sweeping survey and he turned out the gas, opened the door and peered into the hall. It stretched vacant to the window at the far end, a subdued light showing its carpeted length. His nostrils caught its unaired closeness, his ears the heavy stillness of a place enshrining sleep.

Night still held the streets, at this hour dim, deserted vistas, looking larger than they did by day. He stole along them feeling curiously small, dwarfed by their wide emptiness, wanting to hide from their observation. It was typical of what the rest of his life would be, shunning the light, footing it furtively through darkness, forever apprehensive, forever outcast.

His heart sank into blackness, dense, illimitable. It stretched from him out to the edges of the world and he saw himself never escaping from it, groping through it from pursuers, always retreating, always looking back in fear. Poverty would be his close companion; makeshifts, struggles, tricks of deceit, the occupation of his days. The effort of new endeavor rose before him like a mountain to be climbed and for which he had not the strength; the ease he was reft of, a paradise only valued now it was lost. Hate of those who had brought him so low surged in him, dominating even his misery. He set his teeth, looking up at the graying sky, feeling the poison pressing at his throat, aching in his limbs, burning at the ends of his fingers.

There was a faint diffused light when he reached the corner of Pancha's street, the first gleam of the coming day. Like one who sees temptation placed before him in living form and hesitates, reluctant yet impelled, he stood and gazed at the front of the Vallejo Hotel. The lamps showed up a pinkish orange, two spheres, concrete and solid, in a swimming, silvery unreality. Beyond the steps a man's figure moved, walking up the street, his back to Mayer. It was very quiet; the hush before the city, turning in its sleep, stretched, breathed deeply, and awakened.

Mayer went forward toward the lamps.

He had no definite intention; was actuated by no formed resolution; was, for the moment, a being filled to the skin by a single passion. He felt light, as if his body weighed nothing, or as if he might have been carried by a powerful current buoyant and beyond his control. It took him up the steps to the door. Through a clear space in the ground glass panel he looked in and saw that the hall was empty. His heart rose stranglingly and then contracted; his hand closed on the knob, turned it and the door opened. That unexpected opening, the vacant hall and stairway stretching before him like an invitation, ended his lack of purpose. Despair and hate combined into the will to act, propelled him to a recognized goal.

He entered and mounted the stairs.

Cushing, having found the long vigil at the Vallejo exhausting, had contracted the habit of slipping out in the first reaches of the dawn to a saloon down the street. It was a safe habit, for even the few night-roving tenants the Vallejo had were housed at that hour, and if a belated reveler should stray in, the door was always left on the latch. Moreover he only stayed a few minutes; a warming gulp and he was back again, wide-awake for the call of the day. His was the figure Mayer had seen walking down the street.

Pancha was asleep and dreaming. It was a childish dream, but it was impregnated with that imminent, hovering terror that often is associated with the simple visions of sleep. She was back in the old shack in Inyo where her mother had died, and it was raining. Juana was sitting on the side of the bed, her dark hair parted, a shawl over her head framing her face. From the side of the bed she watched Pancha, who was sweeping, sweeping with urgent haste, haunted by some obscure necessity to finish and continually retarded by obstacles. Against the door the rain fell, loud, and then louder. It grew so loud that it ceased to be like rain, became a shower of blows, a fearful noise, never before made by water. Horror fell upon them, a horror of some sinister fate beyond the door. Juana held out her arms and Pancha, dropping the broom, ran to her, and clinging close listened to the sound with a freezing heart.

She woke and it was still there, not so loud, very soft, and falling, between pauses, on her own door. Her fear was still with her and she sat up, seeing the room faintly charged with light. "Who is it?" she said and heard her voice a stifled whisper, then, the knocking repeated, she leaped out of bed and thrust her feet into slippers. She was awake now and thought of her father, no one else would come at such an hour. As she ran to the door she called, "What is it—is something the matter?" Through the crack she heard an answering whisper, "Open—it's all right. Let me in." It might have been anybody's voice. She opened the door and Boyé Mayer came in.

They looked at one another without words, and after the look, she began to retreat, backing across the room, foot behind foot. He locked the door and then followed her. There were pieces of furniture in the way that she skirted or pushed aside, keeping her eyes on him, moving without sound. She knew the door into the sitting room was open and with one hand she felt behind her for the frame, afraid to turn her back on him, afraid to move her glance, the withheld shriek ready to burst out when he spoke or sprang.

She gained the doorway and backed through it and here breathed a hoarse, "Boyé, what do you want?" He made no answer, stealing on her, and she slid to the table and then round it, keeping it between them. In the pale light, eye riveted on eye, they circled it like partners in a fantastic dance, creeping, one away and one in pursuit, steps noiseless, movements delicately alert. Her body began to droop and cower, her breath to stifle her; it was impossible to bear it longer. "Boyé!" she screamed and made a rush for the door. She had shot the bolt back, her hand was on the knob, when he caught her. His grip was like iron, hopeless to resist, but she writhed, tore at him, felt herself pressed back against the wall, his fingers on her throat.

It was a quarter to five on the morning of April 18, 1906.

The first low rumble, the vibration beneath his feet, did not penetrate his madness. Then came a road, an enormous agglomeration of sound and movement, an unloosing of titanic elements—above them, under them, on them.

They were separated, each stricken aghast, no longer enemies, beings of a mutual life seized by a mutual terror. The man was paralyzed, not knowing what it was, but the girl, bred in an earthquake country, clasped her hands over her skull and bent, crouching low and screaming, "*El temblor!*" The floor beneath them heaved and dropped and rose, groaning as the ground throes wrenched it. From walls that strained forward and sank back, pictures flew, shelves hurled their contents. Breaking free, upright for a poised second, the long mirror lunged across the room, then crashed to its fall. On its ruin plaster showered, stretches of ceiling, the chandelier in a shiver of glass and coiled wires.

Through the dust they saw one another as ghosts, staggering, helpless, dodging toppling shapes. They shouted across the chaos and only knew the other had cried by the sight of the opened mouth. All sounds were drowned in the surrounding tumult, the roar of the shaken city and the *temblor*'s thunderous mutter. Rafters, crushed together, then strained apart, creaked and groaned and crunched. Walls receded with a reeling swing and advanced with a crackling rush. The paper split into shreds; the plaster skin beneath ripped open; lathes broke in splintered ends; mortar came thudding from above and swept in a swirling drive about their feet.

He shouted to her and made a run for the door. Hanging to the knob he was thrown from side to side by the paroxysmal leaps of the building. The door jammed, and, his wrenchings futile, he turned and dashed to the window. Here again the sash stuck. He kicked it, frantic, caught a glimpse of the street, people in nightgowns, a chimney swaying and then falling in a long drooping sweep. Somewhere beyond it a high building shook off its cornices like a terrier shaking water from its hair. Grinding his teeth, cursing, he wrenched at the window, tore at the clasp, then turned in desperation and saw the door, loosed by a sudden throe, swing open. Through reeling dust clouds Pancha darted for it, her flight like the swoop of a bird, and he followed, running crazily along the heaving floor.

The hall was fog-thick with powdered mortar, and careening like a ship in a gale. He had an impression of walls zigzagged with cracks, of furniture, upturned, making dives across the passage. White figures were all about; some ran, some stood in doorways and all were silent. He thrust a woman out of his way and felt her move, acquiescingly, as if indifferent. Another, a child in her arms, clawed at his back, forced him aside, and as she sped by he saw the child's face over her shoulder, placid and sweet, and caught her voice in a moaning wail, "Oh, my baby! Oh, my baby!" A man, holding the hand of a girl, was thrown against the wall and dropped, the girl tugging at him, trying to drag him to his feet. Something, with blood on its whiteness, lay huddled across the sill of an open doorway.

Pancha was ahead of him, a long narrow shape that he could just discern. A length of ceiling fell between them, a sofa, like a thing endowed with malign life, rushed from the wall and blocked his passage. He scrambled over it and saw the stair head, and a clearer light. That meant deliverance—the street one flight below. The floor sagged and cracked, he could feel it going, and with a screaming leap he threw himself at the balustrade, caught and clung. From above he heard a cry, "Up, up, not down!" had a vision of Pancha on the second flight, flying upward, and himself plunged downward to the street.

The litter of the great mirror lay across the landing, the light from the hall on its shattered fragments, broken glitterings amid a débris of gold. The balustrade broke and swung loose, the stairs drooped, humped again, and gave, sinking amid an onrush of walls, of splintered beams, of ceilings suddenly gaping and discharging their weight in a shoot of plaster, snapped boards and furniture.

Something struck him and he fell to his knees, struggled against a smothering mass, then sank, whelmed in the crumbling collapse.

Pancha at the stair top, lurching from wall to wall, felt a slow subsidence, a sinking under her feet, and then the frenzied movement settle into a long, rocking swing. A pallor of light showed through the dust rack, and making her way to it she found an open doorway giving on a front room. She passed through; crawled over a heap of entangled furniture toward a window wide to the rising day. She thought she was on the third story, then heard voices, looked out and saw faces almost on a level with her own, the street a few feet below her, a clouded massing of figures, moving, gesticulating, calling up to the windows. The greater bewilderment had shut out all lesser ones. She did not understand, did not ask to, only wanted to get out and be under the safe roof of the sky. Climbing across the sill, she found her feet on grass, stumbled over a broken railing, heard someone shout, and was pulled to her feet by two men. They held her up, looking her over, shaking her a little. Both their faces were as white as if they had been painted.

"Are you hurt?" one of them cried, giving her arm a more violent shake as if to jerk the answer out quickly.

"Hurt?" she stammered. "No. I'm all right. But—but how did I get out this way—onto the street?"

She saw then that his teeth were chattering. Closing his lips tight to hide it he pointed to where she had come from.

She turned and looked. The Vallejo, slanting in a drunken sprawl, its roof railing hanging from one corner, its cornices strewn on the pavement, had sunk to one story. Built on the made ground of an old creek bed, it had buckled and gone down, the first and second stories crumpling like a closed accordion, the top floor, disjointed and wrecked, resting on their ruins.

CHAPTER XXXIV

LOST

A UNT ELLEN ALWAYS MAINTAINED the first shock threw her out of bed, and then she would amend the statement with a qualifying, "At any rate I was on the floor when Lorry came and I never knew how I got there." She also said that she thought it was the end of the world, and pulled to her feet by Lorry, announced the fact, and heard Lorry's answer, short and sharp, "No—it's an earthquake. Don't talk. Come quick—run!"

Lorry threw a wrapper about her and ran with her along the hall, almost dark and full of rending noises, and down the stairs that Aunt Ellen said afterward she thought "were going to come loose every minute." A long clattering crash made her scream, "There—it's the house—we're killed!" And Lorry, wrestling with the front door, answered in that hard, breathless tone, "No, we're not—we're all right." The door swung open. "Mind the glass, don't step in it. Down the steps—on the lawn—*quick!*"

They came to a stand by the front gate, were aware of the frantic leaps of the earth subsiding into a long, rhythmic roll, and stood dumbly, each staring at the other's face, unfamiliar in a blanched whiteness.

There were people in the street, scatterings, and huddled clusters and solitary figures. They were standing motionless in attitudes of poised tension, as if stricken to stone. Holding snatched up garments over their night clothes, they waited to see what was coming next, not speaking or daring to move, their eyes set in terrified expectancy. Lorry saw them like dream figures—the fantastic exaggerations of nightmare—and looked from them to the garden, the house—the solid realities. The ruins of the chimney lay sprawled across the flower beds, the splintered trunk of the fig tree rising from the debris. Stepping nimbly among the bricks, in his white coat and trousers as if prepared to wait on table, was Fong.

"Oh, Fong!" she cried. "Thank heaven, you're all 're all right!"

Fong, picking his way with cat-like neatness, answered cheerfully:

"I velly well. I see chimley fall out and know you and Missy Ellen all 'ighty. If chimley fall in you be dead."

"Oh, Fong!" Aunt Ellen wailed; "it's like the Day of Judgment."

Fong, having no opinions to offer on this view of the matter, eyed her costume with disapproval.

"I get you cover. Velly bad stand out here that way. You ketch cold," and turning went toward the house.

"He'll be killed!" Aunt Ellen cried. "He mustn't go!" Then suddenly she appeared to relinquish all concern in him as if on this day of doom there was no use troubling about anything. Her eye shifted to Lorry, and scanning her became infused with a brisk surprise. "Why, Lorry, you're all dressed. Did you sleep in your clothes? You certainly never had time to put them on."

Lorry was spared the necessity of answering. A violent quake rocked the ground and Aunt Ellen, clasping her hands on her breast, closed her eyes.

"It's beginning again—it's coming back. Oh, God, have mercy— God, have mercy!"

The figures in the street, emitting strangled cries, made a rush for the center of the road. Here they stood closely packed in a long line like a great serpent, stationary in the middle of the thoroughfare. The low mutter, the quiver under their feet, died away; Aunt Ellen dropped her hands and opened her eyes.

"Is this going to go on? Isn't one enough?" she wailed. "I'll never enter a house again, never in this world."

The appearance of Fong, coming down the steps carrying an armchair, diverted her.

"He's got out alive. Don't you go back into that house, Fong. It isn't safe, it'll fall at any moment. There's going to be more of this—it isn't finished."

Fong, without answering, set the chair down beside her, taking from its seat a cloak and an eiderdown coverlet. He and Lorry wrapped her in the cloak and disposing her in the chair tucked the coverlet round her knees. Thus installed, her ancient head decorated with crimping pins, her old gnarled hands shaking in her lap, she sank against the back murmuring, "Oh, what a morning, what a morning!"

A lurid light glowed above the trees and sent a coppery luster down the street. The sun had swum up over the housetops and the people in the roadway; Lorry, on the lawn, gazed at it aghast, a crowning amazement. It hung, a scarlet ball, enormously large, like a red seal of vengeance suspended in the heavens. "Look at the sun, look at the sun!" came in thin cries from the throng. It shone through a glassy, brownish film in which its rays were absorbed, leaving it a sharply defined, magnified sphere. Fong, coming down the steps with another chair, eyed it curiously.

"Awful big sun," he commented.

"It's shining through something," said Lorry. "It must be dust."

Fong put the chair beside Aunt Ellen's, pressing it into steadiness on the lawn's yielding turf.

"Maybe smoke," he answered. "After earthquake always fire."

Aunt Ellen gave forth a despairing groan.

"Anything *more!*"

"Don't be afraid," Lorry comforted. "We've the best department in the country. If there should be any fires they'll be put out."

Aunt Ellen took courage from this confident statement and, life running stronger in her, sat up and felt at her head.

"Oh, I've got my pins in, but how was I to take them out? Lorry, *do* sit down. You're as white as a sheet."

"I'm all right, Aunt Ellen. Don't bother about me. I'm going into the house."

The old lady shrieked and clutched at her skirt.

"No—no, I won't allow it." Then as the girl drew her dress away, "Lorry Alston, do you want my death on your head as well as your own? If you want anything let Fong get it. He seems willing and anxious to risk his life."

"Fong can't do this. I'm going to telephone; I want to find out if Chrystie's all right. I'm sorry but I must go," and she ran to the house.

From the first clear moment after the shock her thoughts had gone to Chrystie. As she had tucked Aunt Ellen into the chair, she had been thinking what she could do and the best her shaken brain had to offer was a series of telephone messages to those friends where Chrystie might have gone. The anxiety of last night was as nothing to the anguish of this unprecedented hour.

That was why her face held its ashen pallor, her eyes their hunted fear. But there was no relief to be found at the phone—a dead stillness, not even the whispering hum of the wires met her ear. "It's broken," she said to herself. "Or the girls have got frightened and gone."

Out on the lawn she paused a moment beside Aunt Ellen.

"Something's the matter with the wires. I'm going to the drugstore on Sutter Street."

"But what for—what for?" Aunt Ellen wanted to know. "Telephoning when the city's been smitten by the hand of God!"

"It's Chrystie," she called over her shoulder as she went out of the gate. "I want to find out how she is."

"Chrystie's at San Mateo," Aunt Ellen quavered. "She's all right there. She's with the Barlows."

The man in the doorway of his wrecked drugstore laughed sardonically at her request to use the phone. All the wires were broken—you couldn't telephone any more than you could fly. Everything was out of commission. You couldn't telegraph—you couldn't get a message carried—except by hand—not if you were the president of the country. Even the car lines were stopped—not a spark of power. The whole machinery of the city was at a standstill. "Like the clock there," he said, and pointed to the face of the timepiece hanging shattered from the wall, its hands marking a quarter to five.

She went back, jostling through the people. Bold ones were going into the houses to put on their clothes, timid ones commissioning them to throw theirs out of the windows. She saw Chinese servants, unshaken from their routine, methodically clearing fallen bricks and cornices from front steps to which they purported, giving the matutinal sweeping. She skirted a fallen stone terrace, its copings strewn afar, the garden above a landslide across the pavement. People spoke to her, some she knew, others who were strangers. She hardly answered them, hurrying on. Dazed, poor girl, they said, and small wonder.

If Chrystie was in the city she would certainly come home. It was the natural, the only, thing for her to do. But it would be impossible to sit there waiting for her, doing nothing. The best course for Lorry was to go out and look for her—go to all those places where she might be. Aunt Ellen would be at the house, waiting, if she came, to tell her they were all right. And Lorry would return at intervals to see if she had come. If by midday she hadn't, then there was Mark Burrage. She would go to him. But Chrystie would be back before then—she might be there even now.

Her rapid walk broke into a run and presently she was flying past the garden fence, sending her glance ahead under the trees. No—Aunt Ellen was alone, looking as if she was participating in a solitary picnic. In front of her stood a small table covered with a white cloth and set with glass and silver. She was inspecting it closely as if trying to find flaws in its arrangement and as Lorry came panting up the steps, said with a relieved air:

"Oh, there you are! Fong's brought out breakfast. He says the kitchen's a wreck and he had to make the coffee on an alcohol lamp. The range is all broken and there's something the matter with the gas in the gas stove. Did you get the Barlows?"

Lorry sank down on the other chair.

"No. the telephone isn't working. We can't get any word to anyone."

"She'll be all right," said Aunt Ellen, lifting the silver coffee pot. "San Mateo's a long way off."

It was an unfortunate moment for a heavy shock to send its rocking vibrations along the ground. Aunt Ellen collapsed against the chair back, the coffee pot swaying from her limp grasp. Lorry snatched it and Aunt Ellen's hands, liberated, clutched the corners of the table like talons.

"Oh, God have mercy! God have mercy!" she groaned. "If this doesn't stop I'll die."

Fong came running round the corner of the house.

"Be care, be care, Missy Ellen," he cried warningly. "You keep hold on him coffee pot. I not got much alcohol." He saw the treasure in Lorry's hand and was calmed. "Oh, all 'ight! Miss Lolly got him. You drink him up, Miss Lolly. He make you good nerve."

But Lorry could not drink much. It seemed to Aunt Ellen she hardly touched the cup to her lips when she was up and moving toward the house again—this time for her hat.

"Hat!" muttered the old lady, picking at a bunch of grapes. "The girl's gone mad. Wanting a hat in the middle of an earthquake."

Then her attention was attracted by a man stopping at the gate and bidding her good-morning. He was the fishman from Polk Street, extremely excited, his greeting followed by a voluble description of how he had escaped from a collapsing building in his undershirt. Aunt Ellen swapped experiences with him, and pointed to the chimney, which if it had fallen inward would have killed her. The fishman was not particularly interested in that and went on to tell how he had been down to Union Square and seen thousands of people there—and had she heard that fires had started in the Mission—a good many fires? Lorry, emerging from the house, drew near and said, as she had said to Fong:

"But there's no danger of fires getting any headway. You can't beat our firemen in the country."

The fishman, moving to go, looked dubious.

"Yes, we got a grand department, no one denies that. But the Mission's mostly wood and there's quite some wind. It looks pretty serious to me."

He passed on and Lorry went to the gate.

"Where are you going *now*?" Aunt Ellen cried.

"Out," said Lorry, clicking up the hasp. "I want to see what's going on. I'll be back in an hour or two. If Chrystie comes, stay here with her-right here on this spot."

Afterward Lorry said she thought she walked twenty miles that day. Her first point of call was Crowley's livery stable where she asked for a carriage. There were only two men in the place; one, owl-eyed and speechless, in what appeared to be a state of drunken stupefaction, waved her to the other, who, putting a horse into the shafts of a cart, shook his head. He couldn't give her a carriage for love or money. Every vehicle in the place was already gone—the rich customers had grabbed them all, some come right in and taken them, others bought them outright. He swung his hand to the empty depths of the building; not an animal left but the one he had and he was taking it to go after his wife and children; they were down in the Mission and the Mission was on fire. He had the animal harnessed and was climbing to the seat as Lorry left the stable.

After that she gave up all hope of getting a carriage and started to walk. She went to every house in that part of the city where Chrystie had friends, and in none of them found trace or word of her sister. She saw people so stunned that they could hardly remember who Chrystie was, others who treated the catastrophe lightly—not any worse than the quake of '68, nothing to make a fuss about—a good shake-up, that was all. She found families sitting down to cold breakfasts, last night's coffee heated on the flicker of gas left in the pipes; others gathered in pallid groups on the doorsteps, afraid to go into the house, undaunted Chinamen bringing down their clothes.

As she moved her ears were greeted with a growing narrative of disaster. There had been great loss of life in the poorer sections; the injured were being taken to the Mechanics' Pavilion; the Mission was on fire and the wind was with it. In this, the residential part, there was no water. Thrifty housekeepers were filling their bathtubs with the little dribble that came from the faucets, and cautioning those who adhered to the habits of every day to forego the morning wash. It was not till she was near home again that, meeting a man she knew, she learned the full measure of ill-tidings. The mains had been torn to pieces, there was no water in San Francisco, and the fire, with a strong wind behind it, was eating its way across the Mission, triumphant and unchecked.

It gave her pause for a wide-seeing, aghast moment, then her eye caught the roof of her home and she forgot—Chrystie might be there, ought to be there, *must* be there. She broke into a run, sending that questing glance ahead to the green sweep of the lawn. It met, as it had done before, the figure of Aunt Ellen in front of the little table, the empty chair at her side. Even then she did not give up hope. Chrystie might be in the house; all Aunt Ellen's pleadings could not restrain her if it suited her purpose to dare a danger.

Before she reached the gate she called, hoarse and breathless.

"Is Chrystie there?"

Aunt Ellen started and looked at her.

"Oh, dear, here you are at last! I've been in such a state about you. No, of course Chrystie's not here. I knew she wouldn't be. They say all the trains are stopped—the rails are twisted. How could she get back?"

Lorry dropped on to the steps. She did not know till then how much she had hoped. Her head fell forward in the hollow of her chest, her hands clenched together in her lap. Aunt Ellen addressed the nape of her neck:

"I don't know what's going to happen to us. I've just sat here all morning and heard one awful thing after another. Do you know that the whole Mission's burning and there's not a drop of water to put it out with? And if it crosses Market Street this side of the city'll burn too."

Lorry did not answer and she went on:

"The people are coming out of there by hundreds. A man told me—no, it was a woman. I didn't know her from Adam, but she hung over the gate like an old friend and talked and talked. They're coming out like rats; soldiers are poking them out with bayonets. All the soldiers are down there from the Presidio and Black Point. And lots of people are killed—the houses fell on them and caught them. It was a man told me that. He'd been down there and he was all black with smoke. I thought it was the end of the world and it might just as well have been. Thank goodness your father and mother aren't here to see it. And, *thank God*, Chrystie's safe in San Mateo!"

Lorry raised her head in intolerable pain.

"*Don't*, Aunt Ellen!" she groaned, and got up from the step.

The old lady, seeing her face, cast aside the eiderdown, and rose in tottering consternation.

"Oh, Lorry dear, you're faint. It's too much for you. Let's get a carriage and go—somewhere, anywhere, away from here."

Lorry pushed away her helpless, shaking hands.

"I'm all right, I'm all right," she said. "Sit down, Aunt Ellen. Leave me alone. I'm tired, I've walked a long way, that's all."

Aunt Ellen could only drop back, feebly protesting, into her chair. If Lorry wanted to walk herself to death *she* couldn't stop her—nobody minded what she said anyway. She sat hunched up in her wraps, murmurously grumbling, and when Fong brought out lunch on a tray, ordered a glass of wine for her niece.

"I suppose she won't drink it," she said aggrievedly to Fong; "but whether she does or not I want the satisfaction of having you bring it."

Lorry did drink it and ate a little of the lunch. When it was over she rose again and made ready to go. She said she wanted to look at the fire from some high place, see how near it was to Market Street. If it continued to make headway they might have to go further up town, and she'd be back and get them off.

She went straight to Mark Burrage's lodgings. She knew the business quarter was burning and thought the likeliest place to find him was his own rooms, where he would probably be getting ready to move out. It was nearer the center of town than her own home and as she swung down the hills she felt, for the first time, the dry, hot breath of the fire. Cinders were falling, bits of blackened paper circling slowly down. Below her, beyond the packed roofs and chimneys, the smoke rose in a thick, curling rampart. It loomed in mounded masses, swelled into lowering spheres, dissolved into long, soaring puffs, looked solid and yet was perpetually taking new forms. In places it suddenly heaved upward, a gigantic billow shot with red, at others lay a dense, churning wall, here and there broken by tongues of flame.

On this side of town the residence section was as yet untouched, but the business houses were ablaze, and she met the long string of vehicles loaded deep with furniture, office fixtures, crates, books, ledgers, safes. Here, also, for the first time, she heard that sound forever to be associated with the catastrophe—the scraping of trunks dragged along the pavement. There were hundreds of them, drawn by men, by women, drawn to safety with, dogged endurance, drawn a few blocks and despairingly abandoned. She saw the soldiers charging in mounted files to the fire line, had a vision of them caught in the streets' congestion, plunging horses and cursing men fighting their way through the tangled traffic.

The door and windows of Mark's dwelling were flung wide and a pile of household goods lay by the steps. As she opened the gate a boy came from the house, stooped under the weight of a sofa, a woman behind him carding a large crayon portrait in a gilt frame. The boy, dropping the sofa to the ground, righted himself, wiping his dripping face on his sleeve. The woman, holding the picture across her middle like a shield, saw Lorry and shouted at her in excited friendliness:

"We're movin' out. Goin' to save our things while we got time."

"Where's Mr. Burrage?" said Lorry.

"Mr. Burrage?" The woman looked at her, surprised. "He ain't here; he's in the country."

"The country?" Too many faces were smitten by a blank consternation, too many people already vainly sought, for Lorry's expression to challenge attention.

"Yes, he went—lemme see, I don't seem to remember anything—I guess it was nearly a week ago. His mother was took sick. He's lucky to be out of this." Her glance shifted to the boy who was looking ruefully at the pile of furniture. "That'll do, Jack, we can't handle any more."

As Lorry turned away she heard his desperate rejoinder:

"Yes, we got it out here, but how in hell are we goin' to get it any farther?"

After that she went to Mrs. Kirkham's. There was no reason to expect news of Chrystie there, except that the old lady was a friend, had been a support and help on occasions less tragic than this. Also she knew many people and might have heard something. Lorry was catching at any straw now.

In the midst of her wrecked flat, her servant fled, Mrs. Kirkham was occupied in sweeping out the mortar and glass and "straightening things up." She was the first woman Lorry had seen who seemed to realize the magnitude of the catastrophe and meet it with stoical fortitude. Under her calm courage the girl's strained reserve broke and she poured out her story. Mrs. Kirkham, resting on the sofa, broom in hand, was disturbed, did not attempt to hide it. Chrystie might have gone out of town, was her suggestion, gone to people in the country. To that Lorry had the answer that had been haunting her all day:

"But she would have come in. They all—everybody she could have gone to—have motors or horses. Even if she couldn't come herself she would have sent someone to tell where she was. She wouldn't have left us this way, hour after hour, without a word from her."

It was dark when Mrs. Kirkham let her go, claiming a promise to bring Aunt Ellen back to the flat. They couldn't stay in the Pine Street house. Only an hour earlier the grandnephew had been up to say that the fire had crossed Market Street that afternoon. No one knew now where it would stop.

With the coming of the dark the size of the conflagration was apparent. Night withdrew to the eastern edges of the heavens; the sky to the zenith was a glistening orange, blurred with shadowy up-rollings of smoke, along the city's crest the torn flame ribbons playing like northern lights. Figures that faced it were glazed by its glare as if a red-dipped paint brush had been slapped across them; those seen against it were black silhouettes moving on fiery distances and gleaming walls. The smell of it was strong, and the showers of cinders so thick Lorry bent down the brim of her hat to keep them out of her eyes. As she came toward the house she felt its heat, dry and baking, on her face.

In front of her, walking in, the same direction, was a man, pacing the pavement with an even, thudding foot-fall. The gun over his shoulder proclaimed him a soldier, and having already heard tales of householders stopped on their own doorsteps and not allowed to enter, she curbed her eager speed and slunk furtively behind him, skirting the fence. Through the trees she could see the lawn, lighted up as if by fireworks, and then the two chairs—empty—the eiderdown lying crumpled on the grass. In the shade of branches that hung over the sidewalk, she scaled the fence and flew, her feet noiseless on the turf. She passed the empty chairs, and sent a searching glance up toward the windows, all unshuttered, the glass gone from the sashes. Were they in there? Had Aunt Ellen dared to enter? Had Fong overcome her terrors and forced her to take shelter? If he had she would be no farther than the hall.

Like a shadow she mounted the steps and stole in, the front door yawning on darkness. The stillness of complete desolation and abandonment met her ears.

She stood motionless, looking down the hall's shattered length and up the stairs. The noises from without, the continuous, dragging shuffle of passing feet, calls, crying of children, the soldier's directing voice, came sharply through the larger, encircling sounds of the city fighting for its life. They flowed round the house like a tide, leaving it isolated in the silence of a place doomed and deserted. She suddenly felt herself alone, bereft of human companionship, a lost particle in a world terribly strange, echoing with an ominous, hollow emptiness. A length of plaster fell with a dry thud, calling out small whisperings and cracklings from the hall's darkened depths. It roused her and she turned, pushed open the door and went into the drawing-room.

The long side windows let in the glare, a fierce illumination showing a vista of demolishment. Through broken bits of mortar the parquet reflected it; it struck rich gleams from the fragments of a mirror, ran up the walls, playing on the gilt of picture frames. She moved forward, trying to think they might be there, that someone might flit ghost-like toward her through that eerie barring of shadow and ruddy light. But the place was a dry, dead shell; no pulse of life seemed ever to have beaten within those ravaged walls. She summoned her energies to call, send out her voice in a cry for them, then stood—the quavering sound unuttered—hearing a step outside.

It was a quick, firm step, heavier than a woman's, and was coming down the stairs. She stood suddenly stricken to a waiting tension, dark against a long sweep of curtain, possessed by an immense expectancy, a gathering and condensing of all feeling into a wild hope. The steps gained the hall and came toward the doorway. Her hands, clasped, went out toward them, like hands extended in prayer, her eyes riveted on the opening. Through it—for a moment pausing on the sill to sweep the room's length—came Mark Burrage.

He did not see her, made a step forward and then heard her whisper, no word, only a formless breath, the shadow of a sound.

"Lorry!" he cried as he had cried the night before, and stood staring this way and that, feeling her presence, knowing her near.

Then he saw her, coming out of the darkness with her outstretched hands, not clasped now, but extended, the arms spread wide to him as he had dreamed of some day seeing them.

CHAPTER XXXV

THE UNKNOWN WOMAN

A FEW MINUTES AFTER the Vallejo Hotel had sunk into ruin, a man came running up the street. Even among those shaken from a normal demeanor by an abnormal event, he was noticeable; for he was wild, a creature dominated by a frenzied fear. As he ran he cried out for news of the hotel, and shouted answers smote against him like blows: "Down—gone down! Collapsed. Everybody in the lower floors dead!" And he rushed on, burst his way through groups, shot past others flying to the scene, flung obstructing figures from his path.

"Mad," someone cried, thrown to the wall by a sweep of his arm, "mad and running amuck."

They would have held him, a desperate thing, clawing and tearing his way through the crowd, but that suddenly, with a strangled cry, he came to a stop. Over the shoulders of a group of men he saw a girl's head, and his shout of "Pancha!" made them fall back. He gathered her in his arms, strained her against him, in the emotion of that supreme moment lifting his face to the sky. It was a face that those who saw it never forgot.

The men dispersed, were absorbed into the heaving tumult, running, squeezing, jamming here, thinning there, falling back before desperate searchers calling out names that would never be answered, thronging in the wake of women shrieking for their children. Police came battling their way through, forcing the people back. Swept against a fence Garland could at first only hold her, mutter over her, want to know that she was unhurt. She gave him broken answers; she had run up instead of down—that was how she was there. The horror of it came back in a sickening realization, and she shook, clinging to him, only his arm keeping her from falling. A man had thrown his

265

coat about her, and Garland pulled it over her, then, looking down, saw her feet, bare and scratched in pointed, high-heeled slippers. The sight of them, incongruous reminders of the intimate aspects of life, brought him down to the moment and her place in it.

"Come on," he said. "Let's get out of this. You want to get something on. Can you walk? Not far, only a few blocks."

She could do anything, she said, now that she knew he was safe, and, her fingers in the bend of his arm, he pulled her after him through the press. Gaining clearer spaces, they ran, side by side, their faces curiously alike, stamped by the same exalted expression as they fronted the rising sun.

She heard him say something about taking her away, having a horse and cart. She made no answer; with his presence all sensations but thankfulness seemed to have died in her. And then, upon her temporary peace, came thronging strange and dreadful impressions, waking her up, telling her the world had claims beyond the circle of her own consciousness. She caught them as she ran—a shifting series of sinister pictures: a house down in a tumbled heap of brick and stone, a sick woman on a couch on the sidewalk, a family dragging furniture through a blocked doorway, pillars, window ledges, cornices scattered along the road. Over all, delicately pervasive, adding a last ominous suggestion, was a faint, acrid odor of burning wood.

"Fire!" she said. "I can smell it."

"Oh, there'll be fires. That's bound to come."

"Where are we going?" she panted.

"Right round here—the place where I was stayin'. There's a widder woman keeps it, Mrs. Meeker. She's got a horse and cart that'll get you out of this. I guess all the car lines is bust, and I guess we'll have to move out quick. Look!"

He pointed over the roofs to where glassy films of smoke rose against the morning sky.

"Everyone of 'em's a fire and the wind's fresh. I hope to God this shake up ain't done any harm to the mains."

They had reached Mrs. Meeker's gate. He swung it open and she followed him across the garden to where a worn, grassy path, once a carriage drive, led past the house to the back yard. Here stood Mrs. Meeker, a hatchet in her hand, trying to pry open the stable door.

"Oh, Lord!" she cried, turning at his step, "I'm glad you've come back. Every other soul in the place has run off, and I can't get the stable door open."

Her glance here caught Pancha, her nightgown showing below the man's overcoat.

"Who's she?" she asked, a gleam of curiosity breaking through the larger urgencies.

"My daughter. She lives right round here. I run for her as soon as I felt the first quake. You got to take her along in the cart, and will you give her some clothes?"

"Sure," said Mrs. Meeker, and the flicker of curiosity extinguished, she returned to the jammed door that shut her out from the means of flight. "Upstairs in my room. Anything you want." Then to Garland, who had moved to her assistance, "I'm goin' to get out of here—go uptown to my cousin's. But I wouldn't leave Prince, not if the whole city was down in the dust."

Prince was Mrs. Meeker's horse, which, hearing its name, whinnied plaintively from the stable. Pancha disappeared into the house, and the man and woman attacked the door with the hatchet and a poker. As they worked she panted out disjointed bits of information:

"There's a man just come in here tellin' me there's fires, a lot of 'em, all started together. And he says there's houses down over on Minna and Tehama streets and people under them. Did you know the back wall's out of that new hotel? Fell clear across the court. I saw it go from my room—just a smash and a cloud of dust."

"Umph," grunted the man. "Anybody hurt?"

"I don't think so, but I don't know. I went out in front first off and saw the people pourin' out of it into the street—a whole gang in their nightgowns."

A soldier appeared walking smartly up the carriage drive, sweeping the yard with a glance of sharp command.

"Say. What are you fooling round that stable for?"

Mrs. Meeker, poker in hand, was on the defensive.

"I'm gettin' a horse out—my horse."

"Well, you want to be quick about it. You got to clear out of here. Anybody in the house?"

"No. What are you puttin' us out for?"

"Fire. You don't want to lose any time. We've orders to get the people on the move. I just been in that hotel next door and rooted out the last of 'em—running round packing their duds as if they'd hours to waste. Had to threaten some of 'em with the bayonet. Get busy now and get out."

He turned and walked off, meeting Pancha as she came from the house. A skirt and blouse of Mrs. Meeker's hung loose on her lithe thinness, their amplitude confined about her middle by a black crochet shawl which she had crossed over her chest and tied in the back.

"A lot of that big building's down," she cried, as she ran up. "I could see it from the window, all scattered across the open space behind it."

Engrossed in their task neither answered her, and she moved round the corner of the stable to better see the debris of the fallen wall. Standing thus, a voice dropped on her from a window in the house that rose beyond Mrs. Meeker's back fence.

"Do you know if all the people are out of that hotel?"

She looked up; standing in a third story window was a young man in his shirt sleeves. He appeared to have been occupied in tying his cravat, his hands still holding the ends of it. His face was keen and fresh, and was one of the first faces she had seen that morning that had retained its color and a look of lively intelligence.

"I don't know," she answered. "I've only just got here. Why?"

"Because it looks to me as if there was someone in one of the rooms—someone on the floor."

The stable door gave with a wrench and swung open. Garland jerked it wide and stepped back to where he could command the man in the window.

"What's that about someone in the hotel?" he said.

The young man leaned over the sill and completed the tying of his cravat.

"I can see from here right into one of those rooms, and I'm pretty sure there's a person lying on the floor—dead maybe. The electric light fixture's down and may have got them."

Garland turned to Mrs. Meeker:

"You get out Prince and put him in the cart." Then to the man in the window: "I'll go in and see. A soldier's just been here who says they've cleaned the place out. There's maybe somebody hurt that they ain't seen."

"Hold on a minute and I'll go with you," called the other. "I'm a doctor and I might come in handy. I'll be there in a jiff."

He vanished from the window, and before Prince was backed into the shafts, walked up the carriage drive, neatly clad, cool and alert, his doctor's bag in his hand.

"I was just looking at the place as I dressed. Queer sight—looks like a doll's house. Bedding flung back over the footboards, the way they'd thrown it when they jumped. Clothes neatly folded over the chairs. And then in that third-story room I saw something long and solid-looking on the floor. Seems to be tangled up in the coverlets. The electric light thing's sprinkled all over it. That's what makes me pretty sure—hit 'em as they made a break. Come on."

He and Garland made off as Pancha and Mrs. Meeker set to work on the harnessing of Prince.

The soldiers had done their work. The hotel was empty—a congeries of rooms left in wild disorder, opened trunks in the passages, clothes tossed and trampled on the floors. As the men ran up the stairs, its walls gave back the sound of their feet like a place long deserted and abandoned to decay. The recurring shocks that shook its dislocated frame sent plaster down, and called forth creaking protests from the wrenched girders. The rear was flooded with light, streaming in where the wall had been, and through open doors they saw the houses opposite filling in the background like the drop scene at a theater.

The third floor had suffered more than those below, and they made their way down a hall where mortar lay heaped over the wreckage of glass, pictures and chairs. The bedroom that was their goal was tragic in its signs of intimate habitation strewn and dust-covered, as if years had passed since they had been set forth by an arranging feminine hand. The place looked as untenanted as a tomb. Anyone glancing over its blurred ruin, no voice responding to a summons, might have missed the figure that lay concealed by the bed and partly enwrapped in its coverings.

The doctor, kneeling beside it, pushed them off and swept away the litter of glass and metal that had evidently fallen from the ceiling and struck the woman down. She was lying on her face, one hand still gripping the clothes, a pink wrapper twisted about her, her blonde hair stained with the ooze of blood from a wound in her head. He felt of her pulse and heart and twitching up her eyelids looked into her set and lifeless eyes.

"Is she dead?" Garland asked.

"No," He snapped his bag open with businesslike briskness. "Concussion. Got a glancing blow from the light fixture. Seems as if she'd been trying to wrap herself up in the bedclothes and got in the worst place she could—just under it."

"Can you do anything for her?"

"Not much. Rest and quiet is what she ought to have, and I don't see how she's going to get it the way things are now."

"We got a cart. We can take her along with us."

"Good work. I'll fix her up as well as I can and turn her over to you." He had taken scissors from his bag and with deft speed began to cut away the tangled hair from the torn flesh. "I'll put in a stitch or two and bind her up. Looks like a person of means." He gave a side glance at her hand, white and beringed. "You might get off the mattress while I'm doing this. We can put her on it and carry her down. She's a big woman; must be five feet nine or ten."

Garland dragged the mattress to the floor, while the doctor rose and made a dive for the bathroom. He emerged from it a moment later, his brow corrugated.

"No water!" he said, as he stepped over the strewn floor to his patient. "That's a cheerful complication."

He bent over her, engrossed in his task, every now and then, as the building quivered to the earth throes, stopping to mutter in irritated impatience. Garland went to the window and called down to Pancha and Mrs. Meeker that they'd found a woman, alive but unconscious, and space must be left for her in the cart. He stood for a moment watching them as they pulled out the up-piled household goods with which Mrs. Meeker had been filling it. Then the doctor, snapping his bag shut and jumping to his feet, called him back:

"That's done. It's all I can do for her now. Come on—lend a hand. Take her shoulders; she's a good solid weight."

Her head was covered with bandages close and tight as a nun's coif. They framed a face hardly less white and set in a stony insensibility.

"Lord, she looks like a dead one," Garland said, as he lowered the wounded head on the mattress.

"She's not that, but she may be unless she gets somewhere out of this. Easy now; these quakes keep getting in the way."

They carried her down the stairs and out into the street. Here the crowd, already moving before the fire, was thick, a dense mass, plowing forward through an atmosphere heat-dried and cinder-choked. The voices of police and soldiers rose above the multiple sounds of that tide of egress urging it on. A way was made for the men with their grim load, eyes touching it sympathetically, now and then a comment: "Dead is she, poor thing?" But mostly they were too bewildered or too swamped in their own tragedy to notice any other.

Prince and the cart were ready. From her discarded belongings Mrs. Meeker had salvaged three treasures, which she had stowed against the dashboard, a solio portrait of her late husband, a canary in a gilt cage, and a plated silver teapot. The body of the cart was clear, and the men placed the mattress there. The spread that covered the woman becoming disarranged, Pancha smoothed it into neatness, pausing to look with closer scrutiny into the marble face. It was so unlike the face she had seen before, rosy and smiling beneath the shade of modish hats, that no glimmer of recognition came to her. Chrystie was to her, as she was to the others, an unknown woman.

Mrs. Meeker, even in this vital moment, knew again a stir of curiosity.

"Who is she?" she said to the men. "Ain't you found anything up there to tell us where she belongs?"

The doctor's voice crackled like pistol shots:

"Good God, woman, we've not got time to find out who people *are*. Take her along—get a move on. It's getting d——d hot here."

It was; the heat of the growing conflagration was scorching on their faces, the cinders falling like rain.

"Get up there, Mrs. Meeker," Garland commanded; "on the front seat. You drive and Pancha and I'll walk alongside."

The woman climbed up. The doctor, turning to go, gave his last orders:

"Try and get her out of this—uptown—where there's air and room. Keep her as quiet as you can. You'll run up against doctors who'll help. Sorry I can't go along with you, but there'll be work for my kind all over the city today, and I got a girl across toward North Beach that I want to see after."

He was off down the carriage drive almost colliding with a soldier, who came up on the run, a bayoneted musket in his hand, his face a blackened mask, streaming with sweat. At the sight of the cart he broke into an angry roar:

"What are you standing round for? Do you want to be burnt? Get out. Don't you know the fire's coming? *Get out.*"

They moved out and joined the vast procession of a city in exodus.

For months afterward Pancha dreamed of that day—woke at night to a sense of toiling, onward effort, a struggling slow progress, accomplished amid a sea of faces all turned one way. The dream vision was not more prodigiously improbable than the waking fact—life, comfortable and secure, suddenly stripped of its garnishings, cut down to a single obsessing issue, narrowed to the point where the mind held but one desire—to be safe.

Before the advancing wall of flame the Mission was pouring out, retreating like an army in defeat. Every avenue was congested with the moving multitude, small streets emptying into larger ones, houses ejecting their inmates. At each corner the tide was swollen by new streams, rolling into the wider current, swaying to adjustment, then pressing on. Looking forward Pancha could see the ranks dark to the limit of her vision; looking back, the faces, smoke-blackened, sweat-streaked, marked with fierce tension, with fear, with dogged endurance, with cool courage, with blank incomprehension. The hot breath of the fire swept about them, the sound of its triumphant march was in their ears, a backward glance showed its first high flame crests. Soldiers drove them on, shouted at them, thrust stupefied figures in amongst them, pushed others, dazedly cowering in their homes, out through doors and ground-floor windows. At intervals the earth stirred and heaved, and then with a simultaneous cry, rising in one long wail of terror, they jammed together in the middle of the street, so close-packed a man could have walked on their heads.

To make way through them Garland was forced to lead the horse. Women clung to the shafts and trailed at the tailboard; the cart stopped by an influx of traffic, men stood on the hubs of the wheels staring back at the swelling smoke clouds. Mutual experiences flashed back and forth, someone's death dully recounted, a miraculous escape, tales of falling chimneys and desperate chances boldly taken. Some were bent under heavy loads, which they cast down despairingly by the way; some carried nothing. Those who had had time and clearness of head had packed baby carriages edge full of their dearest treasures; others pulled clothes baskets after them into which anything their hand had lighted on had been hurled pell-mell. There were sick dragged on sofas, wounded upheld by the arms of good Samaritans, old people in barrows, in children's carts, sometimes carried in a "chair" made by the linked hands of two men.

And everywhere trunks, their monotonous scraping rising above the shuffle of the myriad feet. Men pulled them by ropes taut about their chests, by the handles, pushed them from behind. Then as the day progressed and the smoke wall threw out long wings to the right and left, they began to leave them. The sidewalk was littered with them, they stood square in the path, tilted over into the gutter, end up against the fence. Other possessions were dropped beside them, pictures, sewing machines, furs, china ornaments, pieces of furniture, clocks, even the packed baby carriages and the clothes baskets. Only two things the houseless thousands refused to leave—their children and their pets. It seemed to Pancha there was not a family that did not lead a dog, or carry a cat, or a bird in a cage.

By midday the cart had made an uptown plaza, and there come to a halt for rest. The grass was covered thick with people, stretched beside their shorn belongings, many asleep as they had dropped. A few of them had brought food; others, with money, went out to buy what they could at the nearby shops, already depleted of their stores. All but the children were very still, looking at the flames that licked along the sky line. They had heard now the story of the broken mains, and somberly, without lament or rebellion, recognized the full extent of the calamity.

A young girl, standing on a wall, a line of pails beside her, offered cupfuls of water to those who drooped or fainted. Thirsty hoards besieged her, and Pancha, edging in among them, made her demand, not for herself, but for a sick woman. The girl dipped a small cut-glass pitcher in one of the pails and handed it to her.

"That's a double supply," she said. "But you look as if you needed some for yourself. We've a little water running in our house, and I'm going to stand here and dole it out till the fire comes. They say that'll be in a few hours, so don't bring back the pitcher. There's only my mother and myself, and we can't carry anything away."

Pancha squeezed out with her treasure, and going to the cart climbed into the front, sliding over the seat to a space at the head of the mattress. She bent over the still figure, looking into the face. Its youth and comeliness smote her, seemed to knock at her heart and soften something there that had been hard. An uprush of intense feeling, pity for this blighted creature, this maimed and helpless thing, rescued by chance from a horrible death, rose and flooded her. She moistened the temples and dry lips, lifted the bound head to her lap, striving for some expression of her desire to heal, to care for, to restore to life the broken sister that fate had cast into her hands. Mrs. Meeker came and peered over the side of the cart, shaking her head dubiously.

"Looks like to me she'd never open her eyes again."

Pancha was pierced with an angry resentment.

"Don't say that. She's going to get well. I'm going to make her."

"I hope you can," said the elder woman. "Poor thing, what a time she must have had! Your pa says it seemed as if there was no one there with her. I'd like to know who she is."

"She's somebody rich. Look at her hands."

She touched, with a caressing lightness, Chrystie's hand, milk-white, satin-fine, a diamond and sapphire ring on one finger.

Mrs. Meeker nodded.

"Oh, yes, she's no poor girl. Anyone can see that. You'd get it from the wrapper, let alone the rings. I've been wondering if maybe she wasn't straight."

"She is. I know it."

"How could you know that?"

"By her face."

Mrs. Meeker considered it, and murmured:

"I guess you're right. It has got an innocent look. It'll be up to you, whether she lives or dies, to find out who she is and if she's got any relations."

"Oh, that'll be all right," said Pancha confidently, "I'm going to take care of her and cure her, and when she's good and ready she'll tell me."

They moved on for quieter surroundings and to find a doctor. This was a hopeless quest. Every house that bore a sign was tried, and at each one the answer was the same: the doctor was out; went right after the quake to be back no one knew when. Some were at the Mechanics' Pavilion, where the injured had been gathered, and which had to be vacated later in the day; others at work in the hospitals being cleared before the fire's advance.

Late in the afternoon Mrs. Meeker left them to go to her cousin's, who had a cottage up beyond Van Ness Avenue. Prince and the cart she gave over to them; they'd need it to get the woman away out of all this noise and excitement. Tears were in her eyes as she bade farewell to the old horse, giving Garland an address that would find her later—"unless it goes with the rest of the town"—she added resignedly. In the first shadowing of twilight, illumined with the fire's high glow, they watched her trudge off, the bird cage in one hand, the portrait in the other, the teapot tucked under her arm.

It was night when they came to a final halt—a night horribly bright, the sky a blazing splendor defying the darkness. The place was an open space on the first rise of the Mission Hills. There were houses about, here and there ascending the slope in an abortive attempt at a street which, halfway up, abandoned the effort and lapsed into a sprinkling of one-story cottages. Above them, on the naked hillside, the first wave of refugees had broken and scattered. Under the fiery radiance they sat, dumb with fatigue, some sleeping curled up among their bundles, some clustered about little cores of fire over which they cooked food brought out to them from the houses. A large tree stretched its limbs over a plateau in the hill's flank and here the cart was brought to a stop. Prince, loosed from the shafts, cropped a supper from the grass, and the unknown woman lay on her mattress under the red-laced shade.

A girl from a cottage down the slope brought them coffee, bread and fruit, and sitting side by side they ate, looking out over the sea of roofs to where the ragged flame tongues leaped and dropped, and the smoke mountains rolled sullenly over the faint, obscured stars. They spoke little, aware for the first time of a great exhaustion, hearing strangely the sounds of a life that went on as if unchanged and uninterrupted—the clinking of china, the fitful cries of children sinking to sleep, the barking of dogs, a voice crooning a song, and laughter, low-voiced and sweet.

Presently they drew closer together and began to talk; at first of immediate interests—food to be procured, the injured woman, how to care for her, find her shelter, discover who she was. Then of themselves—how the quake had come to each, that mad, upward rush of Pancha's, Garland's race along the street. That done, she suddenly dropped down and lying with her head against his knee, her face turned from the firelight, she told him how Boyé Mayer had come to her in the dawn, and how he lay buried in the ruins of the Vallejo Hotel.

CHAPTER XXXVI

THE SEARCH

THERE WAS NO INTERCHANGE of vows, no whispered assurances and shy confessions, between Lorry and Mark. After that sheltering enfoldment in his arms, she drew back, her hands on his shoulders, looking into his face with eyes that showed no consciousness of a lover's first kiss. For a space their glances held, deep-buried each in each, saying what their lips had no words for, pledging them one to the other, making the pact that only death should break. Then her hands slid down and, one caught in his, they moved across the room.

During the first moments exaltation lifted her above her troubles. His longed-for presence, the feel of his hand round hers, made her forget the rest, gave her a temporary respite. Only half heeding, she heard him tell how her summons had come, how, with two other men who had families in the city, he had chartered an engine, made part of the journey in that, then in a motor, given them by a farmer, reached Oakland, and there hired a tug which had landed him an hour before at the Italian's wharf.

For himself he had found her, after a day of agonized apprehension, at a time when his hopes were dwindling. To know her safe, to feel her hand inside his own, was enough. All she told him then was that she had come back to the house for Aunt Ellen and Chrystie, and found they were gone. But they might have left a letter, some written message to tell her where they were. With those words her anxieties came to life again, her step lost its lingering slowness, her face its rapt tranquillity.

Dropping his hand, she started on a search, through slanting doorways, by choked passages, across the illumined spaciousness of the wide, still rooms. Nothing was there, and she turned to the stairs, running up, he at her heels, two shadows flitting through the red-shot gloom. The upper floor, more damaged than the lower, was swept with the sinister luster, shooting in above the trees, revealing perspectives of ruin. Every window was broken, and the heat and the smell of burning poured in, the drift of cinders black along the floors.

She darted ahead into her own room, going to the bureau, sending a lightning look over it. Standing in the doorway he saw her start, wheel about to glance at the bed, the chair. A pile of dresses lay in a corner, the closet door was open.

"Someone's been here," she said. "The diamond aigrette, the jewel box—all my things are gone. Even the dress I wore last night—it was on the bed. They've all been taken."

He came in and took her arm, drawing her away.

"Everything of value's gone," he said quietly. "I went all through the house before you came and saw it: the silver downstairs; even a lot of the pictures are cut out of their frames. Looters have been here, and they've made a clean sweep. I hoped you wouldn't see it. Come, let's go."

She lingered, moving the ornaments about on the bureau, still hunting for the letter, and muttering low to herself,

"It doesn't matter. Those things don't matter"—then in a voice suddenly tremulous—"they've left no letter. They've left nothing to tell me if Chrystie's back and where they've gone to."

His hand on her arm drew her toward the door.

"Lorry, dear, there's no good doing this. They were probably put out, had to go in a hurry, hadn't time to do any thinking. When I came in here there was a soldier patrolling along the street. He may have been there when they left; and if he was he may know something about them."

She caught at the hope, was all tingling life again, making for the stairs.

"Of course. I saw him, too, and I dodged behind him. If he was here then he'd know. They might even have left a message with him. Oh, there he is!"

The arch of the hall door framed the soldier's figure, standing on the top of the street steps, a gold-touched statue lifted above the surging procession of heads. With a swooping rush she was at his side.

"Where are the people who were in this house?" she gasped.

The man started and wheeled on her, saw Burrage behind her, and looked from one to the other, surprised.

"How'd you get in there?" he demanded. "That house was cleared out this afternoon."

"Never mind that," said Mark. "We're leaving it now. This lady's looking for her family that she left here earlier in the day."

"Well, I got 'em off—at least I got the only one here, an old lady. She was sittin' there on the grass where you see the chairs. We had orders to put out everyone along this block, and seem' she was old and upset I commandeered an express wagon that was passin' and made the driver take her along."

"Only *one* lady?" Lorry's voice was husky.

"Yes, miss, only one. I asked her if there was anybody in the house, and she said no, she was alone. There was a Chinaman with her that helped me pack her in comfortable—a smart, handy old chap. I don't know where he went; I didn't see him again."

A heart-piercing sound of suffering burst from the girl, and her face sank into her hands. The soldier eyed her sympathetically.

"I'm sorry, lady, I can't tell you where she's gone. But, believe me, it was no picnic gettin' the people started—some of 'em wantin' to stay, and others of 'em wantin' to take all the furniture along. We didn't have time to ask questions. But you'll happen on her all right. She's safe uptown with friends."

Lorry made no answer, and Mark led her down the steps. He thought her emotion the expression of overwrought nerves, and consoled her with assurances of a speedy finding of Aunt Ellen. She dropped her hands, lifted to his a face that startled him, and cried from the depths of a despair he had yet to understand.

"It's Chrystie, it's Chrystie! She's gone, she's lost!"

Then, pressed close to him, two units absorbed into the moving mass, she told him the story of Chrystie's disappearance.

His heart sank as he listened. Disagreeing in words, he saw the truth of her contention that if Chrystie had been out of town she would have been able to get word to them and would have done it.

It looked as if the girl was in the city, hidden somewhere by Mayer. Listening to Lorry's account of the interview in the Argonaut Hotel, he disbelieved what the man had said, rejected her theory of his innocence. Chrystie nerved to a bold deception, the charges in the anonymous letter, all stood to him for signs of Mayer's guilt. He told her none of this, tried to cheer and reassure her, but he saw with a dark dread what might have happened. An hour before he had skirted the edges of the fire, seen the hotel district burning, heard of fallen buildings. Chrystie could have been there keeping a tryst with Mayer. He let his thoughts go no further, stopped them in their race toward a tragedy that would shatter the girl beside him as the city had been shattered.

As they walked her eye ranged over the throng, shot its strained inquiry along the swaying sea of bodies. Chrystie might be among them, might even now be somewhere in this endless army. A woman's figure, caught through a break in the ranks, called her to a running chase; a girl's face, glimpsed over her shoulder, brought her to a standstill, pitifully expectant. He tried to get her to Mrs. Kirkham's, but was met with a refusal he saw there was no use combating. Early night found them in a plaza on a hilltop, moving from group to group.

He had a memory of her never to be forgotten, walking ahead of him, copper-bright, as she fronted the blazing light, black against it, bending to look at a half-hidden face, kneeling beside a covered shape, outstretched in a stupor of sleep. The night had reached its middle hours, the dense stillness of universal repose held the crowded spot, when she finally sank in a helpless exhaustion and slept at his feet. He could do nothing but cover her with his coat, hold vigil over her, move so that his body was a shield to keep the glare from her face. He watched her till the day came, and the noises of the waking life around them called her back to the consciousness of her anxiety.

The loss of relatives and friends was one of the following features of the great disaster. With every means of communication cut off, with a great area flaming, impossible to cross, enormous to circle, with the exodus in some places so hurried no time was left for plans or the sending of messages, with the spread of the fire so rapid no one knew where the houseless thousands would end their march, families were scattered, individuals lost track of. Groups that at dawn had been a compact whole, an hour later had broken, been dispersed, members vanished, disappeared in the inconceivable chaos. To those who suffered this added horror the earthquake remains less a national calamity than the memory of a time when they knew an anguish beyond their dreams of what pain could be.

So it was with Lorry. The wide, encompassing distress touched her no more than the storm does one sick unto death. The growing demolition, spread out under her eyes roused no responsive interest. It was like a story someone was trying to tell her when she was writhing in torment, a nightmare coming in flashes of recollection through a day full of real, poignant terrors.

For two days she and Mark searched. There were periods when she sought the shelter of Mrs. Kirkham's flat, dropped on a bed and slept till the drained reservoir of her strength was refilled, then was up and out again. Mark and the old lady had no power to stay her. He went with her, and Mrs. Kirkham kept a fire in the little oven of bricks in the gutter so that food might be ready when they came back. Returning from their fruitless wanderings, they found the old lady seated in a rocking-chair on the sidewalk, a parasol over her head to keep the cinders off, the coffeepot on the curb and the brick oven hot and ready.

It was Mrs. Kirkham who found Aunt Ellen—safe with friends near the Presidio. Lorry would not go to her, unable to bear her questions. So, Mrs. Kirkham, who had not walked more than three blocks for years, toiled up there, sinking on doorsteps to get back her wind, helping where she could—a baby carried, a woman told to come round to the flat and get "a bite of dinner." She quieted Aunt Ellen, explained that Lorry was with her, said nothing of Chrystie, and toiled home, dropping with groans into her chair by the gutter. When she had got her breath she built up the fire and brewed a fragrant potful of coffee, which she offered to the worn and weary outcasts as they plodded past.

There was not a plaza or square in that part of the city to which Lorry and Mark did not go. They hunted among the countless hoards that spread over the lawns in Golden Gate Park, and covered the hillsides of the Presidio. They went through the temporary

hospitals—wards given to the sick and injured in the military bar-
racks, tent villages on the parade ground. They saw strange sights,
terrible sights; birth and death under the trees in the open; saw a
heroism, undaunted and undismayed; saw men and women, ruined
and homeless, offering aid, succoring distress, gallant, selfless, forever memorable.

Night came upon them in these teeming camping grounds.
Along the road's edges the lights of tiny fires—allowed for cooking—broke out in a line of jeweled sparks. Women bent over them;
men lighted their pipes and lay or squatted round these rude hearths,
all that they had of home. The smell of supper rose appetizingly, coffee simmering, bacon frying. Calls went back and forth for that most
valued of possessions, a can opener. There was laughter, jokes passed
over exchanges of food, an excess of tea here swapped for a loaf of
bread there, a bottle of Zinfandel for a box of sardines. It was like a
great, democratic picnic to which everybody had been invited—the
rich, the poor, the foreign elements, white, black and yellow, the old
and the young, the good and bad, virtue from Pacific Avenue, vice
from Dupont Street, the prominent citizen and the derelict from the
Barbary Coast.

The fire flung its banners across the sky, a vast lighting up for
them, under which they went about the business of living. At intervals,
booming through the sounds of their habitation, came the dynamite
explosions blowing up the city in blocks. When the muffled roar was
over, the gathering quiet was pierced by the thin, high notes of gramo-
phones. From the shadow of trees Caruso's voice rose in the swaggering
lilt of "*La Donna e Mobile*," to be answered by Melba's, crystal-sweet,
from a machine stored in a crowded cart. There were ragtime melodies,
and someone had a record of "Marching Through Georgia" that always
drew forth applause. Then, as the night advanced, a gradual hush fell,
a slow sinking down into silence, broken by a child's querulous cry, a
groan of pain, the smothered mutterings of a dreamer. Like the slain
on a battlefield, they lay on the roadside, dotted over the slopes, thick
as fallen leaves under the trees, their faces buried in arms or wrappings
against the fall of cinders and the hot glare.

In all these places Lorry and Mark sent out that call for the lost
which park and reservation soon grew to know and echo. Standing on

a rise of ground Mark would cry with the full force of his lungs, "Is Chrystie Alston there?" The shout spread like a ring on water, and at the limits of its carrying power, was taken up and repeated. They could hear it fainter in a strange voice—"Is Chrystie Alston there?"—then fainter still as voice after voice took it up, sent it on, threw it like a ball from hand to hand, till, a winged question, it had traversed the place. But there was no answer, no jubilant response to be relayed back, no Chrystie running toward them with welcoming face.

Late on the second night he induced her to go back to Mrs. Kirkham's. She was heavy on his arm, stumbling as she walked, not answering his attempts at cheer. He delivered her over to the old lady, who had to help her to bed, then sat and waited in the dining room. No lights were allowed in any house, and this room was chosen as the place of their night counsels because of the illumination that came in through the open hole of the fireplace, wrenched out when the chimney fell. When Mrs. Kirkham came back he and she exchanged a somber look, and the old lady voiced both their thoughts:

"She can't stand this. She can't go on. She's hardly able to move now. What shall we do?"

Their consultation brought them nowhere. As things stood there was no way of instituting a more extended search. The police could be of no assistance, overwhelmed with their labors; individuals who might have helped were lost in the mêlée; money was as useless as strings of cowrie shells.

At dawn Mrs. Kirkham stole away to come back presently saying the girl was sleeping.

"She looks like the dead," she whispered. "She hasn't strength enough to go out again. I can keep her here now."

Mark got up.

"Then I'll go; it's what I've been waiting for. Without her I can cover a big area; move quick. I want to try the other side of town. In my opinion Mayer had Chrystie somewhere. She was prepared for a journey—the trunk and the money show that—and the journey was to be with him. If he got her off we'll hear from her in a day or two. If he didn't she's in the city, and it's just possible she drifted or was caught in the Mission crowd. Anyway, I'm going to try that section.

Tell Lorry I've gone there. Keep up her hope, and for heaven's sake try to keep her quiet. I'll be back by evening."

So he went forth. It seemed a blind errand—to find a woman gone without leaving a trace, in a city where two hundred thousand people were homeless and wandering. But it was a time when the common sense of every day was overleaped, when men attempted and achieved beyond the limits of reason and probability.

Half an hour after he had left the flat he met with a piece of luck that gave his spirit a brace. On the steps of a large house, deserted for two days, he came upon one of his companion clerks. This youth, son of the rich, had procured a horse and delivery wagon and had come back to carry away silver and valuables left piled in the front hall. Also he had a bicycle, an article just then of inestimable value, and hearing Mark's intention of crossing the city, loaned it to him.

People who live in the Mission are still wont, when the great quake is spoken of, to remember the man on the bicycle. So many of them saw him, so many of them were stopped and questioned by him. Looking for a lady, he told them, and that he looked far and wide they could testify. He was seen close to the fire line, up along the streets that stretched back from it, in among the crowds camped on the vacant lots, through the plazas and the tents that were starting up like mushrooms in every clear space. In the little shack where the *Despatch* was getting out its first paper, full of advertisements for the lost and offers of shelter to the outcast, he turned up at midday. He saw Crowder there, told him the situation, and left with him an advertisement "for any news of Chrystie Alston."

Late afternoon saw him back on the edges of the Mission Hills. The great human wave here had reached the limit of its wash. The throng was thinner, dwindling to isolated groups. Wheeling his bicycle he threaded a way among them, looking, scrutinizing, asking his questions. But no one had any comfort for him, heads were shaken, hands uplifted and dropped in silent sign of ignorance.

He followed a road that ascended by houses, steps and porches crowded with refugees, to the higher slopes where the buildings were small and far apart. The road shriveled to a dusty track, and leaning his bicycle against the fence he sat down. He felt an exhaustion, bodily and spiritual, and propping his elbows on his knees, let his forehead sink on his hands. For a space he thought of nothing but Lorry waiting for news and his return to her that night.

A woman's voice, coming from the hill above roused him,

"Say, mister, have you got a bicycle?"

He started and turning saw a girl running down the slope toward him. She came with a breathless speed—a grotesque figure, thin and dark, loose cotton garments eddying back from her body, her feet in beaded, high-heeled slippers sure and light among the rolling stones.

"Yes," he said, rising, "I've got a bicycle."

She came on, panting, her hair in the swiftness of her progress blown out in a black mist from her brow. Her face, dirty and smoke-smeared, struck him as vaguely familiar.

"I saw you from the barn up there," she jerked her hand backward to a barn on the summit, "and I just made a dash down to catch you." She landed against the fence with a violent jolt. "This morning a man who'd come up from below told me the *Despatch* was going to be published with advertisements in it."

"It is," he said. "By tomorrow probably."

"Are you going down there again?" She swept the city with a grimed, brown hand.

"I'm going down sometime, not right now."

"Any time'll do—only the sooner the better. I've got an advertisement to put in. Will you take it?"

He nodded. He would be able to do it tomorrow.

She smiled, and with the flash of her teeth and something of gamin roguishness in her expression, the feeling that he had seen her before—knew her—grew stronger. He eyed her, puzzled, and seeing the look, she grinned in gay amusement.

"I guess you know *me*, a good many people do. But my make-up's new—dirt. Water's too valuable to use for washing."

He was not quite sure yet, and his expression showed it. That made her laugh, a mischievous note.

"Ain't you ever been to the Albion, young man?"

"Oh!" he breathed. "Why, of course—Pancha Lopez!"

"Come on then," she cried; "now we're introduced. Come up while I write the ad."

She drew away from the fence while he wheeled his bicycle in through a break in the pickets. As she moved along the path in front of him, she called back:

"We're up here in the barn, our castle on the hill. It mayn't look much from the outside, but it's roomy and the view's fine. Better than being crowded into the houses with the people sleeping on the floors. They'd have taken us in, any of 'em, but we chose the barn—quieter and more air. My pa's with me." She turned and threw a challenging glance at him. "You didn't know I had a pa? Well, I have and a good one." Then she raised her voice and called: "Pa, hello! I've corralled a man who'll take that ad."

From the open door of the barn a man of burly figure appeared. He nodded to Mark, bluffly friendly.

"That's good. We didn't know how we was to get in from this far, and we bin lookin' out for someone." Then turning to the girl, "You get busy? honey, and write it. We don't want to waste this young feller's time."

They entered the barn, a wide, shadowy place, cool and quiet, with hay piled in the back. Depressions in it showed where they had been sleeping, a horse blanket folded neatly beside each nest. To the left an open door led into what seemed a room for tools and farm supplies. Mark could see one corner where below a line of pegs gunny sacks, stacked and bulging, leaned against the wall.

"Now if you'll further oblige me with a pencil and paper," said the girl, "I'll tackle it, though writing's not my strong suit."

He pulled out a letter—offering a clean back—and a fountain pen. The girl took them, then stood in dubious irresolution, looking at them with uneasy eyes.

"I don't know as I can," she said. "I don't know how to put it. I guess you'd do it better. I'll tell you and you write."

"Very well." She handed the things back, and going to the wall he placed the letter against it and, the pen lifted, turned to her. "Go ahead, I'm ready."

The girl, baffled and uncertain, looked for help to her father.

"How'll I begin?"

"Tell him what it's about," he suggested. "You give him the facts, and he'll put 'em into shape."

"Well, we've got a sick woman here, and we don't know who she is. We found her in a hotel, hit on the head, and she's not spoken much yet—not anything that'll give any clew to where she comes from or who she belongs to. That's what the ad's for. She's a lady, young, and she's tall—nearly as tall as you. Blonde, blue eyes and golden hair, and she's got three rings—" She stopped, the words dying before the expression of the young man's face.

"Where is she?" he said.

Pancha pointed to the room on the left, saw the letter drop to the floor as he turned and ran for the doorway, saw him enter and heard his loud ejaculation.

For a moment she and her father stared, open-mouthed, at one another, then she went to the door. In the room, swept with pure airs from the open window, the light subdued by a curtain of gunny sacks, the young man was kneeling by the side of the mattress, his hand on the sick woman's. She was looking at him intently, a slow intelligence gathering in her eyes. The ghost of a smile touched her lips, and they parted to emit in the small voice of a child,

"Marquis de Lafayette."

CHAPTER XXXVII

HAIL AND FAREWELL

THE ALSTONS HAD TAKEN a house in San Rafael. It was a big comfortable place with engirdling balconies whence one looked upon the blossoming beauties of a May-time garden. Aunt Ellen thought it much too large, but when the settling down was accomplished, saw why Lorry had wanted so much room. Mrs. Kirkham was invited over from town "to stay as long as she liked," and now for a week there had been visitors from up country—Mrs. Burrage and Sadie.

It made quite a houseful and Fong, with a new second boy to break in, was exceedingly busy. He had brushed aside Lorry's suggestion that with half the city in ruins and nobody caring what they ate, simple meals would suffice. That was all very well for other people—let them live frugally if they liked; Fong saw the situation from another angle. Back in his old place, his young ladies blooming under his eye, he gave forth his contentment in the exercise of his talents. Gastronomic masterpieces came daily from his hands, each one a note in his hymn of thanksgiving.

When the fire was under control he had turned up at Mrs. Kirkham's, saying he had thought "Miss Lolly" would be there. Then he had taken Lorry's jewel box from under his coat and held it out to her, answering her surprise with a series of smiling nods. He had everything safe, down on the water front—the silver, the best glass, all the good clothes and most of the pictures which he cut from their frames. Yes, he had moved them after Aunt Ellen left, having packed them earlier in the day and got a friend from Chinatown who had a butcher's wagon. They had worked together, taken the things out through the back alley, very quiet, very quick; the soldiers never saw them. He had driven across town to a North Beach wharf, hired a fishing smack, and with two Italians for crew, cast off and sailed about the bay for three days.

"I stay on boat all time," he said. "My business mind your stuff. I watch out, no leave dagoes, no go sleep. All locked up now. Chinamen hide him, keep him safe. I bring back when you get good house."

When they moved to San Rafael he brought them back, a load that must have filled the butcher's wagon to its hood. His young ladies' gratitude pleased him, but to their offers of a reward he would not listen.

"Old Chinaman take care of my boss's house like my boss want me. Bad time, good time, ally samey. You no make earthquake—he come—my job help like evly day. I no good Chinaman if I don't. I no get paid extla for do my job."

The girls, after fruitless efforts, had to give in. Afterward, in their rooms when they sorted the clothes—the two beds were covered with them—they cried and laughed over the useless finery. Fong had carried away only the richest and costliest—evening dresses, lace petticoats, opera wraps, furs, high-heeled slippers, nothing that could be worn as life was now.

"We'll have to go about in ball dresses for the rest of the summer," said Chrystie, giggling hysterically. "How nice you'll look weeding the garden in an ermine stole and white satin slippers."

"We've got to wear them somewhere," Lorry decided.

"For one reason we've almost nothing else, and for another—and the real one—Fong mustn't know he's rescued the wrong things. I *will* weed the garden in white satin slippers, and I'll put on a ball dress for dinner every night."

Chrystie was well again now. Drowsing on the balcony in the steamer chair and taking sun baths in the garden had restored her, if not quite to her old rosy robustness, to a pale imitation of her once glowing self. The rest of her hair had been cut off, and her shaven poll was hidden by a lace cap with a fringe of false curls sewed to its edge. This was very becoming and in sweeping draperies—some of the evening dresses made over into tea gowns—she was an attractive figure, her charms enhanced by a softening delicacy.

The dark episode of her disappearance was allowed to rest in silence. She and Lorry had threshed it out as far as Lorry thought fit. That Boyé Mayer had dropped out of sight was all Chrystie knew. Some day later she would hear the truth, which Lorry had learned from Pancha Lopez. Lorry had also decided that the world must never know just what *did* happen to the second Miss Alston. The advertisement in the *Despatch* was withdrawn in time, and those who shared the knowledge were sworn to secrecy. Her efforts to invent a plausible explanation caused Chrystie intense amusement. She hid it at first, was properly attentive and helpful, but to see Lorry trying to tell lies, worrying and struggling over it, was too much. A day came when she forgot both manners and sympathy, began to titter and then was lost. Lorry was vexed at first, looked cross, but when the sinner gasped out, "Oh, Lorry, I never thought I'd see *you* come to this," couldn't help laughing herself.

On a bright Saturday afternoon Chrystie and Sadie were sitting on the front balcony in the shade of the Maréchal Niel rose. Mrs. Burrage and Lorry had gone for a drive, later to meet Mark—who was to stay with them over Sunday—at the station. Upstairs Aunt Ellen and Mrs. Kirkham were closeted with a dressmaker, fashioning festal attire. For that night there was to be a dinner, the first since the move. Beside the household Mark was coming, and Crowder was expected on a later train with Pancha Lopez and her father—eight people, quite an affair. Fong had been marketing half the morning, and was now in the kitchen in a state of temperamental irritation, having even swept Lorry from his presence with a commanding, "Go away, Miss Lolly. I get clazy if you wolly me now."

Sadie and Chrystie had become very friendly. Sadie was not disinclined to adore the youngest Miss Alston, so easy to get on with, so full of fun and chatter. Chrystie had fulfilled her expectations of what an heiress should be, handsome as a picture, clothed in silken splendors, regally accepting her plenty, carelessly spendthrift.

Lorry had rather disappointed her. She was not pretty, didn't seem to care what she had on, and was so quiet. And as an engaged girl there was nothing romantic about her, no shy glances at Mark, no surreptitious hand pressures. Sadie would have set her down as dreadfully matter-of-fact except that now and then she did such queer, unexpected things. For example the first afternoon they were there, she had astonished Sadie by suddenly getting up and without a word kissing Mother on the forehead. Mother, whom you never could count on, had begun to talk about the days when she was waitress in The Golden Nugget Hotel—broke into it as if it didn't matter at all. It made Sadie get hot all over; she didn't suppose they knew, and under her eyelids looked from one girl to the other to see how they'd take it. They didn't show anything, only seemed interested, and Sadie was calming down when Mother started off on George Alston—how fine he used to treat her and all that. It was then that Lorry did the queer thing—not a word out of her; just got up and kissed Mother and sat down. In her heart Sadie marveled at the perversity of men—Mark to have fallen in love with the elder when the younger sister was there!

She spoke about it to Mother upstairs that night, but Mother was unsatisfactory, smiled ambiguously and said:

"I guess Mark's the smart one of *our* family."

In the shade of the Maréchal Niel rose the girls talked and Chrystie, her tongue unloosed by growing intimacy, told about her wild adventure. She could not help it; after all Sadie knew a lot already, and it hampered conversation and the spontaneities of friendship to have to stop and think whether one ought to say this or not say that. It completed Sadie's subjugation: here *was* a romance. She breathlessly listened, in a state of staring attention that would have made a less garrulous person than Chrystie tell secrets. When she knew all she couldn't help asking—no girl could:

"But did you love him *really?*"

Chrystie, stretching a white hand for a branch of the rose and drawing it, blossom-weighted, to her face, answered:

"No, I thought I did at first; it was so exciting and all the girls said he was such a star. But I was always afraid of him. He sort of magnetized me—made me feel I'd be a poor-spirited chump if I didn't run away with him. You don't want to have a man think that about you, so I said I would and I did go. But that night—shall I ever forget it? It was pure misery."

"Do you think you *would* have gone with him?"

"I guess so, just because I hadn't the nerve not to. I felt as if I *had* to see it through—was sort of pledged to it. Maybe I didn't want to go back on him, and maybe I was ashamed to. You can hardly call the earthquake a piece of luck, but it was for me."

She sniffed at the roses while Sadie eyed her almost awed. Eighteen and with this behind her! The more she knew of the youngest Miss Alston the more her respect and admiration increased. She waited expectantly for the heroine to resume, which she did after a last, luxurious inhalation of the rose's breath.

"Wasn't it wonderful that the person who found me was Pancha Lopez? I keep thinking of it all the time. You know I was always crazy about her, but I never thought I'd meet her. And then to finally do it the way I did!"

Sadie's comment showed a proper comprehension of this strange happening, and then she wanted to know what Pancha Lopez was like.

"Oh, she's a priceless thing—there's nobody anywhere like her, in looks or any other way. She's different. You can't take your eyes off her, and yet she's not pretty. Remarkable people never are."

This was a new thought to Sadie who, absorbing it slowly, ventured a safe:

"Aren't they?"

"No, it's only the second-class ones who don't amount to anything who are good-looking. I must say it was a blow to me to hear that her real name was Michaels. But of course actresses generally have other names, and Lopez does belong to her in a sort of way. She told Lorry about it and about her father, too. Nobody knew she had a father."

"What's he like?"

"Oh, he's a grand old dear—rough, but he would be naturally, just a miner all his life. He took care of me as if I was a baby."

"He won't have to be a miner any more now."

They exchanged a glance of bright meaning, and Chrystie, drawing herself up in the chair, spoke with solemn emphasis:

"Sadie, I've always been glad I had money, because I'd be lost without it. But I'm glad now for another reason—because we could do something for those two. If we couldn't they'd have had to go back and begin all over again. Pancha's got some money saved up, but it'll be a long time before she gets it, and Lorry says it wouldn't be enough any way. Think of that kind old bear with his hair getting gray trudging up and down the Mother Lode! If I'd thought that was to go on I'd never have had a peaceful night's sleep again. We'd have had to adopt him, and I *know* he wouldn't have liked that. Now, thank heaven, we can make him comfortable in his own way."

"Did he tell you what it was he wanted to do?"

"No, he wouldn't, but Lorry got hold of Pancha and wormed it all out of her. For years he's been longing to settle down on a ranch—that was his dream. Poor little dream! Well, it's coming true. We've got several ranches, but there's only one that counts—in Mexico. There's a small one down in Kern that father bought ages ago for a weighmaster he had who got consumption. He died there—the weighmaster, I mean—and we've gone on renting it out and the trustees having all sorts of bother with the tenants. So that's going to be Mr. Michael's. Lorry had the transfer made, or whatever you call it, yesterday in town. She's going to give him the papers tonight."

"It'll be the last time you'll see them for a long while, I guess."

Chrystie, suddenly pensive, dropped back in the chair.

"Um, it will. Before we see Pancha again it may be years. She's going abroad to study. But she's promised to write and tell us all about how she's getting on. And when she comes back—a real grand opera singer—won't I be in a state! I get all wrought up now thinking about it. If she makes her first appearance in New York I'm going on there to see her."

"How long will it take—getting her ready, training her and teaching her?"

"No one can tell exactly. People here who've heard her and know about those things say she has such a fine voice and is so quick and clever that she might go on the stage over there in a year or two. She's got a lot to learn of course; even the way I feel about her I can see she needs to be more educated. But no matter how long it takes she's going to be financed—that's what they call it—till she's finished and ready. Lorry's guaranteed that."

"Lorry's awful grateful to them, isn't she?"

"Lorry!" Chrystie's glance showed surprise at such a question. "She's ready to give them everything she has. She's not just grateful, she's *bowed down* with it. Why she advertised in all the papers for that doctor who saw me on the floor, and now she's found him she'd build him a whole hospital if he'd let her. Lorry's not like me. *She's got deep feelings.*"

The carriage, turning in at the gate, stopped the conversation, and Chrystie rose and sauntered to the top of the steps. Mother Burrage, in her new black silk mantle, bought through a catalogue, and a perfect fit, came up the path, Mark and Lorry behind her. Mark waved a greeting hand and Lorry called instructions—please tell Fong to bring out something cold to drink and tell Aunt Ellen and Mrs. Kirkham to come downstairs even if they were in their wrappers—they must be worn out shut up with the dressmaker all day. It was exactly the sort of thing Sadie knew she would say—and Mark only just off the train.

The dinner that night was a brilliant success. Fong had outdone himself, the menu was a triumph, the table a shining splendor. He had insisted on setting it—no green second boy could lay a hand on the family treasures, now almost sacred, like vessels lost from a church and miraculously restored. In the center he had placed the great silver bowl given to George Alston by the miners of The Silver Queen when he had retired from the management. Fong had been at the presentation ceremony, and valued the bowl above all his old boss's possessions. In the flight from the Pine Street house he had trusted it to no hands but his own, and finding it hard to hold had carried it on his head. He had also elected to wait on the table—the reunion had a character of intimacy upon which no second boy should intrude—and to do the occasion honor had put on his lilac crepe jacket and green silk trousers. From behind the chairs he looked approvingly at the glistening spread of silver and glass, the flowered mound of the Silver Queen bowl, the ring of faces, and "Miss Lolly" and "Miss Clist" in the dresses he had saved.

Clothes of any kind were at a premium, and the Misses Alstons' hospitality extended to their wardrobe. Sadie had no need to avail herself of it; she had stocked hers well before coming, making a special trip to Sacramento for that purpose. But Pancha, who had lost everything but a nightgown and slippers, was scantily provided. Before dinner there had been a withdrawal to Lorry's room, whence had issued much laughter and cries of admiration from Chrystie. Now, between Mark and Crowder, Pancha loomed radiant, duskily flushed, gleamingly scintillant, in the white net dress with the crystal trimmings that Lorry had worn on an eventful night.

Yes, it was a very fine dinner. At intervals each told his neighbor so, and then told his hostess, and then told Fong. Crowder, whose customary haunts were burned and who was eating anything, anywhere, sighed rapturously over every succeeding course, and Mrs. Kirkham said she'd never seen its peer "except in Virginia in the seventies." Toward the end of it they drank toasts—to Lorry and Mark on their engagement, to Mother and Sadie as the new relations, to Pancha and Mr. Michaels as the saviors, to Chrystie on her restoration to health, to Crowder as the mutual friend, to Aunt Ellen as the ambulating chaperon, to Mrs. Kirkham as the dispenser of hospitality and wisdom, and finally, on their feet with raised glasses, to Fong.

The party broke up early; there were trains and boats to catch for those going back to the city. With the hour of departure a drop came in their high spirits, a prevailing pensiveness in the face of farewells. Chrystie quite broke down, kissed Mr. Michaels to his great confusion, and wept in Pancha's arms. Father and daughter were to go their several ways early in the week and this was good-by. They stumbled over last phrases to Lorry, good wishes, reiterated thanks. She hushed them, hurried their adieux to the others, herself affected but anxious to get them off; such excitement was bad for Chrystie. As the carriage rolled away she stood on the steps, a waving hand aloft, hearing over the roll of the wheels and the talk in the hall, Pancha's clear voice calling, "Good-by, good-by; oh, good-by!"

When she came back the others were already preparing to disperse for bed. The old ladies were tired, yawning as they exchanged good-nights and moved, heavy-footed, for the stairs. They began to mount, their silks rustling, muttering wearily as they toiled upward. Chrystie had to go too, at once, and straight to bed; no reading or talking to Sadie. She agreed dejectedly and trailed after the ascending group, throwing sleepy farewells over her shoulder.

Sadie, who felt very wide-awake, was for lingering. It was only ten, and what with the unwonted excitement and two cups of black coffee, she did not feel at all inclined toward sleep. She thought she would stay down a little longer, and then her glance slipping from the file of backs fell on her brother and Lorry, side by side, their faces raised, their eyes on the retreating procession. Sadie waited a moment, then seeing they made no move to follow it, bade them a brisk good-night and went up the stairs herself.

FURTHER READING

McTeague. Frank Norris, 1899.

Miss Lonelyhearts. Nathanael West, 1933.

The Big Sleep. Raymond Chandler, 1939.

East of Eden. John Steinbeck, 1939.

The Crying of Lot 49. Thomas Pynchon, 1966.

Play it as it Lays. Joan Didion, 1970.

Less Than Zero. Bret Easton Ellis, 1985.

TIMELINE

1535, First Spanish settlers establish a colony in The Bay of La Paz, thought to be located in present-day Santa Cruz

1545, First *Cocolitzli* epidemic kills millions in Mexico and California. It is hypothesized the fever was introduced by European colonists and exacerbated by drought and overpopulation

1776, The United States declares independence

1820, Mexico gains independence from Spain, now rules California

1846, Start of the Mexican-American war which the Americans will win in 1848, annexing western territory which will become California

1848, Gold discovered in the Sacramento Valley, start of the Gold Rush

1850, California officially declares statehood. It is the 31st state in the union

1866, Bret Harte publishes "Outcropping of California Verse"

1870, Geraldine Bonner is born

1875, First Asian Exclusion Act passed, effectively ends open borders in the United States

1885, Mark Twain publishes *Adventures of Huckleberry Finn*

1887, H.J Whitley begins developing a subdivision of Los Angeles which he names Hollywood

1890, Population of California surpasses one million

1893, First moving pictures shown to a public audience

1899, Frank Norris publishes *McTeague*

1900, Geraldine Bonner Publishes her first novel, *Hard Pan*

1903, Jack London publishes *The Call of the Wild*

1903, *The Great Train Robbery* is shown in American Theaters

1903, Telegraph lines cross the Pacific from San Francisco to Hawaii, Japan and China

1904, Geraldine Bonner publishes her fourth book, *The Castlecourt Diamond Case*

1906, The San Francisco Earthquake kills nearly three-thousand and destroys much of the city, an event portrayed fictionally in *Treasure and Trouble Therewith*

1914, The start of World War I

1917, America enters into the war

1917, Geraldine Bonner publishes her seventh novel, *Treasure and Trouble Therewith*

1918, The end of World War I, an estimated eight million soldiers had died along with seven million civilians.

1920, Population of California now almost 3.5 million

1920, F. Scott Fitzgerald publishes *This Side of Paradise.*

1924, A second Immigration act that supplants the initial Asian Exclusion Act is passed by Congress. Immigrants from Asia are effectively banned.

1927, *The Jazz Singer*, the first "talkie", is shown in theaters. American cinema has become dominant over its European counterparts which are rebuilding following the war.

1929, The Stock Market crashes; chaos and poverty ensues.

1930, Geraldine Bonner dies.

www.ingramcontent.com/pod-product-compliance
Lightning Source LLC
Chambersburg PA
CBHW032148190626
46814CB00005BA/1898